THE
WYNDSHAPER

THE IVENHENCE CHRONICLES, BOOK ONE

Written by
KATE ARGUS

For Sarah.
It all began when you asked me to tell you a bedtime story. Thank you for listening, and believing.

THE WYNDSHAPER. Copyright © 2021, Kate Argus Literary Inc

www.kateargus.com

All rights reserved. No part of this publication may be reproduced, distributed, or transmitted in any form or by any means, including photocopying, electronic or mechanical methods, without the prior written permission of the publisher or author, except in the case of brief passages embodied in reviews. For permission requests, contact the publisher by e-mail at katearguswrites@gmail.com.

This is a work of fiction. Names, characters, business, events and incidents are the products of the author's imagination. Any resemblance to actual persons, living or dead, or actual events is purely coincidental.

Paperback ISBN: 978-1-7368720-0-0

Ebook ISBN: 978-1-7368720-1-7

Developmental edit by: Quinn Nichols, Quill and Bone Editing
@quillandboneediting
Edited and proofread by: Britt Laux, Magic and Moons @magicandmoons
Cover design by: Franzi Haase - @coverdungeonrabbit

Content Warnings

Hello, dear reader. Please note that this story contains themes and situations which could be upsetting or triggering. If you aren't concerned by potential triggers, feel free to skip this page.

This book contains the following;
Violence
Battles
Graphic scenes
Death
Asphyxiation
Mention of sexual assault
Mention of slavery
Prejudice
Physical torment

While many of these themes are only touched on briefly or shown in one chapter, I would never want you to risk your mental wellbeing while you're reading my book. Please be assured that there are no scenes which contain graphic sexual assault. In addition, none of the LGBTQIA+ characters depicted are deadnamed or misgendered. I want you to feel safe as you escape into the world of The Wyndshaper.

May the Wynd carry you ever onward.

THE WORLD OF THE WYNDSHAPER

N

IRONSPINE MOUNTAINS

ILUMENCE

LUMINHOLD

ISLES OF ADEN

IVENHENCE

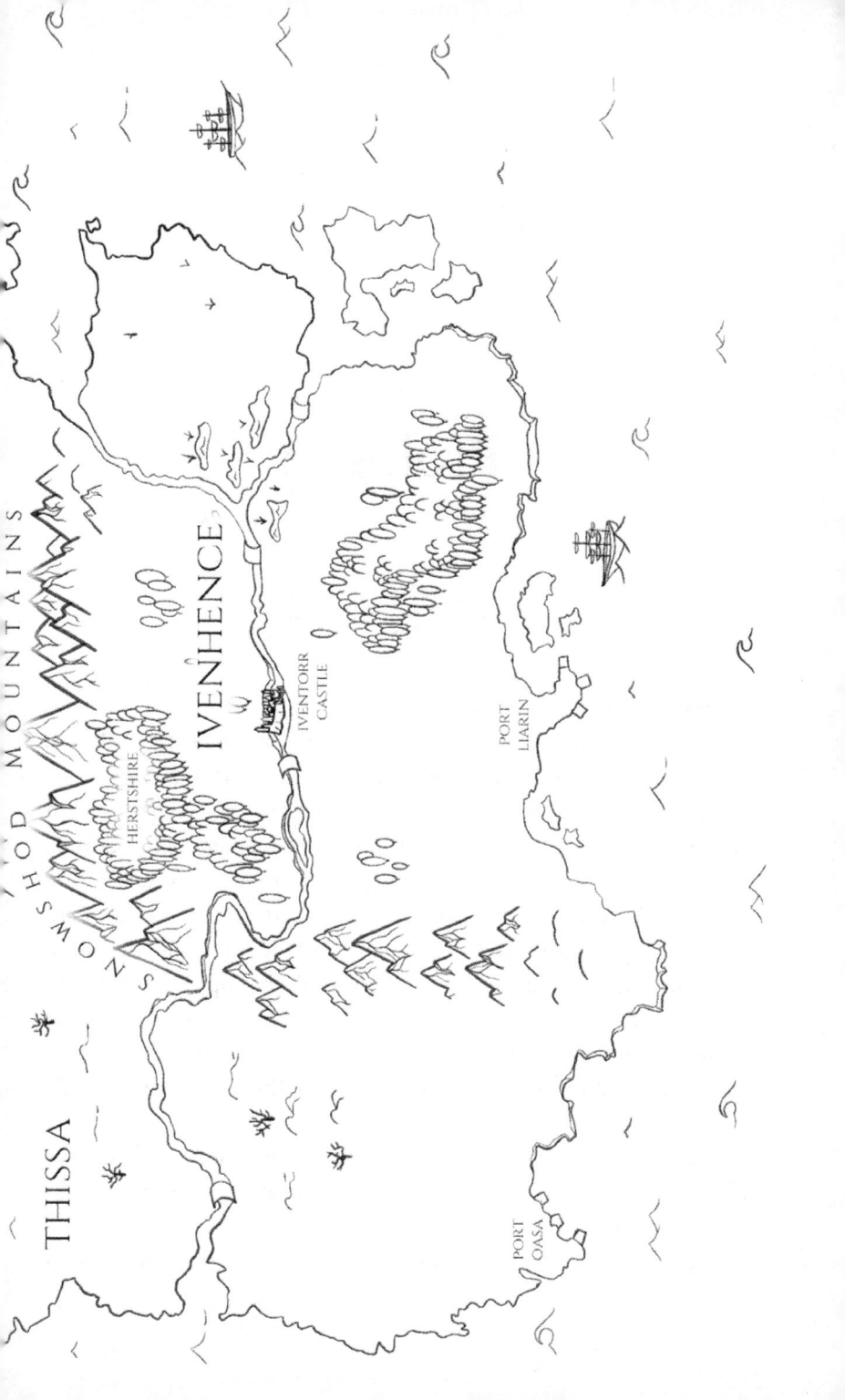

SNOWSHOD MOUNTAINS

THISSA

HERSTSHIRE

IVENTORR CASTLE

PORT LIARIN

PORT OASA

Prologue

It was finally Reclamation Day.

Pushing strands of red-brown hair out of her face, the little girl stood on her tiptoes to peer over the edge of a curved stone banister. Her simple tunic rustled in the same breeze that stirred her unruly locks. Unable to contain her excitement, she beamed, pulling herself up on her elbows to gaze over Iventorr Castle.

Carved from a stone island which jutted out of the Emerald Basin, its ten towers stretched towards the sky, the tallest seeming to touch the clouds. From the tops of the uppermost spires fluttered dark green banners, emblazoned with a silver 'I'. The sinking sun shone amber on the grey walls, lending them warmth and color that reflected brightly off the rippling waters of the wide lake below.

She'd never seen it from this high up before. Her plump cheeks flushed guiltily. Her Papa would scold her if he found her so far up in the guest tower.

Voices and distant laughter drifted up from the streets as if calling to her, accompanied by the aroma of roasting meat. Her stomach growled. Reluctantly, she lowered herself from the railing. Pausing to scoop up a couple oddly-shaped objects, the girl skipped from the balcony to a long spiral staircase and hurried down.

Reaching the end of the descent, she exited the wide double doors into the setting sunlight. The girl paused at the top landing of a much shorter flight of steps, her bright green eyes darting over the mayhem below.

The courtyard buzzed with the energy and activity of the hundreds of people that filled it. Merchants from across the lands and beyond the seas had come; tanners, toymakers, tailors, cobblers, jewelers, armorers, and more. Their cloth-draped booths and wooden stalls hugged the outer perimeter of the stone plaza, a sculpted stone fountain babbling merrily in the center. Other children the girl's age clustered around displays of vivid candies and strange toys with wide eyes, or dashed about laughing and shouting. Youths gazed at gleaming swords, armor, and strands of gems, doing their best to ignore the hawkers who cried out ceaselessly, "Imported straight from the Isles of Aden! You shan't find pearls of this quality anywhere else!" Or "Step up, step up! The finest silks, such as the gypsies carry from across the sea!" Men and women milled about the fountain, chatting and laughing as troupes of performers tried to make their flutes and drums heard above the noise.

Though the tantalizing scents of cinnamon, sizzling pork, garlic, and roasted potatoes teased her nose, the girl didn't budge from the top of the stair. Her flitting glance landed on a small gap in the crowd across the courtyard. There stood a boy several years older than she, looking distinctly uncomfortable as he shifted in the narrow space beside the dining hall's doors. The evening sun glinted off his neatly combed black hair, silver circlet, and shining boots.

With a grin and a bounce, she skipped down the steps and dove into the crowd. Weaving past carts and many pairs of adult legs, the girl paused to shoot a wistful stare at a caramel-covered apple in the candy merchant's display.

"Oy," said a voice at her shoulder. "Those're pretty good. Where'd you get them?"

Turning to the querier, a boy a head taller than herself, she straightened. "I didn't get them," she replied matter-of-factly, squeezing her burden even closer. His face creased doubtfully, but before he could say anything, she scampered on.

Finally breaking past the edge of the crowd, she turned to the dining hall doors with a beam.

"Hello, Prince Dreythan," she said, her cheeks tingling.

The boy glanced briefly down at her, his black eyes absent. "Hello, Fletch," he said, his polite tone barely covering his reluctance. "How fare you?"

"I fare well." Fletch grinned before continuing, "I crafted something. I saw you making the model of Iventorr Castle, when you were whittling the shingles for the roofs, and it gave me an idea!"

The prince looked down at her, one corner of his mouth lifting bemusedly. "Indeed?

The little girl nodded, holding her bundle out. Her childish hands held a quiver full of arrows and a simple bow, just her size. "See?" she chattered as he took them. "Papa showed me how, and I made them all, even the arrows!"

The prince's slender hand ran the length of the bow as he inspected it closely, his smile slowly growing.

"Papa said I did well, ex-cep-tion-al-ly well," Fletch added carefully, then rushed on, "but sometimes he says that even when I don't do well. So I thought you should look at them since you're a craftsman!"

"I, a craftsman?" The boy chuckled, pulling one of the arrows out of the quiver. "No, not compared to you. Look at how well these are made! I should not be surprised if their flight was as true as your father's arrows." Tapping the feathered end of the missile with one finger, he handed the bow back with a wink. "Fletch the

Fletcher, that is how you ought to be called!"

She giggled, her cheeks burning.

Sliding the arrow back into place, Dreythan held the quiver out. "Take pride in your work," he told her seriously, though he still smiled. "Your papa was right. You have done exceptionally well."

Fletch accepted the quiver, bashfully unable to meet the prince's eye. She opened her mouth to thank Dreythan—

"There you are!" roared a voice. A pair of strong, gentle hands closed around her ribs, lifting her high into the air. "There's my magpie!"

The laughter bubbled out of her as her father, Kell Wyndshaper, tucked her into his arms, his beard tickling her face. "Stop it, Papa! I'll drop my bow!"

The tickling instantly stopped. "We wouldn't want that, now would we?" He scowled playfully, and she shook her head, grinning back. "We can't have the castle guard damaging their weapons!"

Planting a kiss on her father's sun-leathered face, Fletch's fingers brushed a piece of his silver-brown hair out of his face as his jade green eyes twinkled at her like dew-dusted leaves.

"Castle guard?" Dreythan interjected. "What do you mean, Captain?"

"Your pardon, my prince," Kell said, bowing. Fletch giggled as she dipped with him. "Fletch is being assigned her first honorary guard duty at the banquet tonight. She's being tasked with patrolling the north stair."

"It's okay, Papa," she interjected. "You can say the way it really is." Turning to Dreythan, she explained, "No one could watch me since Mama isn't here anymore and everyone wants to go to the banquet."

Both Dreythan and Kell's faces fell.

She tucked her bottom lip between her teeth. Had she said something wrong?

Before she could realize her mistake, a rich voice interrupted, "Ah, I had hoped to find you here."

Kell and Dreythan both turned as a man strode toward them. The gentle breeze in the courtyard lifted white hair away from his brow, his weathered face breaking into a kindly smile. A velvet cloak of forest green rippled from his broad shoulders, and the sun's setting light glinted off the ten-pointed silver crown that weighted his head.

"My lord," Kell said, dipping into another bow. Fletch knew better than to titter this time; bowing to King Dreythas wasn't something to laugh about.

The king placed his hand on Kell's shoulder, squeezing. "How many times must I ask you not to bow to me?" He chuckled, his voice deep and rumbling like warm summer thunder.

"However long it takes you to accept that I shall never stop," Kell replied.

The king's twinkling obsidian eyes settled onto Fletch, and she smiled shyly. There was something large about the king, she'd always thought. Something bright and comforting, but large.

"Hello, Fletch," he said with a nod, then turned to Dreythan. "I am sorry I kept you waiting, son."

"Not to worry, Father," the prince assured him. "Fletch kept me company."

The king's eyes softened as his arms circled his son's shoulders. Face reddening, the boy avoided Fletch's eye, giving his father a quick hug back.

"It is nearly sundown," Kell said suddenly. There was an abrupt shift, and Fletch was back on her feet again. "Don't forget what I said, Fletch. You promise to stay on the northern stair?"

She nodded. "I promise."

He planted a whiskery kiss on the top of her head. "That's a good magpie," he whispered. Straightening, he turned to the king. "Come, my lord. The procession awaits."

The king held on to Dreythan for another moment, then pulled away, his face falling. "I must go," he told him soberly. "Will you see Fletch safely inside the dining hall once the ceremony is complete?"

"I shall."

With that, both men hurried away.

"Why is your father carrying a sword?" Dreythan asked.

Startled by the prince's tone, Fletch glanced up to find him staring after their fathers, his black brows furrowed. "I don't know," she said, a chill gripping her chest. "Is that bad?"

He quickly shook his head. "Not at all," he assured her with a smile. "He is the Captain of the Guard, after all. And most of the guards wear swords. It does make sense when one considers it."

Puzzled, Fletch frowned up at him. She was about to ask him how that could possibly make sense when the groan of oak and iron split the air, punctuated by the clear, bright cry of trumpets. The doors of the guest tower gradually parted, the bustle in the courtyard dissolving into quiet. King Dreythas stepped out, followed closely by his brother, King Morthas of Ilumence, and Morthas's son, Prince Morthan. Behind them paced a score of leather-armored, green-cloaked guards and their Captain, Kell Wyndshaper.

As his brother and nephew passed to stand below and the ranks of the castle guard parted around him, King Dreythas paused on the top step of the guest tower, clearly visible above the crowd. With his every glance, people pushed forward to stand below. Many more than had been present in the courtyard emerged from buildings and streets to press in, straining to get as close as possible. Eyes turned up toward the king, they waited as silence settled.

A melancholic smile curved his lips as the king's gaze swept the faces below. "I welcome you, one and all, to Ivenhence and Castle Iventorr," he said, his rich voice rolling over the quiet audience. "Today, we celebrate the anniversary of the Crimson Horde's defeat. We rejoice the day that our subjugators, Vvalk and Sliv, were cast from their dark throne. We remember the sacrifices made, the friendships formed, and the birth of this great nation.

"Forty years ago, we resolved that we would be slaves to the Unbreathing no longer. Through hard work and perseverance, we gathered arms in secret, protecting and uplifting those who could not see an end to their torment. United, we stormed the streets and halls of this very castle, destroying our oppressors with silver and fire. In so doing, we forged our future. The future of Ivenhence and Ilumence, unified against Kazael's dark creations."

The king paused, head bowing. The sun's fading radiance illuminated his crown and white hair, wreathing his stately face in brilliance. Somehow, in Fletch's eyes, he looked even larger at a distance.

"However, in claiming our freedom and our peace, many brave souls were lost. They sacrificed themselves for the tranquility we experience today. Let us now join together to pray for the many who perished during the Battle of Reclamation, and to thank them for the price they paid."

King Dreythas pressed his palms together, fingers intertwining as he closed his eyes, lifting his face to the sky. Around Fletch, the members of the crowd clasped their hands, some looking up as the king, some with heads deeply bowed. Tears slipped down the wrinkled cheeks of many of the elders present, their lips moving in silent thanks. Sensing the sorrow and gravity of the moment, she stared, wondering, and saw that many of the other children looked exactly the way she felt; awed, but confused.

Her Papa had told her that their kingdom, Ivenhence, was like her sister. That Papa had fought hard for the kingdom to live, and that because of him and a great many other people, it finally came to be. She wondered if the 'great many people' he had spoken of were the same people who had lost their souls during the Battle. If they were also like her Papa; brave, strong, warm, and safe. Over the crowd, she could just see him at the bottom of the guest tower stairs, brushing a hand across his eyes.

"Our friends, parents, siblings, and children you were," the king intoned, the timbre of his deep voice reverberating through the streets as his mouth traced the familiar words of the Honoring. "You gave us a future of prosperity and liberty. You gave us hope. Whilst the blood of my veins rules this kingdom, your honor shall remain untarnished. This I swear."

Soft words melded together all around Fletch, swelling with unity and power as the people chanted, "Our loved ones, neighbors, and protectors you were. You sacrificed your lives that ours could be lived fully. Your pride shall remain undiminished for as long as we live. This we swear."

"This we swear," Prince Dreythan echoed beside her. Curious, she glanced up to see him solemnly raising his arm with the crowd, saluting the lost souls as the sun's final rays faded over the horizon.

Resisting the instinct to slump down in his chair, Dreythan sat straight, pushing his empty plate to one side. Below the table at which he sat, three oak tables stretched the considerable length of Iventorr's dining hall. They were crowded with townsfolk, soldiers, visiting merchants, and other peoples from all corners of Ilumence and Ivenhence and beyond. They feasted on roast boar, potatoes, and salted greens, drinking freely of barrels of wine and mead as they chattered and laughed amongst themselves. As the hours had wound on and emptied barrels had begun to stack along the wall, the conversation had grown ever more boisterous, interrupted occasionally with a raucous song. Scores of men and women had staggered or wavered their winding way out of the hall after taking their fill, some of them gently prodded by footmen and maids, only to be replaced by others who had waited their turn for a seat.

The end of the hall where Dreythan sat was raised one step. His table was much smaller than and perpendicular to the others. At this table sat King Dreythas, his brother King Morthas of Ilumence, and Morthas's son Morthan, as well as a handful of notable citizens. They, too, were still eating and drinking eagerly.

And there was no sign of it ending anytime soon. A frown crept onto the young prince's face as he stifled a yawn.

"'Tis a shame we were unable to sign the trade agreement with Thissa," his uncle Morthas was saying to King Dreythas, his voice little more than a buzz over the joyous drunken singing and chattering of the crowd. "But their terms were simply too exacting. Had they been willing to negotiate, I would have considered it. But had we gone forward as Gorvannon wished, we would have been unable to keep up with the demand from Thissa, Aden, and Ivenhence combined. Our trade relations with all would have suffered in time."

"Your decision was a sound one," Dreythas replied. "But I fear that Thissa's dictator will not take rejection well. His country has few enough resources that he may turn to other means when trade fails."

Dreythan cast a quick glance at his father, whose wise, serene eyes were unusually turbulent. What did he mean?

Morthas lifted his goblet to his lips, then paused. "What of Ivenhence's trade agreement with him? Does it not provide enough lumber and foodstuffs to satisfy their need?"

Setting his own cup aside, Dreythas avoided his brother's eye as he replied, "Our caravans have been going missing at the border to Thissa. It has become too dangerous to allow them passage."

Morthas's silver brow creased.

The conversation between the two kings faded into the background as Dreythan's attention wavered. It was late, several hours past sundown. There would be no chance to advance the construction of his little castle this evening. He should have known better than to hope for it, but... He allowed his eyes to shut for a moment, picturing it. The model was nearly done. All that remained was the most challenging part: the bridge that spanned the Emerald Basin, connecting Iventorr Castle to the mainland. He'd intended to finish it earlier, but there had been no time. The pang of disappointment pulled at his chest as a vision of his unfinished work played through his mind.

Something bumped the back of his chair. He opened his eyes to see Kell Wyndshaper pausing at one end of the table. The Captain's sharp green eyes scanned the crowd, a scowl dissolving from his face as he raised an arm. Following his eyeline, Dreythan spotted a tiny figure at the other end of the dining hall, waving a tiny bow.

Fletch. He couldn't help smiling. She was an odd little creature. Pretending to be a castle guard when most girls her age preferred to make dolls and playhouses. And she was always asking questions he didn't quite know the answer to.

Closing his heavy eyes again, Dreythan leaned back in his chair. They were much alike, he and Fletch. Neither of them had their mothers anymore, and both had fathers who were old friends dedicated to the kingdom of Ivenhence. And both he and Fletch liked to craft things.

His mind continued to wander drowsily, comfortable and heavy from the late hour and the generous meal. The cheers and chattering of the crowd below slowly faded as he tread the mysterious place between slumber and wake. It could have been hours or minutes that passed.

"Kell?" said his father's voice. "Is something amiss?"

"No, my lord. 'Tis nearly midnight, and my daughter still keeps her watch. 'Tis high time I relieved her of her duties," Kell said with a chuckle.

"Of course, my friend. I also need my rest." There was a brief pause. "Bring Dreythan after me, and relieve Fletch of her post on the way."

"Yes, my lord. Shall I dismiss the merrymakers?"

"Nay. Let them have their revelry." A chair scraped across the floor, jolting Dreythan closer to consciousness. "There was not a single Thissian merchant in the courtyard," his father murmured, barely audible. "Were there any in Verdance?"

"Nay, my lord," Kell replied quietly. "Not a one. Have no fear. I am prepared should anything happen."

A warmth rested on Dreythan's shoulder, then gently shook. "My prince," Kell's voice said, close to Dreythan's ear. "My lord

Dreythas bids you to follow him. He retires to his chambers for the night."

The prince turned sluggishly toward him, eyelids drooping. He was half certain he was dreaming. "Wh-what?"

"Your chambers, my prince." Kell gestured to the other side of the hall, where the king was just beginning to ascend the northern stair. "You need your rest."

Oh. He wasn't dreaming. Rubbing his palms across his cheeks, Dreythan tried to straighten. "Yes," he mumbled through his fingers. "Rest." Blinking, he nodded up at Kell. "Very well." His chair scraped back over the wooden floor.

Across the heads of the crowd, he could see his father reach the top of the northern steps, the minute figure of the girl bowing and stepping to the side as the guards opened the doors.

There was a strange muffled sound, like silverware falling on a blanket. Suddenly, the south door of the dining hall slammed open. A man burst through, an enormous bow clutched in one hand. Wild hair flying, face twisting, he nocked an arrow, aimed, and released.

A sick crunching thud echoed over the crowd. Across the hall, Dreythan's father dropped to the floor.

As quick as thought, the assassin turned even as guards sprinted towards him. His rabid eye met Dreythan's. With one swift motion, another arrow whistled straight for the prince.

Time froze, as did Dreythan. The world swam in foggy uncertainty. Surely he was still dreaming.

A grip on his shoulder yanked him to the side.

The shocked stillness was torn by a shrill scream. People scattered from their seats, mindless in their panic to escape. The assailant spun to fight off the guards who swarmed around him. A guard's blade pierced the assassin's ribs from behind, and he dropped from sight.

Turning, Dreythan's eye met the shaft of a jet-black arrow inches from his head. The hand on his shoulder fell away as Kell Wyndshaper swayed, his gaze dropping to the missile protruding from his ribs. The prince tried to catch him, but the captain fell heavily, pulling Dreythan to his knees.

Another cry resounded from the northern stair. A splintered thought pierced the prince's numb mind. His father. Surely his father was all right. He turned uncertainly to the north door, but a hand grasped his arm. Looking down, Dreythan stared at the dark stain that was blossoming from under the Captain's armor, spreading to the stone where Dreythan knelt. Frozen still and silent, Dreythan could only watch as Kell strained to lift his head. Lids fluttering, lips desperately trying to form words, the man's eyes emitted an unfathomable plea.

Then the eyes grew hollow. Grey head lolling onto the stone, unuttered words failing, Kell Wyndshaper's last breath rattled from his bloodied lungs.

Chapter 1

Dreythan tried to smooth the wrinkle that had been deepening in his forehead, but with little success. He'd already waited several minutes for the two red-faced men before him to stop bickering, and his patience was wearing thin. Since entering the throne room, they had only paused in exchanging shouts and accusations to bow to him and draw breath.

"Your gods-damned dog wouldn't be dead if he hadn't eaten my chickens, Korstan! I did warn you, twice!"

"That hound was trained to track deer and rabbits, not kill chickens! My family'll starve this winter. I haven't a nose to sniff out game. Perhaps if you'd put up a ruddy fence, as I'd suggested, your chickens wouldn't have—"

"Build a fence?! Damn fool, do you know how much time and lumber—"

Abruptly, Dreythan stood. "That is enough."

The king's command sliced the tension between them. Deflating like limp sacks, the two men turned to face him as Dreythan inspected the one named Korstan. The man's calloused hands kneaded the brim of his straw hat, his eyes cast miserably at his scuffed boots.

"Your neighbor mentioned he warned you," Dreythan said. "What manner of warning was this, and why was it needed?"

Korstan swallowed hard. "My lord," he said, head still bowed, "my neighbor Gorlak here brought a dead chicken to my homestead three weeks ago. It'd been torn at but not eaten, and Gorlak claimed he saw my hound Digby running into the woods when he came out of his barn."

"Thank you, Goodman Korstan." The king turned his attention to Gorlak, who stood with feet planted far apart, burly arms crossed over his chest. "Did you demand payment for the dead chicken?"

"Yes, m'lord," Gorland drawled, tilting his jaw to stare down his nose.

"How much?"

The man blinked, chin lowering. "Er, m' lord?" When the king's gaze didn't waver, Gorlak shrugged. "I asked 'im for five coppers, m'lord."

Five coppers. As much as a man might pay for a young goat, or a week's stay at an inn. His head throbbed. "Odd that such steep recompense was necessary," the king mused. "Five coppers for a chicken... explain this to me."

Gorlak muttered something about 'meat ruined, and feathers too'.

"You mentioned you warned him twice? Why?"

"More o' my chickens went missin', m'lord."

Resisting the inclination to rub his temple, Dreythan turned his attention to his feet. His thoughts matched their rhythm as he paced before the throne. "Goodman Gorlak, you do not deny that you killed Goodman Korstan's dog. How did you kill it?"

"Set a trap," came the short reply. "In th' woods between our farms."

"Are those woods your land?"

"Er, no. M'lord."

"I would suppose they belong to Goodman Korstan."

"Yes, m'lord."

Jaw twitching, Dreythan stopped and stared at the man. Irritation swelled within him, coupled by his pounding head, but he forced his expression into neutrality. "You set a trap for this man's hound on his own land without firm proof that the beast had ever touched your chickens or even set foot on your property," he said deliberately. "You realize this falls within the realm of malignant trespassing."

Gorlak's arms dropped limply to his sides as his face turned the color of spoiled milk. "M-m'lord," he stammered weakly. "I-I—"

"My lord," Goodman Korstan interjected. "Gorlak has always been a fairly... peaceful neighbor. I would not wish ill on him."

Still not turning from Gorlak, Dreythan acknowledged Korstan with a nod. "You wronged a forgiving man," he said. "Be sure not to take advantage of this again. You will give Goodman Korstan ten coppers or one gold so he may purchase a healthy bloodhound pup. You have three weeks to do this. If you have not paid the Goodman by your deadline, you will serve one moon hard labor in the castle and your fee will be paid by the treasury."

The men bowed, Korstan murmuring fervent thanks. Four guards escorted them out of the throne hall as Dreythan lowered himself back into the unforgiving wooden seat.

When the guards returned to their posts moments later, one approached the throne. "That is all for today, my lord."

"Very well. Find Captain Norland and Brinwathe and summon them here."

With a smart salute, the guard swiftly departed.

Finally alone, Dreythan leaned slowly back into the throne and allowed his taut features to relax into a frown.

It had been fifteen years since his father's assassination. Fifteen years since the weight of kingship had been dropped upon him. He'd made many mistakes in the beginning of his reign before learning the value of sound council. The only man he had felt he could fully confide in had been his uncle Morthas. But Morthas lived north of the Snowshod Mountains, with a kingdom of his own to rule. He had always been kind enough to visit during the summers, but keeping in contact with him proved difficult. Over the years, several valuable messenger jays were lost in the Valer-Norst Pass. The young king had eventually come to realize he would simply have to learn to govern on his own.

Dreythan's line of thought was interrupted as the doors to the throne hall groaned apart. A burly bear of a man pushed through. Sheathed blade clinking against his armor, his thick boots beat a steady rhythm as he strode down the center aisle of the hall. A fiery beard bushed over his wide chest. His upper arms, free of cloth and armor, were marked by several slashing parallel scars.

"Captain Norland," the king greeted. "How fare the preparations?"

The man's bright sky-blue eyes met Dreythan's gaze as he briefly knelt below the throne, one gauntleted fist pressed to his heart. "My lord," he said, his rumbling voice echoing through the stone chamber, "I've just come from the stables. Your steeds've been prepared and the saddlebags are being filled as we speak. I've also selected your escorts as requested. One Sentinel and three castle guards. But—" his arms crossed beneath his beard "—I do wish you'd consider taking more of the Sentinels with ye. That is their only duty, after all. To keep ye safe," he finished pointedly.

"Five including myself should be more than sufficient, Norland," Dreythan replied, suppressing a wry smile. "Our objective is speed, and more would only slow us down. You worry too much, though it is appreciated." When Norland's scowl remained, the king added, "The Sentinels deserve rest when they can have it. It happens rarely enough. Fret not, my friend. The road is not dangerous, provided we stay warm. It shall be too cold for bandits."

"It's not the cold nor the bandits that worry me," Norland grunted.

"I have brought the documents you requested, my lord,"

interjected a quavering voice. The two men turned to see another hobbling down the aisle, withered hand clutching a cane as he tucked a scroll close to his chest.

"That is good to hear," Dreythan replied. "I had not expected them to be completed so quickly."

The elder halted at the bottom of the steps, bowing as low as his crooked spine could manage. "Thankfully, there was a template already written, my lord. I have penned the date and stamped it with the royal seal. All that is needed is our signatures."

Standing, Dreythan descended the steps and took the proffered scroll. A swift flick of his wrist unfurled the parchment. Scanning the carefully penned words, he nodded. Not a letter out of place. "This appears to be in order. You have my thanks, Brinwathe."

Brinwathe's face dissolved into a mass of smiles. Rummaging about in a bag slung over one shoulder, he produced a quill and ink.

Dreythan and Norland's eyes met for a brief moment as Norland took the pen, his thick brows unable to hide his troubled glare.

A gentle quiet lay over the forested mountains, a few flakes of snow drifting from the sky to rest on the white-dusted branches of eldertrees. No wind rustled the pines as the moon and stars shone softly down, glimmering across the snow to illuminate the night. The only sounds that broke the stillness were the occasional hoot of a distant owl and the muffled thuds of horses' hooves as Dreythan's small company made its way up the narrow, tree-crowded trail that wound its way up the wooded hills.

Two days had passed since their departure from Iventorr Castle, and it would likely be another two before they reached their destination, Luminhold in Ilumence. They were just approaching the crevice that divided the two tallest mountains in the Snowshod range, Mount Valer and Mount Norst. While being the quickest path to Ivenhence's sister-kingdom, it carried some measure of danger no matter the season. The mountains and their trees were constantly dusted with snow except in the hottest of summers. It was said that blizzards blew in so cold and so sudden through the Pass, they could freeze a man where he stood.

Dreythan shifted in his saddle, pulling the thick wool of his cloak tighter around his shoulders. A stream of white mist escaped his lips as he released a long sigh.

Having to leave Ivenhence under the rule of Warden and Witness made him uneasy. While Dreythan trusted Captain Norland with his life and knew Brinwathe was both wise and intelligent, they were not royalty; they were not accustomed to the burden of power or the weight of justice. Between managing reports from the Foresters and Fishers, settling disputes between his subjects, sentencing punishment for crimes, and overseeing taxation, the king was an overworked man. He could only hope that Brinwathe and Norland would be able to manage between the two of them.

The image of Norland's troubled frown rose before him, and Dreythan sank deeper into his cloak. He didn't doubt the same thoughts had crossed his captain's mind as Dreythan signed him into power as Warden.

"I recognize this part of the trail," Sentinel Raylin said, his breath puffing through the cowl that covered his jaw. "We'll be inside the Pass in two hours."

The others nodded, grunting their acknowledgement. They had exchanged names and conversation during the first several hours of their journey. Mordin, Layward, and Pennick were members of the castle guard, and Raylin was one of the Sentinels, the royal guard. They seemed familiar with each other, though Dreythan had only known Raylin previously. It had been pleasant to exchange discourse, a welcome distraction from the sobering reason for their journey. Now, it was simply too cold to talk. Their breath was already causing minute crystals of ice to form on their scarves and hoods. Trying to speak would only make it worse.

The king glanced at each man, barely distinguishable from each other as they huddled on their mounts, cloaks and limbs tucked close for warmth. None of them seemed to mind the quiet, thankfully. They were likely thinking of their families and duties at home or, like Dreythan, were preoccupied with other matters.

The trail began to wind back and forth across the face of a steep, rocky incline, dodging protruding boulders and trees. The horses' hooves clopped softly against stones lying hidden under the snow. Stray snowflakes danced by, stirred by the chill breeze that cut down the incline. Clumps of snow slid from shifting tree branches to plop softly to the ground.

Then there was stillness. The biting wind halted suddenly and completely, the mountains themselves seeming to hold their breath. Ears flicking, nostrils flaring, the horses stopped. One of them pranced backward, neck arched nervously.

Raylin stiffened. "Something is amiss," he hissed, sliding from his saddle. "Get off the horses. Quickly!"

A whisper sliced the air, then a thud. Mordin toppled from his mount, an arrow protruding from his neck.

The blood froze in Dreythan's veins. Images of Kell Wyndshaper and the jet-black arrow flashed through his mind. A grip on his arm yanked him back to reality and out of his saddle.

"Protect the king," Raylin snapped as the others struggled to dismount. "Find cover!"

More arrows hissed through the air. Pennick tried to throw himself to the ground, a missile burying itself between his shoulder blades. He dangled limply beneath his horse, one foot caught in a stirrup. The creature reared, shrieking in terror, and bolted down the trail, yanking the guard's body across snow and stone.

Raylin's hand tugged Dreythan lower. "Stay down," the Sentinel grunted. He jerked his head at Layward, then down the incline. "We're right behind you. Head for that boulder. Run!"

As the king turned, his heartbeat roaring in his ears, another volley of bolts rained down. Two of the horses lurched, then screamed, tearing off after the first fleeing beast.

Dreythan pushed himself upright into a dash, his legs burning as he forced them into motion. His feet churned snow as time crawled by. Every step was exaggerated, thick, slow. As if the world was steeped in molasses. Each heartbeat was a thunderous crack of lightning, sending a pulse through his vision.

Seconds passed in an eternity. Skidding to a halt behind the boulder, he pressed his back to the icy rock. Raylin dove behind him as an arrow hissed over his head down the hill. Layward was nowhere in sight.

Dreythan gulped in a breath to gasp, "What now?"

The Sentinel ducked lower as another arrow ricocheted off the stone above. "I'm not sure," he replied quietly. "We can't stay here. They'll circle around and pin us down. We have to try to sneak down the incline."

"They will spot us with ease," Dreythan whispered. "Our dark cloaks against the snow?"

The man's eyes brightened. Tugging his cloak free of its broach, he pressed a fistful of the coarse material into the snow. When he lifted it free, the snow stuck.

Catching on instantly, Dreythan whipped his off and copied Raylin's idea. Working in silent fervor, they soon had two white-caked cloaks.

Laying flat on his belly, Raylin re-clasped his brooch and raised his hood. "I'll go first," he said. A drop of moisture rolled down his temple, freezing in a crease beside his eye. "Want to make sure 'tis safe." With that, he wriggled out from behind the boulder on his belly, sliding slowly down the hill.

He made it past several trees before an arrow plunged into his back. Raylin's spine arched, but he made no sound. One hand rose, reaching forward as if still trying to crawl. Another missile found the back of the hood, and the arm collapsed into the snow.

Ice crept through Dreythan's veins. He was alone now. No guards, no possibility for escape. He glanced desperately around, his eyes falling on a dense snow-covered shrub growing against the rock. Wrapping the camouflaging cloak tight, he squeezed his tall frame into the narrow space between them and crouched, scarcely daring to breathe.

"Here's the second guard," growled a dry voice, a strange accent blurring the words. "Stupid bloke. His steed stepped on his head."

Another called, "Another one of them here. That's what I call good hunting! They didn't even have a chance to fight back." A gleeful chuckle echoed eerily between the trees.

Dreythan's fists clenched at his sides. His guards were not game to be gloated over. They were good men who... who had given their lives to defend him.

"What do you think you are doing?"

He huddled even lower beside the boulder, the thudding in his chest pounding too loudly. The flat demand had come from only a few feet away.

"His blood's all over the place," the gravelly voice replied. "You can't expect us not to at least taste it."

"Yes I can." A short, hooded figure passed by Dreythan's hiding place to bend over the snow-cloaked guard. "You know our orders. Leave no trace."

"Is that the clever one?" the cheerful voice asked.

The one closest to Dreythan gave an affirming grunt. One bony hand emerged from the dark cloak to flip Raylin to his back. The man's eyes stared blankly up at the sky, a trickle of blood escaping one nostril. There was an expectant pause. "It's not the king," he announced.

The other two voices cursed in unison as a finger of dread traced Dreythan's spine. Head bent toward the ground, the hooded man turned, taking step after agonizing step toward the boulder until he was only three feet away.

Suddenly, the constant breeze that flowed down the mountainside shifted, blowing freezing air into the king's face. The hooded man stooped low, his shoulders level with his knees.

Dreythan held his breath. His hand inched toward the hilt of his blade.

"Gah," the man hissed. "The snow is too stirred up to make

heads or tails of." Straightening, he tilted his head and sniffed the air.

There was a distant twang and a near thump. The hooded man crashed to his face, an arrow protruding from his back.

"How?" shrieked the bright voice. Sprinting into Dreythan's view came another figure, bow drawn, legs moving faster than any human's. Lurching, he fell. His body tumbled down the incline, bouncing off rocks and trees as it went.

Someone was hunting his hunters. They could use his aid. Heart in his throat, Dreythan leaped from his hiding place, blade ringing as he pulled it free. The final assailant was dodging between trees, zig-zagging down the slope faster than Dreythan's vision could follow. At the sound of a sword being drawn, he stopped, yellow eyes glinting like a cat's toward Dreythan. The eyes grew far too close far too quickly. There was another twang, another thud. The yellow eyes blinked out.

Then the forest was still again. Moonlight gleamed through the trees, casting broken shadows on the ground. A frigid gust swept through the Pass, piercing Dreythan's thick cloak. He shuddered, sword still poised at the ready.

Between two trees appeared a slender cloaked figure. They made their way up the incline, climbing the steep grade as easily as a mountain goat. Stopping by Raylin's body, they bent over him, breaking off the arrow in his back and crossing his arms over his chest. Then they paused, one gloved hand holding the feathered shaft up in the dim light.

"That was a clever hiding place," a feminine voice said, sending a thrill of shock through the king. "Next to the boulder, in the brush." She turned toward him, her face in shadow from the green hood covering her head. "I'm a Forester; I shan't harm you unless you're a poacher, thief, vagabond, or enemy of Ivenhence." She gestured to where the hooded man had fallen. "Whoever you are, you have some powerful enemies. The Unbreathing aren't to be trifled with."

A Forester? Cautiously, heart still pounding in his throat,

Dreythan lowered his blade. "How could you possibly know that?"

Her head cocked to one side, her silhouette stiffening. "Oh," she said softly, then, "How could I know where you hid? Or that your enemies are Unbreathing?"

"The Unbreathing."

"I can see the movement of air and Wynd," she said shortly. "No breath came from any of your attackers, save when they spoke and when this one," she toed the prone form, "tried to sniff you out." She motioned him closer. "Take a look at him now."

He inched out of his hiding place, branches scraping snow off his cloak. When he stood beside the woman and looked down, he choked back a gasp of horror.

The man's skin and flesh were withering before his very eyes. Within seconds, nothing was left but grey, shriveled, parchment-like scraps wrapping bones within clothing and cloak.

"The Devul that possessed this body had done so for a long time," the woman said. "T'was pure luck I picked him as my first target. We might not have survived otherwise." Tucking the broken arrow into her quiver, she turned to the king. "Then again, if you hadn't stood and drawn your blade, I wouldn't have gotten a shot at the last one." Though he couldn't see her face, he heard the grateful approval in her voice. "Come along, my lord," she said, brushing snow off his shoulders. "You need to move around and get some warmth back into you."

It took a moment for Dreythan's legs to obey him. Sheathing his sword, he followed the woman up the trail to where Pennick's body lay. At the sight of his skull, he swallowed hard and turned away, nearly retching. It was a pulpy mess of bone shards and purple-grey and red sludge.

"I'll lay them all beside each other," the woman was saying, taking the dead man's arms. "Could you help me?"

He nodded numbly, careful not to look at the head as he grasped the body's ankles. Together they half-slid, half-carried it down the hill and laid it beside the first.

"I'll call a storm," she said as they went. "Hopefully it'll be enough to cover the bodies, preserve them. Their families should be able to find them and give them a proper burial."

They did the same for the last two guards, breaking off the arrows that had slain them, laying them beside the others and crossing their arms over their chests. For the final guard, the woman removed his cloak, shook it off, and put it around the king's shaking shoulders.

"It'll only get colder, my lord," she told him soberly. "My home isn't far, we can take shelter there. Come along."

With that, she led him through the woods, keeping a steady pace as the gusts began to blow stronger, the cold sprouting bitter fangs.

Dreythan trailed slightly behind, hands clutching the cloaks close about him, forcing his aching legs to keep moving. As the shock and terror faded into weariness, his bleary eyes could barely focus on the ground before his feet, but he somehow managed to keep up with the long-legged woman. A few times, he thought he saw her reaching for the sky or making sudden motions with her hands. But when he blinked and looked again, she was simply shifting her bow from one hand to the other.

Some minutes into their trek, stray flakes of snow began to lift between the trees, borne on the cutting breeze. Just as she had predicted. He would have wondered at it, but a numbness had settled into him, and the trees and ground passed by in a grey blur.

Chapter 2

Black arrows, men falling left and right, flesh shriveling into ash. The memories flooded Dreythan's mind as he rushed suddenly back to consciousness.

Shooting upright, his hand flailed to his side.

"Easy," a calm voice said. "You're safe now, my lord. Your weapon is beside the door, along with your other belongings."

Taking a deep breath, Dreythan tried to settle his pounding heart as he gathered his senses. He lay in a simple bed, a rough woolen blanket covering him. Hewn logs had been stacked atop one another to form the four walls of a small one-room house. His boots, gloves, belt, and scabbard were arranged neatly next to the rough wooden door. A merry fire blazed in a brick hearth on the opposite side of the room, with three cloaks hung to dry on the wall close by it.

A figure bent toward the hearth with their back toward him, the crackling flames illuminating their silhouette.

Lowering his aching legs over the side of the bed, the king

rubbed his bristly, unshaven chin. An uneasy chill crept down the nape of his neck. His guards... The arrows... Assassins. The woman.

"You stopped them," he said slowly, gathering his scattered thoughts. "My attackers. And guided me to safety." He paused. "How?"

"I was hunting," she replied over her shoulder.

The aroma of stewed vegetables and venison wafted through the warm air of the cabin. Dreythan's stomach twisted hungrily.

"There's a good deer trail not far from the path through the Pass. I was tracking an injured doe when I heard horses. They sounded terrified." The ladle circled the pot one last time, then withdrew and tapped on the rim. "'Tis unusual to hear horses at all in these parts, let alone frightened ones. I knew there must be trouble. When I saw the Unbreathing headed right for your hiding place, there was little time to act." Pouring some of the contents from the pot into a clay bowl, she rose and crossed the room, placing the steaming bowl in Dreythan's hands. "I only wish I could've gotten there sooner. Eat up, my lord. I don't have any spoons, but you can drink from the bowl if that's all right."

The woman stood taller than average, slender and lithe. Her face was pale, fine-boned and round, with freckles sprinkled generously over the bridge of her nose and cheeks. Unruly hair had been cut unevenly to about shoulder length. It was bright red-brown, the color of autumn leaves.

Dreythan blinked. She must be part gypsy to have hair of that unusual shade. As he stared into the woman's emerald green eyes, a strange sense of familiarity washed over him.

He watched as she settled back down beside the fire, pouring another bowl of stew. Between puffs to cool down the steaming liquid, she commented, "'Tis unusual to have travelers through the Valer-Norst Pass, my lord. But the king? Why would you take such a dangerous road to Ilumence?"

The question prodded his foggy thoughts, forcing an attempt at clarity. He frowned down at his bowl. So many threads of fear and uncertainty were spinning in his mind, weaving a tangled web of questions. "I was on my way to Luminhold."

Luminhold. Morthas... Morthas's funeral.

He shot to his feet, narrowly avoiding spilling hot stew down his front. A jolt shot through him as his stiff muscles cried out in protest. "I must leave immediately," he managed, blinking through the pain. "The burial is in less than two days."

"Are you all right?" The question was quick, sharp. "Are you injured?"

"No, not injured," he grunted. "Simply unused to riding horseback."

"And clearly in pain. You're in no condition to brave the Pass on foot," the young woman told him firmly. "Not now."

Without a horse, without guards or a guide, there was little chance he would make it across the border without freezing or losing his way. And there was no guarantee he was not still being hunted. "I cannot abandon my duty," he said, trying and failing to push the anxiety away. "Is there any way I might possibly reach Ilumence within the next day?"

She shook her head, a frown etched across her brow. "No, absolutely not. The snowstorm has blocked the Pass. There's no way to make it through, not without the proper equipment and experience." Rapidly, she sketched a figure in the air with her fingers. "Imagine this is the Pass. When a blizzard such as this descends, the snow is driven in from all directions, building and piling against the two sharp angles of the mountains 'til the path is buried under several feet of white powder." Jaw firmly set, she finished, "Having patrolled this area for a decade, I can assure you I know what I speak of, my lord. You would not make it through. Not for at least a fortnight."

He glanced sharply at her. "You cannot be older than I."

A flush colored her cheeks. "I am twenty-two, my lord," she replied, raising her chin defensively.

"And yet you have patrolled here for ten years?"

"Yes... a little longer, in truth."

He stared at her green eyes and red-brown hair, the sense of familiarity so strong now he could nearly touch it. "You have been a Forester since you were a child," he whispered, and then, realized. "Fletch?"

A smile lit up her freckled face. "So you do remember me."

The fifteen-year-old boy looked up as the guards escorted a tiny figure holding a bow and quiver. He knew her long before one of the men announced, "Fletch Wyndshaper to make a request of you, my lord."

The little girl stepped forward, her round face unusually sober as she placed the bow and arrow-less quiver at his feet. "My lord," she said, her voice steady as she folded her childishly plump hands in front of her. "Since my Papa died, I've been living in an orphanage on the outside of the city. The people there are kind, but... I feel crowded and jostled, and I'm not allowed to use my bow." She paused, briskly wiping her nose, and sniffed resolutely. "Your father was king," she said, "and now that he is... gone, you are king. My father was a Forester before he became Captain. Now that he is gone, I wish to be a Forester. He lived to serve Ivenhence, and I want to do the same thing so all his hard work shan't be for nothing."

The guards smiled indulgently. The child was, after all, only seven.

But Dreythan looked into those eyes and saw a pleading. A pleading he'd seen three moons before when Kell Wyndshaper collapsed onto the cold stone with an arrow in his heart, a pleading that he saw every night when he closed his eyes. "Do you understand what you ask of me?" he said quietly. "The life of a Forester is a lonely one. They rarely leave their post, and seldom speak with or meet other people. You would have to learn to become self-sufficient and to live off the land you protect. It would be a difficult and demanding life."

Fletch nodded. "I want to be by myself," she said. "I want everything to be quiet."

Dreythan understood exactly what she meant. The sympathetic glances, the whispering behind hands, the all-too-sensitive inquiries about how he was feeling. He would gladly escape from it all if he could.

"It shall be as you have requested," he said gently.

One of the guards guffawed. "My lord," he protested, "she is only a child! She cannot oversee the safety of the forest, let alone her own safety!"

Dreythan silenced the man with a cold stare. "I am barely more than a child," he said quietly. "Yet I am responsible for the safety of this entire nation. I oversee the taxation and distribution of goods. I decide which men are guilty and which are innocent. Would you say that I am unfit to do these things because I am young?"

The guard ducked his head. "No, my lord."

Dreythan looked at Fletch, and smiled. "If I can be a king, then surely Fletch can be a Forester."

The little girl took his hand and kissed it. "Thank you, Your Majesty," she whispered, and left.

That night, and every night after, Dreythan's dreams had been free from pleading green eyes.

The king sank back onto the bed, absently sipping from his bowl. "I must confess, I did not recognize you," he replied slowly. "It has been many years, after all. But I could never forget the young girl who asked to become a Forester." After a brief pause, he asked, "How is it that you recognized me? Why did you not remind me?"

Still smiling, Fletch lifted her bowl to her lips and drank deeply. "Your voice. I remembered it from the castle," she answered between gulps. "But the voice from the castle was your father's. You sound just like him."

Dreythan searched his stew for a suitable reply, feeling he'd just received an extraordinary and undeserved compliment.

"And I didn't remind you because... Well, you've been through a lot. My identity is unimportant by comparison." She took another long sip from her bowl. "But you never answered my original question. What brings you through the Pass?" She drew a quick breath as if to ask another question, but stopped.

Without looking up, Dreythan said, "My uncle, King Morthas the Benevolent, is to be buried in two days. I was trying to reach

Luminhold in time to attend his ceremony."

There were several moments of silence as Dreythan hid his face behind his soup. He gulped it down past the sudden lump in his throat, blinking the stinging from his eyes. Bits of sweet carrot, celery, and venison mingled in the broth, their flavors delighting him as he chewed. When the swallowed stew reached his hollow belly, it warmed him from the inside out. Gods, but he had been famished.

When he lowered the bowl, Fletch had set hers aside and folded her long fingers over her knees. "I'm sorry," she told him quietly. "I shouldn't have pried. You have my condolences, my lord, for whatever they're worth."

No suitable answer came to mind. The king nodded, carefully not meeting the young woman's eyes.

Several uncomfortable seconds passed before Fletch stood, nodding at the bowl in Dreythan's hands. "You'd best finish quickly," she said. "We'll be snowed in unless we leave soon."

Dreythan cocked a brow at her.

"Iventorr Castle," she replied to his silent question. "You'd normally send a messenger jay to Iventorr upon arrival in Luminhold, correct? When no missive arrives, the castle will be in an uproar. 'Tis nearly thirty miles to the closest town. Since we don't have a horse, the return trip to Iventorr shall take at least three days." Her eyes scanned him up and down. "Judging by how sore you look, I would guess four."

Dreythan turned to the neat pile of his belongings, hands still clutching the simple wooden bowl. When his eye fell on a rust-colored spot on his freshly scuffed black boots, his heart clenched in his chest.

Blood.

Whose blood? Mordin's? No, Mordin had been killed before he could even dismount. It must have been Pennick's, when he tried to throw himself out of the saddle. The image of Raylin's desperately reaching hand flashed before his mind, and he shuddered.

"Would it be at all possible to get a message across the border?" he asked finally. "Morthan expects my presence. I cannot allow him to believe I did not wish to pay my respects. It would be an affront to Ilumence, and a poor way to welcome Morthan to his throne."

"Hmm. Let me think on it," Fletch said. She was silent for a few moments, sipping her stew. When she lowered the bowl from her lips, her head bobbed deliberately. "Hmm. I may be able to make it to the border," she mused. "If I wore my snowshoes and all three cloaks. I know where the Ilumencian Forester outpost is… I should be able to find it and return in a few hours." Though she appeared calm, her eyes dimmed with apprehension.

"I shall not command you to do so," the king told her. "You have already saved my life, and I shall need your aid on the return journey. However, if you would deliver my message, Ivenhence would be in your debt."

To his surprise, she grinned. "No need for such formal language, my lord," Fletch replied with a chuckle. "My duty is to you and to Ivenhence. Your wish is my command." Her mirth faded to solemnity. "What message shall I deliver?"

"Nothing extravagant. Explain that my company was—" he swallowed "—attacked, and the Pass can only be traversed at great peril." Guilt strained through him. Great peril, which he was sending her into. "Please give him my heartfelt condolences, and…"

"And your regret that you're unable to pay your respects?"

He blinked at the soft suggestion, but nodded. "Yes. Yes, precisely. The wording you used is appropriate."

"Very well." Setting her bowl by the fire, she stooped, pulling supple leather boots over her calves. "The sooner I depart, the sooner I return and the less chance we'll have of becoming trapped here." Pulling the three cloaks from their pegs, she donned them one at a time, fastening each around her shoulders and raising each hood. Then she strapped her feet into a clunky pair of vine-strung wooden frames, slipped her hands into a pair of gloves, and snatched her quiver and bow from a peg on the wall.

With one hand on the door, she stopped and glanced over her shoulder. "You'll want to keep your sword close at hand while I'm gone, my lord." Her voice was muffled through the cloaks. "I'm unsure if there are more Unbreathing searching for you. I doubt they would find my cabin with the fierceness of the storm, but you can't be too careful." With a bob of her head, she tugged the door open and was gone in a gust of snowflakes and frigid air.

Dreythan sat back down on the narrow bed, wincing. His back and legs were much the worse for wear after two days on horseback. It wouldn't surprise him if his inner thighs were two large blisters, but it would be wrong to focus on his pain. Not when he still had his life, and his guards and friends had lost theirs.

Too weary and heartsick to do much else, he pulled his blade closer and poured himself another bowl of stew, then another, eating with abandon. Gut comfortably full, he sat sideways on the little bed, back propped against the cabin wall, his sword sheathed over his knees. Fletch's warning echoed in his mind, and he doubted he would rest until she returned.

The blizzard wasn't the fiercest she'd ever traveled in. But it was certainly fierce enough.

Hands clamped inside the three cloaks, pinching their seams together, Fletch squinted into the storm. The world was in reverse. Rivers of aqua and lavender swirled around her, the Wynd so strong it looked solid. Trees and rocks were mere gaps in the rapids, dark shapes which forced the torrential flow to part around it. With a quick exhale and a stiff swirl of her wrist, she reinforced the battered barrier of vermillion that formed a tight cylinder around her, leaning into the gusts as she shuffled cautiously over a snowbank as tall as the lowest limb of a pine.

It was ludicrous. Carrying a message through the Pass in a storm like this. She gritted her teeth against a shiver, pushing the thought away. It was her duty, and she was glad to do it. Even if it was only to give the king some peace of mind.

Inching her way down the other side of the enormous mound, she blew out another quick puff, spinning her hand. The king... Another few moments, and the Unbreathing would have found him. She drew a shaky breath at the thought.

It was a lucky thing she'd chosen to track the injured deer that morning. The doe's limp had been worsening. Better to give the poor creature a quick, merciful end than to let it be torn apart by a hungry wolf or troll. But better to allow a deer to succumb to nature's cycle than to allow the king to be slain by demonic monsters.

Her snowshoe caught on something, nearly sending her stumbling. Barely catching herself, Fletch's heart jumped to her throat as her eyes fixed on the thing that protruded from the snow. She yanked her foot free. A mostly-buried branch went flying, sending white clumps spraying, and Fletch swallowed hard. At first glance she'd thought it was a frozen hand.

With a deep breath, she pressed on. Images of dull white-grey flesh and crusted brown stains rose before her. She could only hope that the events from three years ago weren't repeating. She could only hope another Unbreathing den hadn't claimed the Pass.

Knuckles tightening in the wool fabric of the cloaks, Fletch doubled her pace. She had to get the king to safety as quickly as possible. The people of Herstshire needed to be warned.

"My lord?"

Dreythan started awake with a groan.

"My lord, I've delivered your message to one of the Foresters across the border." A hand helped him sit up, another pushing his boots onto his lap. "We have to leave, quickly. The storm grows worse."

Blearily, he pulled the boots on, clumsy from the soreness radiating through his lower body. Lifting his head, he met Fletch's eye. "How long has it been since your departure?"

"Five hours," she replied over her shoulder, pulling various foodstuffs out of a small cabinet. "I'm glad you were able to sleep. We may not be able to rest for a while once we've left." Tying a cloth sack firmly shut, she slung it over her shoulder and spread another one open. "Stand by the fire. You'll need the warmth in your bones."

He obeyed without thinking, shifting past her to feel the flames seep heat into his back. As he watched, Fletch rapidly packed the second sack and tied it shut as well. She turned toward him, her glance sharp and clear.

"Here," she said. "You'll need these." Removing two of the three cloaks, she pressed them into his hands.

Dreythan opened his mouth to protest, but she shook her head. "I'm used to these Wynds," she said. "It isn't as bad here as in the Pass. But you aren't. You'll need both of them, my lord. Best to put your own cloak on first so the second covers it... Those royal silver buttons would be a beacon to any Unbreathing looking for you."

"I had not considered that," Dreythan admitted, shrugging the cloaks on.

As he donned the rest of his gear, Fletch strode around the tight cabin, putting out the fire, placing the dirtied bowls in a large basin of water, pulling the rough blanket into place over the bed. She turned to face Dreythan just as he finished buckling his sword about him.

"You're ready?"

"I am."

"Very good," she said with a nod. "Before we go, I ought to make you aware of the danger we're heading into."

Dreythan swallowed. More danger than being hunted by

Unbreathing? He nodded, summoning his most neutral expression. "Go on."

"While we travel, we must not lose each other. We'll need to either link arms or hands until we have entirely escaped the blizzard. 'Tis far too easy to become separated and lost in this type of storm. If you leave my side, you'll freeze." She inspected his face carefully, as if unsure he understood. "Also, don't try to drink from the water skins without warming them first. The water can freeze to the walls of the skin in small shards, which will slice your throat if you attempt to drink. So if you become thirsty, tell me before drinking." Pausing, she raised a brow at him. "Do you have questions?"

"None," he said, though he briefly wondered how she would warm water in the middle of a blizzard. And why leaving her side meant he would freeze.

Fletch regarded him deliberately. "I'm sorry you're in pain," she finally offered, her brow furrowing. "I wish I had a salve to ease it, but I don't. Perhaps we shall find some in Herstshire on our way through."

"Do not worry overmuch," Dreythan told her, trying a reassuring smile. The upward curve was stiff on his lips. "I shall manage."

Satisfied, she tucked her bow under her arm, one gloved hand pressed against the door, one held out to Dreythan. "Then let's be going, my lord."

He took the hand, and they stepped out into a world of howling, whirling, blinding white. Fletch immediately began making her way in one direction, wading through snow that was already knee-deep in most places and waist-deep in drifts. Her hand firmly grasped the king's, guiding him behind her.

"Step where I step," she shouted.

He barely heard her before her words were snatched away by the screeching wind.

The cold nipped cruelly at his face and feet with needle-sharp teeth. With his free hand, he pulled his hoods down lower over his face, holding them closed over his mouth and nose to keep the stinging chill at bay.

Leaning into the biting gusts, Fletch kept up a steady pace, vigorously tramping in one direction.

The snow had obliterated any landmarks, and the wind kept whipping around, abruptly changing direction. Dreythan could only see a few yards, the whirling flakes blinding him to everything further. It was desperately confusing. At least it would be impossible for any remaining Unbreathing to find them.

Fletch stopped abruptly and turned. "Doing well enough?" came her muffled shout.

The king nodded. "How can you tell which way?"

"How the land lies," she replied, pointing. "When the mountain snow melts each summer, it wears away the mountainside. Over time, it's formed a ravine all the way to the Emerald Basin. All we must do is follow the slant down. It'll guide us!" With a reassuring squeeze of the hand and a quick smile, she continued on.

The white snowflakes fell in clustered disharmony, piling onto their already fallen comrades. The blizzard whipped them upwards again, forcing them to continue their weary journey, driving them to find another place to rest and be buried. Strangely, it reminded Dreythan of his father's ashes. The day of the funeral, he had poured them out over the Emerald Basin. A sudden wind had blown over the surface, scattering the ashes far and wide across the glimmering water.

Another memory rose unbidden to his mind. His father Dreythas, holding an ornate silver urn, emptying his wife's ashes over the Basin. The water had been unnaturally still that day, with hardly a ripple to disturb the reflections that hovered above. It were as if the Basin itself had mourned the death of Dreythan's mother.

She'd died when he was quite young. He sometimes wondered if the face he thought he remembered was truly hers, or if his subconscious had conjured the image to comfort him. The face was plump and dimpled, with twinkling eyes and a merry smile. It was accompanied by a light-hearted voice that called him 'Drey, my son,' and sung a lullaby without words.

Perhaps it was his mother. Perhaps it wasn't. Either way, the visage visited him in dreams occasionally, comforting and warming him. Sometimes, a gentle hand encircled his and stayed there through his dream...

The hand tugged his urgently. "My lord," a voice said. "My lord! King Dreythan!"

He lifted his head. "Yes." Something warm touched his face. Had he been dreaming?

"My lord, we've escaped the blizzard. Perhaps you'd like to rest?"

"Rest," he mumbled, the words tumbling wearily from his lips. "Yes."

The hand helped him stumble to a bare patch of needles beneath a cluster of evergreens. "There," the voice said gently. "Lay down, my lord."

He did so without protest. As he drifted into slumber, he thought he heard his mother's voice humming a hauntingly familiar melody.

Chapter 3

Fletch shook her head as she bent over the king, adjusting his cloaks to cover his hands and feet. He must have been exhausted. Already his shoulders were shifting rhythmically in deep, slumbering breaths.

She paused, leaning back as she examined his face. It was commonly known that Dreythan was thirty, but he appeared a decade older. His high cheekbones and forehead were pronounced in his thin, careworn face. Frown lines marred the skin between his thick brows and the corners of his eyes. His lips were a constant line of pensive anxiety. Around his temples, streaks of grey mingled with the black hair that covered the rest of his head.

Being a king must be more challenging than she could imagine. It was difficult to reconcile this Dreythan with the one she'd known so long ago; the handsome boy who'd smiled down at her and complimented her bow. This Dreythan looked as though he hadn't smiled in years.

Settling against the trunk of a nearby tree facing the king, Fletch tugged her cloak close. Losing her own father had been world-shattering, but it must have been even more so for Dreythan. Not only had he lost his father, but all his father's responsibilities and burdens had been thrust on him simultaneously.

Lingering on his still-furrowed brow, she found herself frowning as well. He was the reason she'd lost her father. Not him, exactly, but her father's sworn duty to Ivenhence. She couldn't resent the king, not when she'd sworn to honor her father's memory by taking the same oaths her father had. But it was strange to consider, especially after all this time. After the mourning and constant ache for her father had gradually faded.

Had Dreythan ever had a chance to properly mourn his?

Stray snowflakes floated between the tree limbs above on a blue wisping breeze, interrupting her somber line of thought. Raising one hand, she deftly swirled her wrist. The snowflakes halted, whirling away from the bare patch of leaves where she and the king rested as a dome of translucent yellow and orange surrounded them. Satisfied, she pulled her cloak close and settled deeper into the tree roots. But she didn't close her eyes. She couldn't afford to sleep when her king was resting.

Especially not when there were Unbreathing about.

Unease twisted her stomach. Pulling an arrow from her quiver, she inspected the silver-capped bolt and set it across her knees with her bow.

Now that the storm had faded, the forested mountains were still in the early morning hours before sunrise. Distant hoots and the occasional lonely howl echoed between the snow-laden trees, but otherwise, quiet reigned.

Turning her head toward the sky, Fletch watched as it gradually lightened, hours passing as she patiently waited. Waiting hadn't been easy when she'd begun training as a Forester. She smiled as she remembered her younger self, all twitchy feet and bottled energy. How her mentor had shaken her head at her. But over the years and many hours of practice, waiting had become second nature.

Something rustled in the underbrush, and Fletch tensed. The dim light of the not-quite-risen sun barely illuminated the bushes a few feet away where a shape shifted. Leaning slowly forward, she nocked her arrow, staring unblinking into the shadows.

"NO!" The cry burst from Dreythan as he shot upright, hands flying to his side.

The snow-laden bushes erupted, snow spraying everywhere as an enormous white rabbit bounded away, leaving a trail of paw prints.

Swallowing her pounding heart, Fletch slipped her arrow back into its quiver. "Not to fear, my lord," she told him, forcing a smile. "'Twas only a hare."

Dreythan's hands fell away from his blade's hilt. Face regaining some color, he raised it toward the sky. "You kept watch all night."

She shook her head, still smiling. "I've been resting, if not in the same way you have." Kneeling beside him, she opened one of the food bags, pulling out a water skin and a chunk of bread. "Here."

Dreythan took the vessel. His eyes blissfully closed as he took several long gulps. Finally lowering it, he gasped, "I have never had anything like this before."

Fletch cast a curious glance at him. "'Tis spring water," she said. "Nothing special. What do you drink in Iventorr?"

"Well water. 'Tis musty and stale in comparison."

Taking a few sips of her own, she fished another chunk of bread from her pack. "Wells," she mused. "Hmm. I don't recall them... I must not've been allowed near them as a child." Taking a bite of bread, she munched thoughtfully. "Or were they recently added to the castle?"

"It has not changed in all the years I have been there," the king said. "The wells have been part of Iventorr for over fifty years, I believe."

Fletch glanced up, wondering at his strained tone, but he avoided her eye as he ate.

Not knowing how to respond, Fletch hesitated, searching for a change of subject. With a quick wave of her hand, she allowed the dome of warm Wynd around them to dissipate. "I'm sorry about the storm," she said finally. "Shaping the Wynd high above the Hearth is unpredictable at best... I was simply trying to summon some snow to throw any remaining Unbreathing off of our trail, but—"

she gestured toward the dark skies to the north "—as you can see, it turned into something far more than that."

His black eyes finally met hers, confusion etched clearly into them. "I am afraid I do not understand."

She couldn't help smiling at his puzzlement. "My surname is Wyndshaper, after all. You didn't think I'd inherit my father's gift?"

"Gift?" His brow furrowed further. "What gift do you speak of?"

She stared blankly at him. Then she dropped her gaze to her boots, biting her lip. "I thought you knew. 'Tis difficult to explain, but... I suppose I could show you." Bringing her fingertips to her lips, Fletch exhaled, cupping the breath in her palms. With a flick of her fingers, she expanded the gleaming ball of sheer yellow, willing it to brighten to a vibrant orange. "Now, I know you can't see it," she said, "but imagine I am holding a ball. Touch it."

The king glanced doubtfully at her. After a slight hesitation, he slipped his hand between hers. Surprise lit his face. "You warmed the air?"

She nodded. "Wynd-bloods — the Wyndarin and their descendants — can see and manipulate the Wynd. 'Twas how I was able to summon the storm, and the reason we didn't freeze in the blizzard."

"And your father possessed this gift?" Dreythan's lips pinched together.

"Yes," Fletch replied. "I thought it was widely known... His father was Wyndarin, after all." She hesitated as Dreythan's mouth narrowed even further, then added, "But... perhaps it isn't as widely known as I'd thought." Swallowing the last of her bit of bread, she stood, stretching. "The sun shall rise soon, my lord," she said, offering Dreythan her hand. "We ought to get started."

"Indeed," he agreed. He took her hand and she helped him to his feet. A wince broke his sober features. Clutching his back, he rocked forward. "I am unaccustomed to riding horseback," he grunted.

She winced. "Ah. Yes, you mentioned that. Walking for several hours couldn't have helped. Hopefully we'll find some salve in Herstshire." Plucking the second sack from the ground, she tucked it under her arm, giving Dreythan an encouraging nod. "Once you start moving, the stiffness will loosen."

But before she could give him her hand, the king straightened, stoically thrusting one foot forward. Fighting back a grimace, he took another step, and another.

"Good." Fletch turned, walking slightly ahead of him, peering over one shoulder. "Now make a rhythm with your footfalls. One, two... One, two."

"You spoke truly," he said, following her down the slope. "'Tis becoming easier."

His strides were steady enough. She nodded approvingly. "I spoke from experience. The first time I harvested a deer out here on my own, I was exceedingly proud of myself. Until I realized I was a mile away from my cabin."

"What happened?"

"I dragged the carcass through the wood on a makeshift sled. It took me five hours to arrive home." She shook her head at the memory. "I knew the meaning of exhaustion that day, but the following three days were torture. I could barely move without crying out from the pain." Fletch glanced back at him again, startled when his black eyes met hers curiously.

"Why did you not leave it there, and come back to it later?" he asked.

"I couldn't," she said. "Wolves or trolls would've claimed it. I needed the meat to get through the oncoming blizzard."

"How old were you then?"

She squinted up at the trees, considering. "I must have been ten or eleven. I'd only been stationed here for a season or two."

There were a few moments of silence. "How did you become assigned to this post? It is one of the most isolated areas in all of Ivenhence." Was that a hint of admiration in the king's level tone? "You were not afraid to live without any neighbors, any assistance?"

"Afraid?" She slowed her pace, allowing the king to catch up. "What is there to be afraid of?"

He hesitated. "Freezing to death? Being ambushed by bandits? Wolves? Trolls? Starvation?"

She frowned. "I must admit," she said slowly, "I've been afraid of starvation a few times. Particularly when I thought the blizzards would never end. 'Tis one thing to find your way out of a blizzard, but 'tis entirely another to hunt in one. But as to the others, bandits are few in this area... and so long as you respect the territories of the wolves and trolls, they are no danger."

He searched her face carefully. "You have no fear of freezing?"

"No, my lord. 'Tis one of the benefits of being a Wynd-blood. I can trap air and warm it around myself. Although," she admitted ruefully, "a blizzard can snatch the warmed air away as quickly as I make it. 'Tis still dangerous in the Pass, but most other areas I patrol don't grow cold enough or windy enough to present me with a threat of freezing."

They were both quiet for a while, their feet crunching in the snow as the sun's first rays pierced the forest around them, glinting vermillion and crimson through the trees.

When the king glanced at Fletch, his features softened. "I ought to have said this far sooner," he said. "I apologize that I did not. Thank you for saving my life."

"Don't apologize," Fletch replied immediately. "You were weary from traveling, heartsick from losing your uncle, and in shock from the death of your men. Niceties are unimportant, considering."

There was a long beat of uncomfortable silence.

"Morthas was a good man," Dreythan finally offered, his words halting and hesitant. "A kind man." He shot a look at Fletch, and she nodded encouragingly. The curve of his throat bobbed as he swallowed. "When I had just become king, he wrote frequently by messenger jay, giving me council and helping me to understand the duties of a king. Though the journey from Luminhold can be a dangerous one, he visited me each summer until he grew too old to ride a horse." Dreythan paused. "His knowledge and experience were invaluable. I always bid him goodbye with bolstered confidence, knowing that I had learned and grown during my time with him."

"You looked up to him," Fletch said, holding a branch up for the king to duck beneath.

"I did. He ruled his kingdom for over forty years. His reign was peaceful and prosperous, despite Ilumence's complexity. The people loved him, and—" Dreythan faltered, but the words spilled out "—I loved him, as well." He glanced quickly at Fletch as if expecting some kind of reaction, so she nodded again. Squaring his shoulders, he added, "The captain of my guard, Norland Wyntersoul, cautioned me against the Pass. I should have heeded his warning."

Catching the shadow of regret and shame that fell across Dreythan's face, Fletch's jaw tightened. "You couldn't have known there would be such danger as the Unbreathing," she told him gently. "Not even I knew, and I patrol it each day." Doubt whispered in her mind, and she frowned. "Although, 'tis strange they were even there... I've seen no signs of a new den or of any Unbreathing for three years. Not since the den outside Herstshire was destroyed." She stepped over a fallen tree with a shake of her head. "Unless perhaps 'tis on the Ilumencian side of the border? But why would they enter the Pass in that case?"

"They were looking for me."

Stopping dead in her tracks, Fletch spun to face Dreythan. "What?"

The king's countenance was drawn, strained. "When the

Unbreathing nearest my hiding place turned the final guard face-up, he said 'it's not the king', as if he expected him to be."

Her hand tightened around her bow. "I don't like the sound of that." The king reached her side, and they continued walking together. "Though now you've said it, it makes certain sense. They were behaving unlike any Unbreathing I've ever seen. Using weapons rather than their own hands, leaving fresh bodies unspoiled to seek another that eluded them." Her eyes narrowing, she nodded. "The bow would be far easier to use in an ambush than brute strength and speed. They must have lain in wait for you."

Dreythan looked away, his jaw clenching. "One of them tried to feast from the blood of Pennick — the guard who fell under his horse," he told her, the words halting, painful. "But the one nearest me forbade it, saying they had orders to leave no trace."

A clammy hand of dread clenched in Fletch's chest. "They had orders?" she repeated.

"That is what I heard."

"This keeps growing worse and worse," Fletch muttered, casting a quick glance at their surroundings as they walked. The forest's long morning shadows suddenly seemed far more ominous. "Did they mean to not leave any trace of you, or of themselves behind? Were they meant to make it seem as though you had simply gone missing? Why?" She gestured at Dreythan emphatically. "And why you?"

Shoulders rigid, the king added slowly, "Not to mention, if it truly was an ambush, how did they know I would be traveling through the Pass? Word of Morthas's death reached me the afternoon of his passing... very few in Luminhold or Iventorr were aware. Even fewer knew that I would attend his ceremony."

Fletch watched the king's face fall. She could almost hear the thought 'or attempt to do so' cross his mind. Guiltily, she dropped her gaze. She'd apologized for the accidental severity of the storm... it had prevented the king from completing his journey. But now, she was glad it had. It might have very well saved their lives if more Unbreathing were hunting him.

Raising her chin, Fletch drew and nocked a silver-tipped arrow. The Unbreathing would likely follow them all the way to Iventorr; she would have to be vigilant.

"Had you not told me they were Unbreathing," Dreythan said suddenly, "I feared they were Thissian."

Startled, Fletch blinked. "Thissian? Why, my lord?"

"Their arrows are black. As were the ones that killed our fathers," Dreythan replied, his angular features thoughtful. "Just before the assassination, my father was forced to break Ivenhence's trade agreement with Thissa. And I have recently had to decline one. Gorvannon, Thissa's dictator, has become increasingly demanding of Ilumence's and Ivenhence's relations as a result. It seemed as though this was more than coincidence." He swerved to miss a sapling, adding, "I cannot think of any other entity that might seek a leaderless Ivenhence."

Remembering the arrow she'd broken off from the snow-caked guard's back, Fletch slipped her quiver from her shoulder. "The bolt they used is fletched with black goose feathers," she said. Pulling the snapped missile to the light, she peered at it, squinting. "Which is unusual of its own accord. But the shaft is some material I'm unfamiliar with, and the feathers have been bound to it in an intricate pattern of crisscrossing thread so fine it can hardly be felt." She handed it to Dreythan. "This is excellent craftsmanship. Though," she faltered, "it seems odd to say."

The corner's of Dreythan's lips curled in a slight smile. "I am glad you thought to take one," he told her, only handling it for a moment before passing it back. "The arrows which the assassin carried fifteen years ago are kept in Iventorr's vaults. We must compare them upon our return."

Beneath their feet, the snow had decreased to a mere dusting across the forest floor. Patches of it had even melted into puddles, the sun's rays breaking through the trees to glimmer warmly across the little ripples.

"How far have we come from your home?" the king asked,

unclasping the brooch of the silver-lined cloak.

"Eight miles or so," Fletch replied. She suppressed a grin as, out of the corner of her eye, she watched Dreythan struggle to fold the cloak, nearly tripping on the hem. "Thankfully, we've made good time. If we keep this pace, we ought to reach Herstshire before nightfall."

Finally giving up and resorting to rolling the pesky garment up in an ungainly ball, Dreythan tucked it under his arm. "We shall be safe there?"

"As safe as any other town when Unbreathing are hunting you. 'Tis possible that some've made it there before us, hoping you'd pass through, but 'tis unlikely. Still, we ought to be cautious."

As the sun began its downward curve toward the horizon hours later, Fletch peered over her shoulder at Dreythan, her freckled cheeks pink. "Now that we're nearing the village, I'd like to make a suggestion for safety's sake, my lord. T'would be prudent to go by a name other than your own while in Herststhire. If anyone knew your true identity, word would pass like wildfire through the area."

He nodded. "And those who hunt me could find us all the more easily."

"Precisely."

Her long legs slowed as she curved to avoid the trunk of the largest tree Dreythan had ever seen. The rough, grey-barked column was over ten feet across, its gnarled roots stretching out over the forest floor for several meters. The first branch emerged about twenty-five feet above the ground. He could not even begin to guess how high the top of the tree reached. He stared in awe, the knot of anxiety in his chest melting as a sense of awe and insignificance whelmed him.

"The people of Herstshire shall know by your speech and

mannerisms you're well-bred," Fletch continued. "But I doubt any of them shall recognize you." There was a pause as the sound of her feet also stopped.

Dreythan turned slowly to Fletch to find her grinning widely.

"'Tis one of the oldest eldertrees in Iven Forest," she said, affectionately patting a root as high as her knee. "And 'tis also one of my landmarks on the path to Herstshire."

"I have never seen anything like it." The words spilled from Dreythan's lips. He glanced quickly at Fletch, but her gaze wasn't on him. It was turned to the seemingly endless boughs above. A ray of sunlight fell across her cheeks, lighting them with an inner glow as she smiled. "Eldertrees," he mused. "This is the only area of Ivenhence in which they grow, is it not?"

Fletch nodded. "As far as I'm aware, my lord."

"Perhaps I could say I am a Journeyman Librarian of Iventorr, traveling through Iven Forest to study them."

"That's an interesting idea." She turned her smile toward him. "I like it. T'would also justify the need for a Forester escort. Who else would know where in the forest the eldertrees reside?"

Dreythan hesitated. "You... do not believe we should enter the town separately?"

"No, not at all. T'would be safest to enter together." She arched a brow at him. "Why do you ask, my lord?"

"Some... might consider it inappropriate for a young woman to be traveling alone with a man who is not her betrothed," he said delicately.

Much to his surprise, Fletch laughed. "Your Majesty," she said, her eyes twinkling, "You flatter me. But the people of this town know me well. I collect my weekly wages here, and occasionally tell a story or have an ale. They shan't think twice about me escorting a visiting librarian."

When the sun began to glow rosily, drifting lower toward the horizon, the tree line suddenly thinned. Between the shadows and tree trunks, dark squat shapes were outlined by orange light spilling from windows and hanging street lanterns. Their feet met dirt road, and Fletch halted.

"One moment," she said quietly. Raising a hand, she flicked her fingers in a beckoning motion.

Dreythan's eyes widened as a gust of air pushed hair away from her face. She breathed deeply, scanning the village before them.

Seeming satisfied, she turned to Dreythan. "I don't smell any Unbreathing," she told him. "Still, they could be hiding. Keep alert, my lord." Unstringing her bow, she slung it over her back beside her quiver and shifted the leather belt around her waist, sliding a sheathed dagger from her back onto her hip.

The king nodded uneasily. "Lead on."

They proceeded cautiously into the village, following the dirt road as they emerged from the cover of the woods. Dreythan's nerves jangled discordantly in his throat, his hand twitching toward his sword hilt at each rustle of the brush. Likewise, Fletch's eyes darted back and forth across the road, her knuckles white around her dagger.

The tension eased a little as they reached the lit portion of the cart-rutted road. To either side were short, rough buildings made of stacked stripped logs, much like Fletch's hut. Not a single building they passed was constructed of bricks or stone.

A few townsfolk still occupied the street. Most of them wore patched, colorless clothing, their shoulders stooped from years of hard work, tin dinner pails swinging from their hands as they walked. Their faces were covered with soot and grime. Upon seeing Fletch, most of them smiled and waved or nodded, but all of them stared curiously at Dreythan.

"Fletch," he muttered, his gut twisting. "Why do they all appear so… impoverished?"

She glanced back at him with a puzzled frown. "'Tis a mining village," she said. "And those who aren't miners are woodcutters and carpenters, or blacksmiths. None of those occupations offer high reward."

"Inglestead, to the west, is a similar community," he replied, "but they are far more prosperous. How does Herstshire differ?"

"I've heard Inglestead has a trade route close at hand. Its townspeople can sell their goods without any worry. Out here, 'tis a different story. The closest trade route is on the other side of the Emerald Basin. Merchants have no reason to come out here. You might say Herstshire is the most isolated village in Ivenhence."

"But it is on the fastest route to Ilumence."

"Yes, but that route is far more dangerous than the other." She smiled sadly. "A few of the villagers here've tried making the trip to Ilumence before, but the Pass freezes over too often to make it worth the risk."

Dreythan stared at Fletch's back, unable to vocalize a response. To her, this level of hardship was normal. To see folk with hollow cheeks and hungry eyes was commonplace. Hands clenching inside his cloak, he marched on behind his guide, stomach twisting into a cold, hard weight. How could he not have known his citizens were this poorly off? He should have been doing something to help them.

Pausing in front of a set of wooden steps, Fletch looked up at a two-story log building. "Here we are!" she told him, slipping her quiver from her shoulder. "I believe Missy is roasting a boar."

The wooden sign hanging above the door read 'Grubby Mug Tavern & Inn' and featured a faded painting of a clay mug topped off with frothing beer. Dreythan glanced doubtfully at Fletch, but she didn't notice. With a growing smile, she shoved the door open.

He only hesitated for a moment before following her inside.

Chapter 4

Warmth washed over Fletch as she pushed through the door, met by the thick, appetizing scent of roast pork. Her stomach instantly growled. Weaving between the wooden tables that littered the wide room, Fletch side-stepped simple sawed logs that had been pushed up to them to form stools, hearing Dreythan's boots click across the worn floorboards behind her. She knew most of the folk who occupied the tables, nodding to the ones who met her eye and quietly passing those who drank deeply of clay mugs, mumbling to themselves. In the back, a roaring fire blazed in the hearth, a hog turning on the spit above it.

The tension of the day easing, she paused beside a small grey-haired woman in a brown dress and cream apron. Fletch tapped her shoulder. "Hello, Missy."

The woman turned, surprise and delight flashing through her brown eyes. "Why, Fletch dear," she smiled brightly, setting a fistful of tankards at a table, "'tis good to see you whole. I saw the clouds over the Pass yesterday and hoped you weren't out in it.

That storm looked wicked."

Fletch winked at the old worrywart, planting a kiss on her softly-wrinkled cheek. "T'wasn't anything too unusual. The storm, that is. Even were it a mere sprinkling of rain, you still would've fretted."

Missy scowled at her teasing grin, then dusted her hands dramatically. "I shan't deign to answer that. Well, go on, dear. I'm sure my husband will be happy to serve you a drink."

Heading for the long bar beside the hearth, Fletch slid onto a tall stool, waving at the man behind. He wiped clay cups with a dishcloth, humming cheerfully. "Hello, Jon. How fare you?"

The man looked up, his round face broadening with a white smile that was made even brighter by the polished darkness of his skin. "Well, bless the biscuits!" He chortled. "If it isn't Fletch Wyndshaper. What brings you all the way here, this time o' the week?" Before she could reply, his brown eyes transferred to Dreythan, widening. "And who's this? I haven't seen you in these parts before, stranger. Welcome t' the Grubby Mug!"

He offered a huge, meaty hand to the king. Taking it, Dreythan was given a hearty shake. "I am Roderick Galefall, Journeyman Librarian of Iventorr," he said.

Fletch raised a brow at him. Dreythan didn't seem to notice her skepticism as Jon beamed, still gripping his hand. "Good to meet you, Galefall, good to meet you. I'm Jon Pruden, keeper o' this humble tavern and inn. What's your business in Herstshire, if I might ask?"

"I am simply passing through," the king replied, his dark eyes inspecting the innkeeper's face as he managed to withdraw his hand. "The library has assigned me to the study of indigenous fauna. The eldertree, in particular."

"I've been assigned to escort him through the forest," Fletch interjected, nodding toward the hearth. "That hog smells delicious."

Jon glanced from Dreythan to Fletch, his surprise quickly forgotten. "You both look fair famished," he said with a chuckle.

"Forgettin' my manners, I am. Well, welcome again, Galefall! I hope you find the hospitality here to your likin'." Ducking out from behind the bar, he called, "Missy! Bring these here folk some grub."

Patting her grey curls, the little woman hurried to the roasting hog and sliced some off, distributing the meat onto two plates. Trundling to the counter, she slid the plates in front of Dreythan and Fletch. "There you are. Go on and fill your stomach, dears, and tell me what you'll have to drink since my husband—" she shot a teasing glare at the innkeeper's back, "—is busy chatting with our other patrons."

Not hearing his wife's jibe, Jon moved on to another table, shaking the hands of the occupants as he laughed and chatted animatedly.

Fletch cast a quick glance at the king, watching his expression ease into a smile. "I'll have some water."

"What? No ale? A woman can have a drink too, dear, even if the men are present." She winked cheekily at Dreythan. "Very well, then. And what can I get your handsome friend?"

Dreythan's lips widened. "An ale, kind lady."

There, finally, was a hint of the boy Fletch had once known. His shoulders had relaxed, his spine no longer ramrod straight. One elbow propped against the bar, with dirty boots and cloak and an unshaven chin, he looked as though he had grown up in a small town, not on a throne.

Two mugs plopped onto the counter before them. "There you are," Missy said. "Your drinks. Will you be taking a room tonight, perhaps?"

"Two rooms," Dreythan said before Fletch could reply.

Missy nodded. "Two rooms it is. I can take your belongings up now, if you'd like."

Fletch handed their food packs and cloaks to Missy, but kept her quiver and bow. Picking up the pork with her fingers and taking a large bite, she glanced surreptitiously at Dreythan. He stared for a moment at his plate. Then he shrugged, picked up the meat, and began eating ravenously.

"We're safe for now," she muttered out of the corner of her mouth, swallowing back a 'my lord'. "I recognize everyone here. There's no sign of Unbreathing in Herstshire."

Dreythan nodded, still chewing. As Fletch turned back to her own plate, she knew she hadn't imagined the relief that flashed across the king's face.

Master Pruden trundled back behind the bar from collecting empty mugs, humming merrily. Drinking heartily from his own cup, Dreythan wiped his mouth and took a deep breath. "Master Pruden," he said, "This brew is excellent. It has a unique flavor — crisp and sweet, yet salty. Is this your own recipe?"

The innkeeper gave Dreythan his sunniest smile. "Why, yes," he said slowly. "That's terribly kind of you to say. Would you be havin' another?"

"Not at the moment. In truth, there is another reason for my visit to Herstshire."

With a slice of bread halfway to her mouth, Fletch froze.

"I travel on behalf of the king," Dreythan continued. "He desires to find how his reign has affected the kingdom, and he wishes to make improvement in lacking areas."

Master Pruden's shoulders shook with hearty guffaw. "That's a good 'un," he boomed. "The king wants to make improvement! Oh, heheh! Are you sure you're not a jester, Galefall?" He chortled again, setting his cup on the counter with a bang.

A dark frown shadowed the king's eyes.

"The man is serious, Master Pruden," Fletch quickly interjected. "Spread the word to your other customers. He'll speak to them after we've taken our fill."

When both of them stared soberly at him, Pruden's laughter gradually faded until he stared blankly back. "You're serious, aren't you," he said, and shrugged. "Very well, then. I'll let 'em all know."

As he turned and left the bar, Fletch clutched the rim of her plate. Didn't Dreythan understand that this would bring attention to him? Yes, it was unlikely anyone would recognize him, but...

But he was the king, she reminded herself with a scowl. He could do as he liked.

Dreythan shifted beside her. "It is not often that a ruler can speak directly with his subjects and learn their true thoughts," he told her under his breath. "Often their words are colored by their perception of what their king wants to hear. I mean to find out why this town is so badly off, and what can be done to help."

Biting her lip, Fletch resisted the urge to rub her palm against her forehead. "No need to explain yourself, my lord," she muttered. "It's too late to take it back now."

They continued eating in uncomfortable silence, allowing the sounds of the tavern to wash around them. The crackling fire, the hushed voices of Jon and Missy Pruden conversing with the other patrons, the clink of cups and plates against wooden tables.

Fletch cast a glance over Dreythan, whose eyes were fixed on his food. Had he even considered how he would converse with the townsfolk of Herstshire? If she were in his place, she would be staring at nothing, her stomach churning itself into knots as she chewed her lip raw, planning questions and answers in advance. The king, however, appeared intent. Focused. Perhaps he was troubled by Jon's mirth, or perhaps he anticipated the discussion... it was difficult to guess.

Picking up her tankard, Fletch took a long draught, blinking when she realized Missy had given her ale rather than water. "What shall you ask them?"

Dreythan swallowed. "What do you mean?"

She frowned. "You can't simply ask the patrons how the king can improve his reign. You'll be bombarded with nothing but complaints. Everyone has a different opinion of what could be done better."

"Hmm." Dividing another large chunk of bread with his fingers, Dreythan popped it in his mouth.

Fletch raised one brow. He hadn't even seemed to hear. "Perhaps asking targeted questions would yield targeted answers?" she pressed. "Funnel and sieve the feedback into useful information by asking about specific topics." Catching a sharp look from the king, she dropped her eyes to her plate, cheeks flaring. "My apologies, my lord. T'was only a suggestion."

"With what questions would you begin?" he asked after a brief pause.

She nearly choked, and swallowed hard. "You're asking my opinion?"

He nodded, the hint of a smile playing around his lips.

Wondering if he was testing her somehow, Fletch replied hesitantly, "Well, I'd begin by asking if the village's overall condition has improved or worsened since you — er, since King Dreythan began his reign. That would steer conversation in a constructive direction, I think."

"Indeed," he mused, brows furrowed. "Hmm... 'tis a good suggestion. I thank you, Fletch."

Jon approached the counter, brown eyes serious. "I hope you're up for an earful," he said. "Most of the men here have had their share to drink for the night, and may be eager to speak their minds." He wiped his hands on his patched apron and patted them together. "Just give me the word, and I'll let them know when you're ready."

Dreythan nodded briskly. "I am," he said. "Please, go ahead."

Clutching the handle of her tankard, Fletch slowly spun on her stool to face the gathered townsfolk.

The innkeeper leaned to one side, peering around Fletch. "Aye, you lot," he bellowed. "Roderick Galefall is ready. Gather 'round."

The other people in the tavern picked up their log-seats and formed a semi-circle around the bar, facing Dreythan. Many of the men had thick grimy beards, dirty hands, and broad shoulders. Working men. The women present wore patched dresses and tired expressions, their bruised, calloused hands curled around their cups and tankards.

Dreythan looked them all over. There were about twenty of them in all. Most of them looked curious, a few hopeful, and one or two angry. At the very least, none of them were shouting about dead chickens or hounds. He nodded to them, briefly meeting the eye of each person present. How long had it been since he'd spoken with Ivenhence's citizens outside the context of the throne?

"Greetings," he said. "Master Pruden has already told you my business in Herstshire?"

They nodded, and a few murmured, "Aye."

"Good. Your time is valuable, and I shall not waste it. Has Herstshire's condition worsened or improved since King Dreythan began his reign?"

"Both," one man replied, but another, simultaneously, "Neither!"

Dreythan frowned. Both and neither; interesting. "Will you explain? In what way has it improved, and in what way has it not?"

There was a pause in which the patrons glanced hesitantly at each other. "'Tis improved 'cause 'tis much safer for our little ones," one woman finally volunteered. "That Unbreathing den was taken care of a couple years back, and our children have a safe place to play within the town limits."

"It hasn't improved 'cause we work long, hard hours in the mines and in the forest," one man said with a rueful smile. "But that ain't the king's business. We chose our work."

"It would help if more coin came into our hands."

All of the villagers suddenly looked down or away.

"We're also better since we have a steady supply of fresh water," one of the women burst too cheerfully. "The king sent a crew when his reign began, digging a well for each town in Ivenhence. It has helped immensely."

"A paved road to our town would have been better."

This time, Dreythan caught the speaker. It was a huge, burly man whose patched tunic stretched taught across a muscular chest. A woodsman, from the looks of his rough, sap-stained hands.

"You there," he said, gesturing to the woodsman. "What is your name?"

The inn's patrons pulled away from the man, eyes downcast as if denying his voice. But the woodman's blue eyes met Dreythan's unflinchingly. "I am called Ker, and I am not afraid to speak what everyone here is thinking," he replied.

Dreythan nodded, stomach clenching. Ker's eyes weren't angry, or bitter. They were intense, open. Brutally honest. "That is what I had hoped."

Leaning forward, Ker's massive hands clasped over his knees. "This village is struggling," he growled, eyes alight with fervor. "Word has it the king has worked hard to ensure fair tax for every town in Ivenhence. But here, the tax is a persecution to us. The ore we mine, the lumber we fell, the few grains and vegetables we harvest, none of it leaves this village. We scarcely ever use coin. Here, we survive by bartering what we need from each other. For us, taxes are a strain to come up with each year. We have two ways to get the coin — trade something to a shopkeeper, or sell something to Forester Wyndshaper. That's it." He looked down, his jaw set squarely. "It's frustrating to see parents unable to feed their children because they had to sell their harvest for taxes. It's unfair when a blacksmith has nothing to trade because he cannot afford to purchase ore to shape. Last moon, Farmer Tren borrowed his tax coin from Miller Tren because he had to sell his chickens for last year's tax." Taking a deep breath, he shrugged and once again met Dreythan's eye. "Perhaps if there were a safe trade route to our village, things would be easier."

Every word the man spoke was a hammer driving a nail into Dreythan's chest. The tax. How long had he labored over Ivenhence's taxes with Morthas's guidance? And yet he'd still managed to overlook vital details. "How far is the nearest trade route?" the king inquired. Though his heart was thudding dully, he kept his face carefully blank. "I believe Forester Wyndshaper mentioned it was on the other side of the Emerald Basin."

"Three days' walk," Master Pruden interjected. "If there's good weather. The shopkeepers and tradesmen have formed small caravans in the past, but..." He shook his head. "There's no profit to be had on the road. Not to mention, 'tis dangerous."

One old codger who had been sullen and silent the entire discussion suddenly shifted, his age-clouded eyes squinting. "Ilumence would've been far more conscious of our needs," he grumbled. "Ef this shitehole town would've been in Ilumence, that is." Several people tried to shush him, but he snarled, "Why do ye think the king ignores yer plight? What more can ye expect from th' son of a rebel an' an upstart."

It took all of Dreythan's strength to maintain his even expression. "I will ensure that this is communicated to the king," he managed. "Is there other information you believe ought to communicated to him about Herstshire?"

The people before him remained silent, thoughtful frowns on their faces. "I believe that Ker summed it up in what he said," one of them commented.

"Very well. I thank you for taking the time to speak with me. Be assured that the king will hear your concerns." He stood and looked to Master Pruden. "I have traveled far in the last three days," he said. "I must rest."

"Right this way," Missy said from the foot of the steps.

Following her up the tight staircase with Fletch trailing behind, Dreythan found himself in a small hallway as a dark weight settled in him, heavy and cold. The sensation grew, compressing his lungs so he could barely breathe.

"The two doors at the end are yours," Matron Pruden was saying. "There is a bath waiting for you, but I'm afraid you'll have to take turns — we only have one tub. I already warmed it for you, Fletch dear. I couldn't remember if it was water you still struggled with, or flame."

Dreythan tried to thank her, to swallow the rising bile in his throat, but all he could manage was a strained nod.

"Thank you, Missy," Fletch said over Dreythan's shoulder.

"Not a problem, dear. There are clean sheets and blankets on each of your beds."

As Mrs. Pruden left, Dreythan's feet carried him down the hallway and into the last room, Fletch's footsteps echoing behind him. A tin tub, filled to the brim with steaming water, sat in the corner opposite the bed, and two candles cast their dim light on the room.

Fletch turned to him. "You should take the bath first," she said. "I'll wait."

"No," he replied, thankful his voice didn't crack. "You go ahead. I... I must think."

She gave him a long, careful look, which he avoided. "Very well." Entering the room, Fletch shut the door.

Finding his way into the next room, Dreythan sank into the straw-stuffed bed, absently removing his gloves and boots. The suffocating heaviness in his lungs squeezed ever tighter. Burying his head in his hands, he stared blankly at the wooden floor.

The village was impoverished. Despite his attempts to ensure fair taxation, these people were living meagerly — no, suffering. Ker had said they could not afford to feed their children. That taxes were causing them to starve. He shut his eyes and swallowed hard, the pressure on his chest increasing. He should have realized that some villages were removed from trade routes and access to coin. Hadn't Morthas even mentioned this during one of his visits? His oversight was inexcusable. How many other villages in Ivenhence were also struggling? How far had his father's kingdom regressed during his rule?

A soft knock interrupted his spiraling thoughts. The door opened slightly as Fletch poked her head in, her wet hair sticking to her cheeks. "I've finished," she told him. "Your turn."

He nodded numbly and skirted past her without a word.

His mind was far away as he slid into the warm water, not even noticing as clouds of dirt and crusted blood swirled around his skin. His father had worked so hard to ensure the safety and prosperity of Ivenhence. As his uncle Morthas had once his father died. Yet in fifteen years, he'd unknowingly undone their effort and council. He'd overlooked the people who depended on him for their livelihoods. And the one person he could look to for guidance was gone forever.

When Dreythan exited his bath and re-entered the room wearing his white nightshirt, he found Fletch idly tidying the room's sparse furnishings. He sat on the edge of the bed, staring into the distant nothing, hands clutching his filthy stockings.

Fletch settled beside him, and he stiffened. Gently, she pulled the socks from him, folding them neatly and draping them over the foot of the bed. Hesitantly, she faltered, "I'm... I'm not practiced in comforting others, or giving them peace of mind, my lord. But — but I'm listening. That is, if you'd like to speak. If not, I'll leave you in peace."

He turned his head away from her, but she waited patiently, her presence not shifting from the straw mat beside him. The weight on his chest trembled threateningly. "I have failed," he finally grated, hands gripping each other as his knuckles turned to ivory.

"Failed?" Fletch repeated. "What do you mean?"

"I swore to my father's grave I would keep this kingdom strong and prosperous," he said, his voice strange in his own ears. "But the people of Herstshire are struggling because of the taxes I have levied against them." He couldn't bring himself to meet her eye, and stared at the floor, pulse pounding in his temple. "My oversight has cost my citizens dearly. How can that be anything but failure?"

When there was no answer, he glanced over to find Fletch weaving her fingers together, her gaze fixed on the intricate lines of her palms. "Well," she said slowly, carefully, "I wouldn't say you've failed. You've made mistakes, certainly. But mistakes are opportunities to learn and grow. Ignoring or not correcting your mistakes is failure." She nodded firmly. "If the state of the village remains unchanged once your reign has ended, then you will have failed. But until then, you have the opportunity to improve. To change."

Returning his gaze to the floor, Dreythan shook his head. "You do not understand," he said hollowly. "Your lack of action hasn't affected people who depend on you."

There was a moment of silence.

Leaning forward, Fletch propped her elbows on her knees, her face in the edge of Dreythan's vision. "Yes," she said finally. "They have. Do you remember how I mentioned an Unbreathing den outside Herstshire? And that it was destroyed?"

Confused, he examined the side of her face he could see. It was set, grim. "Yes," he said slowly. "One of the townsfolk mentioned it as well."

"There's a lot more to the story." Her fingers wove into and around each other, twisting painfully. "Three years ago, people started going missing. They would suddenly disappear, and one moon later, another, and another. At first we thought an unusually wily troll had come down from the mountain and was stalking villagers as they left the safety of the town." She paused, throat bobbing. "But there was no trace of trolls, nor of the people who'd disappeared. Five moons after the first disappearance, five people were missing. I grew desperate. I combed the village and the surrounding woods for a week. Finally, I found a blood trail. A faint one. I didn't even know if it was from a rabbit or a human, but I followed it deep into the woods and found a frozen hand, sticking up out of a covering of pine limbs. I uncovered the body, and after some searching, found the other four. All of them sported teeth marks on their wrists and necks, some of them even on their ankles. The bite marks were perfect and sharp, and had not torn the flesh, merely pierced it."

With a deep, shaking breath, she released a frustrated huff. "It was obvious, then. A nest of Unbreathing lay hidden nearby. They wouldn't venture far from their den in harsh Wynds, so I knew they hid close to the place they'd disposed of their victims. After searching for several more days, I found a narrow fissure that led into the mountainside. A cave."

"The Unbreathing den?" Dreythan said when Fletch didn't continue.

She nodded. "There were seven of them. I knew I couldn't slay them all with just my father's knife, and had to send word to the Foresters' Head for silver-tipped arrows." One hand rose to rub her damp forehead. "Then I had to wait for his response. Gods, but the waiting was awful. When the arrows arrived, I was able to sneak my way into the Unbreathing den and pick them off one by one." Her weight shifted, and he knew she'd turned to look at him. "Don't think you are the only one who has made mistakes that cost others dearly, my lord," she said. "Had I opened my eyes to the possibility of Unbreathing, Herstshire might not have lost five good people, people who still had many years yet to live. They might have only lost one, or two. Yes, I made mistakes, but I didn't fail. I kept my oath and protected Herstshire. I slew the Unbreathing."

Startled by the adamance in her tone, Dreythan finally lifted his head and met Fletch's eye. Her expression was somehow kind, yet firm. Understanding and unyielding. "How long has the village been in this state?" he heard himself ask.

"I'm unsure, my lord. As long as I have been posted here, there have always been whispers of difficulty paying the yearly tax."

"And whispers of how much better off they would be in Ilumence?" Dreythan asked sharply. He immediately regretted his tone.

Fletch didn't seem to mind. She shook her head with a wry smile. "That was only ornery Trenton. Everyone here knows he's one of those Ilumence Loyalist nuts. He lived in Ilumence his entire life until he grew too old to care for himself. His son brought him here to look after him, but all he does is whine about the glory of ancient Ilumence and her storied history." She rolled her eyes. "He'll tell anyone how he looks down on Ivenhence for being a kingdom of rapscallions and usurpers. Pay no mind to his ire, my lord. He's the only one in Herstshire who follows that line of thought."

"He is not the only one in Ivenhence, however," Dreythan said. "Many who came to our nation after its founding share that view, as do many who reside outside of it. Many proudly claim the title of Loyalist."

She shook her head. "I don't understand it."

"Nor do I."

They were both silent for a few moments. Dreythan noted the weight in his ribs had gone. Perhaps Fletch was correct. She had not failed; once she knew the Unbreathing were to blame, she found them and slew them. Yes, Herstshire was struggling. But now that he knew of Herstshire's poverty, he could take steps to correct it. He could do his best to make things right.

"My lord," Fletch said quietly. "There is something else I'd like to say, but I'm not sure 'tis my place."

"Please," he said, unable to stop the smile that softened his face. "Your council is welcome."

Cheeks flushing, she ducked her head. "My father was a great man," she said. "Even though I was young when he died, I still remember his wisdom. Once he spoke with the men he led about why your father, King Dreythas, was an excellent ruler. Most of them believed it was because he was an inspiring leader — he'd led slaves to rebel against and defeat the Crimson Horde. Others thought t'was because he was highly intelligent, good with numbers. Or because he was kind and wise. But my father told them, ''Tis because he is a man before he is king. He takes his duty to rule seriously, yes, but his duty as man comes first. Every man is here on this Hearth for a reason. We must make ourselves the best we can be, so those closest to us are inspired to do the same. Perhaps we shall never do anything that changes our world, but we can certainly influence others to do so. And that is precisely what King Dreythas does.'" Standing, Fletch hesitated, then softly tapped a hand on Dreythan's shoulder. "Perhaps if you focused more on being yourself, your rule would benefit as well. Just a thought, my lord. I'll let you rest now. Goodnight."

She left, closing the door behind her.

He is a man before he is king... Dreythan had barely enough time to wonder what it meant before he laid his head down on the pillow and fell into a deep, dreamless sleep.

Chapter 5

The following morning, when Dreythan dragged himself out of bed, stretched his sore, stiff body, dressed, and stumbled down the stairs to the tavern, he found Matron Pruden already wiping down the bar, eyes bright and clear as though she had been awake for hours.

"Good morning, Roderick dear," she said with a smile, presenting a plate of fried eggs and some roasted boar. "An ale this morning?"

"No," he said. "Water, if you please."

As a cup was filled and placed before Dreythan, Master Pruden appeared, carrying a precariously stacked tray of freshly cleaned mugs. "Mornin', Galefall," he greeted. "I hope you found your room to your likin'?"

"That I did," Dreythan replied. "Thank you."

"Glad t' hear it." He set the pile of dishware on the counter, his perpetually-smiling brown eyes hiding a frown. "Ah, yes. Fletch asked me t' tell you that she's refilling her quiver. She'll be back shortly." After a brief pause, he propped his elbows on the bar. "I haven't seen her so worried in a great long while," he muttered to Dreythan. "Your work isn't takin' you near any troll lairs, is it?"

"Worried?" The king summoned his most convincing smile. "No, no troll lairs. Why would you believe she is worried?"

Master Pruden's forehead wrinkled skeptically. "I know that young woman better'n most. When she puts on her most cheerful an' optimistic airs, that's when she's really and truly perturbed about summat. She was more chipper this morn than I've seen her in years." Master Pruden's brown eyes scanned his, suddenly sharp. "Though it might not seem so, the solitude of the Lonely Vow has been difficult for her. She's like a daughter to me an' Missy. You keep her out of harm's way, you hear?"

Mouth dry, Dreythan nodded.

"Though," Pruden added, his serious demeanor easing, "I reckon she can keep herself out of harm's way." He turned back to his work with a chuckle, meticulously placing mugs in tidy rows on rough shelves.

An icy gust rushed over Dreythan's tunic as the inn door banged open, then shut. Suddenly acutely aware of his protector's absence, Dreythan examined the newcomer out of the corner of his eye. They pushed their hood back. Auburn hair tumbled around their face, and the king's pounding heart settled.

"There you are," Fletch said with a wink as she hefted her bristling quiver. "All filled and ready to go." Lowering her voice, she added, "Though I wish I could have gotten more silvered arrows." Slipping the quiver over her shoulder, she buckled it into place. "How are your legs?"

"Better than yesterday."

"Glad to hear it. I'm afraid old Hershelle is out of salve." She glanced to Master Pruden. "Unless you or Missy have some, by chance?"

He rubbed his bald head ruefully. "No, sorry to say. We used th' last to treat the miners' burns last season."

"Do not think anything of it," Dreythan interjected, seeing the kindly man's dark face fall. "I shall manage. As I said, the pain has lessened since yesterday." Fishing a gold piece from his belt, he slid it across the bar. "We must be going, Master Pruden. Thank you for your excellent hospitality. Please thank Matron Pruden as well."

After a few quick goodbyes, they exited the tavern, food packs and water skins freshly filled. Together Fletch and Dreythan strode down the dirt road, avoiding muddy cart ruts and puddles of melting snow. In the sun's light, the town looked more alive and less... haunted. Pens held chickens, sheep, and a few pigs, though the fences looked as though they were made to hold more animals than they did. Clotheslines were filled with patched articles that fluttered in the slight breeze. Children in faded pinafores skipped past, some stopping to give Fletch a quick grin or even a hand-squeeze. One of them paused to plead, "Forester Fletch, when shall you tell us a story again?"

"You must be tired of all my stories by now." Fletch laughed, stooping to ruffle the small girl's hair. "I've told them all at least thrice over."

"But you tell them so nice," she said, sulking as she trailed after the others.

When they reached the edge of town, Fletch paused and glanced back.

"Is something amiss?" Dreythan asked.

She shook her head. "I haven't been beyond that tree line in ten years," she replied quietly. "'Tis the boundary of my assigned post. It feels as though... I'm leaving home." The melancholy in her expression cleared as she gave him a wide smile. "I don't know the land from here, my lord. We'll have to guide each other. Iventorr is south-southeast?"

"Indeed," he affirmed.

Turning, she peered through the trees. "T'will be simplest to travel south until we find the Emerald River, then follow that to the Basin." Stepping briskly forward, she said over her shoulder, "South is this way."

As Dreythan followed, their footsteps whispering over fallen leaves and twigs, he found himself wondering what Fletch thought of all this. Was she so willing to escort him because it was her duty to protect Ivenhence and its king? Wasn't she afraid of the monsters who'd killed his guards, who could find and kill them?

He glanced at her back as she stepped over a long-dead tree, her long fingers grazing the peeling bark. Somehow, he doubted she was afraid. Cautious, perhaps, and alert, yes. But not afraid. She'd lived in the forest for nearly fifteen years. For her, it was normal to brave the wilds, to hunt her own game and protect the land she lived on. Endangering her own life for the sake of duty must have been a regular occurrence for Fletch, considering the post she was assigned to.

I was able to sneak my way into the Unbreathing den and pick them off one by one.

Her words echoed through his mind, striking him with their understated simplicity. For one person to destroy seven Unbreathing... he wondered how difficult it had truly been.

They traveled through mid-day, stopping once to eat and drink and take a short rest. By the time the sun had reached its pinnacle, the ground they traversed was flat and verdant with rich grass. A small rolling hill rose and fell here and there. Only a few trees dotted the landscape, and fragrant wildflowers clothed the Hearth in bright patches. It was a stark contrast to the peril they were trying to avoid.

"'Tis beautiful here," Fletch said, pausing to shed her cloak. "Far different from the end of spring in the Pass. Look at how alive everything is!"

Dreythan nodded, then hesitated. "Is it always cold? In the Snowshod Mountains?"

"Nearly always," she replied. "Though you grow used to it after a few years. A warm spell graces the mountains every few seasons and the snow melts each year, but it only lasts for a short time."

Glancing at the lush countryside that surrounded them, the king's footsteps slowed. "I do not think I could live in perpetual cold and snow," he said. "I would grow weary of white."

"'Tis nice to escape it," Fletch agreed. "I did miss the castle garden when I began my training."

The king's face tightened. "It has not changed."

"You've said that twice now, my lord," she observed. "When I mention Iventorr, you say it hasn't changed as if you wish it had."

"You might wish change upon it were you kept within your entire life," he said quietly. Fletch turned to gaze keenly at him, and he shook his head. "Do not misunderstand me. I have no wish to shirk my duty as king. However, being away from Iventorr has been somewhat…" He frowned. "I do not know how to express it. Aside from my uncle's death, and my men's murders at the hands of demonic monsters, it has been… different. Perhaps freeing? Not simply another day listening to citizens' complaints about each other, or studying taxes, or monitoring trade routes and ensuring the Foresters and Fishers have the supplies they need to protect our land and borders." His frown deepened into a grimace. "Apparently I did not study taxes enough."

Another few miles rolled by under their feet. The entire time, Fletch was immersed in thought, biting her lip as she pondered how to word the question that threatened to burst out of her.

"My lord," she said finally. "Do you recall what I said to you last night?"

Dreythan's black eyes met hers, and within them, she saw genuine curiosity. "'He is a man before he is king.' Yes, I recall. What does it mean?"

A frown crossed her face as she looked to the horizon. "Consider this. Were you not the king of Ivenhence, who would you be?"

After a moment, Dreythan replied, "I am not sure I understand."

"Take me, for instance." Fletch gestured broadly. "I may be a Forester, but that doesn't define me. 'Tis simply my profession. Thanks to my father, I'm skilled in the crafting of bows and arrows, and that in turn led me to become skilled in their use. I enjoy speaking with others, but many times I'm misunderstood because I'm too direct and I have an odd sense of humor. I'm fond of the colors blue and purple, and the sound of falling rain." She swallowed, then added hesitantly, "I... don't remember much of my mother, but I know I inherited her blood, her hair, and her skin. And because of her, I learn all I can about the Wyndarin. The 'gypsies,' as most folk seem to call them." Inspecting Dreythan's face carefully, Fletch concluded, "So you see, I would still be myself, even were I not a Forester."

Dreythan nodded. "I see," he said slowly. "So that is why you gave examples of my father's character, of what made him a man rather than a king." His face clouded. "I am afraid I am not much like my father, but... I understand your point. Give me a moment to think."

They kept walking, their boots brushing through the fields of grass and bobbing wildflowers. Still Dreythan didn't speak, the space between his brows wrinkled with the depth of his thought. After a mile of silence, Fletch asked, "What sort of things do you enjoy, my lord? Do you have a favorite place to visit, or a — a pastime?"

"I... appreciate the library," he replied slowly. "Mainly due to the solitude. I need not worry about being disturbed there. I also enjoy sparring with the guards on occasion. It takes my mind off matters." Frown suddenly dissolving, he glanced up with a smile. "Is your pastime storytelling?"

Fletch chuckled. "In a way, I suppose. It seems the little ones corner me and badger me into telling them one of my father's old tales whenever I'm in Herstshire. Or they'll have me read one from the town storybook."

"What sort of tales do you tell?"

"Oh, the usual sort," she shrugged, conscious of her sheepish grin. "The Great Slaving and the fight for freedom, the troll and the swamp wyrm, the taming of the sea. The children especially seem to love the creation of the Hearth and how Luminia, Ivere, and Ohnaedris defeated Kazael and his Unbreathing Horde." Attempting to steer the conversation away from herself, she blurted, "You used to build things. I remember you made a model of Iventorr Castle out of wood shavings, twigs, and flour paste once."

The king's eyes twinkled merrily, and she knew he wasn't fooled. "I do not believe I have heard that tale in quite some time," he mused. "The creation of the world and Kazael's defeat, that is. Could you tell it to me?"

Fletch's face tingled fiercely, and she knew it had turned bright red. She couldn't refuse a direct request from the king... Could she? Struggling silently for a few moments, she swallowed hard. Then she cleared her throat.

"In the beginning, the world was shapeless and dark, a void without light, life, or color. The Nameless One, the ageless being who had no birth and no death, who existed before time itself, decided that he would create four beings. Fashioned after himself, intelligent and imbued with The Nameless One's own power, they were to be his children. With one thought, he created two brothers and named them Ohnaedris and Kazael. To Ohnaedris, he gave wisdom and reason. To Kazael, he gave cunning intellect and a strong will. The two brothers stayed by The Nameless One's side, listening to the purposes and plans he had for them."

She cast a quick glance at Dreythan. To her relief, he appeared to be listening intently, his forehead creased as he stepped over branches and stones.

"After a time," she continued, "The Nameless One decided to create two more beings. This time, he made sisters and named them Luminia and Ivere. To Luminia he gave a kind, gentle, sweet spirit, and to Ivere he gave a vivid imagination and fierce determination.

"Kazael, after listening to The Nameless One for a season,

became distracted by the entrancing beauty of Ivere. She, however, remained fixated on her father, determined to grasp his purpose for her. Kazael, in attempts to gain Ivere's attention, experimented with his immense power. He created many wild and uninhabitable worlds that were strange and colorful, but hostile and dangerous.

"Ohnaedris, however, grasped The Nameless One's plan for the four and gathered them all together. He revealed to them the vision he'd had of a world, filled with light and life, illuminated by one bright burning light, and one soft gentle light.

"Ohnaedris began by shaping the world, taking it in his hands and molding it into a rough sphere. He filled it with ore and rich materials to sustain the life it would hold. 'Come,' he said. 'Let us shape this Hearth.'

"Then it was Ivere's turn. She was to provide the light that would feed all life on the world. In a burst of imagination and wild creativity, she created a great sphere that burned in the sky.

"Thinking that this was his chance to finally gain Ivere's admiration, Kazael poured all of his longing and desire for her into his hands and formed a globe that reflected the beauty and brightness of her Sol, then hung it opposite Sol in the sky.

"Ivere was troubled, seeing his obsession and recognizing it as unhealthy. 'It shall be called Mún, or Mirror,' she said, 'A reflection of its creator.'

"Then, all four, who had prepared endlessly for this event, poured their imagination and ideas out onto the ore-laden sphere that Ohnaedris had crafted. Trees, shrubs, grass, plants, animals. They sprung up all over the Hearth.

"But Luminia saw a potential problem. The Sol was excessively hot and scorched some parts of the Hearth. She guided her calming, soothing spirit over the globe, and water ran in rivers and waved in oceans and trickled in streams across its surface. Then she breathed a soft breath, and the world was separated from the Void by a cloak of Wynd.

"Ohnaedris anchored the Sol and the Mún in the Void, setting them in an eternal pattern, governing the growth and life of the

Hearth below.

"The Nameless One saw his children's creation and was pleased with all but Kazael. He warned his son that his 'love' was nothing more than lust, and would poison his heart, but Kazael would not listen.

"Ohnaedris, bent on perfecting the Hearth, thought it was missing something. It lacked order and rule. He conferred with Ivere, who agreed to help him, and together they created the first humans.

"Luminia, upon seeing this new life form, was delighted and intrigued by them. She and her sister spent much time with Ohnaedris, teaching the humans the order of the world and their duty within it.

"Upon seeing the object of his obsession with his brother, Kazael grew livid. 'I will show Ivere how weak the humans truly are,' he said, and from the blackest reaches of his heart he made formless spirits that he named Devuls. He filled them with his jealousy, malice, and hunger. Then he descended on the Hearth, offering men immeasurable power in exchange for their fealty. Some of the men, enticed by his promises, swore themselves to him, and he devoured their spirits and inserted Devuls inside their bodies. These Devuls within human Husks then fed off the strength within other humans' veins, weakening their souls so another Devul could consume them and claim a new Husk.

"Ivere, repulsed by the horrifying creatures that Kazael had made and the cycle of corruption sweeping the Hearth, went to the Nameless and pleaded with him to erase them from existence. But The Nameless One could not. 'His crimes are against your creation,' he said. 'You must find it in yourselves to confront him.'"

Catching a glimpse of the king smiling out of the corner of her eye, Fletch abruptly stopped. "You're poking fun at me, my lord."

"No, you have my word I am not," he protested, attempting to hide the smile and failing. "I simply understand now why the children love your stories so. You have a flair for the bardic arts.

Please, do continue."

"Therefore, Kazael was bound inside the Hearth by Luminia, Ivere, and Ohnaedris," she mumbled. "There's an excessively long story about the battle, which says that the sparks from their swords created the stars, but it always bored me." Her whole face stinging, she hurried forward, hand clenched around her bow.

Thankfully, Dreythan hung back for some time, giving Fletch's embarrassment the chance to wane. "Do you believe the story is accurate?" he asked eventually. "That Unbreathing are Devuls inside human bodies?"

She slowed, glancing over her shoulder. "I don't know, my lord," she admitted. "There's a lot that is unknown about the Unbreathing. Many believe the tale. Many also believe that the Unbreathing become more powerful when they feed from the blood of the living. And that so doing weakens the human's soul, allowing it to be devoured by a Devul which then claims that body as its home. But, to be truthful, 'tis all speculation." Fletch hesitated. "I believe my father knew more about them, due to his time in the Great Slaving. He rarely spoke of the monsters or his experiences, however. Doing so brought him pain." When Dreythan caught up to her, she asked, "Are there any books in the castle library on the subject?"

He shook his head. "I have looked countless times and only found accounts from the Siege that detail the battle itself, but nothing about Unbreathing origin. Nor of the process in which a Devul takes a human body to become Unbreathing."

They turned slightly to the east as their path began to weave in, out, over and down a series of rolling hills. The setting sun painted an ethereal rainbow of smoky purples and blues and vibrant pinks and oranges, highlighted by golden-tinged clouds. Ahead and to the right, less than a mile away, a line of water traced its way across the land, crowded on either side with willow trees and thick bushes, occasionally reflecting the melding colors of the sunset sky.

"That must be the Emerald River," Fletch said.

The king nodded, but Fletch didn't hear his response. Her feet automatically slowed. For the briefest moment, she thought she'd smelled the sour hint of salt.

Turning, Fletch scanned the landscape behind them. Nothing out of place stirred on the hills. No odd shadows shifting from place to place, no sudden movements. In fact, nothing stirred at all. No fluttering birds or hooting owls, no other sounds of wildlife. Heart sinking to her gut, she raised her hand and flicked her fingers, summoning a gust of Wynd.

The stench of rust slammed into her nostrils.

"What is amiss?" Dreythan barely got the words out before she whirled towards him.

"The Unbreathing have found our trail." She whipped a finger toward the river. "Run. I'll guard our rear." Whipping an arrow from her quiver, she nocked it to her bowstring, scanning the way they'd come.

One white-knuckled hand gripping the sheath at his side, the king broke into a dash, heading for the line of dense trees.

"Don't look back," Fletch panted between footfalls. "It'll only slow you."

Legs pumping, chest tight, Dreythan jerked his head.

Behind him, Fletch kept pace, her gaze darting back and forth. There was still no sign of movement. Perhaps they hadn't been sighted. Switching her bow and arrow to one hand, she shaped a steady gust of Wynd shifting across their path. Dreythan stumbled in front of her, sending her heart dropping to her gut. "Keep going, my lord," she pleaded. "We're nearly there."

It was only a white lie; they were over halfway. The comforting cover of trees and the scent-deadening waters of the Emerald River were still minutes away.

They might have been the longest minutes of Fletch's life. She could have pushed herself into a dead run. But she would have left the king in the dust. His hands and arms milled through the air as if trying to propel his body forward, his knees clearly shaking as he tried to maintain his sprint. But finally they were dashing through the shadows of willow trees, skidding to a halt at the bank of the river.

The tunic over Dreythan's spine was dark with moisture. He nearly doubled over, gasping for breath.

Fletch didn't hesitate. She slid down the muddy incline, her feet splashing into the gentle current of the Emerald River. They had been lucky; here the river wove toward them and away again, creating a curve of riverbed where the water was only a foot deep. "Come, my lord," she urged, reaching up to take Dreythan's elbow. "We must hide. Hurry!"

He stumbled behind her, pale face wincing as the cold water seeped into his boots and trousers. Following the edge of the water, they sloshed rapidly along. Beside them, the riverbed rose, morphing from an incline to a five-foot drop-off.

"It appears the dirt washed away during a flood," Fletch whispered over her shoulder, pushing her way under the overhanging roots of an old willow. It was dark and damp, and smelled overpoweringly of rotting vegetation. The perfect place to hide from an enemy that tracked by scent. Removing her cloak, she glanced at Dreythan as he parted the fringe of roots. "Wet your cloak — t'will mask your smell." She dunked hers in the now-knee-deep water and bit her lip as she wrapped it around her shoulders. The wet and the chill soaked into her skin, her cuirass offering no protection from the sopping cloth.

The king copied her, and they huddled awkwardly, dripping, shivering, hunched in the hollow of the bank.

"Do you believe they spotted us?" he asked hoarsely.

"No," Fletch replied. "But they'll track us all the same, my lord." Unstoppering a water skin, she handed it to Dreythan, watching as he gulped rapidly from it. "As long as we stay here, we ought to be safe. But we should be quiet. They could be close."

Fear is the greatest enemy, she remembered her father saying. *Under its influence, wise men do horribly foolish things and intelligent beings act on impulse rather than thought.* Peering through the darkness at the frantic vermillion puffs of Dreythan's breath, she frowned. "I have two more silver-tipped arrows," she whispered to him. "The Unbreathing are stronger and quicker than men, 'tis true. But we can still defend ourselves against them if we have the element of surprise. 'Tis why we needed to hide here."

"I wondered," came Dreythan's near-inaudible reply. "What is the significance of silver-tipped arrows? Would normal arrows not slay them?"

She shifted, the river gurgling around her legs. "No, as far as I know, only silver and fire can destroy the Husk of an Unbreathing." Before he could ask another question, she added, "We're well hidden. They shouldn't find us if we're quiet."

There was no response. As the sun's light died completely, sending one last wash of light between the trees, the only thing Fletch could hear was the sound of water. It burbled, gushed, gurgled and trickled all around her, tugging at her ankles and wicking up her clothes. Finally unable to keep her aching back bent any longer, Fletch slowly lowered herself into a crouch, holding her bow carefully above the water. The king copied her, gritting his teeth.

Through gaps between the roots, slivers of sky could be seen. Stars had begun to twinkle in the velvety expanse, shining their soft, pure light on the rippling river.

Suddenly, the hair on the back of Fletch's neck stood on end. "Be very still," she breathed.

Dreythan didn't move. The sound of muffled voices drifted to them, distant, but growing slowly closer.

"—tellin' you, it's a fool's errand. They've already made it back t' Iventorr."

"We have to make certain. I, for one, would prefer not to return empty-handed."

"As would I. Shut your flapper and use your nose, Telkk."

"How would he react if he saw how easily you abandoned your orders, I wonder."

Four. Fletch's fingers tightened on her bow. There were four distinct voices.

"Their scent faded miles ago," the first voice whined. "An' it wouldn't've done that unless they'd passed through hours an' hours b'fore us. I'm jus' tryin' t'—"

"You are trying to shirk your duty," the last voice snapped, sharp and crisp. "You are trying to find an excuse to hunt fresh blood."

Silence fell.

Heart pounding in her throat, Fletch eased arrow onto bowstring, her eyes fixed on the current of cool yellow-green Wynd that revealed the river's flow. Lines zipped across the surface as insects flitted to and fro. Beneath the water, the Wynd flowed lime green and strong, unstoppable. There were gaps in the current; fish, she assumed. And two bent shapes close beside her; Dreythan's legs and feet. The red-orange puffs of Wynd from his nostrils were short and quick.

There was an odd squishing noise directly above them.

"No sign of them." The closeness of the voice sent Fletch's heart shooting into her throat. "No scent trail, no tracks."

"'Tis odd how quickly their scent faded," another commented.

The sharp voice barked, "You fools. Have you no sense of urgency? Back to where the trail ended. They only left Herstshire this morn, they cannot have made it to Iventorr yet. Go!"

They waited in silence for what felt like years. The sky fully darkened, the stars only obscured by the occasional drifting cloud. Finally, Fletch stood, pulling Dreythan upright. "We should be safe for now, my lord," she whispered. "Come, let us move on."

Breath slowly steadying, Dreythan pushed through the willow roots. A muffled cry escaped him, and he nearly fell, catching himself on the muddy bank.

Slipping her arrow back into her quiver, Fletch unstrung her bow and slung it beside her quiver, circling the king's back with one arm. "Are you all right?"

"I shall be." The moon shifted across his strained face, his frame stiff as he and Fletch struggled upwards. "My legs. Running like mad then crouching in cold water has turned them into driftwood."

She shot a quick glance at him, startled into a smile at his attempt at humor.

When the ground beneath their feet firmed and grass brushed beneath their boots, Fletch half-expected the king to collapse and rest. Instead, he straightened slowly, meeting her eye. "Had you not thought or acted so quickly, we would have been caught," he said simply. "Thank you."

"Don't thank me." She shook her head. "My work is not done yet."

"When they do not find a divergence from the scent trail, will the Unbreathing return?"

"Without a doubt."

"And so long as we are soaked, shall we leave a trail for them to follow?"

"'Tis unlikely."

Squaring his shoulders, Drethan's jaw clenched decisively. "Then let us move as quickly as we may. How far is Iventorr?"

"I'm not certain, my lord," Fletch confessed. "It's been many years since I've traveled this way... Considering we'll have to circle about half the width of the Basin to reach the bridge, perhaps eight leagues."

"Then we shall travel through the night and hope to reach the gates by morning."

She raised a skeptical eyebrow, inspecting his breathing. It was still short and quick. Painful. "It would be wise to do so," she said carefully. "For safety's sake. But you're already weary — are you certain you wish to continue, my lord?"

"I am. Do not worry for me. I shall manage."

Chapter 6

When the sun's warmth spread itself across the kingdom of Ivenhence the following morning, the king and the Forester barely looked up or acknowledged it. They trudged along, their feet and legs only moving through sheer force of will, arms limp at their sides. Half the night they'd followed the river's curve. After crossing the bridge spanning the narrowest point of the Emerald River, they'd turned south, following the rim of the Emerald Basin.

Crossing the bridge in the dark had been an eerie experience. The roar of rapids, the constant distant crash of a waterfall, yet nothing to see but shadow and the cobblestones underfoot. Fletch had tried multiple times to summon flame in her hand the way so many other Wynd-blood could, but as always, the Wynd simmered to cinnamon-red without sparking, then sputtered away.

Through the trees, the moon had glinted brightly off the stone spires of Iventorr Castle, as if sending a welcoming signal. Upon seeing it, Dreythan's shoulders had sagged — whether from relief or dread, it was hard to say.

"Don't let your guard down, my lord," Fletch had said, her voice as heavy as her body. "It shall be hours before we reach Iventorr's bridge."

Now, with the sun finally peering over the horizon, Fletch allowed her shoulders to loosen. Traveling by night when the Unbreathing were strongest had been risky, but with the dawn, they would be weakened. Tilting her head back, she took a deep breath, filling her lungs with sweet air. Blossoming trees hung laden branches over them, from which birds chirped and warbled cheerfully. A breath of Wynd stirred the long grass and tree limbs, which shifted in a gentle whispering melody.

"We're nearly there, my lord," she told the king. "'Tis a shame we'll likely sleep the rest of the day away... it promises to be glorious."

To Fletch's surprise, Dreythan's eyes were alert, his shoulders straight, though he walked with a slight limp. "I am glad for it," he replied. "I shall not be able to rest for several hours yet, I am afraid. But this... glorious day, as you described it, shall make my weariness bearable."

Suddenly, their feet were no longer brushing through grass, but crunching over cobblestone. Distantly, the sound of crashing water reached their ears just as the trees around them fell away. An immense wooden bridge suspended from twisted ropes as thick as a man's waist stretched out over the wide lake far below, joining seamlessly with the stone gates of Iventorr Castle. To the west, from the way they had come, the Emerald River turned into the Emerald Falls. It crashed into the Basin, mercilessly pounding the rocks below with a roar that could be heard even from this distance, sending white foam spraying.

Halting in her tracks, Fletch gazed at the familiar stone castle with its ten towers and fluttering green banners, a strange sensation stirring in her chest. Her childhood home... The place her father had fought to liberate, then died defending.

"'Tis far bigger than I remembered," she breathed. "Or is it smaller? I can't decide. The tallest spire nearly seems to touch the clouds. I wonder how far one could see from the top. Perhaps five leagues?"

A smile cracked Dreythan's drawn face. "Your guess is an excellent one. The falconers have measured the line of sight at five leagues, two miles. They say it is the perfect place for training sun jays."

Fletch ducked her head. She hadn't realized she'd spoken aloud until the king replied. Unwrapping the silver-trimmed cloak from her food pack, she said, "You'd best don your own cloak, my lord. We wouldn't want you returning to Iventorr liken to a peasant." Shaking the garment out vigorously, she held it up to the sun. "'Slightly stained from the snow," she muttered, frowning. "But it'll have to do."

Drethan took it, swapping it with the plain cloak he'd worn for the past few days. As he rolled the cloth into an untidy bundle, Fletch held her hand out to him.

"A king should not be a beast of burden," she said with a wink.

He put the cloak in her hand, but didn't release it until she met his eye. For a moment, his lips tightened, a wrinkle forming on his brow as if he couldn't find words for his thoughts. "Thank you, Fletch," he said finally. "For everything."

Warmth closed around Fletch's chest, but she shook her head. "My duty is still incomplete, my lord. Don't thank me until we're safely within the castle walls."

They resumed their pace. Within minutes, their feet were tapping hollowly against the tightly-seamed wooden planks of the Great Bridge of Iventorr. Shadows of enormous support beams loomed over them, the lake swishing gently fifty feet below.

"My lord?!" came a startled voice. "King Dreythan?" A man appeared from the shadow of the castle's open gate, hand over his heart. "It is you! Thank Ivere. Captain Norland feared the worst when he did not hear from you, my lord. He is in the stables, preparing a search party as we speak."

"Lead me to him," Dreythan commanded, motioning for Fletch

to follow.

The guard's entire body bobbed with the vigor of his nod. "Yes, my lord."

As they strode swiftly down the cobbled street, Fletch stared, taking in as much as she possibly could. Turning away from a straight avenue lined with flowering bushes, they took a path that followed the high stone wall of Iventorr. Vague memories stirred within her as they passed a low, open, triangular structure to the left. Soft bleating, clucking, and mooing could be heard inside. The odd structure housed assorted livestock, Fletch guessed, wrinkling her nose at the smell.

To the right loomed an octagonal guard tower. Soldiers strode about in a circle on top, peering alertly down at the gates and the Basin below. Past the tower, a row of strange houses appeared to have been partially carved into the castle wall, then completed with hewn timber and decorated with arched doors and iron hinges. She stared at them, puzzled by their unfamiliarity. Had they been built after she had become a Forester?

Turning abruptly left, they entered a long, high building of stone, completed with a timber roof. The stables.

It was a madhouse. Soldiers and stableboys scurried hither and thither as a huge red-haired, red-faced man bellowed, "Where are the gods-damned supplies?! Every minute we waste is another the king could be dead. Find Torwell and get him back here, now!!"

Behind Dreythan, Fletch instinctively shrank.

"Captain!" the guard in front of them called. "Captain, the king has returned!"

All activity halted. Every eye turned as one to where the guard stood, then beside him. The large red-haired man was the first to kneel. The rest quickly followed

Shifting awkwardly, Fletch wondered if she ought to bend her knee. She was spared a decision when the red-faced man rose and strode directly to Dreythan, smacking his open palm on the king's shoulder. "My lord," he rumbled, relief etched into each line of his open face. His bright blue eyes glanced behind Dreythan and, seeing only Fletch, grew dark.

"My company was attacked, Norland," the king said quietly. "None of them survived. I must tell their families in person."

Norland hesitated, glancing again at Fletch, then back to the king. "Attacked," he repeated, his voice like low thunder. Then he nodded. "As ye wish, my lord. But your safety is more important. I need to know what happened out there."

"Of course." Dreythan motioned Fletch forward. "This Forester — Fletch Wyndshaper — saved my life. Ensure she gets rest, food, and fresh clothing. I shall wish to speak with her later."

"Yes, my lord." Motioning to one of the guards nearby, Captain Norland whisked the king out of the stables.

Fletch stared as their backs disappeared through the stable doors, startled by the sudden departure.

"That happens quite often," a congenial voice said. A hand entered Fletch's line of sight.

Turning, she looked up from the hand into a ruddy-cheeked face sprouting curly brown whiskers. The young man grinned.

"The name's Klep. Klep Ironshod."

Taking the proffered hand, Fletch received a firm shake. "Fletch Wyndshaper. What happens often?"

"The king gives the Captain instructions that he passes off. Then they march away." Klep's brown eyes twinkled in amusement. "So which part of the king's order ought I guide you to first? Rest, food, or fresh clothing?"

Rest. Gods, that word was music to her ears. She bit her lip, frowning. The king had said he would wish to speak with her later... but he'd also said he wouldn't be able to rest for several hours yet. Odds were, he'd likely call on her within those hours to give a report to the captain of the guard.

"I'll have to replace this cuirass," Fletch said, poking the nearly board-stiff leather. "And I'd pay five gold for a bath about now."

"A bath, you say. Well, the king didn't mention a bath." He grinned widely at his own joke. "But I'm sure we can lump it under the 'rest' command and none will know the difference.

Right this way, Forester Fletch."

Klep was as good as his word. In short order, he escorted Fletch past the great dining hall to a tower connected to it. After disappearing for a short time, he reappeared with a swarm of servants wearing cream-colored aprons or neat brown robes. They carried a set of fresh clothing, pails of water, and armloads of firewood. When Fletch told them they didn't need the firewood since she didn't need the water heated, they glanced dubiously at each other and at her, but trundled back the way they had come, casting odd stares back over their shoulders.

It didn't take Fletch long to warm the bathwater. She stirred the Wynd shimmering in the tub, gradually shifting its translucent shades from peridot and yellow to orange and red, then glinting cinnamon. It felt odd to bathe in the privacy of a far-too-large, far-too-luxurious-looking room. When she finished, she donned her fresh clothing and stepped back into the tower's spiral hall, ruined armor tucked under her arm.

Klep straightened from where he'd been leaning against a wall, nodding to the cuirass. "How bad is it?"

"As bad as I feared," she replied glumly. "I'm unsure if the leather can even be re-tooled."

His brown eyes started to travel from the armor to her face, but froze half-way. Ears reddening, Klep cleared his throat. "Gods, I… I did not realize you were a woman. I should have, of course," he stumbled awkwardly, visibly forcing himself to meet her eye. "The king did refer to you as 'she', and your voice and your face are quite fair, after all, but for some reason I assumed you were—"

"A man your age," Fletch finished for him with a quick smile. "Many make the same mistake. I think 'tis because they are unused to seeing women in trousers."

"True," he admitted. "But still, it is no excuse." He swallowed, his entire face and neck red. "Come, let me show you to the armory."

"Actually," she called, following slowly, "I'm fair famished… could we… stop by the kitchens on the way?"

Dreythan ran a towel over his freshly-shaven face, casting a glance over his shoulder at Captain Norland. The man stood in the far corner of the room, thickly bearded face set in a deep scowl. "I know my report was not a detailed one," he said quietly. "My mind is as clear as mud. I have been awake and on the run for more than a day. Ask me any questions you might have."

"Your 'report' is clear enough for now, my lord." Norland's arms crossed over his burly chest as he propped his shoulder against the wall. "We can muddle through finer details later. What's important is that these attempts on your life present hard questions."

"Such as?"

"Such as, who'd've known you'd be traveling through the Pass? On the day ye left, only a few here in Iventorr were even aware King Morthas — Luminia rest his soul — had passed. Even fewer knew you'd be traveling to Ilumence. And I'd wager the same'd be true for those who dwell in Luminhold." Norland's sharp blue eyes met his, a storm brewing within. "There must be a spy or traitor in one of our strongholds."

Setting the towel beside the washbasin, Dreythan crossed his quarters to the wide window and leaned against the sill. Though it felt as though it ought to be approaching twilight, the morning sun beamed brightly down on the grey stone walls, the gentle waves of the Emerald Basin, and surrounding cliffs, piercing the glass to glow on his face. The contrast to the dark matter they discussed wasn't lost on him.

"I have thought of that possibility," the king said quietly. "'Tis also possible that our messenger jays are being intercepted. But you mentioned questions, plural. What are your other concerns?"

"Why'd the Unbreathing initiate an attack on ye, and to what end? It's not like them to work for any but their own... If they're acting independently, why target ye? And if they aren't acting of their own volition, who're they working for?"

Dreythan smiled bitterly. "Some of these are oddly familiar questions," he said. "I seem to recall them being asked of my father's assassination." A memory of black blur and crimson spray flashed before his eyes. His chest tightened. Was the memory from fifteen years ago or three days?

"But that was the Thissians."

"We were never able to confirm. They never claimed responsibility." The weight of his painful, tired body was steadily growing. He shifted, trying to stay alert, resisting the need to rub his eyes. "The Unbreathing used black arrows, Norland. Fletch brought one for inspection. We'll need to compare it to the one that killed my father."

Norland scowled. "You believe those who're responsible for your father's death are trying to kill ye now?"

"I am not certain, but it would make sense. I would have died the night my father did had it not been for Kell Wyndshaper. The arrow he took was meant for my heart."

Once he said it aloud, it struck him deeply. Fletch's father had laid his life down for Dreythan's, and Fletch herself had saved his life twice.

He owed much to the Wyndshaper name.

"We should train a couple spies, have them infiltrate Thissa," Norland was muttering to himself. "Maybe they'd find more than smoke'n mirrors."

Plucking a simple black cord belt from the dressing table, Dreythan tied it around his waist, fingers shaking. "The families of the slain guards," he said quietly, keeping his voice level. "They have been summoned to the throne hall?"

"Aye."

"Summon Fletch Wyndshaper as well. She knows where their bodies lay. When she returns to her post, we must send a group with her to retrieve them for proper burial." The words sent a cold, hollow echo through his chest. "I am certain you have questions you wish to ask her, as well."

"Indeed I do. I'll summon her immediately, my lord." He turned to leave.

"Norland, wait." Dreythan hesitated, the thought forming simultaneously with his words. "It could be prudent to transfer Forester Wyndshaper to the guard here in Iventorr."

The captain's only response was a skeptical raised brow.

"She has the ability to identify Unbreathing. And she has combat experience against them. Consider it, if you would."

Eyebrow still raised, he replied simply, "As ye wish, my lord."

The captain's boots thumped against the stone floor, receding out of the room. When he was gone, Dreythan stared down at his table where a sober black cloak and a slender silver crown on a velvet pillow lay.

With an inward grimace, he donned them both.

Though the immediate tension of being hunted had faded, a cold void still gaped in Dreythan's gut. A void he couldn't name. It wasn't fear, exactly. And it wasn't worry, or frustration, or uncertainty. It neighbored all of these in its uncanny, insidious insistence.

Shoving the feeling to the back of his mind, he straightened. It was time.

Shifting from foot to foot, Fletch bit back a wince as her armor squeaked rebelliously through the ominous quiet of the throne hall. The castle armorer, Jorga Soothand, had been most generous. She'd insisted Fletch take not only a new leather cuirass that was actually made for a woman's body, but also a set of matching dark brown boots and forearm guards that she called vambraces. The leather was new and still stiff. It felt rather odd to be wearing armor that allowed for the shape of her breasts rather than pressing them into her ribs.

Moving as little as possible, Fletch glanced around. Lofty arched ceilings stretched above, supported by criss-crossing sandstone arcades. A rich green rug traveled the center of the stone floor from the enormous arched double doors, past rows of wooden pews on either side, up a flight of five steps, and ended beneath the throne of Ivenhence.

She wasn't the only person who'd been summoned. There was a young woman only slightly older than she, a sleeping toddler on her hip. Her eyes were pink and swollen, her cheeks tearstained. Also present were an elderly man and woman, clutching each other with bowed heads. A young man, his rough hands clenching and unclenching at his sides, stood near them. Last in line, an older woman, wearing all black, her face pale and strained.

As her eyes passed over them, Fletch's heart sank into her stomach. The king must have summoned the family members of the slain guards.

Captain Norland appeared from a shadowed door behind the throne, announcing, "King Dreythan Dreythas-son." Descending the stairs, he turned and knelt.

The families knelt with bowed heads, and Fletch, unsure of what to do, copied them, staring down at the grey stone floor under her knee.

"You may rise," said Dreythan's rich voice.

They did so in unison. The king stood before them, dressed entirely in black except for his silver crown and silver threads woven into his belt. His angular face was freshly shaven. His regal brows were drawn together and his eyes, wreathed in dark circles, soberly surveyed the men and women before him.

"Four days ago," he said quietly, "those dear to you were escorting me to Ilumence to witness the burial of King Morthas. Layward, Mordin, Pennick, Raylin, and myself were attacked just before we reached the Valer-Norst Pass. I only survived because they laid down their lives for mine." The king paused, looking into each face before he continued, "Their bodies lie at the entrance to the Pass. Currently, they are preserved by snow. This Forester," he gestured to Fletch, "is familiar with the location. She shall lead a retinue of soldiers to retrieve your loved ones' remains for proper burial."

Fletch blinked. There was a long beat of dread-weighted silence, punctuated by a half-choked sob.

"My lord," the elderly man began respectfully, "I know not how the others here feel, but... my son's body need not put others in harm's way." He glanced at his wife, who nodded tearfully, and added, "He lived to protect others, and he died doing so as well. I know he has earned his place in Ivere's sun. Let his body lie where it is. The Pass need not claim any more lives."

The king frowned. Turning to the other families, he asked, "How feel you on this matter?"

The young man folded his hands behind his back. "My lord, I do not disagree," he said huskily.

The matron nodded without a word, as did the young mother.

Dreythan nodded. "Very well," he said heavily. "It shall be as you wish. They shall remain at rest near the Pass." He hesitated. "I am indebted to each of them, and thus to each of you. I believe it only just to pay out their due wages to you as if they were still in my service, for the rest of your lives. For they, and you, have made the ultimate sacrifice for this kingdom. I shall never forget this."

Tears began trickling down the young woman's puffy cheeks. Boldly stepping forward, she took the king's hand, knelt, and kissed it. "Bless you, my lord," she whispered, and quickly left, her shoulders trembling.

The others followed suit, kneeling and rising before hurrying out, until only Fletch, Captain Norland, and the king remained in the chamber.

Heaving a deep sigh, the king lowered himself into the throne, his countenance dark and troubled.

One of Captain Norland's gauntleted hands motioned Fletch closer. "Come, Wyndshaper. I must ask ye some questions about the Unbreathing in the Pass."

Fletch nodded. Shrugging her quiver from her shoulder, she

pulled out the broken black arrow that had killed the clever guardsman and placed it in his hand.

He inspected it carefully, a pensive wrinkle deepening between his eyes. "All their arrows were alike?"

She nodded. "Yes. By the feel and look of the feathers, I'd say the fletchings are black goose."

Norland's scowl deepened. "I've seen wood like this before," he said, weighing the shaft in his hand. "The gypsies trade it. Ebonite, 'tis called. Unusually dense and durable, but light."

Gypsies. "That's... interesting." Fletch nodded, heartbeat pounding in her ears. "I suppose that would explain why Unbreathing use them. They could withstand a stronger pull than most men have. And," she added, her heart gradually settling into a normal rhythm, "since 'tis dense but light, the missile would be faster, more accurate. With an Unbreathing's strength behind it, I'm not surprised it pierced armor." Glancing up, she found Dreythan staring intently at her.

"You previously mentioned the arrow has unusual fletchings."

Again, she nodded. "There are grooves carved into the head of the shaft." Taking the arrow from the Captain, she pointed them out to him, then brought it to the king. "See there? The fletchings are bound in the grooves by exceedingly fine thread. Silk, perhaps? I've never seen an arrow such as this. The components are likely difficult to find, or expensive. Not to mention an arrow such as this could only be created by a master craftsman."

A gruff harrumph punctuated the end of Fletch's sentence. She glanced curiously at Captain Norland, who had pointedly cleared his throat, then at Dreythan.

The corner of Dreythan's mouth lifted in a smile. "Captain Norland believes you are disrespecting my rule by standing on level with the throne," he told her gently. "When a king is sitting in his throne, it is proper to stand one step below him at all times."

"Oh." She quickly took a step down, heat creeping into her cheeks. "Your pardon, my lord."

Had she imagined the brief twinkle in the king's eye? Her

attention was interrupted by Captain Norland asking, "You're certain all three assassins were Unbreathing?"

"Yes, sir. None of them drew breath, and all crumpled into dust or rapidly decayed when silver pierced their hearts."

"None drew breath," the Captain repeated, eyes narrowing. "How did ye know?"

Fletch stared blankly at him for a second. Did no one remember her father or his abilities? "I can see the Wynd's movement," she replied past the lump forming in her throat. "Breath is easy to see in the frigidity of the Pass, stark yellow-orange against the cold blues and purples of the mountain air." She raised a brow. "Why are you holding yours?"

The Captain turned to the king, blue eyes thunderous as he released a gust of persimmon from his lungs. "I've no other questions, my lord," he grunted.

"There is another item I wished to mention," Fletch said to Dreythan, then hesitated. "But, it is... it is a bit forward of me to say it."

"By all means." He gestured with an open hand. "As I have said previously, your council is welcome."

She shook her head. "You misunderstand me, my lord. I don't have council, not exactly. 'Tis... 'tis difficult to put into words." Swallowing hard, she took a deep breath and blurted, "I believe I am needed here in Iventorr."

This was met with a flat stare from the Captain, but the king leaned forward, his expression thoughtful. "I had thought the same. Speak your mind."

"Well," Fletch said, her sleep-deprived mind whirling dizzily, "I'm able to pick Unbreathing from the living on sight. I possess some experience defending against them and slaying them. 'Tis possible you need a guard in Iventorr with these qualities, considering the recent attempts on your life. If there are Unbreathing here, or if they attempt to enter Iventorr, I'd be able to see them and expose them." This last sentence she addressed to the red-haired Captain, who stood with his feet planted wide beneath him, burly scarred arms crossed over his wide chest.

Norland's bearded face bent in a frown as he glanced up at the king. "Her presence here would be beneficial, my lord," he admitted. "And she's more than served her allotted seven years in the Foresters. A transfer could be made with little effort."

Fletch blinked. Norland knew how long she'd been part of the Foresters?

Dreythan's black eyes surveyed Fletch carefully. It was impossible to guess what he was thinking; the expression on his face was one she'd never seen. Alert? Startled? Relieved? "Are you certain that a transfer to the castle guard is what you desire, Fletch?" he asked.

Straightening to her fullest height, she saluted, right hand clenched over her heart. "My lord," she replied, her soul ringing with the conviction of her words. "My desire is to serve my kingdom. If I can serve Ivenhence better in Iventorr than in the Snowshod Mountains, so be it."

"So be it, indeed." He rose, hands disappearing inside the rich folds of his velvet cloak. "Norland, begin the transfer process. I assume you shall hold a trial to determine the best candidate to replace Raylin. Fletch shall take part in that trial as well. See that she is given her own quarters and one hundred gold with which to purchase new belongings."

Fletch was already shaking her head incredulously. "One quarter of that is far more than sufficient," she protested.

Dreythan's lips set in a thin, firm line. "One hundred gold coins," he repeated. "I insist. Thank you, Captain. Thank you, Fletch. You may go."

The Captain bowed deeply, hand over his heart. "Very well, my lord." Turning, he glanced at Fletch, then walked briskly past her. "Come along, Wyndshaper."

Fletch hesitated, then quickly dropped a bow, hand over heart. "Thank you, my lord," she said, and trotted after the Captain.

Dreythan leaned back in his throne, his heart and head strangely light. She had chosen to stay. Lifting his eyes to the arched ceiling, he whispered a quiet prayer of thanks to Ivere, then paused. There were carvings set into the stone high above. The details were so fine that he could not make out what the lines formed, but they flowed across the stone like water flows over sand.

It was beautiful, he thought. How had he not noticed it before?

Fletch followed the Captain as he trotted up a flight of stone steps, armor clinking as he went. "Captain Norland?" She stretched her legs into even longer strides to catch up with his rapid pace. "How did you know I'd served more than seven years as a Forester?"

"I served as the Forester's Head for five years," he replied shortly. "In that time, I signed off on a post assignment request from a ten-year-old. 'Tisn't something ye forget," he replied. His blue eyes cast a piercing glance over his shoulder.

"What brought you to Iventorr?"

The gaze softened. "Same thing as brought ye here. The king."

Close on his heels, Fletch trailed behind Norland as he entered the propped-open doors of a long building. In seconds they were weaving their way between men and women wearing cream robes and white aprons who carried platters filled with dishes. The air in the open room rose warmly from a multitude of plates, stoves, ovens, pots, pans, and bowls to swirl in delightful cyclones of color on the ceiling. Delicious aromas teased her from every direction; bubbling stew, roasting chicken and vegetables, fresh bread, melted butter, and — they paused beside a hearth oven — apple pie.

A woman stood at an oven door, her thin frame stooped so she could peer at the glowing embers within. "Confound this old thing," she muttered, pushing waves of grey hair away from her face. "Can't see if these crusts are browned."

A memory flashed through Fletch's mind; a long, sallow face, an unexpectedly warm smile, and sausage rolls. The face that peered into the oven had shrunk and shriveled a bit with age, but the eyes were the same. Slanting brown eyes, with frown lines crinkling the space between the thin arched brows.

"Matron Gulden," Captain Norland said, his tone markedly respectful. "D'you have a moment?"

Slamming the door shut, the woman turned to the Captain, a singed wooden paddle gripped in one hand like a battleaxe. "What is it? Can't you see I'm trying not to burn these pies?" She whirled to the closest footman, thrusting the paddle into his hands. "Here, check them."

The Captain shifted, his large frame filling too much of the cramped space. "Sorry to intrude," he said, clearing his throat. "This's Fletch Wyndshaper, previously of the Foresters. She'll be transferring to the castle guard, but she's to have quarters of her own. Do ye have a room for her?"

The woman paused, the ill-tempered scowl dropping from her face. Stepping forward, her brown eyes searched Fletch's as she reached for her hand. "Fletch? Do you remember me?"

Fletch nodded slowly, letting the liver-spotted fingers intertwine with hers. "You were kind to me at the orphanage. Did... did you put sausage rolls in my pockets? I remember sneaking them into my lessons at the library."

Matron Gulden nodded, chuckling. "Indeed I did! I suppose I'm the reason some of our texts have grease stains within their pages." She shook her head. "Ah well. Welcome home. They aren't ready at the moment, but when they've cooled down, you're welcome to stop in for some pie." Putting one of her slender arms through Fletch's, she turned to the Captain. "I think I know of just the room, Norland," she said. "I imagine you'd like to begin your daily patrol since you haven't had a moment thus far."

The Captain nodded. "Thank ye, Matron. Report to the barracks tomorrow an hour after sunrise," he told Fletch. "Understood?"

Her right hand flashed over her heart in a quick salute. "Understood, Captain."

As he left, Matron Gulden turned a dry smile towards her. "I think you'll like the place I've in mind. Right this way."

Leading Fletch out of the kitchens, she nodded at a high wall across the cobblestone road.

"This section of wall separates the castle from the royal garden and royal quarters tower, where the king and his family hold their residence," she told Fletch matter-of-factly. "Well, just the king now, but many still have hopes that he will marry. After all, your father was over fifty before he married your mother."

Fletch's heart leaped into her mouth, but Matron Gulden kept on, not seeming to notice.

"This is part of the north-west wing, which connects to the northern wall. Your room is not in one of the towers, but... you'll see."

Leading her up a spiral staircase of wrought iron, the Matron paused at an arched wooden door and pushed it open. "Here it is. Your new home."

It was a square stone room with a bare stone floor and walls. To the right of the door, the wall was occupied by a bare wooden bed and a dusty chest of drawers. The other side of the room housed a screen, a small tub, washbasin and tarnished mirror, and a table with two chairs.

Directly across from the door, a wonderful huge window with a wide stone seat opened over the flower garden and pond. Fletch crossed over to it as if in a dream, and looked out.

Her window appeared to be two or three stories higher than the spacious garden. Directly outside was an enormous oak tree, its trunk engulfed with ivy and surrounded with beautiful, bright flowers. From one of its gnarled branches hung a tattered rope swing.

"Higher, papa, higher!" she cried, exhilaration rushing through her as she rocketed towards the sky. The swing beneath her hovered for one breathless moment. Then it sank back down to the Hearth, and her father leaned in, a smile spread across his bearded face.

"Higher?" He chuckled. "I do not believe it can go any higher. One more push like that and you'll sprout wings and fly away!"

"One more time," she pleaded, and burst into a fit of giggles as Kell complied, planting his strong hand on her back and giving her a mighty but gentle push. The rope swing creaked as she reached what felt like the highest point she had ever swung, her heart beating in her ears as a beam stretched across her face.

The grin slipped away as her father plucked something from the grass, a frown etched across his brow.

He straightened, cradling something in his palm, then held it out to Fletch. The sun glinted off the sharp tip of a silver arrowhead. "Fletch," he said, his voice deep and a bit strange, "This fell from your pocket. Did you take it from the table?"

She bit her lip.

"Did you?"

A sheepish nod.

There was a moment of silence. Finally daring to peer up at her father, Fletch was just in time to see Kell slip the bit of silver into a pocket. "What am I to do with you," he chuckled. "Picking up every shining thing you see, wanting to swing ever higher into the sky! Why, if I didn't know, I'd think you were a little magpie, not a human girl."

"A magpie?" Fletch giggled. "I'm not a magpie, papa."

There was another great push, sending her gliding up towards the clouds. She shrieked with laughter as Kell chanted teasingly, "Magpie, magpie, flying high in the sky!"

Fletch stared. The sight of the old swing... the very swing her father used to push her on... For a moment, it was nearly too much.

"I'll have a mat and bedding brought up for you, of course, but I hope it's to your liking," Matron Gulden's voice was saying.

Whirling around, she wrapped her arms around the woman's narrow shoulders and squeezed as hard as she could. "It's perfect," she breathed, tears blurring her eyes.

Chapter 7

Dreythan wove through the maze of over-laden bookshelves and ladders, brow creased in deep thought as he made his way to the back of the library. Usually he found the scent of paper and ink and leather-bound books comforting, but this morning he scarcely noticed it. Reaching a door partially hidden behind another shelf, he opened it and stepped into a cozy study lit with hooded lamps.

A table took up most of the room. Painstakingly neat piles of books had been stacked on top. One small shelf hugged a wall, holding not books or scrolls but sheafs of parchment, bottles of ink, and bundles of feather quills. To one side of the table, an ancient little man struggled to his feet. His white hair billowed in a puffy cloud around his head as he managed a small bow.

"My lord," Brinwathe's reedy voice quavered.

Dreythan pulled a chair up on the opposite side of the table. "There is no need for that, old friend," he said gently. "Please, sit."

The head librarian sank back into the cushioned chair, evidently relieved. He gave a small, embarrassed cough. "I gathered all records of Ivenhence's taxation since the beginning of your father's reign, just as you requested." He gestured with one swollen-knuckled hand, indicating the neat books before them. "It shall take quite some time to go over them, my lord. May I ask what information you seek within them? Perchance I can direct you to the correct tome."

"I am attempting to pinpoint the flaws in Ivenhence's system of taxation," Dreythan replied slowly. "It is my hope that you might also recommend others to assist in this endeavor."

Brinwathe's head bowed deeply, a frown deepening his jowls. "I am at your disposal, my lord. A flaw in our taxation system, you say? Could you elaborate?"

When Dreythan had relayed everything he'd seen and learned in Herstshire, Brinwathe bobbed his head thoughtfully. "I see." Rubbing his chin, Brinwathe leaned forward, peering down at a map. "Indeed, indeed. The value of coin versus their goods is imbalanced due to the lack of access to trade." He pulled one book from its stack, thumbing it open as a sudden spark kindled in his watery eyes. "Hmm, yes, trade... trade routes... yes!" One spindly finger hovered over the center of the page. "Here we are. When the trade agreement with Thissa fell through fifteen years ago, Hertshire would have been greatly affected. They are so close to the border, it would be simple to cross into Thissa and return, and they also have resources greatly valued in Thissa — lumber and iron."

"I had not considered that." Dreythan nodded, also craning his neck at the parchment spread over the table. "When trade with Thissa failed, so must have Herstshire's economy."

The corner's of the old man's mouth creased into a wide smile. "It seems we have found the flaw, my lord," he quipped. "Or, at least, one of them. Am I correct in assuming your aim is to mend it?"

"Indeed you are," the king replied, returning the smile. Quickly sobering, he stared down at the map. "Now we must simply determine if there are other towns or villages similarly affected, and if there are, how we may mend them."

"That ought not be too difficult, my lord," Brinwathe assured him, whipping another book from another pile. "The records ought to show us which towns would have been most dependent on the shared route with Thissa."

Dreythan took the proffered volume, barely glancing down at it. "Ought the tax rate in Herstshire be lowered?" he muttered, still staring at the map. "That would not solve the problem... They must have coin in order to pay the tax to begin with. But how to get it to them?" The image of felled logs and sooty miners flashed through his mind, followed by nearly-empty livestock pens and children dashing about, clothes mostly made of patches fluttering around their thin frames. His fingers tightened around the book's spine.

The librarian cocked a bushy eyebrow at him. "There are a few ways, my lord. But the simplest and most beneficial way to get coin flowing in and out of Herstshire is to develop trade to and from there." He paused, squinting up at the ceiling. "Perhaps trade with Thissa could be renegotiated? The trade route from Verenshire to Herstshire would reopen soon after."

Suppressing the instinct to shake his head, Dreythan blinked away the memory of a crazed, wild-haired man and a pool of sticky crimson. "It could be possible," he said, thinking of Norland's comment about spies. "Perhaps that is the best first step. But still, there must be something more we can do. Something that will still effect change in the event that trade can't be renegotiated."

Jon and Missy Pruden's faces rose before him. A smile spread slowly across his lips.

Two hours later, Dreythan exited the library, a small scroll clutched in one hand. His chest was strangely light, as if a constricting weight around his ribs had eased and he could breathe freely.

His polished black boots clicked quickly against cobblestone as he strode down the nearly-empty street. It was still early in the morning, the sun only barely peeking over the horizon. He nodded absently to the few passers-by who bowed to or saluted him as he mentally listed the day's tasks he had yet to accomplish.

The most important two were already complete. Or, at least, nearly complete. He and Brinwathe had feverishly poured over sections of books and scrolls, exchanging ideas and thoughts. When everything had been written out on a single scroll, they both looked it over, then exchanged a significant nod. The cornerstone for reform had been settled on.

That was the first and most important item completed. The second was clutched in his hand; a letter to his cousin, newly-crowned King Morthan.

To King Morthan, rightful ruler of Ilumence and son of the late King Morthas,

It is with great sorrow that I offer my deepest condolences on the passing of your father and my uncle. With sincerest regret, I must apologize for not being present at the burial ceremony. My company was waylaid at the Pass through Mount Valer and Mount Norst, and it is only by sheer good fortune that I escaped with my life.

I also wish to pledge my continuing alliance with Ilumence upon your ascent to the throne. Should you need any council or aid, I am more than willing to lend it, as your father did many times to me.

Dreythan Dreythas-son

It was short and to the point. Dreythan hoped it was appropriate; he didn't want to subject a man in mourning to a long, drawn-out missive.

Reaching the door to the falconry, the king paused. Steeling himself against the rancid smell of bird droppings and urine, he shoved it open.

A falconer hurried forward, gloved hand over his heart. "My lord," he stammered. "It is early yet — the sun is barely risen. Do you require my services?"

Dreythan handed him the scroll, nervously eyeing the large bird on the man's arm. It cocked its head at him, bright orange crest wobbling. "See that this reaches King Morthan of Ilumence," he choked, turned on his heel, and left.

During his childhood, one of the sun jays had emptied its bowels on his head. Ever since then, he couldn't stomach the smell of the falconry. Or of birds.

So, that was two tasks completed. He returned to his mental checklist, frowning. After breakfast, he would return to the library to confer again with Brinwathe. It was unfair to place so much responsibility on him, but he seemed willing enough. Hopefully, the missives would be ready by noon. Then he would make his way to the throne hall, which would be open to the commonwealth until all disputes had been settled for the day.

Dreythan wondered if he would have time to observe the trial that Captain Norland was holding. He hoped so; he was curious to see how Fletch's archery compared to the other guards. Or rather, how the other guards measured up to her.

Entering the dining hall, he seated himself at the royal table to the end of the room. Several servants swarmed instantly around him, placing small platters, dishes, and a cup of water before him.

When they had finished, the king tucked in heartily. Pausing mid-sip, he grimaced, wishing for more of the clear, sweet water from Fletch's spring.

Raising his head from his plate, he gazed keenly over the hall until his black eyes fell on a familiar face, smiling and laughing as she chatted with one of the castle guards.

"You jest with me," Klep said with a grin. "You've never held a sword? In your life?"

"I'm not jesting," Fletch insisted, her cheeks aching from smiling so wide. "The bow, arrow, and knife are all I need."

"Are you skillful with it? The knife?"

She hesitated. "Not particularly. I can throw it accurately, but I've never needed to use it for close combat. The only close danger I've ever encountered was two bears, and they were clumsy and slow."

Klep regarded her with wide, shocked brown eyes. "You've bested mountain bears? Just as Captain Norland did?"

She shook her head vehemently. "No, not mountain grizzlies, only small black bears. When I tried to take shelter in their den, I accidentally woke them from their winter sleep. They were furious."

Hesitantly, Klep asked, "You... you didn't kill them, did you?"

"Thankfully I was able to escape without harming either of them."

His shoulders drooped in a sigh of relief. "Thank Ivere."

He was a kind soul, Fletch thought as she inspected his round, youthful face. After the misunderstanding the day before, he'd not only made sure the castle armorer outfitted her, but also that she had a place to rest and knew how to get from there to the dining hall, all the while keeping up a steady stream of cheerful conversation. On top of that, he'd invited her to sit with the other guards in the dining hall, and had remained with her when she'd declined. Others, put off by the uncomfortable exchange, would have followed their command to get her food and fresh clothing and left it at that.

"Nervous about the trial?" he asked after swallowing a large bite of egg-laden toast.

"A bit," Fletch replied. "I fear I didn't sleep well. Are you taking part?"

"Indeed, though—" he glanced at the row of hourglasses shelved above the southern door "—we ought to hurry, now that I'm thinking of it. The bell for the upfirst hour will ring soon."

Hurriedly, he rolled the last of his sausage up in his toast and shoved it into his mouth, pushing his plate away. Following his example, Fletch downed the last of her water. A harmony of clinks resounded around them as those in suits of metal and leather armor pushed plates and cups aside to pick up their weapons from the tables. It was an interesting sight, so many people so used to their routine. As if they were dancing around and with each other.

"That's our signal," Klep said.

The tramping of dozens of booted feet echoed in Fletch's ears as she and Klep made their way along the cobbled streets of Iventorr Castle, carried along in the river of armored figures who were headed in the same direction as they. Lush gardens passed by to either side, bursting with greens and grains. Ahead was a long stretch of the high wall of Iventorr, hugged by a low building which joined to a tall stone tower.

Fletch swallowed back a lump in her throat, trying to ignore the unease that bubbled in her stomach. All the noise, and the people. It was... more. Almost too much.

"That's the barracks," Klep muttered to her, pointing at the squat timber construction. His finger transferred to the stone spire. "And that's the barracks tower. Most of the guards who live in Iventorr live in one of those two places. Those that don't reside in the castle live in Verenshire just on the other side of the Basin."

A sizable patch of packed dirt and heavily trodden grass occupied the grounds in front of the barracks. Archery targets had been set up on this barren field, a dozen of them in a straight row. Their bright red bullseyes and yellow secondary rings resembled twelve miniature suns.

Beside the doors to the barracks waited Captain Norland. Bare arms folded across his barrel-shaped chest, his blue eyes flitted amongst the guards as they slowly filtered out from the barracks and in from the streets. They formed a semi-circle around him, each one coming to attention as they took their place, chins up, chests out.

Many of them cast sideways glances at Fletch. A nervous prickle settled at the base of her neck as she took her place and mimicked their stance, standing as tall and straight as she could.

The last man filed into place, and quiet settled over the small crowd. Removing his helm, Norland tucked it under his arm and said, "Ye all know I'm not one for speeches."

There was a general murmur of agreement. A few bobbed their heads.

He cast a glance around, a muscle in his jaw working. "Let's have a moment of silence in honor of Layward, Mordin, Pennick, and Raylin. We'll not forget the sacrifice they made."

In unison, those around Fletch bowed their heads, staring down at the dirt and yellowed grass. Some pressed a fist to their hearts, foreheads creased earnestly.

She followed their example, examining her boot toes guiltily. She hadn't known the guards who'd been killed. She had no right to pretend to mourn them. Peering at the guard beside her, she bit her lip. Had they done something similar when her father died?

After a long minute of respectful quiet, Captain Norland cleared his throat. "Raylin was the Sentinels' best archer. As he's now gone, I'll have to find a replacement for him. And quickly." He jammed his helmet back onto his skull, scowling. "If ye fancy yourself a bowman, stay. If not, go on about your duties." He shifted to one foot as if to turn, but paused.

"We have a new addition to our ranks," he said. "The Forester who saved the king's life. Her name's Fletch Wyndshaper."

Fletch's heart sprang into her throat. She swallowed hard as a few of the men and women exchanged looks and mutters, casting looks in her direction. Their eyes were like needles poking at her skin; some skeptical, some curious. One or two were openly virulent. In spite of the heat roaring in her cheeks, she kept her head held high, meeting the gaze of any who looked her way.

Two men in particular stared with outright hostility. One was a plain fellow with sallow, saggy skin and watery grey eyes like sour toadstools. Standing beside him was a thick, squat guard with a shaved head and wide whiskers. They met her eye with arms crossed over their chests, sneering.

But beside them stood a few more figures, all of whom regarded

Fletch curiously. Two appeared to be twin brothers, similar in face if not in build. One wore a greatsword strapped to his broad back, while the other, more slender man had a longblade belted at his side. Beside them was a man only a few years older than Fletch, his steel-blue eyes smiling, and — Fletch's heart leaped into her throat — a severe woman with short-shorn grey hair and deep brown eyes. An enormous yew longbow was strapped to her back. When their gazes met, the woman nodded approvingly.

"She's one of our own," Captain Norland growled sternly, cutting off the stare of the wide-whiskered man as he tongued his cheek, seeming ready to spit in Fletch's direction. "Served more'n a decade in the Valer-Norst Pass. She's earned the right to be here." He turned slowly, glaring as if daring anyone to disagree. "Yes, we've never let a newcomer trial for the Sentinels. I know some of ye shan't like the exception, but ye don't have to like it. This will not be the cause of any disputes or disturbances. Am I understood?"

"Yes, Captain!"

Fletch swallowed again, this time the lump of iron in her gullet slowly easing downward. Most of the guards' voices at that last sharp question had been firm in their assent. But there were a fair number who'd muttered their reply, and a few who had grumbled. The cold lump sank from her throat to her stomach as the grey-eyed man squinted at her, lip curled in a smirk.

"Very well," Captain Norland said. "Those wishing to join the Sentinels, remain. All others, to your posts."

Something touched Fletch's elbow. She turned to find the severe woman standing behind her, a smile softening the angles of her brown face. "Fletch Wyndshaper," she said quietly. "It does me good to see you well."

"Master Aeda." She took the woman's offered forearm, gripping it tight as her former master did the same. "Thank you."

"I am certain we'll see more of each other soon." Aeda glanced at Captain Norland's back. "For now, I must take my leave. Ivere's luck with you." Her smile briefly broadened. "Not that you'll need it."

With that, she turned and departed as the guards quickly dispersed, leaving only seven men and Fletch standing in front of Captain Norland. He nodded briskly. "Right then. First, target practice. Line up before the mark, one of ye to each target."

"I'll eat my beard if that's all he tests us on," said a friendly voice. Klep grinned as Fletch turned to him. "Captain Norland is a bit infamous for his 'tests.'"

"Is he now?" Fletch chuckled. The relief at seeing Klep's cheerful face quickly drained into the knot in her stomach, feeding the growing tension.

They took their places behind a line that had been carved in the dirt seventy paces from the targets.

"Might I ask how you know Sentinel Yewmaster?" the young man asked, pulling his bowstring tight. "She doesn't talk much. No one here seems to know her well enough to speak of her."

Fletch slipped her own bow from her back, a smile rising to her face. "She was my mentor," she replied quietly. "When I began training as a Forester, she was the one who volunteered to take me in."

Klep paused, brown eyes wide. "She was a Forester?"

She nodded. "For many years. From what she told me, she was actually one of the first Foresters of Ivenhence. As soon as the Great Slaving ended and the order was founded, she asked to be assigned."

"Ah." He let the bow fall to his side, quiet for a few moments. "Well," he ventured, "I doubt I can hold a candle to a Forester who was trained by the legendary Aeda Yewmaster, let alone the one who saved the king's life." Klep winked. "But I may as well try." Smile falling a bit, he nudged Fletch's elbow with the tip of his bow. "Don't let the others get to you," he added quietly. "Do your best. Show them why you deserve to be here."

Captain Norland made his way down the line, placing a handful of practice arrows at the feet of each archer. "You'll have six bolts," he said. "Make them count."

As the other guards readied their bows, shifting their feet and staring down the range, Fletch examined the field before her. Klep was right. She was here for a purpose; to protect the king and the kingdom. She couldn't let stares or frowns distract her from that. The ball in her stomach faded as her lips curled slightly. It was nice to know that at least one person wanted her to succeed.

The targets were roughly one hundred and fifty feet away, as near as she could judge. A slight breeze coursed over the stone wall to drift into the castle yard, the Wynd shifting from cool greenish yellow to warm vermillion. It would be a tricky shot; she would have to compensate for the breeze, but would have to be cautious not to overcompensate since the current stopped about twenty feet above the target. The twangs of bowstrings rang in her ears. For a moment she was tempted to glance at the other targets, to see how the contestants were doing, but she pushed that out of her mind. Now was not the time to become distracted.

Nocking her arrow to the string, she pulled back and aimed directly at her target. Then, accounting for distance and Wynd, she aimed barely up and to the left.

Taking a deep breath, she relaxed her hand, letting the shaft of the arrow slip past her fingertips.

Sssssssssthick! The arrow buried itself in the target, a few inches below the red bulls-eye. One of the onlookers snorted.

"Not enough distance," she muttered. Drawing another arrow, she raised the tip only slightly more than her previous shot and released. This time it hit the mark. Her next four arrows were all inside the red bulls-eye.

Satisfied, she turned to face Captain Norland, who was nodding approvingly down the range. "Well done, all of ye," he rumbled. "Your next test'll be speed. Run to your respective targets, retrieve your arrows, and return here. Ye may not lay down the weapons you have equipped. Ye may not drop any arrows ye retrieve. On three. One—"

On instinct, Fletch leaned forward, one foot toeing the line of overturned grass.

"—Two—"

She crouched, her chest almost touching her knee.

"Three!"

And she was running with the Wynd rushing past her face, her toes digging into the green turf as she sprinted toward her target. Then she was there, hastily breaking off the six arrows. Grasping them all in one hand, she turned on her heel and ran back to the line, her fists pumping in rhythm with her feet.

When all of the men had returned, puffing and panting, Captain Norland pointed at Fletch. "This one made it there and back in under twenty seconds," he said, then scowled. "Torsh and Torrin, ye both dropped arrows and have been disqualified. Ye may go back to the gate."

The two men bowed their heads and left, shooting incredulous looks Fletch's way.

"Faster than — faster than greased lightning, as my pa would say," gasped Klep, bent nearly double with his hands planted on his knees.

"And now," Captain Norland said. He grinned wickedly, eyeing the panting contestants as he plucked a thick staff from a pile on the ground. "For my favorite part of the test. Hand-to-hand combat."

The oak staff whistled past Fletch's ear as she ducked, bringing her own staff up just in time to knock aside another blow.

"Come now, Wyndshaper." A white grin gleamed through Captain Norland's beard. "This's a spar, not a dance."

Scowling, she blocked his swing, her palms numbing with the impact. Sweat beaded on her brow and down her back, her fingers throbbing. Stares pressed in on her, but she ignored them, glowering back into the mirthful blue eyes before her. "If this is a spar," she panted, "why haven't you landed a single blow?"

The amusement disappeared.

Thwack, wumptht, crack!! The blows came fast and earnest. The captain was no longer playing, the force of each strike sending

Fletch reeling closer and closer to the edge of the sparring ring. Desperately she ducked and swung her staff at Norland's knees. He blocked it lazily. With one final blow, he sent her stumbling backwards out of the ring.

Face stinging, she picked herself up, avoiding the smug smirk from the wide-whiskered man across the ring. She dared to glance at Klep, whose brown eyes were as wide as sunflower heads.

"Ye should be disqualified for stepping out of the ring," Captain Norland rumbled. The one guard chuckled quietly, spitefully.

Fletch turned to Norland. Disappointment and embarrassment swelled inside her, but she forced her spine upright and her chin up. "Yes, Captain," she managed. "I understand, sir. Thank you." Hand still numb, she gave an awkward salute and began to turn away.

"Not so fast, Wyndshaper." The giant man gazed through her, his head dipping thoughtfully. "I wasn't able to break your defenses even after pinning ye against the edge." One hand rubbed his beard as he glanced at the three bruised he'd already beaten. "Can't say the same for them, and I trained 'em myself." Turning back to Fletch, he nodded firmly. "Remain here. We'll see how the rest of this lot compares."

Stunned, Fletch could only lower herself to the grass a few paces away as the Captain barked, "Right, you next, Gorrin. Then you, Ironshod. Ready?"

"That was bloody brilliant," Klep breathed. "I wish you could have seen the look on that bastard Gorrin's face."

She wiped the sweat off her forehead, heart still pounding in her chest. "That might have been one of the most difficult things I've ever done," she admitted. Her tongue was like a porous stone in her head, parched and rough. "I... I feel I'll be quite sore tomorrow."

Klep's chuckle was punctuated by a sharp crack and a cry in the background. "Well, at least you can be sure of one thing. Your knife is much more useful in your hands than you thought."

The doors to the throne hall parted as citizens began filing slowly out, some of them muttering and casting frustrated glances over their shoulder. Captain Norland brushed past them, and Fletch hurried to keep up.

"Norland?" The king's voice called. He lowered himself back into the throne, his angular face taut. "What ails you?"

"We've got ourselves a new Sentinel, my lord," Norland told him. One hand flapped behind his back.

Guessing at the signal's meaning, Fletch slipped into place beside the nearest guard, trying to copy their attentive stance.

"But she has no experience as a castle guard," Norland continued. "I'll have to train her from the ground up." He shook his head, his beard whisking across his cuirass. "She's the swiftest runner I've ever seen, not t'mention she's a wonder with a bow. I ought t'be able to make a passable soldier out of her within a season."

The strained lines of Dreythan's face eased a bit as he glanced to where Fletch stood. "Guard Wyndshaper, approach," he called. "I would speak with you."

She did so, moving stiffly across the carpeted floor in an attempt to keep her new armor from squeaking. When she reached the bottom step, she paused, glancing awkwardly between the king and the Captain.

"When the king summons ye to the throne, always kneel or bow below it," Norland pointed out.

Fletch bent to one knee with a quick nod. "Yes, Captain." Rising, she met Dreythan's eye with an uncertain nod. "Do you require—"

"And don't speak to the king in the throne hall unless ye've been addressed first."

"Lighten your mood, Captain," the king said gently as Fletch's ears burned. "These petty rules need only be enforced whilst the throne hall is occupied with other citizens." Turning to Fletch, he returned her nod. "Before you begin learning your duties as a Sentinel, I have an assignment for you. I trust you are able to write fluently?"

"Yes, my lord," Fletch replied, biting back a 'why'. "Although it's been some time since I've used a quill. Charcoal sticks are easier to come by in Herstshire."

A thud echoed through the stone chamber as the double doors opened. A withered little old man with a wild cloud of wispy white hair entered, followed by four young men carrying scrolls.

"These scribes are all fluent readers and writers, my lord," the old man said proudly. "And capable horsemen, as well. They have worked for me in the library since they were children."

King Dreythan examined the four, then gave a brisk nod. "Very good, Brinwathe," he said. "They shall do well for the task at hand."

Brinwathe's cloudy eyes shifted to the other side of the carpet where Fletch stood. "Am I correct to assume that this is our fifth messenger?"

"You are."

A smile crossed Brinwathe's face, wreathing it in wrinkles. "Very well, my lord." Crossing the carpet, he placed two neatly bundled scrolls in Fletch's hands.

Fletch turned them over, inspecting the fine rolled parchment. Both were sealed with emerald green wax, and the larger of the two was labeled, 'Herstshire'.

"We are... testing a new method of record-keeping and taxation throughout the kingdom," Dreythan said, addressing the four men before him. "Your task may be difficult. It may be ludicrously simple — I am unsure. You shall each travel to three of Ivenhence's major cities, which I shall assign to you, and deliver the messages I have written. You shall then collect a sort of census from the townspeople. Firstly, the name of the man or woman giving their choice. Secondly, the name of the person whom the townsperson is choosing to represent them. No person may choose themselves."

As she stared down at the scrolls in her hands, a spark kindled within Fletch's chest. The king had wasted no time in trying to correct his mistakes. A new taxation system? Perhaps a new start for Herstshire.

The young men all nodded deliberately, seeming to understand the importance of what they were setting out to do. Dreythan gestured to Brinwathe, who stepped forward and turned over the scrolls in the mens' arms, inspecting the seals on each before nodding and stepping back into place.

"You shall record each town's censuses in the scrolls you hold," Dreythan continued. "They are labeled with the names of the towns you must travel to. Once you have collected the censuses from your three assigned towns, you shall return and report directly to me. You have a fortnight to do this." He turned to the man on the end. "Which cities must you visit?"

The man glanced town at the scrolls in his arms. "My lord, I must travel to Limbwood, Inglestead, and Darmator."

"Very good. You know what you must do. Prepare accordingly. I expect you all to have departed by tomorrow's dawn. Am I understood?"

"Yes, my lord," they replied in unison.

Dreythan nodded, satisfied. "Very well. You may go." His eyes followed the men as they filed out of the throne hall.

"Have no fear, my lord," Brinwathe wavered, leaning on his knobby oak cane. "I have no doubt that they shall be quite thorough."

"Indeed." Turning to Fletch, he asked, "Do you have any questions, Guard Wyndshaper?"

She hesitated. "I am to be a messenger to Hersthire, my lord?"

"Indeed," Dreythan nodded. "And to Herstshire only. The smaller scroll you shall give to the innkeeper, Master Pruden."

She turned the scrolls over again. There must be something else inside: they were too heavy to contain only paper and wax.

"You shall return here and report directly to me once you have completed this task," Dreythan was saying. "You may borrow any of the steeds in the stables." He paused, his black eyes inspecting Fletch carefully. "You also have a fortnight to accomplish this," he said finally, gently. "You may wish to say goodbye to your home and collect your belongings whilst you are there."

"As you wish, my lord," Fletch murmured. Two weeks to bid goodbye to the place where she had grown up, to the people who had become her family. It could be a gift... or it could be torture. She turned to Captain Norland, whose beard curled.

"Your training will begin as soon as ye return," he grunted. "It shan't be easy, so be prepared. And don't get yourself killed on this journey. I don't want to have to find another royal archer."

With a brisk nod and a quick salute, Fletch turned on her heel and strode out of the throne hall, head whirling. Only four days ago, she'd been content with the prospect of living alone in the forested mountains near Herstshire. Today, she'd been chosen to train as a member of the Royal Sentinels of Ivenhence. She could scarcely believe it, especially after being knocked out of the sparring ring by Captain Norland. Flexing her shoulder, she winced at the bruise he'd left when he'd clapped his giant hand there in congratulation.

In a way, she was reluctant to leave Iventorr so soon after arriving; she had so much to learn, to see, and do. But it would be good to return home before transferring permanently. To say goodbye to the familiar deer trails and eldertrees, to the people of Herstshire.

Fletch's step faltered. The Prudens' smiling faces rose in her mind, sending a twinge of apprehension through her. The faces' smiles faded into sorrow and longing.

Suppressing the image, Fletch hurried toward the stables.

The king had said she could borrow any steed. When a king gave a subject permission that hadn't been requested, she was fairly certain it was a subtle command. Thus, she'd been commanded to pick a steed.

She swallowed nervously. It had been nearly fifteen years since she'd last ridden a horse, and she'd never done so on her own. But then again, the king had commanded her to retrieve her belongings, and she couldn't do so without a pack animal of some sort. She adjusted her squeaking cuirass, her forehead pinching ill-temperedly. It was too cold for horses in the Pass. Perhaps the castle kept donkeys.

She decided not to get her hopes up.

When she entered the long, stall-lined building, she found the four other messengers Master Brinwathe had selected already bustling about, readying saddles and bridles, blankets and saddlebags. She skirted around them, careful not to get in their way, peering into each stall as she passed.

There were over twenty horses. Some of them paced restlessly, their shining coats rippling over chiseled muscle. A few lifted their heads from grain buckets to snort at her as she passed, the whites of their eyes signaling they were as unsure of her as she was of them.

They were all so... large, Fletch decided. Large and twitchy. Smells and sounds could spook them as easily as a deer. The image of being thrown from one's back to the ground forced her to suppress a shudder. She continued passing stall after stall, hoping to find an old gentle mare or an ornery donkey, but with no luck. Pausing, she glanced over her shoulder. The other messengers had already put bridles on their mounts and were leading them out.

Perhaps it would be best if she were to set out on foot, Fletch reasoned desperately. She didn't know how to take care of a horse or how to feed it, and—

"Heeeeeeerich?"

She yanked away from the cold damp at her neck. Heart in her throat, Fletch whipped around to see a large pair of black eyes rimmed with long white lashes set in a narrow furry face. It arched over her on top of an impossibly long neck. A white horn protruded from a forelock between a set of rabbit-like ears, one pointed straight up, the other half-drooping to the side. The creature blinked placidly, and inquired again, "Heeeeerich?"

"You gave me quite the fright," Fletch laughed nervously, her heart slowly fluttering its way back into her chest. "For a moment I thought a horse was about to bite me."

It blinked again, then lifted its neck to peer over the wall into the stall beside it. Curiously, Fletch stepped up to the door to see the animal's large deer-like body, awkwardly gangly legs, and wide cloven hooves. "You're an elbecca," she said, inspecting the thick black coat speckled with white. "Farmer Tren had one like you a few years back." She craned her neck to get a look at the animal's belly; no udder. "You wouldn't be as useful to him, I'm afraid. No way to make milk, you see."

He put his curly-haired head over the door, nudging Fletch's face with his wet nose. She grinned. "Is that why you frightened me? You needed a few neck scratches?" Obligingly, she buried her fingers in the thick, soft fur, and the elbecca's eyes half closed as he gave another little bizarre hiccup of contentment.

"You must not receive much attention," she mused. "After all, what use is a male elbecca when there are horses to do all the work?" Her eye fell on a small cart in the back corner of the stall. "I suppose you do tasks that a horse isn't much good for or is too large for. Hauling vegetables or waste between the garden and kitchens, pulling small loads in tight areas... Not a very glamorous life, hmm?"

The elbecca bobbed his nose against her hand as if agreeing, and she couldn't help but grin.

It had to be a lonely life, she thought as she smoothed a lock of longer hair off his forehead, parting it to pass around his horn. Waiting for someone to come and attach a cart, waiting for food and water, waiting for attention. The smile faded from her face as the creature's eyes met hers, large and soft.

"Well," she said, an idea suddenly dropping into place, "I think you shall do splendidly. Do you have a saddle?" Tucking the two scrolls under one arm, she stood on tiptoe, peering over the elbecca's back. Sure enough, there it was hanging on the wall above the cart. She lifted it down and slid it over his back, checking the fit. He watched her curiously the entire time, head turned completely backwards on his spindly neck.

"I'd guess you'll need a saddle blanket on first to avoid getting your fur caught," Fletch mused, standing back to inspect. "But that is certainly a full-sized saddle." Hands on her hips, she asked, "What do you say, fellow? Are you up for a bit of adventure?"

To her astonishment, the elbecca's head bobbed.

"Right, then," she said with a grin. "I wish I knew your name... I'm certain you already have one." Her eyes wandered over his long face, the black eyes and lock of black hair that had already tumbled over his forehead again. It occurred to her that he might not have ever left the castle. He could very well have been born and raised in Iventorr. Would he see the wide grassy plains and forests and hills of Ivenhence for the first time when she rode him out of the gates?

An elbecca would fare far better in the cold near the Pass than any horse. And they were capable of carrying a decent amount of weight. Not as much as a horse could carry, but her essential belongings would not weigh much. Perhaps she could give her other things to the people of Herstshire, or ask Missy and Jon to do so for her.

Her stomach gave a sudden lurch, and she bowed her head, burying her face in the elbecca's soft neck. "For now, I'll call you Roderick," she mumbled into the fur.

Chapter 8

"This is simply untoward," King Dreythan growled, glaring down at the two young men as they bowed their heads sheepishly before him. "Four times you both have been in my court in as many moons! If you cannot learn to coexist with each other, one of you shall be forced to leave the castle. You are dismissed." He watched as the pair were ushered out, turning to Captain Norland. "I feel there is more to their bickering than they are willing to tell," he said quietly. "Will you speak with their families?"

The captain nodded. "My lord."

As Dreythan returned his attention back to the rest of the hall, the guards led a young woman forward from the pews. She wore a cream-colored dress with flour-dusted sleeves and a white apron; clearly a kitchen maid. Her head of wild wheat-colored curls remained bowed as she paused at the bottom step before the throne.

"King Dreythan," one of the guards announced, "this citizen wishes to report a theft of royal property."

Dreythan nodded. "Very well. You may speak."

The young woman shifted, her hands clenching into white-knuckled balls at her sides. "My lord, my name is Sariah. I work in the kitchens, you see. And my duty is to ensure that our vegetables are fresh and come straight from the gardens. My elbecca — that is, your elbecca — and I use a cart to take the vegetables from the gardens to the kitchens. Well, I went to the stables this morn since 'tis vegetable day, and the elbecca was gone, as well as his saddle. The cart had been left untouched."

The king steepled his fingers, elbows propped on the arms of the throne. "That is strange," he mused. "Why steal an elbecca from the royal stables when near anyone is allowed to borrow a horse?"

Beside the young woman, one of the guards grinned widely. He quickly ducked his head, covering his mouth with one hand.

Ignoring his odd behavior, Dreythan continued, "And for that matter, where would one hide an elbecca, once stolen? Anyone would notice a beast in the castle if they were not kept in the livestock pens or stables."

The guard began shaking with silent laughter. It was the same young man Dreythan had seen Fletch breaking fast with the morning before. "I do not see how a theft of this manner is cause for mirth," he said with a frown.

Head still bowed, the guard choked, "My sincerest apologies, my lord."

"Er, King Dreythan," Captain Norland interjected. "I know who... borrowed... the elbecca. Wyndshaper was seen... riding him out of the castle yesterday noon. I believe she took 'im as her steed for her errand."

At this, Sariah finally lifted her head, fury in her eyes fading into confusion. "So my elbecca wasn't stolen?"

Dreythan stared blankly at the guard, then at the maid, and finally at Captain Norland. "She took an elbecca," he repeated, unsure if he ought to believe it.

"Yes, my lord," the guard chortled. "And she looked about as happy as if she were riding a unicorn."

Sariah's freckled cheeks blushed. "I beg your pardon, my lord. I assumed he was stolen... Who would take a male elbecca for anything but cart-pulling or breeding?"

Dreythan shook his head. "Fletch Wyndshaper, apparently. Do not apologize, you cannot be blamed for assuming such. You may borrow one of the workhorses from the stables until the elbecca is returned. You are dismissed."

Captain Norland shifted abruptly, muttering something about 'damn fool, riding a bloody elbecca out of the castle' and 'needs to learn castle manners' and 'backwoods Forester'.

"You shall not chide her when she returns," Dreythan said quietly. "I did tell her she could borrow any steed." A sudden picture rose in his mind of Fletch sitting on an elbecca's high back, riding proudly out of the castle gates as she swayed from side to side.

He couldn't help chuckling.

Several leagues from the great bridge of Iventorr Castle, Fletch and Roderick were just turning west away from the lip of the Emerald Basin. It was a marvelous day. A cool Wynd carried across the fields, whirling in buttercup and moss-colored wisps over the wildflowers and long shifting grass. Puffy clouds drifted overhead like white sails across an endless sea. Birds and other small creatures called to each other, filling the air with their melodies.

Roderick stared at everything as they passed, his wide-set eyes taking it all in. His head pivoted slowly to keep an object in his gaze as they progressed, yet somehow he kept walking in a straight line. Occasionally, he would look back at Fletch perched high on his saddle and hiccup inquiringly.

"You'll see where we're going when we get there," she told him with a grin, patting his wooly withers. "You'll like it, I think."

Perhaps she'd been too weary, tense, or focused when she'd passed over these fields before. She didn't remember them being this beautiful, this serene. Glancing up at the sky, she marveled at the wide blue expanse. It felt close enough to touch. Near the Valer-Norst Pass, the trees were so thick she rarely saw more than a patch of sky between leaves and limbs. Here, the Wynd flowed freely over the land like a translucent ocean. In the forested mountains, it streamed between trunks and around boulders and through crevices like rapids pushing along a rocky riverbed. It was a strange and beautiful contrast.

By sundown, they had reached the small stretch of flat land between the rolling hills of the plains and the foothills of the Snowshod Mountains. On the horizon, the snow-laden caps of Mount Valer and Mount Norst were just visible.

"Your long legs cover quite a lot of ground," Fletch commented as she pulled a sack of oats from Roderick's saddlebag. "I wouldn't be surprised if we reached Herstshire by noon tomorrow."

He nudged her shoulder with his nose, his horn missing her ear by a few inches. "Hickeerick."

Making camp was simple enough. In little time Fletch stretched out on her bedroll and turned her face toward the sky as her mind raced onward to Herstshire.

When she had been introduced to the people of the village as their new Forester, many of the townsfolk had been incredulous, even outraged. She still remembered standing beside her mentor in the warm inn, trying to look taller and older than her ten years while red-faced men and women argued around them.

"Look at her. Just a little twig of a thing!"

"How's a child supposed t' protect our village, eh?"

"My Lisbet's stronger than she is, I'll warrant, and she's only eight."

"What's that saying about counting your bushels b'fore the harvest?" a jolly voice had suddenly boomed. The roundest, darkest-skinned man Fletch had ever seen suddenly appeared, carrying a tall cup of steaming tea. Beaming, he'd pushed the cup into Fletch's hands and turned to the room, smile vanishing. "Give her a chance at th' very least before passing your judgements. If Forester Yewmaster says she's ready, she's ready."

This had been followed by a lot of grumbling, but no more complaints were voiced. Missy Pruden had clucked and cooed over Fletch, bringing her plate after plate of hot food. When Fletch finally fell asleep, belly full enough to burst, she did so in the best room in the inn, with a little fire crackling merrily in the hearth.

By the end of that first week in Herstshire, Fletch had come to like and trust both of the Prudens, and by the end of the first year, they were akin to adoptive parents. She visited as often as she could, sometimes twice per week in the warmer seasons and once per moon in the winter.

One year, soon after her thirteenth birthday, she had stumbled into Herstshire, blood streaming slowly but steadily from between her legs. Her swollen abdomen had felt ready to burst, the pain ripping through in waves. Jon had sat her down in one of the rent rooms and called for his wife, reassuring her that she was going to be all right.

Fletch smiled up at the stars at the memory. How could she have known that this horrible phenomenon happened on a frequent basis to many people? Missy had cooked up one of her herbal remedies, then shown Fletch how to make it so she wouldn't have to return to Herstshire each moon. She also had given her an interesting speech about how her body was changing into that of an adult, and what that meant.

Drawing a deep breath in, Fletch released it slowly, watching her breath gradually fade from red to orange to yellow, carried away on the breeze that still flowed between the hills. All of these thoughts and memories, and yet she couldn't bear to face the reason she couldn't fall asleep. Flopping onto her side, she curled into a tight ball, forcing her breathing to slow. Perhaps when she told them of the relocation, they would understand. She winced. Perhaps they wouldn't.

She reached Hersthire close to noon the following day, just as expected. Roderick's hooves clipped against the cobbled road as a chill Wynd streamed between the trees, lifting Fletch's hair away from her ears.

Reaching the center of the huddled village, they found the well crowded with sooty men and women who were washing black grime from their skin into long wooden troughs, then drinking deeply from pails of fresh water. They looked up as she approached, many of their familiar faces breaking into smiles as they lifted a hand to wave. Among them, a bald brown head gleamed, bobbing cordially as he passed around a basket of fresh rolls. Spotting Fletch, his face crinkled into a wide beam of relief.

"Fletch!" he boomed, hurrying towards her. "You're all right! Thank the goddesses."

"Of course I'm all right." She grinned as she dismounted Roderick. "Why wouldn't I be?"

The innkeeper pushed his way to her through the maze of miners, shoving the basket into someone else's hands as he went. When he reached Fletch, he enveloped her in his arms.

Not knowing what else to do, she patted his shoulders, taken aback by the tightness of the embrace. Dread hollowing her chest, she didn't pull away. "Jon?" she asked quietly. "Why would I not be alright?"

He embraced her still for another moment, then let go. "The day you departed with Librarian Galefall, men were here askin' after you," he told her, brown eyes uncharacteristically anxious. "Strange men, unsavory types. They asked where you'd gone. I was loathe t' answer, but they said they were in the service of King Dreythan. Anyhow, I told 'em you were escorting the librarian through the forest t' study trees." He shook his head. "They didn't like that answer one bit, and took off in a huff. I didn't trust the look of 'em so I asked Benton to make the trek out t' your cabin and check on you, but..." Master Pruden wavered, swallowing hard.

Mouth dry, Fletch nodded. "Go on, Master Pruden. He came to look in on me and then—?"

"I'm sorry, Fletch," he stumbled, shoulders drooping. "Benton found your cabin, but he said it'd been torn clear apart, as though it'd been blasted by lightning. The logs walls were scattered and everything — all your belongings — were torn and strewn about. Even your books."

Dazed, Fletch swallowed the cotton in her throat. It must have been the Unbreathing. They must have found her cabin, found the king's scent and her own, and tracked them to the river. Looking down into Jon's eyes, she suddenly understood the relief and confusion there. Wrapping her arms around his shoulders, she pressed her cheek against the top of his head. "Don't apologize. They were only possessions, and possessions can be replaced." Pulling slightly away to inspect his face, she hesitantly asked, "Did they... threaten anyone? The strange men who were searching for us?"

"No, though there was little need to," Jon muttered darkly. "Every man, woman and child was frightened of them. They could've asked for a whole roast boar and we would've given it gladly, if only t' get them to leave. Thankfully we haven't seen hide nor hair of 'em in the past few days." He glanced over at the elbecca who peered curiously back. "We'd best get your... steed to the stables and let Missy know you're alright. We've been worried sick."

"I can look after him whilst you pass out the remaining rolls, if you'd like," Fletch offered, and the innkeeper nodded.

"Go on, then. I'm glad you're safe, Fletch." He trundled off into the cluster of miners, who averted their eyes, pretending not to have seen anything.

Turning to Roderick, she gave his rope reins a soft tug. "I'll have to put you in the stables for the time being," she told him. "Come along."

Obediently, he followed her into the low, open-sided building, ducking his long neck over her shoulder. As soon as she had found a clean stall strewn with fresh straw, he walked right in and stood patiently while she removed his harness and saddle.

"I promise I'll return later to give you a thorough brushing," she told him, patting his velvet nose. "But for now, here's a bucket of water and a basket of hay."

As she left his stall, she glanced back to see his head poked over the door, jaw moving in circles around a mouth stuffed with hay, eyes blissfully half-closed.

Never in her life had she seen a creature look more content.

"Never cause me fright like that again," Missy pleaded, her voice a near-hysterical cluck. "For the love of Ivere, tell us where you're truly going next time!"

"I'm sorry to have caused both of you such worry," Fletch wheezed as her ribs received another strong squeeze. "But I promise it wasn't for naught."

"Not for naught, indeed, seeing as you're well and whole," came the muffled reply from the short woman. Her husband winced apologetically over her head. "But please, Fletch," she said, finally releasing her embrace to pull away, "Tell us what this is all about. Should we worry still? What if those men return?"

"I don't think they shall," Fletch replied slowly. "They were after Dreythan — that is, Roderick. Not me." Both Prudens' eyes widened at the same time, and Fletch sighed. "'Tis a bit confusing. Let me start from the beginning." Taking a deep breath, she frowned at the wooden ceiling.

"Unbreathing?" Jon broke in after she'd finished the tale of the past few days. "Not another den, not again."

"No," she quickly reassured him. "I highly doubt it. There have been none of the signs that were present last time. No, these Unbreathing had traveled to the Pass to intercept the king's journey. For what reason, it's unclear. That's why the king decided to conceal his iden—"

"The king?" Missy interrupted, eyes wide. "The king himself?" She turned to her husband, putting a hand to her lips. "Oh, my."

"Roderick Galefall." Jon nodded sagely. "I thought he spoke too well for anythin' less'n' a nobleman."

"Er, yes." Fletch nodded, trying to keep her thoughts collected. "But that is why he concealed his identity. After the fright at the river, we managed to reach Iventorr safely." She swallowed, mouth turning dry. "One of the men whom the Unbreathing slew was a member of the king's Sentinels. An archer. Now the king needs someone in Iventorr who can easily identify Unbreathing."

Missy and Jon suddenly grew still. Knowing their eyes were locked on her face, Fletch took a deep breath and finished, "I've been reassigned as a Sentinel at Iventorr." It came out far more blunt than she had meant it to.

Before he could hide it, the innkeeper's face fell. Missy didn't move, her expression unchanged. "When?" she asked.

"The king has given me a fortnight to retrieve my belongings and return." That still wasn't right. It sounded so hollow and unfeeling, but... "But... but the king also sent me here for another purpose." The words tumbled from Fletch's lips, her heart twisting painfully in her chest. Handing the smaller scroll to Jon, she said, "This message is for you, from the king. The other is for the whole of Herstshire. Could I ask for your help in spreading the word? It must be heard by everyone who lives here."

Jon stared blankly at the roll of parchment in his calloused hands.

"It shan't bite," Missy smiled tearfully.

"It's a message of thanks, I've no doubt," Fletch told him. "You'll see."

Wiping her eyes, Missy nodded at the other scroll in Fletch's hands. "You say the other is for the whole of Herstshire?"

She nodded.

"Very well. Once Jon has gotten over his astonishment, we'll let the others know." The little woman patted her husband's elbow. "We'll make sure they're all gathered at the inn tonight." When her husband still didn't react, she peered up at him. "Jon?"

"I... I don't know what t'say." Before Fletch could react, he reached over the counter and patted her arm reassuringly. "I'm sorry, Fletch. I'm happy for you, I am. It's just, well…" He shrugged. "I'm a selfish old man, and you've become like daughter to Missy an' me. Watching you become the woman you are today… It's been one of our life's greatest joys."

"You speak the gods' truth, dear," Missy agreed, her eyes moistening again. "You've been a true gift to us, Fletch. And not just to us, but to the whole of this town."

"We shan't be the only ones in Hersthire that miss your presence. Even if most of the villagers don't know what you done for them." Plucking a clay mug from the dish tub, Master Pruden began scrubbing, blinking vigorously.

There were a few moments of uncomfortable quiet. Fletch bit her lip, peering down into her cup. "I cannot even begin to express how much the both of you mean to me," she finally said. "To say you're akin to family… That is, you are my family. I… I'm sorry this is such a sudden and unexpected change. You deserve better than to have something like this thrown at you."

"Nonsense." Missy wrapped one arm around her, pressing her graying head to Fletch's shoulder. "This isn't about what we deserve, dear girl. It's about the opportunity opening before you. And a wonderful opportunity it is."

Jon nodded firmly. "Agreed. I'm truly happy for you, Fletch. You've earned more than t' be stuck on the back end of nowhere all your life. You're a grown woman, with a life of your own." His usual smile finally dawned, warming her from the inside out. "I can't wait t' see what that life holds for ye."

Biting her lip, blinking back tears, Fletch motioned Jon out from behind his counter, and enveloped both the Prudens in the tightest and most tender of hugs.

Hours later, Fletch sat on the wide rough steps leading up to the inn, watching the sun set over the little village. The weary, soot-smeared men and women of Herstshire filed through the dusty streets, the last red rays reaching between the trees to touch their pale, dirty faces. Fletch had already drawn several buckets of water, filling washbasins in front of the well. They stopped, one by one, to rinse their calloused hands and shake loose grime from their clothes, their movements deft with the familiarity of daily routine. The inn's porch steps creaked as they trudged up and in.

She waited until the street was emptied just as the sun finally sank below the tree line. Taking a deep, quivering breath, she stood and straightened her new cuirass.

Jon opened the door and nodded. "They've all gathered."

"I know." Fletch's stomach lurched anxiously as she followed him inside.

One by one, the folk of the town fell quiet as she entered, each turning and meeting her eye. There was Tren with his wife Kailea, their youngest asleep in his broad arms, and Dorwell the smith. Then there was the miller and his eldest son, Lonnec. Most of the people present Fletch knew by name, but all by face. The thought of addressing them all at once was so alien that she found her hands trembling.

"Hello," she heard herself say. That was a good start. At least her voice was working. "Thank you all for gathering here on such short notice. I bear a message from the king, from King Dreythan Dreythas-son. He bid me deliver this to the whole of Herstshire. Please listen well."

Clearing a sudden burr from her throat, she snapped the wax seal holding the scroll shut, unfurled it, and began to read.

"Citizens of Herstshire Village. Firstly, I would like to thank all of you for extending such hospitality to Roderick Galefall during his brief stay in your homestead. I would also like to thank you for your honesty and outspokenness. It has caused me to understand that the taxes that have been levied against you were far too high for a town so far away from a viable source of trade, and that, because of this tax, you have all been suffering.

"I aim to mend this, in two ways. Firstly, a new taxation method shall be implemented. Three times per year, one upstanding citizen of your town shall prepare a report containing their estimation of a fair tax for each individual or family in Herstshire. You yourselves shall choose this person. They must be utterly trustworthy in your eyes, for greedy folk would take this as a chance to benefit themselves."

"What's that supposed to mean?" one shrew-like man interrupted indignantly. His neighbors immediately shushed him, shooting apologetic glances at Fletch.

Swallowing a nervous chuckle, she kept reading.

"You shall elect Herstshire's representative in this manner: My messenger, Fletch Wyndshaper, shall take down the name of each individual, and the name of the person that individual wishes to represent them. Each individual may select a single representative. No person may select themselves. My messenger shall then seal the list of names and bring them back to Iventorr Castle, where they shall be tallied. The person with the highest tally shall be chosen as Herstshire's record-keeper and representative, should they accept the responsibility."

A woman in a long shawl nudged Missy's elbow. "I can't think of any who'd turn down the chance for change," she whispered, and Missy nodded.

"As to the second manner of amendment, your town shall be supplied with a stable trade route," Fletch continued, her mouth numbly forming the incredulous words. "I shall be purchasing a number of Master Pruden's barrels of fine ale, which shall be brought directly to Castle Iventorr by a retinue of guards. This shall create the opportunity for merchants to expand their current trade into Herstshire, as well as for Hertshire to send wares to Verenshire and Iventorr.

I am truly sorry my lack of attention has caused your village pain, and I shall do everything in my power to right it. Thank you again for your honesty and hospitality. Signed, Dreythan Dreythas-son."

There was silence for a few moments, until a tumult of incredulous voices burst forth.

"The king himself sent a missive. That hasn't happened in years,

I don't believe."

"Wasn't his father doing something similar before he was slain? Gods rest his soul."

"Who was it that taught all the children to read, back in those days? The one good at arithmetic? Wasn't it Elder Pruden, Master Pruden's father?"

"A trade route, thank Ivere. Can you imagine what that will do for us? For the smith?"

"Fletch?" Master Pruden placed his hand on her shoulder. "You all right there?"

"Yes," she replied absently, still staring at the scroll. "I'm quite all right, thank you."

Dreythan had originally started the message with 'we would like to thank you', but had crossed out the royal 'we' and replaced it with 'I'. He'd also written her name quite beautifully, a flourish crossing the 't' to join a swirl below the 'h'.

How many years had it been since she'd seen her name on parchment, written by another hand? It was the strangest feeling, as if she'd found something that had been lost and long forgotten.

Shaking herself out of her reverie, she lifted her arms, quieting the joyfully restless crowd. "I'll be here in the inn to collect your names and choices each morning and evening. The king has bidden me return within a fortnight, so I must leave within ten days. Be sure to present your name and choice before then." With that, she sank onto her stool, carefully re-rolling the scroll as the murmuring crowd filed out behind her.

A frothing tankard of ale clapped onto the counter at her elbow. Startled, her eyes darted up to Master Pruden's broad face.

"The king himself." He grinned, white teeth positively glowing. "The king himself praised my great-grandfather's ale."

"Indeed he did," she replied, smiling back at his delighted astonishment.

"He's asked for five full barrels every season!" He rubbed his calloused hands together gleefully. "That's twenty barrels each year! Missy and I can give Tren and old potter Menwell coin for the crops and livestock and for the cups and mugs we replace. Not t' mention the other sundries the inn needs to keep going. Coin'll flow through the town from one hand to another. No one'll struggle t' pay tax." Lifting a mug of his own, he clinked it to Fletch's with a broad wink. "Gods bless the day that King Dreythan passed through our town."

Had Dreythan heard that, it would have filled him with relief, even joy. Smiling, Fletch tipped her mug back and drank deeply, savoring every drop.

The following three days, Fletch rose before the sun and tended to Roderick: cleaning his stall, giving him fresh straw and water, brushing him down. Their early morning strolls in the forest surrounding the village gave Fletch a chance to reminisce, to hope, and to dread. Then she returned to the inn and quickly broke her fast before the townspeople began lining up at her table. And line up they did, full dinner pails clasped in their hands, ready for another day's hard work. After recording the names and votes of all who waited, she carefully put away the scrolls, pen, and ink Librarian Brinwathe had given her and lent a hand around the inn with whatever Jon and Missy Pruden needed.

Cleaning dishes, sweeping, clearing the hearth, even climbing up on the roof to patch a leak or lending aid with other things around Herstshire. She didn't much mind what tasks they needed her for. It was strange and wonderful to be able to spend so much time with them, though the days passed too quickly. It made her heart ache if she allowed herself to dwell on it. Perhaps it would only make her miss them all the more once she was gone. Or, conversely, perhaps her absence would be felt more keenly by the Prudens. She tried to push those thoughts away, but frequently she caught herself staring at their faces as if trying to memorize every detail.

Just before the sun began to set each day, Fletch returned to the tavern, setting out scrolls, ink, and quills in preparation. When the flood of weary townsfolk arrived, she took their names and votes, and when she had finally got through all of them, she ate supper and waited for the tavern to empty so she could help Jon and Missy clean up. Then she returned to the stables to make sure Roderick had plenty of water and hay before patting him goodnight.

But the third night, Fletch entered the stables to find Roderick pacing uneasily in his stall. Both ears standing straight up and turning this way and that, his wide-set eyes blinked rapidly. Seeing Fletch, he shook his long neck, letting out a strained, "Huuuuuhuhuhuh."

Hesitantly, she put a hand over the stall door. He put his nose against it reluctantly. "What's wrong, friend?" She asked, peering around him. "Did something startle you?"

He gradually slowed his stomping as Fletch rubbed his neck and along his jaw. Finally his ear lowered into its usual half-folded state and his white lashes fluttered. With a shake of his head, he let out a long, squeaky sigh.

"That's right," she cooed, patting his shoulder. "No need for that." Easing open the stall door, she slipped past him and edged sideways in the tight space. His water bucket was nearly empty. She plucked it up and headed outside.

Reaching the well, Fletch drew a couple of pails of fresh water, first rinsing out Roderick's bucket, then filling it to the brim. She lowered the lid onto the well and turned.

The hair on the back of her neck stood on end. A soft puff of Wynd brushed past her cheek, carrying the faint but unmistakable scent of salt.

Her knife rang as she yanked it from its sheath. She put her back to the well, slowly circling it, scanning the moonlit rooftops.

The smell faded just as suddenly as it had come. An owl hooted in the distance, the familiar sound eerie and haunting. Seconds passed, then minutes. Heart still pounding in her throat, Fletch sheathed her knife and lugged the bucket into the stables, mind racing. "That was an Unbreathing, no doubt," she told Roderick as she set the water pail down in his stall. "That's why you were so spooked, isn't it?"

The elbecca just looked at her with large, soft eyes. Patting his nose, she made her way cautiously back to the inn, nerves jangling with each step. There was no further sign of Unbreathing, but the uncomfortable prickle on the back of Fletch's neck told her she was being watched. That night, she stayed awake for hours, hovering at the window of her room, heart in her throat. Eventually, knowing she had to rest, she fell asleep with her knife under her pillow.

"Why in Luminia's name would they have returned here?" Jon asked when Fletch told him about it the following morning. "Ye said they came t' the Pass for the king. The king's in Iventorr. Why not go there?"

"I haven't any idea," Fletch replied, uncorking the ink pot with a frown.

"Perhaps they know you helped the king evade them and they wish harm to you, Fletch." Missy slid a steaming plate of toast and eggs onto the table, round face pale.

"That's what I'm afraid of," Jon agreed.

Picking up her fork, Fletch scooped absently at her plate, gut twisting. They had a fair point. What if the Unbreathing were lying in wait for her when she left Herstshire? Or were they intent enough and eager enough to enter the town itself?

In her mind's eye, she saw them. Monsters in mens' skins skulking the streets of Herstshire, not caring if any stood in their way. She looked up into Jon's and Missy's anxious eyes. There was no doubt they would hold their ground before the Unbreathing. And it was certain the foul creatures would harm them when they did.

Fletch swallowed hard. "I believe t'would be better if I asked for all votes to be turned in by sundown," she said, hating the words as they left her lips. "As much as I'm loathe to leave you... I don't wish to risk Unbreathing attacking Herstshire. It can't be coincidence they're here after I've returned."

"Don't you worry, dear." Missy gave her arm a reassuring

squeeze, some color returning to her dimpled cheeks. "Though I'm sure you could handle any Unbreathing that dared showed its face, I'd rather you get safely back to the castle where there are others wielding silvered weapons behind high stone walls."

Jon nodded firmly. "Agreed. I'll spread the word around town that those who've not chosen a candidate yet ought t' do so soon."

"Don't mention Unbreathing," Fletch interjected. "Let's avoid unnecessary panic, if we can help it."

The innkeeper was already turning away, calling over his shoulder, "What Unbreathing? If the votes are collected sooner, that simply means the king can send the trade caravan on t' us as quick as he may! That'll light a fire under their merry arses."

Back aching, Dreythan straightened in the wooden throne, smoothing his brow into a passive expression as the man before him prattled on, hands waving emphatically in the air.

It was already past sundown. The lanterns beside the throne hall's stained glass windows had been lit, their dancing glow casting refracting shards of colored light across the floor and pews. Though Dreythan would normally have finished with any remaining supplicants hours before, still he sat, motioning individual after individual forward.

In the few days he'd spent away from Iventorr, the issues waiting for his attention had rapidly accumulated. The past five afternoons, he had been forced to dismiss a large number of folk still waiting at the close of the usual hearing hours. Though some of them took it well, departing with a simple bob of the head or an understanding smile, most were not so gracious, and Dreythan couldn't blame them. Many of them had muttered to each other, casting narrowed glances over their shoulders as the guards had shown them to the doors. A few had openly shaken their heads.

He couldn't help wondering what they were whispering.

Perhaps they were simply complaining about having to wait, he tried to tell himself. But perhaps they were asking why he'd had to delay, why he'd taken so long with the other citizens. Were they saying he was incompetent, or too deliberate? Too unlike his father?

"—and that's why I just can't abide this decision, my lord," the man before him was insisting. "Please, I beg of you, forbid this union."

Dreythan stirred. He'd heard the same query from other supplicants in his fifteen years as king. Far too many times to count. "How old is your daughter, goodman?" he asked.

The bald head dipped. "Nearly twenty."

"And the woman to whom she is betrothed, how old is she?"

Saggy cheeks reddening, the man's jowls deepened as he frowned. "The same."

"They are both adults, then?"

"They are," he said reluctantly.

"And will they adversely affect the lives of others by joining their hands in marriage?"

The man's face twisted as he sought an answer. It was clear he couldn't find one that didn't portray him as the selfish old windbag he was, for his mouth opened and shut again, once, twice, three times.

"I thought not," Dreythan said, hands clenching on the arms of the throne. "Were I to forbid the two from marrying, I would impose my own will above those of my citizens." His voice was distant in his ears, hard and sharp. "For what reason? To prevent their happiness? To force your daughter to bed a man that you might have the grandchildren you so desire?"

Dreythan cut himself off as the man's jaw dropped. His pulse pounded in his ears. Peeling his fingers from the throne, Dreythan looked down, swallowing. His stomach had curled hollowly within him for hours. A steady beat of white-hot pain throbbed behind his eyes, and his spine was stiff from the long day in the unforgiving seat. And he had let these things break through the wall he'd so carefully constructed around himself. Sucking in a long, slow breath, he held it, counting to ten.

"I shall not forbid their union," he continued finally, raising his head to meet the father's eye. "And I would encourage you to rethink your perspective of this matter. Which is worth more to you? Your daughter's happiness and the relationship you share, or her obedience to you? You cannot have both." Gesturing to the guards, he finished, "You are dismissed."

Too stunned to protest, the man allowed himself to be ushered out without another peep.

The pews were finally empty.

Dreythan was just about to rise from the throne and allow himself to stretch when the doors to the throne hall parted. A chorus of raised voices echoed into the chamber. Past the guards, a small crowd huddled, some pushing in towards the doors, others hanging back with arms crossed over their chests.

"She'll be here any minute," one of them insisted, his voice carrying as he craned around the guards' shoulders to peer into the hall. "The king still holds the throne. Please, if you would ask him to wait but a moment!"

"You've been sayin' as much for five hours," the guard replied, staunchly positioning herself as a blockade. She added something else that Dreythan couldn't hear. The crowd was clearly displeased. Broken phrases and exclamations rose to shouts. One of the protestors from the back started forward, only to to be stopped by another.

The enormous doors began to swing shut behind the exiting father. Turning to the nearest guard, Dreythan's jaw tightened. "Why are there angry citizens outside the hall?"

"I'm not entirely sure, my lord," the guard replied, shifting uncomfortably. "I don't believe they are citizens. Most of them wear garb from the Isles. They've been waiting for someone to arrive for most of the day."

Abruptly, one of the doors swung back open. The woman guard's long split skirt rustled around her ankles as she hurried down the carpet, the nose guard of her helmet unable to hide her glare. Stopping at the bottom stair, she jerked into a bow. "My lord. Ambassador Alicianna Kekona has just arrived from the Isles of Aden. She is requesting to speak with you, my lord."

Mouth instantly turning to sandpaper, Dreythan could only stare. Alicianna Kekona. A name he'd seen hundreds of times on trade documents from the Isles. "Very well," he heard himself say weakly. "Show her in."

As the guard retreated back to the doors, Dreythan straightened his robes, checking the crown's position on his head. For an ambassador to arrive unannounced...

The doors parted again, and a woman entered. Head high, she strode down the center of the carpeted aisle, seeming to glide with the effortless grace of her measured steps. Silk robes of amethyst swirled around her sandaled feet, gems flashing from the hem as they caught the low lantern light. Gold threads gleamed from the intricate, jewel-studded braids of her dark hair. One sash with masterfully embroidered orchids and lilies was draped over her right shoulder and tied at her left hip, while another of solid shimmering gold was tied from left to right. Though her stature was diminutive, her presence filled the hall, powerful and poised.

"Welcome, Ambassador Kekona," Dreythan greeted, rising. "It is an honor to finally meet such an esteemed citizen of the Isles of Aden."

Pausing at the foot of the throne's steps, the ambassador looked up, her eyes the color of ocean shadows. "The honor is mine, Your Grace," she replied, her full lips widening in a smile. Her voice was near-musical, deep and resonant, her accent familiar but crisp as it rolled off her tongue. "My apologies for arriving so late in the day. I had intended to reach Iventorr at a much sooner hour." Her generous hips dipped in a curtsy, the jewels in her braids glittering as her head tilted. "Am I correct to assume you did not receive the missive I sent two days ago?"

Missive? Dreythan shook his head ruefully. "I am afraid I did not," he admitted. "It must be urgent business for you to have traveled here from the Isles, and with such haste."

The ambassador's dark eyes narrowed. "It is indeed. Four days ago, I received word from several merchants of the Isles currently within Ivenhence. They claim a new system of taxation is being implemented. Is this the case?"

"Indeed it is." Uneasiness twisted with the hunger in his gut. "At the very least, it is being tested."

"I see. The Guild members were quite insistent I speak with you immediately." She shifted, sweeping the room with one hand. "You can understand their concern. A change in taxation can have extreme effects on trade and trade routes. Before I departed the Isles, eight more missives arrived. My representees are panicking, Your Grace. They have heard nothing as to how this change will affect them."

Merchants. Trade routes. The words drummed through Dreythan's mind, paralyzing him. Knowing he was staring, he tried to stir, to blink, but couldn't.

"I could understand the lack of communication were Ivenhence in duress," Ambassador Kekona continued. Her tone was diplomatic, reasonable, but her expression was thunderous. "However, given the current state of matters, I must warn you that many of the Merchant's Guild of Aden have threatened to withdraw from Ivenhence. They cannot afford to remain whilst taxation shifts if they are not informed as to how these changes will impact them." Gold earrings chimed as she shook her head. "Import and export is taxed at the Ivenhencian border, yes. But will each town we visit now require some form of tax as well? Will the rate of customs increase at the border?"

She paused, hands folding at her waist, her gaze expectant.

Mouth dry, Dreythan tried to swallow and failed, a knot clenching in his throat. "I confess I am at a disadvantage," he faltered. His hands were sweating. Clasping them together to keep himself from wiping them, he added, "It had not crossed my mind that Ivenhence's trade partners would need to be aware of changes within our borders. I assure you, there has been no intent thus far to change the tariffs of trade."

Doubt flashed across Kekona's face. "You cannot expect your citizens to accept a new tax system if nothing will change for your allies' imports and exports. You'll be accused of expropriation. There will be riots in the streets of Verenshire before the season is done."

Her words, though uttered matter-of-factly, hit Dreythan with the force of a battleaxe. He could only stand before the throne, staring down at the gilded woman in shock as if her statement had disemboweled him.

Head tilting slightly to one side, the ambassador's eyes softened. "My queries do not require an immediate answer," she told him quietly. "But the Guild will expect resolution to their concerns quickly. I can remain in Verenshire until I receive word that you are prepared to negotiate."

"That is appreciated," Dreythan managed. "You are welcome to take residence in our Guest Tower until a proposal has been formulated. I will send word as soon as I am able. Thank you, Ambassador Kekona."

"Thank you, Your Grace. I will look for your summons." She dipped again in a bow, then turned and glided out, her jewelry tinkling with each swift step.

When the throne hall doors closed behind her, it took every ounce of strength in Dreythan's weary body not to sink into the throne and bury his head in hands. He asked one of the guards to have a meal brought to his quarters and escaped to his tower as quickly as possible, his footfalls matching the rhythm of the pounding in his head. But when the meal arrived and he stared down at the bowl of steaming soup and fresh bread, he couldn't bring himself to reach for it.

The ambassador had spoken the truth.

While the new system would be beneficial to towns and families that had previously struggled to make ends meet, it would likely cause the tax to rise for some of Ivenhence's more affluent citizens. Dreythan took a sip of water, his stomach clenching queasily.

Those affluent citizens, upon learning the tax hadn't changed whatsoever for Ivenhence's trade partners and merchants, would undoubtedly raise a stink. Remembering how outspoken they'd been years ago about the installation of wells in every town, he rubbed his aching head. He should have foreseen this inevitability. He should have known he would have to adjust trade customs accordingly.

And to have an ambassador show up unannounced, to be caught grasping desperately for answers like a guilty child caught in a lie... He cringed. Utterly humiliating. Even if he had received her missive, it would have only given him a few hours' lead notice of her arrival. He would have had to dismiss the citizens waiting for his ear yet again, to see the disappointed expressions, the shaking heads.

At this point, he wished that had been the case instead. At least he wouldn't have looked like a fool before the Ambassador of the Merchants' Guild of Aden.

He forced himself to take a bite of bread, wondering why the message hadn't reached him.

The notion that the trade caravan might arrive more quickly spurred the people of Herstshire into action. Those who had already cast their votes prodded their neighbors and family members who were undecided, while those who'd procrastinated finally stopped by the inn to have their names and choices for representative recorded.

By the time the sun had begun to set, Fletch counted a total of one hundred and eighty three villagers' names in her scrolls. Master Pruden had told her there were only about two hundred adults in Herstshire. Hopefully the last few would provide their information before nightfall. She sat on the inn's steps, stomach in her throat, foot tapping anxiously as she tried to wait for the stragglers.

Thankfully, just as the last rays of sunset faded over the horizon, the members of one large extended family filtered in, arguing quietly as they formed a queue at her table. When she jotted down their names and glanced up at Missy, she received a quick nod. The final votes had been collected.

Fletch swiftly packed the scrolls and supplies. Senses jangling with alert discomfort, she shrugged on her quiver and bow and stepped outside.

The livestock of Herstshire had been restless the entire day. The air had been filled with the discordant sounds of cowbells ringing, dogs barking, and pigs grunting and squealing. Roderick, on the other hand, was much calmer than he'd been the previous night. As Fletch entered his stall, he blinked placidly at her, chewing on a bit of hay. It didn't take long to outfit him with his blanket, saddle, pack, and rope harness. As if sensing her tense mood, he nuzzled the hair on top of her head, then nudged her shoulder.

"I'm sorry," she whispered, maneuvering the rope over the tip of his horn. "I know you can't see in the dark, but we need to be going as quickly as we may. The longer we stay here, the more likely Herstshire's danger."

She led the elbecca back to the inn to find two figures standing on the porch, the dim moonlight etching each worried line on their faces. Missy wordlessly wrapped Fletch in her arms as Jon hovered behind her, glancing into the treeline.

"Go on, now, Fletch." Missy stepped back, tears glimmering in her kindly eyes. "Please be careful, my dear. And do write, if you can."

"I shall." Fletch nodded, swallowing against the burning lump in her throat. "I promise."

She turned to Jon, who clasped both her hands in his with a tearful smile. "I wish you all the best, dear girl. You shan't be forgotten by us."

At that, a hysterical half-sob, half-laugh burst from her. "And I shan't forget you either," she blurted. "As if I could. Not in a thousand years."

For one wild second, she clearly saw two paths before her: the path she'd known and traveled most of her life, and a new, strange, dangerous one. A clamoring voice within her begged to stay on the familiar trail, but she knew in her heart she couldn't. Her choice had already been made. The kingdom needed her now. The king needed her.

She couldn't turn back.

Not trusting herself to say another word, Fletch hoisted herself into Roderick's high saddle, casting one last glance at the inn and its porch before her vision became a swimming blur. Urging Roderick into a trot, she blinked harshly, forcing the moisture from her eyes to spill down her cheeks. Within moments, they had clip-clopped past the well and log buildings of Herstshire and were traveling deeper and deeper into the forest.

They traveled at the same brisk pace for two hours, Fletch's chest fluttering at each unexpected movement, every strange sound and smell. Occasionally she pulled the Wynd toward her from random directions, taking a quick sniff as she did, but she didn't once smell the tang of rust.

After they left the trees and began making their way through and over rolling grassy foothills, the tension eased a little. It would be far more difficult for Unbreathing to ambush her in the open rather than in the dense cover of the forest.

Shifting in the saddle, Fletch scanned the surrounding hills. She'd thought the Unbreathing would try to prevent her from reaching the open fields, staging a trap in the shadows of the trees where she could only see by the Wynd's shimmering streams. But they hadn't. Glancing over her shoulder at the distant edge of the woods, a twinge of guilt struck her. What if she'd imagined the Unbreathing scent? What if she'd left Herstshire seven days early for no reason whatsoever? She would have robbed herself of more time with Missy and Jon, acclimating them and herself to the knowledge that she might not see them again for many years.

Remembering the cold finger of dread that had traced up her

spine preceding the abrupt rust scent, Fletch shook her head. She hadn't imagined it.

"'Where there's one Unbreathing, there's more'," she muttered to Roderick, glancing up at the stars. "'Tis what Papa said once, and he's never been wrong yet."

The elbecca bobbed his head in agreement.

Wynd stirred over the hills, swirling over the grass and wildflowers in gentle cyclones and streams of translucent peridot and yellow, carrying with it the scent of spring. It brushed against Fletch's face, lifting her hair away from her cheeks and whispering past her ears.

Reaching out, Fletch grasped the Wynd from the hills to her right and pulled it toward her, inhaling sharply. She did the same to her left as Roderick tossed his head, ears twitching.

Rust pierced her nostrils.

Her fingers tightened in Roderick's reigns, mind racing. They were trying to cut her off from the east. She hurriedly strung her bow and felt in her quiver. Gritting her teeth, she pulled out a silver-tipped arrow and nocked it to the bowstring. Only one other precious missile remained in her quiver; the others were ordinary iron-capped bolts. She cursed herself silently, furious she hadn't asked for more at the castle.

Roderick capped a particularly large hill, then trotted into the little valley below. His long ears alertly upright, they twitched nervously side-to-side.

Three dark figures appeared to Fletch's left, their legs a blur of impossible motion. Her heart leaped into her throat. The thought flashed through her mind to spur Roderick on. But even as she leaned forward to urge him, the shadows slipped closer. Pulling back the arrow, she aimed, softly exhaled, and loosed. One of the dark figures stumbled and fell. The remaining two approached rapidly, gaining on her even as Roderick broke into a gallop.

One silver arrow left. Bending forward, she stood in the stirrups and shouted, "Run, Roderick!"

The elbecca snorted, his hooves flying even faster across the meadow. Drawing the arrow from the quiver, she nocked it and squinted down the shaft, steadying her breath. The two Unbreathing were almost on her. Their eyes gleamed like sickly lanterns in the moonlight, their elongating yellow fangs stark in their ravenous grey-white faces.

The stronger they were, the less human they looked, and the more she hated them.

Fixing her sights on the closest, she exhaled slowly, letting the arrow slip from her fingertips. The monster crashed face-first into the dirt.

Fletch slung her bow across her back. Just as her hand reached the hilt of her silver hunting knife, something slammed her just below the ribs. The air was yanked from her lungs as she crashed to the grass, Roderick screeching in terror as he bolted on without her. Rolling to her feet, she stumbled and turned, gasping.

The last one skidded in the grass twenty paces from her, circling warily to one side. Sweat beading down her temple, Fletch drew her knife.

Seeming to realize her remaining arrows were useless, the Unbreathing stalked closer, teeth bared in a sinister leer. "I know your scent," it hissed.

An icy finger traced down her spine. "Do you, now?"

"The fragrance of Wynd-blood is more tantalizing than I was told. Perhaps the taste will match."

As quick as thought, it hurtled towards her, all shadow and fangs. She ducked and stabbed as its bare hand swiped the air above her. Too slow. A vise-like grip seized her from behind by the shoulders, lifting her kicking into the air. The Unbreathing's hands were like iron vises, crushing the blood from her veins. "Now I shall feast from you," it gloated. Its breath, hot and dry, washed over Fletch's face, the scent of rot and death thick enough to choke her.

"I think not," she snapped. Yanking her chin to her chest, she rammed her head back. Her skull collided with the monster's face. Stars burst in her vision as the Unbreathing's grip loosened on her shoulders. Through her half-blind pain, she struck, thrusting the knife past her own side. It sank into the monster's chest.

She dropped to her knees as the hands released. Rolling aside, she heaved herself to her feet, fists wobbling to the ready.

The Unbreathing was lying on the grass, hands clasped around the blade in its chest as its flesh shriveled into bits of ash. Within seconds, there was nothing left but a cloth-covered skeleton and grey papery flakes.

Gulping a breath of relief, Fletch knelt beside the destroyed Husk. Gingerly, she poked through the remnants, searching for pockets, trinkets, jewelry. Anything to identify why he sought her, who he'd been sent by. Nothing but cloth. She frowned as she retrieved her knife, scanning the hills behind. Spotting the remains of the Unbreathing she'd killed with her final arrow, she approached it and crouched, feeling, patting—

Something crinkled beneath her searching hand. From an inner pocket of the Unbreathing's cloak, she tugged a piece of folded parchment. Incredulous, she stared for a moment, fingers trembling. Then, with a painful grimace, she straightened and began walking, opening the bit of parchment as she went.

Dreythan Corwynter's assassination was hindered by a Wynd-blood who has taken up residence at Iventorr. We must eliminate her for our plans to succeed. Intercept her on the road between Herstshire and Iventorr, but take caution. She is skilled in distinguishing our kind and has robbed several of their Shells.

That was all. There was no signature. The note was penned in a hurried hand with blue ink.

Refolding the parchment, Fletch tucked it away and broke into a hobbling run, crossing throbbing arms over her chest. She had no idea if any more Unbreathing would come after her, and if any did, she couldn't hope to survive. Not without at least a few silvered arrows.

How inconvenient that the precious metal dissolved with the

defeated Husk's flesh.

She wouldn't be safe until she reached Iventorr. And perhaps not even then. The king wasn't the only one with a target on his back anymore, it seemed.

Chapter 9

When Dreythan woke, he marveled he'd been able to sleep at all, then wondered if he had. Ambassador Kekona's words kept playing through his fog-riddled mind as he dressed and made his way to the dining hall for breakfast. He would have to do more research in the library. Surely there were records of—

"My lord?"

Dreythan glanced up from his plate, spoon paused mid-way to his mouth. Before him stood one of the royal guard, his gauntleted fist clenched over his heart. "Yes, Sentinel Alwick?"

The man bowed. "Your pardon, my lord, for interrupting your meal. Captain Norland bade me report to you once you'd woken. He's left Castle Iventorr, Captain Norland has."

"What?" The king stared, confused. Norland — left Iventorr? "Why?"

"A riderless elbecca arrived at the castle gates a couple of hours before dawn, my lord," Alwick replied, his steel-blue eyes reflecting Dreythan's own puzzlement. "When the guards woke the Captain to ask if they should allow the creature in, he... Well, he was greatly concerned." He shook his head. "Understatement. He pulled on his armor like Iventorr itself was ablaze and dashed to the barracks, then the stables. He was leaving with four guards and five horses just as I was summoned to the gate. He bade the elbecca be looked after, and it is, and also instructed me to give you these."

Numbly, Dreythan accepted the rolls of parchment the guard offered, his heart sinking. He didn't recognize the handwriting, but they were neatly labeled 'Herstshire Ballots'.

Fletch.

"Captain Norland wasn't certain when he would return, but he made arrangements for us Sentinels to provide additional protection while he is gone. Have no fear, my lord." With that, the youngest of the Sentinels turned and settled back into his usual place against the wall.

Any appetite Dreythan had vanished.

He forced himself to eat and drink. When he had finished, he rose. Tucking the ballots within his robe, he made his way to the throne hall. Focusing on the daily appeals from the citizens of Ivenhence distracted him for several hours, but eventually the hall emptied and his worried thoughts could not be quelled any longer.

He paced the length of the throne hall over and over, hands folded behind his back, thumbs spinning against each other. Brow creasing, he glanced up through the high stained glass window nearest him. The position of the light on the floor told him it was only noon, but it felt much, much later.

A thousand possibilities were darting through his mind, few of them likely and many ghastly. Perhaps Fletch had sent one of the people who lived in Herstshire back with the elbecca and a cart of her belongings. Perhaps the cart had overturned and spooked the creature... but he doubted it. Fletch did not seem the sort to ask others for help if she could accomplish something on her own. Perhaps she'd finished collecting the ballots. Unable to bear prolonging the goodbyes to her home and her friends, she had set out early to return. But why then would the elbecca have returned without her, clearly terrified?

Turning on his heel, he stalked across the strip of green carpet for the thousandth time. That was what concerned him the most: the state of the elbecca. It was widely known that they were docile, intelligent creatures, difficult to spook and easy to train. What had frightened one so, terrified to the point of collapse?

One of the tall, arched doors to the throne hall creaked open, admitting the fresh-faced guard, Fletch's friend. He hurried down the aisle and halted a few paces away, bowing deeply. "My lord," he gasped, wiping his face the back of his hand. "I've just come from my patrol. Captain Norland has returned."

"Where is he?" The words spilled from his lips. Clearing his throat, Dreythan stopped and turned to the guard. "Is Fletch Wyndshaper with him?"

"Yes, my lord, she's with him. He's taken her to the infirmary."

At that, more gruesome images flashed before Dreythan's eye. He shook them away, quickly descending the stairs. "Let us go at once."

"Yes, my lord."

They arrived at the infirmary to find the door and windows crowded with curious guards. Inside, Fletch was propped up in a bed, her eyes wreathed with blue and purple shadows as two apprentices carefully cut the sleeves off her tunic. Captain Norland stood to one side, fiery brow furrowed as Fletch protested weakly, "Tisn't necessary, ruining a perfectly good shirt. T'was brand new."

One of the women tut-tutted down at her. "Your mind isn't working properly," she chided gently. "You just let us do our duties and tend to your wounds, see?"

Sharing a nod, the two apprentices gingerly pulled the sleeves away. The room drew a collective gasp. Horrible purple, blue, maroon and sickly green bruises mottled Fletch's shoulders, the shape of perfect hand prints.

"Wyndshaper," Captain Norland breathed. "Holy Lady

Luminia... How did ye escape?"

Fletch's head turned to him. She blinked in bewilderment, green eyes glazed. "Escape?"

Dreythan's chest tightened. "No questions now, Norland," he said quietly. "She needs food and rest before anything else."

"Yes, precisely," a reedy voice agreed. A tall, clean-shaven man edged around Dreythan, handing a clay pitcher to one of his apprentices. He wore pure white robes which shifted around his feet, barely brushing the tops of his sandaled toes. "Here. See that she drinks at least half of that before she falls asleep again." Turning to the other, he gestured to the bruises. "Those shall need frankincense oil. Please retrieve it from the herb cabinet." As the apprentice hurried away, he turned to the king, sallow face solemn. "I know you have only just arrived, my lord, but I must insist that this young woman be allowed to rest. I suspect she is in shock. She may not be capable of answering your questions at this moment."

"I am not in shock," came a feeble voice from the bed. "I am perfectly mind of... sound of mind."

The corners of Dreythan's lips curled.

"Of course you are," the remaining apprentice smiled soothingly. "Here, drink this."

Raising an eyebrow at the patient, Norland turned to the physician. "So, Trithinnis," he said, "how long until I can begin training her?"

Sytres Trithinnis's narrow face soured. "Her injuries must be given the chance to heal. A fortnight at the very least, likely longer."

Norland heaved a sigh, glancing toward the bed. "New orders, Wyndshaper. Rest an' recover. Understood?"

But Fletch's eyes were already closed, her head slumped against the pillows, red-brown hair askew.

The physician shook his head with a sigh. "I doubt anything shall wake her now. Ah well. We shall have to treat her while she sleeps."

"Thank you, Master Trithinnis." Dreythan nodded to the Captain, turning toward the door. "Please send word to Captain Norland and myself once she has awoken."

The two men exited the infirmary to find the cluster of guards slowly scattering, casting guilty looks in their commander's direction. He scowled broadly as they skulked away. "Nosy busybodies," he grumbled. "Off to your duties! You've been trained better'n this."

Dreythan watched them leave, smiling ruefully. "I cannot say I blame them. After all, I also came running once I heard that Fletch had returned." Sobering, he asked, "Did she tell you what happened?"

"As well as she could. Three Unbreathing attacked her in the foothills of the Snowshod Mountains. She found this on one of 'em." Norland pulled a bit of crumpled parchment from his coinpurse, offering it to Dreythan. "I don't like what it says, my lord."

Ironing the paper between his fingers, the king's eyes darted over the hastily penned words, forehead gradually knitting. "How could they have known Fletch Wyndshaper is a Wynd-blood?" he muttered finally, handing the parchment back and massaging his temple. "Or that she was traveling the road between Herstshire and Iventorr?"

"I'll do my best to find out, my lord," the Captain grunted, a muscle in his jaw twitching. "But one thing is certain. I'll need to increase security about the castle. We have a spy in Iventorr."

"Make whatever arrangements you deem necessary," Dreythan told him. As the anxiety surrounding Fletch abated, he remembered; he had work that urgently needed attending to. "I shall wish to speak in depth regarding this later, but you need rest, and I must manage other matters. I shall be in the library."

"Aye, my lord."

With a nod, the two men went their separate ways.

In minutes, Dreythan was seated in the library study, books and scrolls steadily piling around him as he poured over page after page and parchment after parchment. One of the librarians had informed him that Brinwathe had returned home early due to his rheumatism. They weren't as quick to find the exact materials the king needed as Brinwathe was, but the scribes present helped each other locate the required records, a small army of worker ants depositing a steady stream of paper on the desk.

Eyes rapidly sweeping line after line of written text, Dreythan suddenly found himself wondering what he was doing. Research, yes. But why? He was already familiar with the customs for trade between Ivenhence and Ilumence, Thissa, and the Isles. They had hardly changed over the years. Reading the records again was a waste of time. There would be no answers in their pages, and he knew it. So was he simply trying to stave off the feeling of helplessness that threatened to drown him? He couldn't afford to lose trade with the Isles. Every town and village on Ivenhence's coast would be thrust into the same hardship that Herstshire had borne for years.

The thought was enough to make him physically ill.

His hands tightened on the book. Did he hope that by reading his father's accounts of the kingdom's taxes for the thousandth time, he would suddenly receive a miraculous insight into his current circumstance? That he would have a vision of what his father would have done in his stead?

"If I might ask," a soft, lilting voice said, "is there a specific piece of information you're looking for, my lord? I have read many of the tomes you peruse. Perhaps I could help you save some time?"

"I am not certain," Dreythan muttered, setting the volume aside and picking up the next. "Perhaps if there were a book regarding the customs the Isles requires of Ilumence, or that Ilumence requires of Thissa. Record of trade taxation between kingdoms other than our own. Perhaps then I might find some answers."

"Hmm. I do not believe there is a book containing that information. Perhaps I ought to make that my next writing project." The voice paused, then added, "I'm quite familiar with the trade between the various nations, my lord. What questions do you have?"

Not quite sure he'd heard correctly, the king lowered his book and looked up. Across the desk stood a tall, lanky figure swathed in loose maroon robes. Their hands were tucked into their sleeves. A length of cloth that matched their robes had been tied around their head, securing their mass of coily greying hair away from their face in an hour-glass like shape. Umber eyes peered at Dreythan over a pair of mismatched pieces of polished glass, which perched in a carved wooden frame on the bridge of their long, slender nose.

"I do not believe we have previously met," Dreythan said slowly. "Librarian —?"

"Anshwell," they replied with a smile, dipping in a slight bow. "Journeyfolk Librarian. Happy to be of service, my lord."

He gestured to the empty chair across the desk, noting their gender-neutral title. "Please, join me. How long have you been part of the library staff?"

The librarian obligingly sat, their long limbs tucking neatly in the generous folds of their robes. "Fifteen years. Though I've served the kingdom since its foundation."

Dreythan inspected their face, surprised. Their androgynous features didn't bear many signs of age, aside from the greying of their dark hair. Their light brown skin was smooth, marked only by the slightest signs of crows' feet at the corners of their smiling eyes. "You survived the Great Slaving?"

They nodded. "I did. I hadn't quite reached adulthood at the time, so I was one of the youngest to fight in the Battle of Reclamation. Afterwards, I was one of the strongest and fittest to remain in Iventorr. Kell Wyndshaper — Ivere rest his soul — trained me to ride a horse and made me one of Iventorr's official messengers."

"At the foundation of the kingdom?" He stared at them, stunned. "You bore messages outside of Ivenhencian borders?"

One of their hands slipped from their sleeve to push the wooden frame further up their nose. "Indeed. My official duty was to bear messages negotiating the formation of trade routes and their regulation within Ivenhence." A wistful smile rose to their face as they looked out the window, reminiscing. "I'll never forget the first time I set out on my own, freshly minted coins of solid silver belted at my side. King Dreythas — Ivere rest his soul — was keen on securing relations with Ilumence, and—" Abruptly, they shook their head. "But here I am, wasting your valuable time when I offered to help save it. What questions might I answer for you, my lord?"

Hope stirred in Dreythan's chest as he met the librarian's intelligent gaze. "You are most certainly not wasting my time," he reassured them. "Please, tell me more. There are few records from the foundation of the kingdom. I often wondered how our trade was so quickly established."

"Ah, yes." The dusky face mellowed. "So much was happening, and much of it arranged by King Dreythas's own hand. There is little wonder he had not the time to pen it all. 'Twas his idea to take the silver ore the Unbreathing had forced us to mine and use it as Ivenhence's primary export. He assigned me to travel first to Ilumence, then to the Isles, and finally to Thissa."

Pulling sheets of blank parchment towards him, Dreythan filled an inkwell and snatched up a pen. "Which nation was the most difficult to secure trade with, and why?"

Anshwell paused, lips pursing. "I would say 'twas Thissa, my lord," they answered finally as Dreythan feverishly scribbled, recording their every word. "Though there were difficulties with each. Thissa's dictator has always been a wary sort, expecting a knife behind each gesture of goodwill. The governors of the Isles already had access to precious metals, and thus didn't see as much value in our primary export as we hoped. And Ilumence." They sighed, shaking their head. "While King Morthal was open to the possibility of trade, the members of his court and his citizens had already formed their own negative views of our kingdom."

"Founded by an upstart prince who irked Ilumence's rule,"

Dreythan said, quill scratching away. It was strange to remember that not everyone remembered his father Dreythas in a positive light. "How did you secure trade with each?"

"T'was fairly simple for the Isles. You see, they had ready access to gold, but silver was harder to come by due to the risk their ships faced crossing the Luminian Ocean. Thus, I was able to convince them..."

The cadence of their voice carried on, regaling Dreythan with the story of the kingdom's trade cornerstones. Several times, Dreythan had to ask them to pause while he refilled his inkwell or replaced his pen. By the time the sun had begun to set, the stirring of hope had blossomed into ideas.

When Fletch opened her eyes, she found herself in a dark, still room. The faintest bit of flickering light played across the timber walls as if from a single candle or a distant fire.

She was lying in a bed, partially propped up by pillows. Her arms pressed awkwardly against her, heavy and stiff as logs. Glancing down, it made sense. They were bound in slings. Crumbly yellow-white paste coated her dully throbbing shoulders. A blanket covered her, but she had the distinct and uncomfortable feeling that her armor and clothing had been removed, and not by her own hands.

Struggling into a sitting position, she could see the rest of the room; long and narrow, with a row of simple beds just like hers butted against one wall. At the furthest end of the room, a dwindling fire crackled in a small hearth. A woman sat fast asleep in a chair beside the glowing embers, the light softly illuminating her white apron and closed eyelids. Beside Fletch's bed was a small table, empty save for a pitcher of water.

Water. She tried to swallow, but her tongue grated against the roof of her parched mouth. Picturing the water rising from the clay pitcher, Fletch focused, swirling her wrists —

And nearly cried out as pain erupted in both shoulders. Thousands of white-hot needles buried themselves in her flesh, burning and piercing.

Gritting away tears, Fletch sucked in a deep, shaky breath. She scooted to the edge of the bed and eased her bare feet down to the smooth, cool stone floor. Arms dangling uselessly, she wavered to her feet. When the room stopped spinning, she stooped over the table, clamping her teeth onto the edge of the pitcher. Gingerly, she tilted the container until liquid sloshed against her upper lip. In the middle of the very last greedy gulp, she realized how musty it tasted.

Straightening, she hesitated. The last thing she remembered was a vague impression of Captain Norland's rough voice and his azure eyes. Had they made it back to Iventorr? She glanced uncomfortably back at the woman beside the fire. It felt wrong to be sneaking about while she was sleeping, but... Judging by the pale light from the two windows, it was still hours before sunrise. Waking her felt like a bad idea.

Crossing slowly to a window, her feet whispering across the stone, Fletch peered out at the unmistakable wood-and-rock amalgam structures of Iventorr Castle. That was comforting, but... in this unfamiliar place, she wouldn't be able to fall asleep again. And she wasn't sure if she could simply lie awake in the dark, waiting for sunrise or for someone to notice her.

She glanced down. A simple loose tunic covered her to below the knees. At the very least, if she ran into someone, they might think she was a peasant and leave her be.

The chill of the floor seeped into her toes, and she shivered. Timidly, carefully, she tip-toed to the door and nudged it open with her hip. Her feet met cobblestone, and she stopped, trying to find a familiar roofline in the maze of shadows and moonlight.

"Who goes there?"

She whirled, a figure already approaching rapidly, footfalls as quick as her heartbeat. "Fletch Wyndshaper," she managed. "Er, sir. Could you, er, tell me where the Garden Wall is? I'm a bit lost."

"Fletch?" The voice chuckled. "What are you doing out of the infirmary? You ought to be resting!" Under the shadow of his helmet, Klep Ironshod's eyes twinkled.

"I'm glad you found me, of all the guards in Iventorr." Fletch grinned, her relief immediate. "How can I rest if I feel as though I'm trespassing?"

His whiskered cheeks flushed slightly. "Aye," he agreed, ducking his head. "I felt the same when I was there last summer for downing fever." Pulling his hood back up, he nodded to the west. "The Garden Wall, you said. Might I escort you? T'would take less time to show you than to describe the route."

"If you can spare the time," Fletch said gratefully. "Thank you, Klep."

"Right this way. I can't leave my post for long." He took off at a brisk pace down the cobbled street, Fletch close on his heels. "How are your arms?" he asked.

"I can barely move them," she replied. "But they'll heal. Thank Luminia they aren't broken."

Klep turned, giving her a curious look as they turned a corner into a wide, open, thankfully empty square. "You and Captain Norland both say that," he observed. "You thank Luminia instead of Ivere. I hope this isn't too forward of me to ask, but... is your family also of Wynterhead Mountain?"

A familiar cold hollow shivered open in Fletch's chest. "No," she replied quietly. "My blood and heritage are of the Wyndarin — the gypsies, as most in Ivenhence know them. They also revere Luminia since they believe she's their creator."

"I wonder why the Wynterhead Clan reveres her," Klep mused, not seeming to notice Fletch's discomfort. "They don't believe she created them as well, do they?"

"I'm not certain." Swallowing, Fletch quickened her pace as they passed the kitchens. "But 'tis an interesting thought. Perhaps we ought to ask Captain Norland."

The young man was already shaking his head, helmet

swiveling. "Not a snowball's chance in the Thissian desert, as my pa would say. The Captain's a bit touchy about his past, Fletch. I do my best to avoid the subject with him."

They walked a little further in quiet until Klep abruptly halted, pointing. "There you are — the Garden Wall."

And there it was, a shadowed thirty-foot-high grey stone barrier framed behind by the shifting shapes of tree limbs.

"Thank you again," Fletch smiled, a bit uncomfortably. "Had you not come along, who knows how long I would've had to sneak about in the dark."

"You're welcome." He beamed back, melting her awkwardness with his warmth. "Goodnight to you, and rest well."

He hurried off as she crept silently into the wall's spiral stairwell, climbing two stories and down a short hall. There was a brief moment of panic and confusion as she doubted which door was hers. But she guessed, opened the door, and there was her room.

She sank onto her bed, embarrassment whelming over her as she stared down at her stockingless legs. "Curse Kazael," she muttered, ears burning in the dark as she cringed. "He saw my bare feet."

Before she slumped onto her bed for a nap, Fletch managed to painfully change into a fresh set of clothes. Her armor was nowhere to be seen. Guessing it had been tucked away somewhere in the infirmary, she swept that thought away as drowsiness overtook her.

When she woke, the first rays of sunshine were pushing past the horizon. As she left her quarters to retrieve some breakfast, she glanced in the mirror and grimaced at her now-wrinkled clothes.

The dining hall was a humming hive of activity. Servants hurried here and there along the room-length tables, distributing steaming plates or cups and rushing through the doors to the kitchen for another load. Guards and gardeners took their fill of breakfast, preparing for another day of work in the sun. Others bustled in and out, taking their places at the tables or rising with a clatter of dishes and silverware. The king's table at the end of the hall was the only still, empty place; an oasis in a bustling sea.

Fletch took a seat and was immediately served a hot plate of jam-smeared toast, eggs, and potato mash. Mouth watering, she gingerly picked up her fork. While changing clothes, she'd discovered she could move her lower arms with little pain, but the slightest shift of her shoulders was enough to make her see stars. Abandoning the fork, she plucked the toast off her plate and ducked her head, taking half the slice in one bite.

"Good morning, Fletch," Klep said, winking as he sat across from her. "I hope you slept well?"

She smiled around the toast. "I bib."

Removing his helmet, Klep set it on the table and ran a hand through his flattened brown curls. "I heard you defeated a group of Unbreathing single-handed." He leaned forward, eyes wide. "Is that true?"

Fletch nodded, grateful that he hadn't mentioned their earlier meeting. "I suppose three could be called a group. But it wasn't easy."

"How? What happened?"

"I'm not sure I ought to share," she said hesitantly, glancing behind. Several other guards had seated themselves close by and were pretending not to listen. Two of them, she recognized: the sour-eyed man and his bald compatriot, the ones who'd sneered at her during the test. "I must ask Captain Norland—"

The Captain himself settled onto the bench next to her, holding a plate of steaming eggs. "Ask me what?"

"Captain," Klep said eagerly, "Fletch Wyndshaper is unsure if she can disclose her battle with the Unbreathing."

The guards seated close by shifted uncomfortably as Norland turned to glare at them. Swiveling back to Fletch, he inspected her gruffly. "The physician threw a right fit when he found ye gone from the infirmary, Wyndshaper," he said.

Heat rushed to Fletch's cheeks. She hoped she hadn't imagined the twinkle in the stern man's eye.

"I do need your report of what happened," he continued. "I'd guess the reason ye left Herstshire so quickly had something to do with the Unbreathing."

Fletch gulped, setting her toast down. "Yes, sir. When I arrived in Herstshire, I was told that men had been in town after the king and I had departed, asking after our whereabouts. I believe they were Unbreathing, sir. My home and belongings had been destroyed. The strange 'men' were likely responsible.

"During my third day in Herstshire, my fourth day away from Iventorr, I smelled an Unbreathing while tending to Roderick — er, the elbecca, sir. It was only there for an instant, then gone, but..."

"But ye knew something was amiss," Norland interjected, his tone approving.

Reassured, she nodded. "Exactly."

Dreythan slipped into his seat at the usual lonely table, eyeing his breakfast with mixed spirits. He had spent hours in the library the previous day, plying Anshwell for information. The librarian's insights into the trade customs of the other kingdoms had already proven invaluable. Through the course of their conversation, several ideas had sparked to life between them, enough for Dreythan to begin drafting a proposal for Ambassador Kekona. He intended to continue with Anshwell's help that afternoon, and hoped to go over Herstshire's ballots with the keen-minded soul as well.

But the ominous possibility of a spy and of unknown hostile 'plans' had placed Dreythan's nerves on a knife's edge. Even after meeting with Norland and discussing the issue at length, he'd kept himself awake late into the night, trying to anticipate what machinations the Unbreathing's master had and why they were so intent on eliminating Fletch's presence in the castle.

Glancing about the Hall, he spotted Fletch and Captain Norland seated beside each other with the young guard across from them. Fletch's slender hands were folded bashfully before her, eyes fixed on the Captain as her lips moved. Her words had captivated the attention of a squad of guards who had abandoned all pretense of breakfast and were turned about in their seats, listening intently.

"The final Unbreathing caught up and yanked me off the elbecca as I drew my knife," Fletch told the Captain, trying and failing to ignore Klep's slightly agape stare. One table over, the grey-eyed man snorted. "He gripped me by my shoulders, lifting me from behind. Driving my head back into the Unbreathing's face forced his grip to loosen, and I thrust my knife back." Looking down at her fidgeting fingers, she admitted, "Ivere's luck must've guided it to the Shell's heart. It was a blind strike."

"I've heard the bruises on your shoulders are perfect handprints," Klep interjected. "Is that true?"

"I'm not certain," Fletch replied, curiosity piqued. "I haven't seen them."

Captain Norland shoved his empty plate away. "You're fortunate your bones weren't crushed," he grunted. "I've seen the strength of the Unbreathing, and it isn't something to take lightly. You're right, Wyndshaper. Ye were lucky." Standing, he gestured at her plate. "But ye also kept your wits about ye and acted decisively. Eat up an' meet me at th' castle gates." His whiskers curled in a hinted smile. "We've got training to do."

"I'd best be off," Klep said, standing as Fletch obediently tried to wolf down her food. "I wish you the Lady's fortune. Not that you'll need it, but—" he shrugged, "—you never know what Captain Norland might throw your way."

Gulping down a mouthful of egg, she managed, "Thank you,

Klep" before he trotted off, armor clinking.

As Fletch approached the castle gates, Captain Norland's voice reached her ears, bellowing, "Torsh, Torrin. Report!"

She rounded the corner to find the Captain striding toward her, the two guards to either side of the gate saluting at his back. "All's well, sir," they replied in unison.

Lending Fletch a brisk nod, Norland brushed past. "This way, Wyndshaper. Ye shan't be able to train with them until ye've healed, but ye might as well meet the rest of th' Sentinels."

She fell into step behind him, feeling suddenly naked without her armor. "Yes, sir."

As Fletch hurried to keep up with the Captain's long paces, a sweet, crisp scent danced through the air. She looked up to find clusters of blooming tree limbs reaching over the top of a wrought-iron fence. An orchard? Before she could pause or ask, they had already passed it. Gardens hugged the path to either side, filled with neat rows of vegetables. Behind the garden to the right rose the kitchen and welcome hall, and beyond the garden to the left was the throne hall. Carved entirely out of stone, it protruded from the inner wall of the castle, its high peaked roof level with the top of the wall.

Continuing past the throne hall, Captain Norland turned sharply left. Ahead of him, nestled into the wall of Iventorr was one of the castle's ten towers. Unlike many of the others, this tower was entirely stone. Roofless, the flat top was ringed with stone blocks, a guard armed with a crossbow stationed atop. An emerald banner fluttered above the single door, the silver 'I' of Ivenhence proudly gleaming in the sun.

Shoving the door open, Norland paused, then stepped aside, holding it open. "Go on," he said gruffly when Fletch gave him an inquiring glance. "This oughtn't take long."

She ducked inside to find a simple circular room, scattered with a couple tables and chairs. As she entered, several figures turned towards her.

"Sentinels," Captain Norland said, stepping to her side. "Meet Fletch Wyndshaper. Wyndshaper, I believe ye already know Aeda Yewmaster."

Meeting her old mentor's warm gaze, the tension in Fletch's throat eased a little. The woman smiled and nodded, as serene as always.

"That over there's Darvick and Harrild Hammerfist," the Captain continued, nodding at two men in the corner. "Both swordsmen, and brothers."

They were the twins she'd seen before the test, one with a longblade and one with a greatsword. The lithe one lent her a friendly nod and a quick smile, while the other grunted, jerking his head as if forced to.

"I'm Matteo Alwick," another interjected, offering his hand. "Your self-defense during Norland's melee combat test was top-notch."

A pair of steel-blue eyes met Fletch's. She pretended not to see the extended hand, lending him a sheepish smile. "You're too kind," she told him, and meant it. "I've a lot to learn. But thank you."

Puzzlement flashed across his tan face, then embarrassment as his glance flashed to her slings. Rubbing the back of his neck, he grinned ruefully. "Sorry about that."

"I told you to remember she was injured," the slimmer twin said, then to Fletch, "He shakes hands with everyone he meets. Please pay him no mind."

"And lastly," Captain Norland said, gesturing to the table on the far side of the room, "Parfeln Holden, our veteran. He's been part of the castle guard longer'n ye've been alive."

Fletch's eyes followed the captain's hand, falling on a man who turned toward her. Bitter grey eyes met hers, and her stomach clenched.

It was the same man who'd jeered at her during the trial, the one who'd leveled cold stares at her across the dining hall.

Lip curling in a gross parody of a smile, Parfeln crossed his arms over his narrow chest. "Heard your account of your injury," he commented, his tone as dry as desert sand.

"As did I," Aeda interjected, her smile gleaming proudly. "You did well, Fletch. Your skills have clearly continued to improve over the years."

The bulkier of the twin brothers shifted, giving Aeda a keen stare. "Is this the child you trained during your Forester days?" She nodded, and he peered at Fletch. Something in his face that had been closed off suddenly opened. "She told us about you once," he said.

"Wait," the youngest Sentinel interjected. "You were the girl who requested to be assigned to the Valer-Norst Pass?"

"Show respect, Alwick," the bulky twin snapped. "She served in one of the most dangerous, isolated posts in all of Ivenhence for over a decade."

Alwick bristled as the slender brother delicately interposed, "I'm certain he meant no impudence, Darvick." Casting an apologetic glance at Fletch, he added, "It's an honor to meet you. Your father was one of my personal heroes. I hope that isn't strange to say."

"Not at all," she replied. Harrild, was that his name? It was impossible not to instantly like his honest, open expression. "He's my hero as well, after all!"

To Fletch's surprise, Captain Norland's beard parted in a grin. "Look at ye lot," he said with a chuckle. "Chummin' along already. You're dismissed to your usual schedules. Harrild, I've assigned two bowmen and an additional swordsman to your purview. They're with the king as we speak." Turning, he nodded to the door. "Let's be going, Wyndshaper. Time to remind ye of Iventorr's layout."

Giving the room at large an awkward nod, Fletch ducked out of the tower into the sun's warm light. The captain skirted past her, turning left. As they proceeded through the castle, the streets became increasingly congested with men and women hurrying to and fro, children laughing and playing, and clusters of people pausing to chat. Somehow, Captain Norland didn't slow. Helmet and shoulders above all but the tallest of men, he strode head up, arms swinging. Any who saw him coming were quick to make way for his rapid approach.

They headed north past the Garden Wall. When they approached the barracks and trodden field of brown, patchy grass, the Captain's pace finally slowed.

It took them quite a while to make it out of the 'military village', as the Captain called it. Many who passed were soldiers, and most of them greeted Norland as he and Fletch strode by. He made a point of speaking to each individual, asking questions and acknowledging their work.

As they finally left the barracks and headed south, a slow smile split the Captain's fiery beard. "And now for my favorite part of the castle rounds," he told her. "Wyndshaper, up ahead is the library, assembly hall, and school."

Fletch glanced up at him curiously. "I didn't take you for someone who would enjoy reading, sir," she said.

Norland's smile faded. "Ye need to think before saying something alike to another," he told her soberly. "Someone else may've taken that as an insult, lass." She felt her cheeks flush, and opened her mouth to apologize, but Norland waved her off. "I said, someone else. I know ye meant nothing by it."

The door to the schoolhouse slammed open. Two little boys with curly red heads came barreling out, grinning from ear to ear as they charged. "Papa!!" one of them shouted, leaping at Norland.

Catching the child in mid-air, the Captain spun him about his head, then scooped the other up with one arm. "Och, ye wee monsters," he groaned. "Ye'll be th' death o' me. What'll your school teachers say? Back in there with ye b'fore I catch a skinnin'!"

The older boy giggled uproariously, while his brother stared shyly at Fletch and tried to hide his face in his father's beard.

"Go on, ye rascals," he growled, setting them both down on their feet. "I'll see ye in about an hour or so."

Having completed their mischief, the little miscreants skipped happily back into the schoolhouse past a scowling adult and slammed the door behind them.

"Your sons?" Fletch asked.

Norland nodded, his whiskers twitching. "Jormund is the eldest, and Solund the younger; Jor and Sol for short."

His accent had come and gone just as suddenly as the children, she noted, grinning. "They're precious."

"Precious troublemakers, aye," he grumbled, leading her back the way they had come. A reluctant smile creased the corners of his eyes. "Last moon Jor decided he wished to make cheese, and hid a pail of milk under 'is bed. It took us a week to discover where the stench was coming from."

Approaching the Garden Wall, Norland suddenly changed his course. At the northernmost part of the wall where it joined with a tall tower, an arch formed a passage through the twenty-feet-thick stone. An iron gate hung open, allowing their passage into the Royal Garden.

Two ancient oak trees sprawled their gnarled roots into the ground, surrounded by rose bushes, daffodils, sunbursts, star lilies, and other flowers that Fletch couldn't name. Lotuses floated in a sparkling pond under the shade of one of the trees, the bits of sunlight that peeked through sparkling in the water. Everywhere Fletch looked, there was vibrant color, every breath laden with the scent of sweet spring. She absently followed the Captain to a small building tucked beside the wall and tower, staring over her shoulder.

"Come in, Wyndshaper," Norland said, pushing open the door and ducking inside. "Petrecia? Are ye home?"

"In here, love," a light voice replied.

Reluctantly tearing her eyes away from the beauty behind her, Fletch hesitantly followed the Captain through the door. She found herself in a tidy single-roomed house with walls of stone and a timber roof. Drying herbs hung from the rafters, filling the home with a clean, comforting scent. A roughly hewn wooden table occupied the center of the room. Six stools were pushed under it and a sewing basket sat on top, scraps of cloth spilling out over the sides. One far corner of the room was concealed by a hanging curtain, and the opposite corner was occupied by two small beds. An assortment of toys was piled in a basket between them.

Curiously, much of the home was decorated by furs. A bear-pelt covered both of the small beds, elk antlers hung proudly on the wall beside the fireplace, and doe hides covered the wooden stools. It felt very much like a cottage one might find in the most remote mountain reaches of Ivenhence.

It reminded Fletch of her own cabin. She swallowed.

"Is our visitor outside?" the light voice said, and Fletch realized there was a woman standing by the hearth, dusting the wooden mantle with a scrap of cloth. Her golden hair was gathered at the base of her neck in a simple knot. She stood on tip-toe to reach the back of the shelf, her small stature emphasized by her husband's largeness.

"Nay, she's here," Norland replied, stepped to the side. "Wyndshaper, this is my wife, Petrecia. Petrecia, this is Fletch Wyndshaper."

"Oh!" The woman folded the cloth neatly and turned, a bright smile pinking her high cheekbones. "Welcome to our home, Fletch. 'Tis a pleasure to make your acquaintance." Suddenly, she stopped. Lighting crackled in the stare she leveled at her husband's dust-covered feet. "Norland, how many times must I ask you to remove your boots outside?"

He shifted, avoiding her eye. "Sorry, love," he mumbled, seeming to shrink several inches. Ducking out the door, he glanced back at Fletch. "When you're done here, head back t' the infirmary, Wyndshaper. The physician didn't get a chance t' finish sewing your sling b'fore ye disappeared. Then report t' me in the throne hall." With that, he turned and abruptly left, leaving a bewildered Fletch standing in his home.

"You appear confused." Petrecia appeared at Fletch's elbow, chuckling. "I suppose my husband failed to explain why you're here?"

Fletch, unsure of how to respond, substituted a shrug for a bewildered head tilt.

"Oh, Norland," Petrecia sighed. "My husband has asked me to teach you the niceties and courtesies of castle life, seeing as how you've lived much of your life in some degree of seclusion. Only while your wounds are healing, of course. There are far more important things to occupy your time once you have mended."

She stared at the woman, uncomprehending for a moment. Abruptly, she was acutely aware of many things. Her height, head and shoulders above Petrecia's. Her trousers, tunic, and boots, in stark contrast to the small woman's dress, bodice, and soft moccasins. Her unbound breasts tucked beneath her sling-supported arms.

"He wishes you to teach me etiquette, you mean," Fletch said doubtfully.

Petrecia's eyes softened. "Now don't think 'tis a reflection on yourself, Fletch. My husband was much like you when he was young. When he came into service in Iventorr, he had to learn manners the difficult way, through years of observation. He simply doesn't want you to experience the hardships he did as a result."

Despite the acute self-consciousness creeping over her, Fletch could see the sincerity and kindness in the woman's eyes. The first signs of wrinkles were just beginning to show around them; laugh lines. "I understand," she said slowly, remembering her exchange with Norland and Dreythan in the throne hall. "I didn't know that standing on level with the king while he sat in the throne was a sign of disrespect, or whether or not I should bow at certain times. And I'd rather avoid embarrassing anyone, the captain and the king most of all."

"Precisely," Petrecia agreed. "There many lessons I teach the kitchen maids and serving girls that you shan't need, such as how to carry yourself and how to walk properly—"

"Walk properly?" The incredulous words spilled out before

Fletch could stop them.

"—but he seemed most anxious of your speech, and of your knowledge of courtesy in the king's presence." Pulling out a stool, she gestured encouragingly. "Come, sit. We have much work to do."

Thus began two of the most challenging weeks of Fletch's life. Every morning she took breakfast in the dining hall, then stopped by the infirmary to have her shoulders checked and to have foul-smelling paste smeared on them, then followed Captain Norland for his first circuit of the castle. They parted ways at the Garden Wall, where Fletch met Petrecia and began four hours of... lessons? It was difficult to put a label on their meetings. Most of the time, Petrecia presented theoretical scenarios and asked Fletch how she would respond to them, then explained what the most ideal response would be and why. How would she speak to the mother of a missing child? What should she do if she were to catch a fellow guard stealing or cheating? How ought she respond when commanded by the king to summon someone, and how would she summon them? When was it appropriate to sit in the king's presence?

Most of the scenarios Petrecia presented involved addressing the king or carrying out duties as a guard. But there were also lessons on table manners. And how to dress according to one's station.

After several hours of this each day, the cozy home began to feel more like an overdecorated prison. When she escaped at noon, Fletch was all too glad to breathe deeply of the fresh air and stretch her long legs.

She would then make her way back to the dining hall for mid-day dinner, where she could usually find Klep. Or he would find her. He was an island of cheer and calm in the roiling sea of strange new things that surrounded her, always willing to exchange a laugh or a story, always asking Fletch if she wanted to sit with the other guards. When Fletch was in his company, she found stares and murmurs easier to ignore.

And stare and murmur the people of Iventorr did. It wasn't just the guards anymore, but the kitchen maids, gardeners, families... Everyone seemed to be unsure of what to make of Fletch. As she walked down the streets, she caught them gawking at her trouser-clad legs and boots or her arms bound up in the special sling the physician had made. Or, if she felt the prickle of prying eyes on her while on rounds with Captain Norland, she would turn just in time to see eyes darting away from her, embarrassed at being caught.

One small mercy was that most of the guard had lost the looks of mistrust and skepticism. But on the other hand, the negativity of the few who still pointedly eyed her had deepened, darkened. Especially that of Parfeln Holden and his bald, bewhiskered friend. It was too much to hope they didn't resent her. All she could do was ignore them and go on about her business.

And so she did. After the mid-day meal, she followed Captain Norland on his second round about Iventorr for the day, paying close attention as he pointed out buildings, alleyways, and residences of note. At the end of the day, she took dinner in the dining hall and retreated back to her own quarters.

On the thirteenth day of this routine, Fletch entered Norland and Petrecia's home to find the golden-haired woman waiting for her with two garments, one draped over each arm.

"Good morn to you, Fletch," she smiled sunnily. "Which color do you prefer, light blue or violet?"

She eyed the long folds of swaying cloth, one eyebrow raised. "Those are dresses," she said.

"Indeed they are," Petrecia agreed. "Which color?"

Fletch met the small woman's brown eyes. Though Petrecia's smile didn't waver once, there was danger glinting there. Dropping her gaze, Fletch bit her lip. "Blue," she mumbled.

"Wonderful." Standing on tiptoe, Petrecia draped the frock carefully over Fletch's shoulder. "Now go behind the curtain and get undressed." Pausing, she cocked her head curiously. "Will you need any help, dear?"

"No," Fletch blurted, then quickly amended, "No thank you," remembering her lesson from three days ago. Always give thanks for offered kindnesses. "I've been managing on my own." Her feet remained glued to the floor. Taking a piece of fabric between her fingers, she rubbed it absently. It was stiff and light, and promised to be unbearably scratchy. "Is there... is there a need for this?" She asked desperately. "I haven't worn anything like it since... since I last lived in Iventorr."

The dangerous glint in Petrecia's eye manifested on the rest of her countenance. "You shall dress yourself behind the curtain," she said, her voice like steel. "And then I shall explain to you the purpose. Not before."

Reluctantly, Fletch withdrew behind the curtain, easing her arms from their slings. It was fascinating that such a small woman could give off such an intimidating presence. She remembered Petrecia giving Norland's dirty boots the same icy stare, Norland's towering height wilting under her baleful gaze. The image nearly made her giggle.

As she squirmed out of her tunic, Fletch called around the curtain, "Petrecia?"

"Yes, do you need help?"

"No, no," she replied too quickly, covering herself as the edge of the curtain shifted. When the cloth and her heart settled, she swallowed. "I was simply wondering. My father, when he was captain, was known as Captain Wyndshaper to all, and was never addressed by his first name. But Captain Norland is addressed just so — by his first name only and never his surname. Is there a, a... well, is there an etiquette-related reason for this being so? Is it not more proper to refer to one's superior by their surname?"

There was a lengthy silence. Fletch stepped into the dress and struggled with the cinch, her mind fumbling as quickly as her fingers.

"I suppose that wasn't a proper question to ask," she said finally.

"Nay," Petrecia said quietly. "'Tis all right, Fletch. You are new to Iventorr, and thus would not know. My husband has... relinquished his family surname. You're familiar with the Wynterhead Clan?"

Giving up on the cinch, Fletch stepped out from behind the curtain, nodding. "From what I remember of my father's stories, they attempted to invade Ivenhence years after the Crimson Horde was defeated." Her eyes fell on Petrecia's face, and froze.

"Norland was born on Wynterhead Mountain," Petrecia said slowly. Forehead creased, lips thin and tight, she sat straight and still at the table, fingers folded together. "His father, Norjund Wyntersoul, was the patriarch of the Wynterhead Clan. When he incited his people to attack Ivenhence, Norland tried to stop him by challenging him for patriarchal rights, though he was little more than a boy. When his father defeated him and exiled him from the mountain, Norland came directly to Iventorr to warn King Dreythas of the impending attack." She paused, her hands shifting to press flat against the table's surface. "His actions saved many lives and prevented an unnecessary war, but he can never return to his home. As such, he's asked that his surname be forgotten." With a sigh, she finally looked up. "That is why he is called by his first name only."

Her eyes fell on Fletch, widening as they travelled over the dress. Fletch's cheeks burned. "I had difficulty with the ribbon," she explained.

"No, you did well!" Petrecia quickly reassured her, standing to take a closer look. "I actually quite like what you've done, wrapping it around your waist to tie in the front. 'Tis usually secured in the back with a large loose bow, but this works nicely since your shoulders are healing."

Her words were kind, genuine. But behind the smile that had risen so easily to her laugh-lined eyes remained the ghost of melancholy.

"I'm sorry I asked," Fletch said. "'Twas an indelicate question... I ought to have known better than to pry."

Petrecia's smile broadened, then faded. "I understand your curiosity. Truly, I do. But this is the very reason we have been meeting this last fortnight, Fletch. Remember, as a Sentinel, you represent the king with each word and deed. If you were ask something alike of a visiting lord or lady, t'would be a terrible affront. The gypsies shall be arriving before we know it, after all. I should hate to see you say something out of turn and bring shame to your king."

Those words punched all air out of Fletch's lungs. It was all she could do to gulp and shake her head.

There was a long, awkward pause.

"Perhaps we can end today's lesson early," Petrecia ventured. "'Tis market day in Verenshire. I'm certain your new abode could use some furnishings, and you might find other things to interest you there. You ought to go and see if you find something that catches your fancy."

Chapter 10

Dreythan scanned the scroll one last time, then lowered it, sucking in a deep breath. Across the table, Anshwell paused in arranging writing materials to give him a reassuring smile, nudging the glass-set frame further up the bridge of their nose with one finger.

Every day for the past fortnight, Dreythan had returned to the library to consult with the Journeyfolk Librarian. Anshwell was a wealth of knowledge. They had been to many places and experienced firsthand the variety and hardship of politics. Negotiating trade routes, transporting coin and valuables, observing the cultures and customs of other nations, and learning how those differences informed their economies. In the span of two short weeks, Dreythan felt he had learned more about the other kingdoms' inner workings than he had in the previous five years.

They had also reviewed the ballots from Herstshire together. The results were conclusive: Master Pruden would serve as the representative for the tiny town. Without a doubt, Dreythan knew the kindly innkeeper would do well in his elected post.

"Tis an excellent strategy, if I might say so," Anshwell had offered while peering through their mismatched bits of glass at the ballots. "Pledging to purchase ale from the innkeeper. In supplying coin to the most frequented business in the town, the coin will flow from the inn to craftsman, farmers, and laborers alike. Not to mention, it'll guarantee enterprising merchants the chance to establish trade close to Thissa." They had tapped their forehead, then pointed upwards. "Well reasoned, my lord."

"I hope so," Dreythan had replied soberly. "Herstshire needs the chance to flourish again."

Now, as they prepared for what was likely the most important diplomatic meeting of Dreythan's life, he found his thoughts drawn to the small town. The trade-route scouting party was departing Verenshire for Herstshire that morning. It would be the first true test of his strategy. Without a safe route, no sane merchant would be willing to undertake the journey.

"A good day to you, Your Grace," said a voice from the door, and Dreythan straightened.

"Ambassador Kekona," he said with a slight bow. "Thank you for joining us. I trust your quarters in the Guest Tower have been to your liking?"

The lowest floor of the tower had been converted into a meeting room for the negotiations. But Ambassador Kekona had not appeared from the stairway that led up to her temporary residence; she stood in the doorway of the tower's entrance, silhouetted by the mid-afternoon light. Behind her stood an array of merchants dressed in traditional Adenite garb. The protestors from two weeks ago, Dreythan realized with a jolt of shock. They looked as unhappy as they had then, perhaps even more so. One of them deliberately turned his back as he met the king's eye.

The ambassador stepped inside, a guard shutting the door behind her as she returned Dreythan's bow. "Indeed. 'Tis a pleasure to see you as well, Librarian Anshwell. Thank you for relaying King Dreythan's updates over the past fortnight. You have allowed me to reassure my representees of your ceaseless efforts and buy us time."

Pulling out a chair, Anshwell gestured. "The pleasure is mine, my lady," they replied. "Please, join us."

She crossed the room as easily and smoothly as silk slides over skin, settling into the seat Anshwell offered. "I have just come from meeting with the merchants of the Guild who are within Iventorr and Verenshire," she said, folding her hands on the edge of the table. "They are most anxious to hear your proposal."

Upon an encouraging nod from Anshwell, Dreythan also sat. Though he had rehearsed his words at least a hundred times over the past three days, his gut still clenched nervously as he began, "After intensive research and careful consideration, I believe we have formulated a change which the Guild will find acceptable, if not agreeable." Palm open, he gestured to a scroll which sat to Ambassador Kekona's right. "Since Ivenhence's foundation, her trade arrangement with The Isles of Aden — which Journeyfolk Anshwell helped negotiate — has not changed. Upon arrival at Ivenhence's border, an Adenite merchant must provide a written record of all goods they are transporting into Ivenhence, and must pay customs according to the type of product and applicable percentage. Upon exit at Ivenhence's border, the same applies."

Ambassador Kekona didn't reach for the scroll, her stormy green-blue eyes fixed on Dreythan's. "I am aware, Your Grace," she said, her tone pleasant, yet prodding.

"However," Dreythan continued, swallowing, "A merchant of the Isles may remain in Ivenhence for an indeterminate amount of time without ever paying additional customs on goods they accumulate during their time here. Thus, many of the Guild travel our kingdom for years at a time." He indicated the scroll to the Ambassador's left, grateful his hand wasn't shaking. "According to our records, the average amount of time a merchant spends within Ivenhence is two years and two seasons. Compared to the taxation required of Ivehence's citizens, this seems disproportionate."

This time, the ambassador's hands unfolded. Her jeweled rings shimmered in the lamplight as she unfurled the parchment, lips curving downward. "This is quite a detailed summary," she said finally.

He hadn't imagined the approval in her tone. He was sure of it. Taking a deep breath, Dreythan went on. "In the interest of keeping taxation for our citizens and the customs of trade for your merchants fair and balanced, I propose the following. Merchants of the Isles of Aden shall provide a detailed list of goods at the border, as they always have. However, they shall not pay customs at that time —"

Ambassador Kekona lowered the scroll, staring incredulously over the top.

"—Unless they happen to cross during one of the year's three tax periods." Chest tightening, he paused, trying to regulate his breathing. "Each merchant shall provide an updated account of goods on hand at the opening of spring, mid-summer, and autumn's end in whichever town they find themselves in. The town's representative shall include the merchants' ledgers in their reports for their town, and the Royal Treasurer shall then calculate each merchant's tax rate based on the quantity of goods the merchant has sold or traded since entering Ivenhence."

Anshwell glanced sharply up, their glass-set frames sliding alarmingly down their nose.

"In this manner, merchants shall be taxed by the goods they have sold only, not by the amount of goods they have on hand," Dreythan added, inwardly smacking his own forehead. He'd forgotten to mention that bit to Anshwell. "Merchants who have not been able to offload goods shall not be punished for their lack of business, and those who have been able to trade freely should not have troubles with the customs. It is our hope that this will not only encourage members of the Guild to bring larger amounts of goods across the border, but also to allow merchants to return to the Isles frequently without worry of punishment by tariff."

A bead of perspiration was forming on Dreythan's forehead. He ignored it as he met the Ambassador's piercing gaze across the table.

Alicianna Kekona didn't move or bat an eye. She stared through Dreythan's soul, her gold hair chain resting in a furrow above her brow.

"Your proposal is an interesting one," she said finally. "It is straightforward, though not as simple as our current arrangement. At the very least, 'tis clear you have put extensive thought and effort into its creation, which is more than I can say for our other trade partners." Casting a glance to Anshwell, she said, "I assume you have transcribed a copy of this proposal?"

"That we have, my lady," they nodded, producing a scroll from the folds of their robe.

The ambassador took it, her smooth brown features tensing as she scanned it and turned back to Dreythan. "I thank you for taking this matter seriously, Your Grace. Though I cannot guarantee my representees shall view your proposal positively due to the requirement for detailed record-keeping, you have my word that I shall do everything in my power to convince them of your good intentions and your evident desire to retain trade with the Isles. I shall return to present your proposal to the Guild in person." Her expression darkened. "Given our recent interactions with Thissa and Ilumence, I suspect they shall not be as receptive as they once might have been. I would recommend the preparation of a second proposal in the event that this is the case."

As Kekona rose, Dreythan hurriedly copied her motion, nodding. "Of course, Ambassador. I shall look forward to your return."

As the woman glided swiftly to the stairs and up out of the room, Anshwell appeared at the king's elbow, polishing the bits of framed glass with the hem of one sleeve. "Well," they offered, "That went as well as I could have expected."

Dreythan's shaking hand rose to wipe the film of cold sweat from his forehead. "I cannot believe I did not stutter once," he admitted. "I have not been that nervous since—"

Since he had crouched between a boulder and a tree, shivering in his boots, or under a riverbank beside an intense, keenly alert Forester.

He shook himself free of the memories as Anshwell placed the frames back on their nose. "It escaped my memory before the meeting," Dreythan said. "And it would be remiss of me to allow it to escape again." Meeting the librarian's eyes, he added, "You have been of great assistance over the last fortnight, Anshwell. Your experience and knowledge are invaluable, and I believe they would better serve in a new application. Would you accept the position of Royal Treasurer?"

They hesitated, their greying head of thick, coily hair bowing as they inspected their sandaled feet. "I am honored that you would consider me fit for such a lofty appointment, my lord," they told him. "Might I ask what my duties would entail?"

"You would be responsible for reviewing and approving the tri-annual tax reports, both from Ivenhence's townships and from Aden's merchants." After a short pause, Dreythan added, "It would be a lot for one person to handle. If you needed to select assistants, I would not be opposed."

To his relief, when Anshwell raised their head, their eyes glinted with anticipation. "A new challenge," they said, rubbing their slender hands together. "Who would have thought it, at my age! Yes, my lord, I accept. I assume the ballots from Ivenhence's other towns require review?"

"Indeed they do. Come, I shall show you to them."

Heart still throbbing dully in her throat, Fletch strode away from the Garden Wall, dressed in her tunic, trousers, and armor. She'd finally managed to pull on the cuirass and vambraces without having to grit her teeth against waves of pain. With her quiver and bow slung across her back and her hunting knife belted at her hip, she finally felt like herself again. Walking around with her arms in slings and without any physical protection had made her as uneasy and embarrassed as if she were naked.

Despite the familiar weight of the leather hanging from her shoulders, Fletch felt little comfort as she headed toward the castle gates.

The gypsies shall be arriving before we know it.

Two passing guards glanced her way, then hurried past, their breath puffing shortly as they murmured to each other. Stomach hollowing, she ducked her head. Was she a curiosity, an oddity to them? A strange, ill-bred, wild woman who'd never known decent society? Or maybe they thought of her as a foreigner, or a ladder-climber.

It didn't matter, she tried to tell herself as she nodded to Torsh and Torrin, the castle gatekeepers. She barely noticed them salute in return.

Once she escaped the shadow of the castle gates and her footfalls transitioned from the hollow clunks across the long bridge to the soft crunching of gravel, Fletch took a long, deep breath. The sun's warmth lit the crown of her head, a soft breeze carrying with it the scent of apple trees and wheat fields. On either side of the road, acres of neatly planted farmland sprawled like a knitted afghan of varying shades of green. Birdsong and the rustling of crops and tall grass caressed her ears. Tilting her chin toward the wide sky, she watched a cloud shift across it, borne by a stream of mint green Wynd. Tension eased slowly from her shoulders as she let herself smile. She hadn't realized how crowded she'd felt in Iventorr. How watched.

Two miles of the quiet road passed far too quickly, and soon a low, sprawling mass of brick and stone buildings lay before her. She made her way slowly down the main road of Verenshire, trying to take in her surroundings. Young birch trees lined the avenue on both sides, separating the road from homes and shops. Tidy flower beds surrounded the bases of the trees, filled with daffodils and lilies. Nearly every window and shutter Fletch saw was thrown open, as if inviting in the Wynd and fresh summer scents. Men and women stood in small clusters here and there on street corners, conversing in jovial tones as children ran past them, screeching with laughter as they played.

Fletch swallowed hard. Suddenly conscious of her hands dangling awkwardly at her sides, she tucked them into the crooks of her arms, hugging herself. It was easy to understand now why the king had been so dismayed at the state of Herstshire. Compared to this, it may as well have been a ghost town.

Fletch's feet slowed to a stop. Images of Jon and Missy Pruden's faces flashed before her eyes, a weight settling over her as stinging heat rushed to her eyes. The sudden urge, the desperation of longing was too much to bear. She missed the cool, shadowed forest and the chill Wynd against her face. The deer trails she knew so well, her little log hut, the familiar pines, and eldergreen trees.

She didn't belong in Iventorr.

She belonged in the mountains, in the company of ancient trees and forest creatures, protecting Herstshire from the terrible storms that threatened to bury it with snow. She belonged with friendly townsfolk who would offer her tankards of ale and ask her what she had hunted recently, and would bring her a plate piled with roasted boar and poached eggs. Not in Iventorr or Verenshire, where people appeared offended by her very existence.

Her cheek was damp. Wiping the tear quickly away, Fletch scowled. Hands trembling, she tucked her arms around herself and took a deep, shuddering breath. "You requested to be transferred here," she reminded herself angrily. "Idiot."

Forcefully shoving those thoughts away, she began to turn back toward Iventorr.

Out of the corner of her eye, something white fluttered.

She paused. Across the street in a small square stood a wagon. Its cloth cover was an amalgamation of disparate weaves and patterns, upon which was stitched the outline of a book. Several rectangular bits of sheer material had been secured to the outline to simulate pages, which rustled and shifted with the breeze.

Other wagons and stalls occupied the square, each with a merchant out front hawking their wares. But not the book wagon. Its entrance was markedly empty.

Without knowing why, Fletch crossed the street, ignoring the traders as they called out to her. Circling to the back of the curious vehicle, she poked her head around the flap and peered in.

To either side of the interior, from the front to the back of the wagon, were shelves. Books of every size had been stacked and leaned together like a puzzle. Scrolls were stuffed in the gaps above them, as if making sure not to waste any precious space. On one shelf squatted a row of dark bottles. On another above it, piles of parchment squares were pinned down by glass weights. In the back of the wagon, a man sat on the wooden floor, his legs folded so his brown feet rested on opposite knees. A large book lay open on his shins.

"Welcome," he said without looking up. His quiet voice contained remarkable authority. "Please browse as long as you'd like."

"You're the proprietor?" Fletch asked, burning with curiosity.

"I am."

Still, the man didn't raise his head. His long, copper brown, grey-streaked hair was gathered at the base of his neck with a strip of leather. A rough robe of burlap-like material was his only garment other than simple sandals.

Fletch hesitated, wondering if she ought to wait for him to look up. After an awkward moment, she pulled herself up into the wagon, scanning the scrolls and book spines. Each had a simple title burned into their leather bindings or penned onto the outer edge. Many were of ordinary things, such as *Constructing a Home: Five Methods from Varied Cultures*, *Planting a Balanced Garden*, or *Culinary Meats*, but some of them caught Fletch's eye, such as *The Winding Way* and *The Isles of Aden: A Brief History*.

She had begun thumbing through a worn copy of *Elbecca Care and Training* when her eyes paused on one small, dark volume. The word stamped onto the spine almost looked like — she picked it up and dusted it off, heart leaping into her mouth — *Unbreathing*.

"You have found the gem of my collection," the voice behind her said. "It has taken me many years to collect and record the information within those pages."

As Fletch turned and met the man's eyes for the first time, the strangest feeling passed over her. It were as if, for a moment, she could almost remember her father's face.

His gaze was grey and piercing. One corner of his whiskered mouth curled in a bemused smile above a neatly trimmed beard. It was impossible to guess how old he was; his skin was weathered as if by many years of harsh sun and Wynd, and laugh lines crinkled the corners of his eyes, but his physique was that of a man in his prime.

Standing, he gave a small bow. "I am called Naraan the Nomad."

Remembering Petrecia's lessons, Fletch inclined her head. "Fletch, Sentinel-in-Training," she replied. "I'm pleased to make your acquaintance." Her lips parted again, but she clamped them shut.

"I see a question burning in your eyes," Naraan observed. "My life has been dedicated to learning and the passage of knowledge, young Sentinel. If you desire to know something, you have only to ask."

She quickly shook her head. "No, sir. T'would be prying. I've no wish to make a fool of myself again today."

"'Again today'?" The man's grey eyes twinkled. "I see. In that case, might I make a query of you, in exchange for what you wish to ask me? A trade of information, if you will."

After only a moment's hesitation, Fletch nodded. "Very well."

"You don't strike me as someone who holds your tongue for the sake of niceties. Your eyes are open, direct. Why are you hesitant to ask me your question? Are you concerned you shall offend me?"

Biting her lip, Fletch considered. "I don't believe my question would offend you," she replied. "However, I asked someone else regarding their personal matters earlier, and… well, t'was painful for them. I'd rather not repeat the same mistake."

When Naraan's grey eyes didn't leave hers, as if waiting for her to continue, she swallowed. "In addition, I'm now in direct service of the king. So I must mind my words and actions. Should I misstep, t'would reflect badly on Iventorr."

The nomad peered closely at her for a moment, then nodded, satisfied. "I see. Thank you for your honest answer, Fletch. Please, make your inquiry of me."

Unprepared for the blunt request, she blinked, then blurted, "Are you a Wyndarin?"

Naraan's eyes lit up. "Indeed," he replied, "Though most Ivenhencians would call me a gypsy. Are you also of the Wyndblood?"

"Yes," she said with a nod. "Through both parents. Do the Wyndarin people not travel in one large group?"

"They do," he said. "I left them many years ago." His teeth flashed in a smile, white and bright. "As to that, I must ask you not to inquire."

"Oh. I see."

Mind whirling, Fletch realized her hand still clasped the small *Unbreathing* book. She ran a hand over the dusty cover, excitement pushing away any remnants of doubt. "You wrote this yourself?"

Naraan nodded. "Indeed. Most of the materials you see here are the results of my wandering."

"This is truly remarkable," she said, mostly to herself. "I have searched the library in Iventorr for any information on the Unbreathing and Devuls, but, as the king said, there was nothing. Not a single scroll."

Naraan's thick brows drew together. "It was all stolen," he told her. "Just before the assassination of King Dreythas, Luminia rest his soul. 'Twas one of the strange happenings that led to his death."

Before Fletch could ask what he meant, he turned, rummaging

through a shelf stuffed with scrolls. "There were other such occurrences," he said, "and I am certain they are connected to his death, although 'tis unclear how." Taking a smaller scroll, he held it out to Fletch. "You must take it. 'Tis my account of each incident, and my thoughts." She accepted it hesitantly, and he reached past her to another book. "This one is a bit dry," he admitted, holding it up. It read, A History of Ivenhence. "But vitally important if you must know more about the Unbreathing."

"I shall take all of them," she said with a grin. "How much?"

"Two gold pieces."

Shifting all her items into one arm, she shrugged off her quiver and tipped out three coins. "Here," she said, pressing them into his brown hand. "Please take it. I have no need for gold."

Naraan hesitated, peering into her eyes before his craggy features softened. "Very well," he said. Wrapping the purchase deftly in a square of burlap, he pressed it into her hands.

"Thank you, Naraan." Fletch smiled. "I hope we meet again."

"The same to you, Fletch Wyndshaper."

As Fletch hopped down and started out for Iventorr, it suddenly occurred to her that she hadn't actually told the nomad her surname. Turning, she glanced over her shoulder to shoot a long, curious look at the lone Wyndarin's wagon.

The dining hall was as clamorous and crowded as any other evening when Dreythan finally entered and sat at his solitary table. Since the conclusion of the meeting with Ambassador Kekona, a wrinkle he couldn't iron had puckered his forehead, and it was evolving into a headache. Yes, the presentation had gone well, but the ambassador had been clear; he should expect rejection from the Guild. How was he supposed to prepare an additional proposal if he had no clue what the Guild's expectations were?

On top of this, a messenger had stopped him outside the Guest

Tower with two messages. One missive was verbal, informing him that the small collection of Verenshire merchants had left for Herstshire. The trade caravan was on its way. The second message was physical; an elegant scroll. Wrapped in wax-coated parchment and bound tightly with ribbon, it was sealed with the Great Tree of Ilumence. A letter from his cousin, Morthan, no doubt.

When he had sat down in the private room in the library and opened the letter, these words met his eyes:

To King Dreythan Dreythas-son, rightful ruler of Ivenhence and dear cousin,

We are deeply grateful, both for the verbal message upon being unable to complete your journey and for your words of comfort upon reaching Iventorr safely. Allow us to assure you that no offense was taken; we are relieved upon learning you escaped harm.

Our father Morthas (may Ivere provide him rest) has been laid within our ancestral tomb. I know he regarded you as a second son, cousin, and so took the liberty of laying a second silver blade by his side. It saddens me that you were unable to witness his burial, but I hope this will put your mind at ease.

Before his passing, my father coached me in all manner of taxation and fair judgement, but I fear I am overwhelmed by the magnitude of his legacy. So many things need attending. Our trade routes within the island nation state of Aden alone number far more than I had imagined. I do have three advisors from whom I can draw wisdom and strength, but they are not kin. They feel the need to soften harsh truths. I have only just discovered that the fishing villages along our eastern coast were ravaged by a terrible storm mere days after my father's passing. The townsfolk had been hungry and suffering for nearly a moon before I was able to send aid. I am ashamed to think of what my father would say.

I am sorry to burden you with my troubles. But it is my hope that, having far more experience in matters of state than myself, you might offer some insights. How does one man rule a nation?

I know we were never close, cousin. But I do thank you again for your words of comfort and your offer of council. It means more to me than I

can express.
Morthan Morthas-son

Still ruminating over the letter, Dreythan absently scooped food from his plate to his mouth, chewing as he turned the words over and over in his mind.

Morthan had three advisors... He wondered if they were the same men that had counseled King Morthas, Ivere rest his soul. If so, was Morthan delegating any tasks to them? Was he putting their experience to use? Or did he feel the burden of rule was his to bear alone?

All that came to Dreythan's mind was a phrase he'd only heard weeks before; *He is a man before he is king.*

Raising his head, he scanned the dining hall, fixing on a figure not too far away. A bow and quiver lay haphazardly on the table beside her, as if placed and immediately forgotten. Her cinnamon red hair formed a fringe around her face, her head bent low over a book.

Realizing he was smiling, Dreythan lowered his eyes to his plate. A little jolt of shock ran through him. He'd been eating potatoes, stewed greens, and beef, one of his favorite meals, and hadn't even noticed.

Trading his fork for a spoon, he tucked into his meal, his thoughts churning. Ambassador Kekona had seemed to think his proposal was an acceptable one, but why was she cautious of the Guild's reaction? After her hint that Ilumence's and Thissa's trade was also in danger, it was clear that the Guild of Merchants' expectations were not being met.

Perhaps he should ask Morthan what had changed between the Isles and Ilumence.

He grimaced, taking a sip of well water. Asking such a question could sound ignorant, even impudent. But for negotiations with Ambassador Kekona to be successful, knowledge of the Isles' ill favor with Ivenhence's ally could prove invaluable.

As he finished his meal and left the dining hall, these thoughts kept spinning through his mind. He could offer Morthan what little insight he had, and close his reply letter with his own inquiry. Morthan could perceive it as a favor requested for a favor given. Or he would wonder why he'd hoped Dreythan could help him at all; he was clearly not the king Dreythas had been.

Dreythan stopped. He was standing in the middle of the cobbled street of Iventorr. The setting sun glowed on the horizon, the fading rays bleeding over the clouds like the doubt that had bled into his pondering.

He was a man before he was king.

His footfalls resumed automatically, echoing in his ears with his heartbeat. He wondered if his father Dreythas would have asked for help, were he in his place. An image rose of the outline of his strong frame raised above the crowd of Reclamation Day, his white head crowned in golden sunlight as it bowed in prayer.

His father wouldn't have allowed his kingdom to slip to a place in which precarious negotiations were needed.

The wrinkle in Dreythan's forehead deepened. *But what if he had?* a small voice whispered. What if he did need to ask for help. Would he have been humble for the sake of his peoples' wellbeing, or would he have been stubbornly prideful to save face?

His stomach tightened.

Ascending the stairs of the royal tower, he entered his study and sat. As soon as he filled his inkwell and picked up a pen, words began to flow from his fingertips.

To King Morthan Morthas-son, rightful ruler of Ilumence and our cousin,

Your request for honest advice is one I understand all too well. When my father perished, I had none to turn to who would not attempt to protect me from seeing my own mistakes. None, that is, excepting your father Morthas. I owed him much, and will attempt to repay that debt in any manner that I can.

A sage friend recently opened my eyes to a bit of wisdom that has eluded me these last fifteen years. One must be a man before he is king.

There is only so much we can do, cousin. We are flesh and bone and grow weary and overwhelmed just as any other. We must know our strengths and weaknesses and adjust our rule to compensate.

I have recently come to understand I have neglected the smaller hamlets in my kingdom, and thus, a new system of taxation is being tested in Ivenhence.

He penned a concise explanation of the new system, then paused. The question would need to be worded delicately.

Perhaps a similar concept could be of benefit to you. If Ilumence were divided into sections based upon population, one representative or a committee could be elected to oversee each section, to whom citizens could bring their concerns and grievances. It could also be beneficial for you to directly oversee the section containing Luminhold. In this manner, the citizens of Ilumence would still see you as approachable.

I must caution, however, that the system I am implementing is not entirely polished. It has raised concerns with the merchants of the Isles of Aden; they threaten to remove their trade routes should any change in customs not agree with them. 'Tis my understanding Ilumence recently experienced this difficulty as well. Could you perhaps provide some insight into their expectations?

Should you not wish to divulge these details as a confidential matter of state, I shall understand. I sincerely hope this missive has been of some help to you. Do not hesitate to write again. I shall look for your reply.

Dreythan Dreythas-son

When his eyes scanned the parchment critically, re-reading the words that had flowed so steadily and firmly from his mind, they fell upon the phrase 'a sage friend'. His lips curled in an unconscious smile.

A sage friend, indeed.

As soon as Fletch returned to her quarters that evening, she loosened her armor and sat at her table, pulling the cloth bundle of books towards her. She'd already read a bit of *Unbreathing* during supper, which appeared to have been written in Naraan's own hand. Separated into categories of information, the chapters contained titles such as *'Folklore and History'*, *'The Nature of a Devul'*, and *'Vulnerabilities'*.

She'd poured over the *'Vulnerabilites'* chapter, absorbing the information. She was all too familiar with the scent of salt or rust that hung around the monsters, and she'd been aware of their aversion to sunlight. She'd believed that only Wynd-bloods could smell the stench, and that the Unbreathing were weakened by strong Wynd, but these beliefs had never been confirmed by another. Until now. They were also weakened by ice and fire. These elements were not as damaging to them as silver, but, according to Naraan, in a blizzard the Unbreathing were only as strong or fast as the average human.

And all that information was in one chapter alone. Hands clumsy with excitement, Fletch untied the knotted bundle and spread the reading materials out. The little dark-covered book she immediately set aside, then the scroll labeled *The Conspiracy and Assassination. A History of Ivenhence* she pushed aside and —

And there was still one more book in the bottom of the sack, wrapped in its own layer of cloth.

Fletch stared at it for a moment, puzzled.

When she lifted it out, the burlap square fell easily away to reveal an aged journal. Cured leather wrapped entirely around the pages, secured with a leather strip. The crackled volume had no title.

Though she hadn't seen in it in nearly fifteen years, Fletch recognized it immediately.

Wonderingly, she tugged at the leather strip. Stiff with disuse and age, it finally fell open toward the back, revealing two separately penned words; 'Fletch' and 'magpie'.

Kell Wyndshaper sat at a wooden table, a quill in his left hand with an ink pot close by, the pen scratching carefully across the age-crinkled pages of his journal.

Fletch stood on tip-toe, straining to see over the edge of the table. "Papa," she piped curiously, "What are you doing?"

Kell glanced down, green eyes smiling as he replied, "Well, my little magpie, I am writing."

"What are you writing, Papa?"

Setting the quill and ink pot down, he scooped her up in his his strong arms and set her on his lap. "Look here," he said, thumbing a few pages forward and placing a few scratched lines in ink. "That is your name."

"Magpie?" Fletch giggled, fidgeting with the leather string.

"Nay," Kell laughed. "This is 'magpie'." Taking up the quill again, he penned it into the parchment.

A wide, wobbly smile spread across Fletch's face. Her heart swelled against her ribs as she stared down at the two penned words, only barely visible by the flickering candle-light.

Cradling the book in her hands, she flipped to the first page and peered at the handwriting, squinting as the lines swam before her eyes.

The fifty-seventh year of Ohnaedris, in the fifth week of spring

I've been assigned to escort Prince Dreythas across the Ilumencian border to the south on a scouting mission from the king. 'Tis my personal belief that this mission has been designed by Dreythas's own hand; it is no secret the Prince grows weary of the Capitol. Nonetheless, King Morthal has commanded that I am to document the journey and our findings, and so I shall.

Our mission is a fairly straightforward one; to ascertain why old

Ivereland has had little to no communication with Ilumence over the past few hundred years. We occasionally receive the odd trade caravan or immigrant, but these are excessively few and far between. Does the Wyntersoul Clan of ancient history still exist? If so, how does their kingdom fare? We are to find answers to these questions and report to King Morthal.

The Prince has asked that I treat him as a commoner, and to call him Dreythas Corwynter during our journey. I find him to be pleasant in his own way, though he has certainly had a softer life than most. If I am to treat him as a commoner for the next few moons, then I shall have to train him in a commoner's ways.

Fletch's brows wrinkled together. Her father must have begun writing the journal when he was roughly her own age, serving as a Forester of Ilumence. Chewing absently on her lip, she continued to read.

The fifty-seventh year of Ohnaedris, in the eighth week of spring

It has been one week since we crossed the border into old Ivereland, and very little of note has occurred. Dreythas carefully charts our path, drawing maps and taking notes of the positions of the stars when they are out. Though it is clear our path has no direction, I don't feel lost. Rather, it seems we are explorers, much like the ancient Wyndarin. Traveling land rather than sailing the open seas.

Dreythas successfully hunted and harvested a young doe today. We carried the carcass together to a farmer's house we had seen in the distance, and traded most of the meat for jerky and bread. I congratulated him on his improvement with the bow, and he turned his thoughtful black eyes upon me.

'I must ask you,' he said, 'You are part gypsy, are you not?'

I explained to him that my father was, in fact, a Wyndarin who had fallen in love with a village girl and moved on with the rest of his kin when they departed, not knowing that my mother was with child. Dreythas was greatly curious about my ability to shape the Wynd, and when we retired for the night, he said, 'I shall call you Kell Wyndshaper, if I may. It is a better-suiting surname than Fornost."

I feel I must note that the farmer was extremely suspicious of us. He would not allow us to enter his home, and would not speak to us of common matters. His fearfulness does not bode well for our mission.

Fletch stared at the last sentence, her heart thudding against her ribs. Closing the pages gently, she held the journal to her chest as tenderly as if she were hugging the author.

"Good to see you again, Papa," she whispered, heat prickling her eyes.

How on Hearth had Naraan known who she was? Whose daughter she was? She should have gone back to ask, she reflected. If she saw him again, it would be first thing from her lips.

As badly as she wanted to keep reading her father's handwriting, she hesitated. The knowledge within the Unbreathing book needed to be relayed to the king, as well as to Captain Norland and the rest of the guard. What if the same were true for the other two materials, the conspiracy scroll and the history book?

Reluctantly, she re-wrapped the journal in the bit of burlap. The king needed the knowledge the other books contained. She had to finish them as quickly as possible.

◆

Chapter 11

To Fletch, it was strange to simply go about her business, following daily routine when demonic monsters wanted her king and herself dead. Captain Norland was making every effort to gather information from across the kingdom: requesting reports of Unbreathing sightings, formulating plans to infiltrate Thissa with spy merchants.

But she could only wait. It was maddening.

Her one comfort was the knowledge she was doing everything she could; learning about the Unbreathing and preparing to equip other people with the same knowledge. Letting her body heal so she could be strong enough to fight again.

Still, it was worrying to think that one of the monsters could slip into the castle gates at any moment. The guards would see a simple peasant, not a demonic monster. The thought turned Fletch's stomach. She kept her knife at her side at all times, even when at Petrecia's. The little woman thankfully didn't say anything.

After a bit of experimentation, Fletch discovered the small *Unbreathing* volume was the perfect size to slip inside her quiver (minus a few arrows). And breakfast, dinner, and supper were ideal times to devour a chapter along with her meal. Every opportunity she had to read, she took it.

In the 'Folklore and History' chapter of *Unbreathing*, Naraan had written, *'It has been said that the first Devuls Kazael ever created were not created at all. Many believe that, just as the Unbreathing are capable only of corruption, never creation, so is their progenitor.*

It is said that when Kazael first lured men to his side with promises of power and glory, he warped their souls, twisting them into dark mirrors of themselves. I cannot say for certain that this is the case, nor can any, for very little is known regarding the true nature of a Devul or of an Unbreathing.'

"Well, that's not very helpful," Klep commented, peering across the table as Fletch finished reading the passage aloud. "Why did he so title the chapter if he doesn't know their true nature?"

She frowned down at the page, her eyes scanning the paragraph again. "I believe he wanted to draw attention to that fact. He also mentions that when Unbreathing feed from the blood of a human, it isn't clear if the act of draining blood is what weakens the prey, or if they are truly latched onto the soul as is popularly believed."

Shaking his head, Klep returned his attention to his plate. "How is there so much about them we don't know?"

Later in the same chapter, Naraan pointed out that there had never been record of a female Unbreathing, only of women who were referred to as 'witches'.

'It is my personal belief that Kazael's true purpose for the Devuls was to show Ivere how weak the souls of men were. Perhaps the Devuls are fractions of Kazael's own being, for they seem to share the view of women that he held for Ivere: to them, they are objects with which to fulfill their lustful desires. It is only logical to think their view towards men would also be the same as Kazael's. Thus, a man's body is the only form they see fit to possess.

In the rare instance that a woman pledges herself to Kazael, it seems he rewards them with a measure of his power, binding their will to his own in exchange for the ability to corrupt and manipulate. These women then lure men to Kazael's service, promising glory, power, pleasure, and never-ending life... and so the cycle goes on.'

Upon reaching this sentence, Fletch stopped, her finger pausing on the page. She found herself wondering why in Luminia's name anyone would commit themselves to the subjugation and corruption of humanity. But even beyond that, why would a woman commit herself to serving a god whose monsters raped and tortured women as if it were sport?

A flash of frost-bitten flesh blinked before her mind's eye, and she shuddered, rubbing her arms.

It took her the better part of a week to finish reading *Unbreathing*. Once she had, she set it carefully aside on the table in her quarters. Though her father's journal still sat wrapped securely on her table, she left it be, promising herself to finish the other materials first for Dreythan's sake.

The following day, she had no reading material to stuff in her quiver. The scroll Naraan had given her was too small and fragile to jostle around amongst sharp arrowheads, and the history book was too big. So she rose before the sun, lit a few candles, and sat down to read before she started her day.

The Conspiracy and Assassination contained a tidy list of events and the dates on which they occurred, as well as notes carefully referenced below.

The first event was the disappearance of reading material from the library.

'It would seem that the thief was an Unbreathing or was under their employ,' Naraan had written. *'Removing the only physical record of our collective knowledge would indicate that the Unbreathing felt it gave humanity some advantage. I know for a fact one of the scrolls listed the four known ways to destroy an Unbreathing's Shell, and also indicated ways for a normal human to identify the monsters.'*

Fletch frowned, unconsciously leaning closer as she continued to read.

'I believe that the tomes and scrolls were stolen to weaken all of Ivenhence. When facing an enemy, one's most powerful weapon is knowledge. Knowledge of how the enemy thinks, what it hates, what its weaknesses are. Without this knowledge, Ivenhence is open to infiltration and attack.

Certainly, there remain a few men from the time of the Great Slaving who can remember all that there is to know about the Devuls and their folklore, but these men are now old. No longer fighting men. The only threat they pose to the Unbreathing is the passing of their knowledge from one to another. Which leads to the next point of conspiracy.'

Naraan went on to point out that, just before King Dreythas's death, many of the survivors from the Great Slaving and the ensuing battle had died gruesome and mysterious deaths. Many of them had been *'seemingly set upon by wolves and half-eaten'*, or had been *'found in their beds forever asleep'*. He had recorded where they had lived and died, and on which dates. Fletch's eyes widened at the length of the list, and how short of a time span the elders' deaths had fallen in.

'The pattern continues,' Narran said. *'Wiping all knowledge from Ivenhence. Yet Ilumence was left alone, unscathed. None of her numerous libraries were raided. None of her elders were attacked. Why? Would not Ilumence be a larger threat? She is an ancient nation, with roots going back to the beginning of recorded history. Why would the Unbreathing not concern themselves with her bright, beaming light?*

There is a simple answer: Kazael's prison.'

Fletch stared blankly at the scroll for a moment, then scanned the following paragraph. Naraan did not explain himself or his 'answer', but there was a small notation below that last sentence.

See 'A History of Ivenhence', Chapter #1

Sliding the scroll to one side, Fletch pulled A History of Ivenhence towards her. "Thank you, Naraan," she muttered, opening the book to the first chapter. "That was quite thoughtful of you."

It began with the story of the Nameless One and the creation of his four children. In great detail, it expounded on the creation of the Hearth, Kazael's betrayal, and then, of course, the part that Fletch always found boring. The Great Battle.

A smile curled her lips as she remembered Dreythan's coy glance, his request for a story as if he were a mischievous child.

But before the war, the book recounted a time when humanity was threatened by the tide of Unbreathing that swept it. Fletch hovered over this section of the page, stunned. She'd never known the Great Battle had been fought with such overwhelming opposition, or that humankind had very nearly been lost forever. It was a chilling thought.

It went on to recount Kazael and Ohnaedris battling in the form of huge winged men on the surface of the Hearth, shining swords locked together.

'Armies of men, Wyndarin, and Unbreathing battled all around them. The battle took a turn for the better when the Archer, the leader of the army of men, slew Kazael's general Velthran with a silver arrow. Kazael bellowed in rage.

Seeing their opportunity, Lady Luminia caused a great wave of water and Wynd to wash over Kazael, knocking him off of his feet, and Lady Ivere turned to flame and blinded him.

Ohnaedris then bored a great hole into the Hearth, casting Kazael into it as the remaining Unbreathing fled. Fashioning a great pillar in his hands, he turned to Ivere and Luminia, and together they filled the enormous rock with veins of silver. With this silver-laden stone they blocked the chasm, and Lady Luminia surrounded it with water to further prevent any attempt at escape.'

Looking up from her book, Fletch wondered why that last paragraph tugged at her so. She bent her head down and read it again, and it pulled at her even harder.

There was no explanatory notation.

Frustrated, Fletch snapped the history book closed and tossed it to one corner of the table.

The sun's first violet-red rays were just peeking over the edge of the castle walls. Reluctantly, she lurched to her feet and snatched up her quiver and bow. After a brief pause, she plucked her father's journal from the table and tucked it under her arm, then ducked out her door.

Dreythan entered the still-quiet dining hall, resisting the urge to rub sleep from his eyes, all too aware of the droop in his shoulders. Since Ambassador Kekona's departure, the merchants of Aden had grown restless, appearing outside the guest tower every afternoon to see if she'd yet returned. One of the guards, the woman who'd acted as a barricade in the throne hall, had been stopped by the merchants earlier that day, and their exchange had grown heated.

On top of that, no reply missive from Morthan had arrived. He had begun to worry that he'd have to formulate a backup trade proposal for the Guid without any insights from Ilumence. Thousands of varying scenarios had run repeatedly through his mind as he laid staring up at his ceiling, wishing for sleep.

"My lord." A young woman appeared at his elbow as he lowered himself into this chair. "An urgent message for you from the citizens of Limbwood."

He accepted the offered scroll, nodding blearily. "Thank you." As the courier swiftly departed, Dreythan broke the wax seal and unfurled it. His drowsiness drained away as several sheets of parchment unrolled over the table, each one penned in a different hand. From the citizens of Limbwood? He scanned each letter, some short and to the point, others elaborate and overly courteous. All had been signed by a different resident of Limbwood, and all claimed that a man named Darman Lollma had tried to bribe them to vote him into the position of tax representative for the city. Each letter concluded in practically the same words; *If Darman Lollma tried to force me to pick him as our town's representative, I'm certain he did the same to others.*

Feeling the rough, unshaven skin of his jaw with one hand, Dreythan squinted down at the papers. If he remembered correctly from his conversations with Anshwell, Darman Lollma had been the most-voted-for name in Limbwood, beating out the top-most competitor by only five votes.

Dreythan reached for his water glass and downed it all in one deep draught, avoiding the taste. He would have to ask Captain Norland to send his most capable man to look in on the matter, but... it made him restless. He hated to think what a dishonest person could do with improperly collected taxes in Limbwood. The town was Ivenhence's primary source of lumber. A smart man could be rich in a decade. A greedy man could be rich in a year.

Stomach churning, Dreythan reluctantly pulled his plate closer as his eye fell on Fletch, once again bent over a book. Something in the way she read, her arm circled protectively around the pages, her spine rigid as she leaned into the words, made him wonder what could be so intriguing.

Strolling down the aisle towards her was the young guard she was always with, Dreythan noted as he reluctantly took a small bite of potato, forcing himself to eat. The man had taken nearly every meal with Fletch since her return from Herstshire. Sure enough, the guard approached and greeted Fletch, setting his scabbard and belt atop the table beside her bow and quiver. They immediately fell into earnest conversation, Fletch's eyes alight with intensity as her slender hands articulated her every word. The young man's arms crossed skeptically at first, but gradually relaxed to his sides, then propped up on the table as he leaned forward, paying keen attention to whatever Fletch was saying.

Head throbbing, Dreythan shut his eyes, blaming his headache for his inexplicably foul mood.

Completely absorbed in her father's tale, Fletch was oblivious to all else as the dining hall slowly filled up around her, the usual hubbub and cacophony drowned out by the melody of words in her mind. It had been a full season since Dreythas and Kell had departed Ilumence, avoiding frost troll lairs and wyrm-infested swamps. She'd just finished reading an entry about the discovery of an abandoned town when she came across the most interesting entry of all;

The fifty-seventh year of Ohnaedris, in the eleventh week of summer

Dreythas and I stumbled across a great mystery this day. We have found an island of stone in the midst of a wide, recessed lake. The island is connected to the land by a massive wood and rope bridge. We witnessed men and women carting raw ore from the island across the bridge. They then discarded the ore in the forest, and returned with carts empty.

Something about the people and the island puts me ill at ease, but Dreythas insists we must find out more. 'Tis the largest group of gathered people we have seen since our arrival in Ivereland. We have no way to know if the people who live here would be hostile to us. I have cautioned Dreythas that we must avoid discovery, and he has agreed. Tomorrow we shall locate the ore dump and find what we may there.

The next entry wasn't dated and was written poorly, barely legible.

Our discovery of this island is far more significant than Dreythas and I could have imagined. We found the ore dump before dawn, and we were immediately confused. The people were discarding mined silver out in the forest as if it were lumps of mud. We searched among the piles of stone and ore for more clues, but turned up nothing. Hearing footsteps, we hid. A group of men and women arrived with their carts, making new contributions to the piles.

Their overseer caught my attention. He was bare-chested and watched the slaves with slitted eyes. I could smell him from my hiding place; his stench filled my nostrils with a coppery tang. Something about him was off; was badly out of place, but I did not know what it was until he raised his head and sniffed the breeze.

He did not draw breath unless he was tasting the air. He was a Devul hiding in a human body, an Unbreathing.

The troop of slaves could not leave quickly enough. As soon as they crossed over the bridge and the gates clanged shut behind them, I told Dreythas we had to return to Ilumence immediately. He did not understand. I explained to him that the miners were slaves, subjugated by a nest of Unbreathing. They likely served as cattle to slake the beasts' thirst. This explained why we had seen only abandoned settlements since crossing the border, and why the farmer was so afraid.

Dreythas's eyes narrowed, and he turned to look at the stone island. He stared at it for several minutes before saying quietly, "Kell. What does that remind you of?"

I looked at the island.

"A stone island," he muttered. "Surrounded by water and filled with silver."

My heart sank into my stomach. "Kazael's prison."

"The Unbreathing are forcing the people to mine for them because they cannot touch the silver themselves." His face paled. "They mean to release Kazael."

I could not deny the sense of his words. They rang with truth. We cannot be sure how far down the Unbreathing have already delved, and we cannot be certain how long we have before they reach Kazael in his Pit. We do not know if we have time to return to Ilumence for reinforcements. So, tomorrow, we shall allow ourselves to be captured and put to work by the monsters. We can only hope that we will be able to stir up the slaves to fight back.

I shall place this journal in a hollow tree near our campsite. If we shall succeed in our endeavor, I shall return; if not, then we have failed.

"Fletch! Will you join us?"

Fletch jumped at the sudden voice, her heart slowly settling back into place after her eyes met Klep's curious gaze.

"You look like you've seen a ghost."

"I'm sorry," she breathed, carefully folding the journal shut. "'Tis just… this belonged to my father."

"Don't apologize," he said, his whiskered face softening. "I didn't mean to disturb you. Ought I leave you alone?"

She shook her head numbly. "No, that's quite alright. Are you familiar with the story of the Great Battle? How Kazael was defeated and imprisoned?"

"As familiar as any other bloke, I suppose."

"According to legend, Kazael's prison is blocked by a stone filled with silver, surrounded by water. Do you... do you suppose we're sitting on that very stone at this moment?" Tilting her father's journal towards him, she pointed out the entry she'd just read.

Once he'd finished digesting the scrawled words, one of Klep's brows arched upward. "I suppose 'tis possible," he admitted after a moment's consideration. "If you believe the legends. But if that were the case, wouldn't we all know? Wouldn't that sort of tale have been passed down to each generation?"

"I would hope so," Fletch replied slowly. "But time has a way of turning truth into tales, and tales into legends. And as you've just said, legends are difficult to believe." She paused, the weight of that thought settling slowly on her. "How much knowledge has been lost to time, I wonder. And how much truth remains in legend."

Ding. Bong. Ding, bong.

At the sound of the bell, they automatically rose. Tucking her father's journal under one arm, Fletch slung her quiver and bow over her shoulder, flashing Klep a quick smile. "Thank you for listening," she said, though there was much more she wished she could say. *Thank you for asking if I'd like to sit with the other guards, even if I always decline. Thank you for meeting my eyes when you speak to me. Thank you for not staring when you think I'm not looking. Thank you for being my friend.* "I know most would find this subject a bit... off-putting."

He returned the smile with his usual broad grin. "Just because something's unpleasant or challenging to think about doesn't mean we oughtn't think about it." As he straightened his tunic, the grin faded. "You'll tell Captain Norland about this, right?"

She nodded.

"I thought as much. Ivere's luck to you, Fletch. I'll likely not see you again 'til the morrow since 'tis my day of rest. Pleasant day!"

"Pleasant day," she echoed, suppressing a chuckle as he gave her a mock salute and marched away.

The back of her neck prickled. She turned instinctively towards the stare, prepared to meet a set of disdainful or distrustful eyes. But it wasn't a guard or a kitchen maid that met her glance. It was the king.

He looked as though he hadn't slept well. Dark circles puffed under his eyes, and his forehead was creased in worried lines. Even so, his cheeks looked a little fuller, and his eyes brighter. More hopeful.

With a slight smile, the king inclined his head. A grin sprang to Fletch's lips as she returned the nod.

Captain Norland was waiting for her outside the southern door to the dining hall, arms crossed across his chest. As soon as she appeared, he grunted, "Wyndshaper."

She started to reply with a snapping salute, but he was already gone, turning on his heel to stride down the cobbled road. Head down, arms swinging at his sides, he looked ready to bowl over anything that dared stand in his way. Men and women parted to either side, unwilling to be caught in his path. Fletch could barely keep pace jogging after him. He reached the castle gate, snapping, "Report!"

Torsh and Torrin, the gate-keepers, stood to attention instantly, their hands pinging against their helmets as they saluted. "All's well, sir!" They chorused.

Norland nearly ran into Fletch with the force of his swivel. Barely even giving her a glance, he pushed past, footfalls echoing off the stone of Iventorr.

Swallowing hard, she took a few running steps to catch back up to the giant man.

"Captain?"

"Hmm," he grunted.

He was in the foulest mood Fletch had ever seen. Butterflies rose in her throat, but she pushed them away, swallowing again. "Captain," she repeated, "May I speak with you? It regards the Unbreathing."

He glanced back finally, thick brows bristling. "Go on, then."

Shifting the journal to her hands, she hesitated, then reluctantly held it out to him. "This belonged to my father, Captain Kell Wyndshaper."

Finally slowing, Norland took the journal, giving her a piercing look as he turned it over. It looked like a child's toy in his enormous calloused hands. Gingerly, he handed it back to her as if it were a holy relic that could break at any moment. "What of it, lass?"

As Fletch told him what she'd read of the island and of the slaves mining silver ore, of Kazael's prison and the eerie similarities between the two, Norland's tempestuous demeanor slowly evaporated. When she finished, a thoughtful furrow had replaced the ill-tempered one.

"I suppose I ought to be glad ye thought to tell me," he said finally after a long pause. "Most would've written it off as folklore and paid no mind to it. Or ye could've kept it to yourself for fear of looking foolish."

"But you don't believe 'tis simply a tale?" Fletch asked hopefully.

Norland shook his head. "Nay, not I. I've seen too much of the world to think that tales are only that, or to be foolish enough to think the gods are a mere myth." He paused. "It makes a certain sense, after all. The Unbreathing might not be working for someone... they might be working with them, striving for a common goal. The downfall of Iventorr." With a scratch of his beard, he nodded. "Aye, that'd explain it."

"If the Unbreathing intend to overtake the island and continue their efforts to free Kazael, that could be why they would be willing to slay the king," Fletch said, too relieved that Norland believed her to notice he'd already reached the same conclusion.

His eyes crinkled in a smile. "Indeed, lass."

His feet slowed to a stop in front of the Sentinel tower. Fletch raised her brow at him.

"Today ye begin your training in earnest," he told her soberly. "'Tis time to begin learning what a royal guard is and does."

Her heart jittering against her ribs, she tried to suppress the grin that rose to her face. "Does this mean no etiquette lessons, Captain?"

His expression glinted dangerously. "For today only, or for the rest of the week?"

The reply 'for the rest of time and eternity' sprang to her tongue, but she caught it before it slipped out. It would be churlish to thank Petrecia for her exceeding patience with such words. Straightening, she said, "Whichever you would allow, Captain."

"I suspect your initial response was quite different," Norland said, nodding approvingly. "Yet ye replied with respect. Perhaps there's hope for that tongue of yours." His meaty hand clapped her lightly on the shoulder. "I shan't make ye attend any more torture sessions, lass. I only needed ye to learn to think before speaking. Go practice your archery when ye've finished here, but stop by the armory for some practice arrows. Wouldn't want to waste your silver-tipped bolts." He gestured to the door. "I've other matters to attend to, but I've left orders for your training. Pay attention, and do me proud, lass." With an encouraging nod and one last shoulder-pat, he opened the door and ushered her inside.

Mentally preparing himself for another few hours in the stiff, uncomfortable high-backed wooden monstrosity most called 'the throne', Dreythan entered the rear door of the throne hall to find it surprisingly bare. Only a handful of citizens awaited him in the rows of pews, sitting quietly as they watched him approach his daily object of torment.

"My lord," a voice muttered. Captain Norland appeared, intercepting his path to the throne. "A matter has been brought to me that requires your attention. It concerns one of the guards. Two of 'em, actually."

It was unlike the stolid Captain to come to the king with his subordinates' matters. Interest piqued, Dreythan nodded. "Speak, Norland."

But the Captain hesitated, shifting his considerable weight from one foot to the other. "Klep Ironshod wishes to... to court Fletch Wyndshaper." He scratched his bushy jaw, then tugged it harshly. "He came to me this morn and asked how he ought to proceed. I can only see trouble coming of it... And so I thought it best to ask for your insight."

A cold, hard fist clenched in Dreythan's stomach. "He has only known her for a season — less than, even."

"My words exactly, my lord. He said he can't say he loves her, but—" a vein in his temple pulsed "—he'd like to discover if he would, in time."

"I see." A throb echoed through the king's skull. He closed his eyes, inhaling sharply through his nose. "Have you asked Fletch how she feels about this... Klep?"

"Nay, my lord. I thought this matter needed your attention first."

The pain subsided. Dreythan nodded, mental gears churning. "You were wise to do so. Whether Fletch were to accept or decline such an offer, rumors would spread like wildfire." His frown deepened. "The guard might come to resent her."

"Some of 'em already do," Norland said bluntly. "They think she's an ambitious back-stabber because she's training as a Sentinel before serving the required years as a castle guard."

"I see." He tapped his lips thoughtfully. "We shall have to proceed carefully. After the last citizen has been cared for here, summon Klep Ironshod. I shall speak with him."

The Captain bowed and turned away, and the guards ushered

forth the first peasant.

The king's mind was divided then, one portion focused on dealing justly with his subjects, and the other quietly pondering what needed to be done regarding Fletch and Klep. By the time the last mete had been given and the final citizen left, he thought he might have a solution.

"Norland," he said quietly. "Dismiss the other guards, as well."

The Captain nodded briskly, turning and barking at those who stood in their posts as Dreythan sank back into deep thought. In little time, Norland returned, a familiar young guard trailing slightly behind him like a lost pup.

Removing his helmet from his mess of curls, Klep Ironshod bowed his head and knelt at the bottom step before the throne. The fluffy whiskers along his chin and jawline couldn't conceal the round boyishness of his cheeks. Tan hands trembling, he tucked his helmet under his arm, eyes fixed on the emerald carpet beneath his knee.

"Klep Ironshod," Dreythan said. "You wish to court Fletch Wyndshaper?"

"Yes, my lord," came the respectfully subdued reply.

The king nodded. "You were wise to seek the council of Captain Norland before making your intentions known." Pausing, he inspected the top of Klep's curly head. "You need not remain kneeling, Klep. Please, stand. How many years are you?"

Breathing a visible sigh of relief, the guard did as requested, head dipped in the semblance of a deferential nod as he met Dreythan's gaze. "I'm four and twenty, my lord," he replied.

Four and twenty. Dreythan was only six years Klep's elder, but it might as well have been two decades. "And how long have you been part of the guard of Iventorr Castle? From whence do you come?"

"Two years, my lord. Before I came to Iventorr, I lived on my father's farm in Ingling." As if bolstered by the thought, he gulped, adding, "Helping with the cows and elbeccas, and with planting and harvest, mostly."

As Dreythan looked into the man's clear, honest, bright eyes, he reflected on how vastly different they were. Kep's countenance didn't bear the weight of loss, nor the hardness of responsibility. He hadn't yet tasted the bitterness of life, only the sweetness. "I see," Dreythan said, mostly to himself.

"I hope you can understand why I'd wish to court Fletch, er, Sentinel Wyndshaper, my lord," Klep said, eyes shining fervently. "She's honest, brave, and a thousand other things."

Dreythan smoothed his brow into neutrality. "Yes," he allowed reluctantly. "She is keen of wit and spirit. But consider this carefully." He paused to lean forward, directly meeting Klep's eye. "What if Fletch Wyndshaper were to give you her hand? Your courtship would serve as an item of gossip across the castle, especially amongst the guard. It would cause an excess of distraction, not only for those who gossip, but for both you and Fletch as well. Given the recent attempt on my life, I cannot afford to have distracted guards. To prevent this, Captain Norland would have no choice but to remove one of you. He cannot remove Fletch. Even though she is in training, she is the only one who can readily identify Unbreathing, and is therefore invaluable." Images of Fletch and Klep together at the dining hall flashed through his mind. He clenched his fists against them, thrusting them forcefully away. "You, then, would be the one removed from the guard. I would be glad to write a letter of commendation, but once you had settled into new employment, would you be content? And once you were removed from the castle guard, who would be blamed for your departure? It would be Fletch. Many amongst your fellows already resent her for her sudden and well-deserved promotion to Sentinel. Some of them would leap at the opportunity to sow seeds of malcontent against her. Were she to give you her hand in courtship, she would have to suffer much resentment."

Keeping his gaze fixed on Klep's, he watched realization and dread dawn on the young man's face. "You must also consider the possibility that Fletch may decline your offer of courtship. If word spread, what then? The same dilemma arises, but worse. Fletch's embarrassment would only be matched by your shame at her rejection. One of you, then, must leave the guard. Once again, it cannot be Fletch. It would be you. And Fletch would most certainly bear the full weight of the blame."

The young man bowed his head, the consequences of his desire finally clear. "What would you have me do, my lord?" he asked huskily.

"You must decide if you wish to take the next step. Will you ask for Fletch's hand? If so, I would require you to preemptively find other employment. You must work outside the guard for at least a moon before approaching Sentinel Wyndshaper. This would disconnect the perception that you were cast from your position because of Fletch, and would allow her to be blameless in your fellow guards' eyes."

"And if I do not ask her?"

"You may remain a guard of Iventorr." He rose at long last from the throne, but paused. "I would allow myself time to make such a decision, Klep. It may very well affect the rest of your life."

"Yes, my lord," he replied, head still bowed.

Satisfied, Dreythan nodded to Captain Norland, then walked away. As the roiling inferno in his chest slowly extinguished, he took a long, deep breath. Though the pounding in his skull was now a steady drumbeat, his hands were steady. His father might have been proud of how he'd handled himself, he thought. Especially considering how badly he'd wanted to forbid Klep from asking Fletch for her hand at all.

His ears burned. After a decade and a half of standing up for his citizen's rights to court whomever they wished, he'd nearly broken his principle. For two of his castle guards? The thought prickled at his conscience, as if he'd guessed his own mind incorrectly. Brushing it aside, he hurried on to the library.

Chapter 12

Upon entering the royal guards' tower, Fletch was surprised but pleased to find the slender twin Sentinel, Harrild Hammerfist, waiting for her.

"There you are," he said with a warm smile as the door swung shut behind her. "Ready to start learning what it means to be a Sentinel?"

"I thought no one would ever ask," she replied with a grin.

As they left the tower for Iventorr's cobbled streets, Harrild turned to her. "There're many pieces to this responsibility. Our first priority is to keep the king safe. Our second is to respect his privacy."

She nodded. "Safety, then privacy."

"It may sound impossible to constantly watch over the king and leave him in peace at the same time. But it isn't. It takes loads of care and skill, which is what I'll mainly be training you in." Halting abruptly, he tapped the side of his head with a finger. "To watch over the king, a Sentinel must always communicate with their partner. Where the king is likely to head next, what sort of weather we're likely to have, how crowded the streets are. Anything and everything you notice, always pass it on to the other Sentinel on duty." He lent her a nod, gesturing ahead. "In so doing, you form a bond of trust. Not to mention, you heighten your awareness of your surroundings, and your partner's awareness as well."

Their first stop was the throne hall, which they accessed easily by a short stone path that led directly from the Sentinel tower to the back of the hall.

"Is that the door the king uses each day?" Fletch asked as they approached it.

His hazel eyes twinkled as he nodded. Slipping inside the door, he paused, pointing. "See those stones protruding from the wall? They form a tight stair. Follow me." He climbed easily up the precariously tiny steps and around the inside corner of the stone chamber, one hand on the wall. It was much like climbing a tree, Fletch thought as she followed. Reaching a hidden balcony in the high shadows of the arcaded pillars, she found herself at the very top of the hall. Below, the sunlight filtered through stained glass windows to fall in broken shards of color on the empty throne and pews, an eerie quiet filling the room.

"I can see this post is excellent for an archer," she whispered. "But a swordsman is of no use, so far away from the king."

Harrild's pockmarked face split in a grin. "Right you are. My usual post is next to that pillar there, just behind and to the left of the throne. That spot is nearly always wreathed in shadow. Come, I'll show you."

And so the afternoon went on. They followed the king around the castle, staying out of his sight but always keeping him in theirs. He spent several hours in the library, speaking with a withered little man who Harrild called 'old Brinny', poring over scrolls.

The sight reminded Fletch that the king needed her books. It sobered her to realize she'd gotten frustrated and turned to her father's journal. Especially when Dreythan didn't know about

Kazael's Prison.

After the library, Dreythan walked around the royal garden for some time, brow creased deeply. He kept stopping and staring at the cobbled path under his feet as if completely lost in thought.

"He does that quite often," Harrild murmured. "Sometimes he'll call one of us down and we'll talk for a while." He paused, lips thinning, and added, "He's a lonely man, the king. But I'm not sure if he realizes it."

When they went their separate ways at the dining hall, Fletch hesitated, then blurted, "Sentinel Hammerfist?"

"You sound as though you're addressing my brother," he chuckled. "Please, it's just Harrild."

She nodded, relaxing. "Harrild, then. Thank you for... for answering all my questions today, and for your courtesy."

"Of course. I'm glad to add another able comrade to our ranks." As if reading her mind, the Sentinel grinned ruefully. "Parfeln Holden shan't be so willing to help you learn, I'm afraid. But the others will, especially my Matteo and your former master, Aeda." Resting one long-fingered hand on his blade's pommel, he added, "As for my brother, I think he's on the fence about you. Give him a season or two, and he's bound to come around." He lent her one more easy smile, then turned away, waving over one shoulder. "Rest well!"

The next morning, Fletch met Harrild again at the Sentinel tower. After some brief instruction, they split up at the throne hall, Fletch climbing up into the lofty nest she'd been shown the day before while Harrild slipped into the shadowy post behind the throne.

Captain Norland was standing beside one of the guards near the bottom step below the throne, speaking in as quiet a rumble as he could muster. Conspicuously, the post directly across from them was empty.

Fletch watched with growing curiosity as one of the door guards unceremoniously hurried down the aisle to Captain

Norland, whispering something in his ear. Norland scowled and growled a reply. The guard nodded and shifted to take the empty place.

Only four citizens needed the king's attention. He finished with them within two hours, Fletch's curiosity building the entire time. Where was the missing guard? For them to be this tardy? It was unheard of... And she had experienced firsthand how intolerant Captain Norland was toward lateness. He'd fired a man for sleeping past the upfirst bell only a week prior. It had been an awful thing to witness, the pale guard trying to stammer an apology while Captain Norland waited, his red beard bushing further and further as his face remained still as stone.

As the final citizen left the hall, the arched doors booming closed behind them, Captain Norland stepped to the throne and began speaking with the king in a low, hurried growl. It was impossible to see the king's reaction or to hear the exchange. But moments later, the Captain nodded briskly, turned on his heel, and rushed out. Dreythan stood deliberately and moved toward the throne hall's rear door.

That was Fletch's cue. Exiting the alcove, she clambered down the stone hand-holds to find Harrild waiting for her. His scar-pitted face was creased worriedly, a dark shadow hovering behind his eyes. "Let us attend the king," he said quietly. "Captain Norland has gone to attend to some business and may be away for the remainder of our watch."

Fletch nodded, following him silently. From Harrild's closed expression, she gathered the 'business' the Captain was attending to should not be subjected to inquiry.

The remainder of their watch passed uneventfully. The king wandered through the garden for an hour or so before making his way to the library, and then to the dining hall. There was an air of restless uncertainty about him that she didn't like.

As much as she tried, Fletch couldn't keep her mind from attempting to piece together the day's mysterious puzzle pieces. She could well imagine that Captain Norland would have been angered by the guard's failure to appear for his watch. But would he have reported this to the king? No, she didn't believe so. The Captain seemed to operate the guard independently, not wanting to burden Dreythan with issues he could resolve himself. Even if Norland had reported the guard's tardiness to the king, why would this matter be one that Harrild felt he could not discuss? Where had Captain Norland gone? What business was so urgent?

These thoughts swirled around and around in her head until the bell finally rang the hour before sundown, setfith, when she left her post to Aeda Yewmaster.

Striding quickly to her usual spot in the dining hall, Fletch scanned the surrounding tables for a familiar head of curly brown hair, but Klep was nowhere to be seen. Confused, she frowned down at the table.

Where was Klep? She hadn't seen him after breakfast the day before, but that wasn't unusual. It had been his week's day of rest.

And then, it fell into place.

She hadn't seen him all day. The guard who'd been tardy and never reported for duty... Klep.

A kitchen maid brought a plate of food and a tankard of water. Though Fletch absently thanked her and tried to eat, her appetite was gone. Where on Hearth had Klep disappeared to?

"Wyndshaper."

Her fork clattered to her plate as she jumped. Turning, she gulped, "C-Captain Norland, sir."

His scarred face was carefully expressionless. Shoulders squared, helm tucked under one burly bare arm, he might have been the perfect picture of impassive strength. But his clouded eyes didn't quite meet hers as he said quietly, "Finish eating, lass. Meet me at the eastern door when you've done."

Fletch's heart sank into her stomach. Features dissolving into a deep frown, Norland hesitated. One gauntleted hand descended gently on her shoulder. Abruptly, he turned and strode off.

Shoving her plate away, Fletch snatched up her weaponry and dashed after him. He didn't look back. "I was finished, Captain," she said. Her gut had worked itself into a hopeless, nauseated knot. Not even one of Matron Gulden's pies could have tempted her. "Is something amiss?" she asked, trotting to keep up, her heart fluttering with each step.

He glanced back to show that he'd heard, but didn't slow or respond. Instead, he shoved his way through the dining hall's eastern doors and continued walking. His footfalls were hard and quick, his boots pronouncedly beating out a rhythm on the cobblestones. Stomping between vegetable gardens, past the stables, Norland approached the library tower, Fletch close on his heels.

They were heading for the infirmary, Fletch realized. Her knotted stomach turned to ice. Her thoughts immediately jumped to the king, but she shook that away. She'd just left him with Aeda and Darvick. Surely he was all right.

Captain Norland stopped just outside the door of the low stone structure. Turning, he finally met Fletch's eye, fiery brows creased. "I don't know how to tell ye this, lass," he said quietly, his strange accent stealing into his words. "So I'll just say it." He stopped and gazed at her, one brow raised in a silent question.

She swallowed hard and nodded.

His frown deepened. "Klep Ironshod was attacked." Before she could manage any query, Norland added, "By Unbreathing."

The world spun and blurred. All sense of direction, sight and sound hazily turned slowly over. When it stilled, Captain Norland's face and voice swam back into focus. "—horribly weakened. The physician can't get much out of him... He barely has the strength to speak."

"Unbreathing?" Fletch managed, her voice strangely thick in her own ears. "In Iventorr?"

"Nay," Norland said, shaking his head. "Nay, lass. Klep went to the tavern in Verenshire last night. According to the barkeep, he left tipsy just after sunset."

They had reached the infirmary. Norland's head lowered as he placed a gentle, calloused hand on her shoulder. Turning, he

217

opened the door to the infirmary, and they entered. Numbness settled into Fletch's face as the color drained from it.

Inside, they passed a cluster of guards, their helmets tucked under their arms as they huddled together, pale and still. Two women and a man wearing white robes were speaking in hushed tones, and there was a moment of glances and whispers, anxiety and tension. Then Fletch was standing beside a simple cot.

In it lay the shadow of Klep Ironshod. His face was chalky pale, nearly grey in tone. Eyes closed, his breath was shallow and fast. A fine film of sweat covered him, seeping through the thin cotton robe that rested on his collarbone.

Fletch's chest clenched painfully.

"Tell me," she said, barely recognizing her own voice. "Tell me what happened."

Shifting his helm from one arm to the other, Norland quietly said, "It was Gorrin who found him. Says he saw a figure bent over him. When he approached, the figure fled. He found Klep lying there on the cobblestone, pale and unmoving." His hand twitched up to his beard, tugging half-heartedly. "The physician has no doubt it was an Unbreathing. The wound on his neck, the loss of blood. His weakened state. It all adds up."

Fletch felt her head bobbing and stopped, wondering how long she'd been nodding. She allowed her eyes to travel over Klep's neck.

Contrasting against the pallor of Klep's skin were two minuscule wounds, a puncture directly adjacent to a bruise. It looked as if a small, sharp object had pinched down on his vein and a dull object had met it from underneath, crushing with enough power to force the opposing sharp object in.

"A bite," Fletch said.

"I believe you are correct," said a calm, quiet voice. She turned to see Sytres Trithinnis standing beside her, his hands folded into the sleeves of his simple white robe.

"How…" she started, then swallowed. "What do you…" But again the words failed.

"How do I believe Klep will do in time?" Sytres frowned thoughtfully. "I am afraid I cannot say. Were the wound inflicted by a mere beast or by weapon, I would say that he could recover given weeks or moons." His brown eyes met Fletch's gaze frankly. "But this appears to be the work of the Unbreathing, and... we possess precious little knowledge in that realm."

"I have books," she remembered abruptly, but just as quickly as she thought of it, she realized that not one chapter of Naraan's *Unbreathing* had addressed their feeding or turning. The 'Regeneration' chapter had only contained Naraan's theories on how the Devuls who inhabited human bodies were not destroyed when their husks were, and how the few Devuls who had certainly been destroyed met their doom. "But none of them contain any information pertaining to this," she added miserably.

"According to folklore, once a man's lifeblood has been drained enough to weaken his mind, he is susceptible to Devulish influence at the full moon." The physician glanced toward Captain Norland.

"The moon's full tonight," he said bluntly, red brows furrowed so tightly they nearly joined over the bridge of his nose.

It took a moment for Fletch to understand. "You're saying," she said slowly, "That Klep will be... that a Devul will Turn him... tonight?"

Sytres nodded reluctantly. "According to folklore," he repeated. "We may learn a great deal this night that has long been the source of speculation."

"I'm sorry, lass," Norland said, his voice a startlingly gentle rumble. "I know you've spoken with the lad often since arriving here in Iventorr. It may not be my place to say this, but I think you're the closest friend Klep has here. He needs a friend with him now."

That last quiet statement yanked Fletch's remaining equilibrium mercilessly from her. There was no mistaking the message. Eyes stinging, she bobbed her head again.

None of them left the infirmary as the evening wore into dusk, and the dusk to night. Captain Norland paced restlessly, his boots clomping on the smooth stone floors. Physician Trithinnis calmly made his way here and there between beds, speaking quietly with his white-robed assistants and apprentices, treating the other patients but frequently returning to Klep's bedside to listen to his breathing and heartbeat.

Fletch remained at Klep's bedside, staring absently into his still face. Though her body was still, her mind whirled incessantly. She had no doubt that the Unbreathing in Verenshire had intended to Turn a castle guard. How convenient it would have been; a spy in the king's own ranks. The drunk Klep would've made a simple target.

But the Unbreathing had failed on two counts. It hadn't dragged Klep far enough back into the alley before settling down to feast. Its hunger and greed must have gotten the better of it. And, it had assumed the Captain of Iventorr's guard wouldn't notice one missing guard for one short day.

Captain Norland always noticed.

At least the attack had taken place outside of Iventorr, she tried to reassure herself, but it rang hollow in her own mind. The Unbreathing had turned their attention to Iventorr's guards.

"Captain," she said as his pacing brought him close, "Do you believe Klep was attacked because he was alone?"

"Aye, lass," he replied shortly. "I've since ordered the guard to travel in groups to and from Verenshire. They know danger's about and are on high alert." Stopping at the foot of Klep's bed, he turned on his heel and strode off again.

Occasionally, Klep's eyes would flutter open. Each time, he tried to lift his head and speak, but the most he could manage was to roll his head to one side and stare glassily at the room around him. During these moments Sytres would rush to him, raise his head to a cup of water, and tell him to not speak, to rest. An expression of blank confusion swam in those glazed brown eyes.

Once the physician hurried off for the third time, Fletch inched her chair closer to Klep's bedside. The short, quick puffs of breath flared from his nostrils in small clouds of yellow-orange. Normally, one's breath was a nice vermillion, the color of bright sunlight shining through eyelids.

Resting her right hand in her lap, palm up, fingers relaxed, Fletch carefully laid her other hand's on Klep's arm. Swirling and flexing the wrist of her now-hidden right hand, she warmed the Wynd around Klep's cot to a toasty orange-red. Then, gently, she eased the Wynd into his nostrils.

His chest rose and fell fully for the first time she'd seen that day, his pallid face gaining the slightest hint of color. Encouraged, Fletch repeated the movement. His chest rose and fell again. For the next half-hour, she kept funneling warm Wynd into Klep's weakened body. Against her better judgement, hope began to grow within her.

Physician Trithinnis bent over Klep again, pressing a bronze instrument like a trumpet to his chest. As he placed his ear against the narrowed end, a surprised but pleased smile crossed his face. "He has improved." He nodded, straightening. When he lifted Klep's eyelid with his thumb, the smile disappeared.

"What's wrong?" Fletch asked, already leaning forward.

Sytres did not remove his thumb immediately, allowing Fletch to see the cause for his sudden dismay.

The veins in the white of Klep's eye were spreading, spidering across the surface.

But they weren't red, the color of blood. The choking veins in Klep's eye were bright yellow.

"I have not seen anything such as this," the physician murmured uneasily.

The eye stirred under his thumb as the other opened.

"W-where?" Klep's voice said weakly.

The physician withdrew his hand, startled. Fletch squeezed Klep's arm gently, heart in her throat.

"'Tis all right, Klep," she lied reassuringly. "You're in the infirmary. That was Physician Sytres Trithinnis just now. He's caring for your wound. Captain Norland is here also."

"Fletch," Klep's voice whispered. His chest lifted slightly, slowly, as a tiny stream of Wynd entered and exited his lungs. "It's so cold, and so... empty. Why is everything so empty?"

Cold and empty, like the hollow in her gut. "I don't know," Fletch said, her fingers tightening on her friend's wrist. "But I'm here, alright? Try to focus on my voice."

Sytres bent closer over Klep's glazed, jaundiced eyes, squinting into them. "You have been bitten by an Unbreathing." His voice was strange, fervored. Excited? "It's quite possible that you are being Turned. We need to know everything that you are experiencing, so please, elaborate."

Shooting a startled glance over the physician to Captain Norland, Fletch caught a deep scowl and a barely perceptible shake of the head. She settled back into her chair, watching uncertainly.

Eyes lolling in his skull, Klep squirmed feebly. "There's something here," he said. The dread and terror in his voice was echoed on his moist, chalky face, his hand trying to grip Fletch's. Her fingers found his, and she squeezed as hard as she dared. "There's something old... twisted here. I can't see it, but... It's empty, and ravenous, and it's all around me."

The physician passed a hand over Klep's face, staring closely as the young man gazed beyond him, unblinking. "Can you see me?"

"I... I think it's waiting for something," he said, and his hand trembled in Fletch's.

Turning towards her, Sytres frowned. "I do not believe he can hear me. Repeat my inquiry. He seems to be more aware of your presence than anything else."

Again, Fletch glanced hesitantly past his shoulder to Captain Norland, who dipped his head slightly in a nod. "We should be trying to help him, not interrogating him," she heard her voice say, rough and raw.

The physician's eyes narrowed. Behind him, Captain Norland looked down and away.

Turning back to her friend, Fletch clenched her teeth against the rising tide of heat within her and asked, "Can you see me, Klep?"

His eyes swept past her, empty and uncomprehending. "No," he whispered.

The hushed horror in that one word sent a shiver down Fletch's spine.

A scream ripped from Klep's throat as his eyes rolled back in his skull. Sytres and his assistants rushed forward, shoving Fletch aside. Their hands pinned Klep's limbs to the bed as his spine arched in agony. He writhed against the restraint, still screaming as sweat poured from his skin.

A hand closed on Fletch's shoulder. She jumped.

"Stay back, lass," Captain Norland said grimly.

The shriek abruptly stopped, Klep's body consumed with violent convulsions that nearly shook the physician and assistants free. Even from where she stood, Fletch could still see the yellow veins spreading in the whites of his eyes. He heaved one deep, shuddering breath, lips stretched away from gritted teeth. The exhale was a drawn-out screech of terrified anguish that filled the infirmary with dread.

She stood there, helpless, heart pounding in her throat as Captain Norland's grip tightened and more nurses came running to help hold Klep down. Even with nine people surrounding his bed, their knuckles were strained white, grasping his wrists, elbows, knees, and ankles. The convulsions stopped. His back bent horribly upwards as if an invisible force had him by his middle, pulling him toward the ceiling. Blood trickling from one nostril, he drew a moaning breath and released it in a brutal cry, collapsing into spasms that rattled the bed he was pinned to.

Tearing her eyes away, Fletch glanced up at Captain Norland. He didn't seem to notice, his apprehensive gaze transfixed on the awful scene before them. Over his shoulder, through the open window looking out over the Emerald Basin, the full moon's pale, eerie light played over the rippling waters. In a bizarre, detached moment of clarity, Fletch realized it was nearly midnight.

The crowd around the cot abruptly stopped and pulled away.

Klep lay still, his eyes now completely yellow, each breath a horrible, painful, wheezing gag.

"Fletch."

She moved forward without thinking, Captain Norland's hand wrenching free of her shoulder. One of the nurses stumbled as she shoved them aside to grasp her friend's arm. "I'm here, Klep," she told him desperately. "I'm here."

His head lolled toward her, and for the first time since breakfast the previous morning, his eyes met hers, rimming with tears which rolled down his cheeks. Two identical rivulets of blood. "Don't let it take me," he whispered, a crimson trickle slowly rolling from one nostril. "Please, Fletch. Don't let me Turn."

Stunned, she could only stand there when his screams started anew and she was pushed aside. This bout was even worse than the last, his body writhing with such horrible strength that they could barely hold him. Then, distantly, the bells of Iventorr's welcome hall began to ring, punctuating Klep's weakening howls. With each resounding gong, his struggling subsided until, at the bell's seventh peal, Fletch finally understood.

Sweeping an arm at the assistants crowded around, her other hand closed around the hilt of her father's silver hunting knife. "Get back," she hissed.

Startled, they eyed the weapon and stepped away without a word.

"Wyndshaper?" Sytres snapped. "What—"

The short blade flashed through the air. Soft resistance and a sickening pop resonated up the handle into Fletch's hands as the knife plunged through Klep's heart and sank up to the hilt in his chest.

The writhing stopped. His eyes focused, transferring from the pommel of the weapon in his ribs, to Fletch's fingers, up her arm, and finally to her face. Another tear of blood escaped to spill down his cheek as peace washed over his features. His lips parted as if to speak, but his eyes fluttered closed. Limbs going limp, head falling back into the pillows, Klep Ironshod's last breath escaped him, the faint trail of marigold orange Wynd merging into the surrounding stream.

He was gone.

Something tapped Fletch's boot. Numbly, she glanced down. Bright crimson dripped from her blade. Her hands went cold and clammy as if plunged into a bucket of ice, and the knife clattered to the floor.

A long moment of strained silence reigned. No one moved or made eye contact, but the air in the room was tense and strained as if ready to snap.

"What in Ivere's name have you done?" Sytres snapped. Sallow brow furrowed, thin lips pressed into a fine line, his glare was like needles piercing Fletch's skin. "You have just robbed all of Ivenhence the chance to finally uncover some truth as to the nature of the Unbreathing!"

"Easy there." Two large, gentle hands closed around Fletch's shoulders. "Prepare Klep Ironshod's body for embalming and transport," Captain Norland said to the apprentices, ignoring the physician. "His family'll want to bury him at home." Not waiting for acknowledgement, he began to guide Fletch from the room.

Sytres's nostrils flared, his eyes widening in rage. "You cannot be serious!" He intercepted them at the door, blocking the way with arms crossed over his narrow chest. "We could have learned how a man is Turned, how quickly the Devul takes control of the body, how long it takes them to reach their strength. And you threw this opportunity away."

Fletch stared at him, a pinpoint of diamond-hard ice forming inside the void: the seed of cold rage. "It was his final wish," she choked past the lump of bile in her throat. "And he's my friend."

"Nothing happens in this infirmary against my command," the physician continued railing. "I can have you imprisoned for the action you have taken here! You murdered a fellow guard!!"

He abruptly cut himself off as Fletch again escaped Captain Norland's grasp. Her blood-splattered boot toes inches away from Sytres's spotless sandals, she stared down at him, watching all pretense of bravado evaporate from his face. "'Tis a good thing you didn't command me to leave Klep be, then," she said, distantly amazed at the cool calm in her voice. "And 'tis also fortunate so many others here heard his final words, begging to be ended. Murder?" Her hands balled into fists at her sides. "No, what you wanted for him was murder — continued agony and certain death. If you think putting a man through that is justified, you're as sick and as twisted as a Devul yourself."

As she finished speaking, a strange thing happened. One of the guards standing behind Sytres met Fletch's eye and nodded firmly, silently triumphant. An assistant bowed their head and gently drew a sheet over Klep's body. As Fletch turned away, time muddled and slow, she saw the other nurses and apprentices, and Klep's fellow guards all watching her with the same expression: agreement.

"Come on, lass," Captain Norland told her quietly, circling her shoulders with one arm. "Let's get you home."

They left the infirmary, a wake of stillness behind them. The hollow in Fletch's chest grew heavier with every step, the numbness fading into a tight ache. It was the only thing she was fully aware of; everything else, the sound of her boots against the cobblestones, the clink of Captain Norland's greatsword against his back, the yellow-green breeze that drifted through the streets. It was all a distant haze.

"Ye did right by him," Norland said finally, and the conviction in his voice made Fletch look up. Eyes clouded, he shook his head. "Sytres spoke truth, in part. When in the infirmary, not even the king can contradict the physician's commands. That's why... that's why I couldn't do anything. Why I stood aside and stayed quiet." He glanced down at her, sorrow etched deep in his scarred face. "I'm truly glad ye did what ye did, lass. And... for what it's worth, I'm proud of ye."

The void in Fletch's ribs shattered like a glass pane splintering in response to the perfect pitch. The tight ache rushed out, spilling through her in a shuddering wave. The horror of the night, the suddenness of it all, the blood on her hands. Klep's blood. It was all too close and too clear.

Lungs seizing, vision blurring, Fletch's feet stumbled. She couldn't stop the sobs when they gripped her mercilessly, wringing tears from her stinging eyes and wracking her chest so she could scarcely draw breath.

The hand on her arm didn't move, but gently squeezed. The kindness and warmth in that simple touch infused with the pain coursing through Fletch, and for a moment, she wept even harder, her breaths short and ragged between shuddering exhales.

When she finally managed to force her lungs into some semblance of compliance, she gasped, "I'm sorry, Captain."

"Don't ye even say et," Norland replied, his strange accent as thick as when she had seen him with his children. "Don't ever apologize for showin' your feelings, Fletch. Et takes a strength t' allow th' truth o' your soul t' show." The hand patted her shoulder, and a few more tears rattled loose over her cheeks. "Come along, we're nearly home. I shan't expect ye for guard duty tomorrow, lass, but if ye need th' distraction, you're welcome to et."

The truth of one's soul.

He was a man before he was king.

Drawing a deep, cleansing breath, Fletch straightened as much as she could. Here was a man who was stern, but kind. Who hid his gentle heart behind a prickly exterior. A rough-around-the-edges giant who treated others with consideration and respect. A loving father and husband before the captain of the guard. Someone she was proud to know, and proud to serve under.

In some ways, he reminded her of her own father.

"Yes, sir," she said hoarsely, and let him lead her onward to the Garden Wall.

Chapter 13

It was strange to feel such pain over someone she'd only known for a moon.

Most of the time, it kept its distance from her. As Fletch learned the duties, posts, and pathways of a royal guard, staying out of the king's way and listening closely to every word from the mouths of the other Sentinel veterans, time passed in comfortable numbness. Sitting in her quarters, working her way stubbornly through the *History of Ivenhence* book, she could focus on the words, though they became duller and more difficult to absorb the closer the end came.

Each meal taken in the dining hall, however, was a precarious event. Several times, she looked up at the sound of a familiar voice, instinctively expecting to see Klep's wide whiskered smile and his twinkling eyes. Then the memory of the full moon crashed over her. If she squeezed her eyes shut and took several deep breaths, she found she could force the tears away, but the ache in her gut sometimes prevented her from eating.

Two weeks slowly passed, the sun rising earlier and setting later as summer progressed, the days growing warmer and drier. Each day without fail, Fletch woke before the sun peered over the horizon, rose, washed herself, dressed, and donned her weapons and armor. A few times, when the ache was already present in her stomach before she even set foot in the dining hall, she stopped by the kitchens for a sausage roll and an apple from Matron Gulden. The old woman's eyes were full of sorrow, though, and it was just as difficult to meet her softened smile as it was to avoid the increased looks from the guards in the hall.

But one evening, six weeks after arriving in Iventorr for the first time, Fletch snapped the history book shut triumphantly, holding it over her head in a long, delightful stretch. She had finally finished the last chapter.

The next morning, she rose especially early and hurried to the dining hall as the horizon began to glow a soft pink, shining through the translucent streams of Wynd that blanketed the Hearth below. Books and scroll tucked close to her chest, she ducked through the door and made her way to her usual lone seat. She'd thought long and hard about how to present them properly to the king; according to Petrecia, such things had to be done through certain channels.

One of the kitchen servants paused with a tray of food as soon as Fletch sat, setting a plate in front of her. "There you are," the young woman murmured, nudging a curl that escaped her kerchief away from her face.

"Thank you," Fletch replied.

Rather than scurrying off as she usually did, the maid hesitated. Her brown-speckled cheeks pinked. "Er, I'm Sariah," she offered finally, shifting her tray to her other arm. "You're... you're Fletch, right?"

"That I am," she said, heart sinking slightly.

But rather than tell her how sorry she was for her loss, Sariah lent her a bashful smile. "You borrowed my elbecca for your messenger errand some weeks ago." The pink in her cheeks deepened. "That is, he isn't mine, he's the king's. But I'm his caretaker, and I thought... maybe you'd like to visit him sometime?"

She stared at her for a moment as the words settled in. "If you wouldn't mind," she breathed, "I would love to. Is there a time that would be best?"

Sariah shook her head. "Anytime." Glancing down at the platter of food in her hands, she grinned sheepishly. "I must be back to my duties. Pleasant day to you!"

As Fletch turned to her meal, still smiling, her eyes passed over the group of guards that usually sat one table away. Most of them were looking in her direction. The bald, bewhiskered man met her eye and stood.

Pretending not to have noticed, she busied herself with cutting a slice of pork.

A shadow passed over the table in front of her. "Mind if I sit here a moment?" asked an unfamiliar voice.

Looking reluctantly up, Fletch looked up into the eyes of the man whose spiteful stares she'd endured many times. Today, though, his expression was neutral. "Certainly," she replied, wishing Petrecia's lessons hadn't included giving seats to strangers.

The guard settled onto the bench across from her, his hand extending across the table. "I'm called Gorrin."

Reluctantly, she accepted the hand. The strong, firm shake she received startled her. "'Fletch. 'Tis a pleasure."

"No, I'm quite sure it isn't," Gorrin snorted. "I shan't take much of your time, guard Wyndshaper. I just wanted to say... I'm sorry I treated ye with such disdain for the past weeks. 'Tisn't any excuse, but a few of us have been in the castle for over twenty years, hoping to one day serve the king as part of the Sentinels. It didn't seem fair that ye were chosen above us, and I took it badly." His forehead pinched into several ridges. "But I've seen ye practicing on the training grounds, even so soon after your shoulders were wounded, and it's clear your skills are equal to any of ours. Not t' mention ye outran us all in the test." He looked down, studying the many scars and callouses on his wide, spade-like hands. "I guess none of us wanted t' admit ye deserved th' post until a fortnight ago."

Fletch's heart plunged into her stomach.

"I'm doing a terrible job of this," the man muttered to himself. "What I'm trying t' say is, we know what ye did for Klep Ironshod, honoring his last wish despite that damned leech parading about. Ye did well by your friend. And... well... I'm honored t' have a woman— a person of such integrity and strength serving in Iventorr."

With that, his face beet red, he gave a respectful nod and pushed away from the table to rejoin his friends.

Stunned, Fletch stared after him for a moment, then down at her plate, heart throbbing in her gut. From the many whispers and increased number of glances from the guards, she'd thought they were condemning her for Klep's death. Not quietly saluting her for what she'd done.

Hurriedly wolfing down her breakfast, she left the dining hall, all too conscious of the stares that followed her out. Arriving shortly at the library, she dodged in and out of the high rows of shelves until she spotted the short, bent figure of the head librarian. Stooped over a raised podium, he scratched rapidly away in an unfurled scroll.

"Excuse me," she said quietly. "Master Brinwathe?"

The white head turned, blue eyes sparkling curiously. "Yes?"

"I have some materials here that I believe would be of great interest to our king." She held them out to him.

Taking one book in each hand, he peered at their covers. "Hmm, hmm. Yes, indeed," he murmured, mostly to himself. "'*Unbreathing*', '*A History of Ivenhence*'. Quite interesting." He transferred them to the podium and took the small scroll from her as well. "'*The Conspiracy and Assassination*'. Fascinating! May I ask how you came by these?"

"There was a merchant in Verenshire a few weeks ago. Naraan

the Nomad, of the Wyndarin. His wagon was filled with books and scrolls written in his own hand." She hesitated, and added, "The king had previously made mention of the lack of information on these subjects."

Brinwathe scratched his wispy white cloud of hair and nodded, his face breaking into a wrinkled smile. "My lord shall be pleased. I shall set these aside for him. He has planned to be here this afternoon." Rheumatic spine creaking into a slight bow, he inclined his head towards her. "Thank you, Fletch Wyndshaper. Your father would be right proud."

Fletch blinked. "Thank you also, Master Brinwathe."

The old man chuckled. "'Tis only Brinwathe, Fletch. I am no man's master. You had best be on your way. The Sentinels shall be gathering in the tower soon."

The king finally made it to the library at setthir, three bells past noon. All too conscious of the prickling tension in his shoulders, he hurried into the study.

"It's strange that one man has gained so much power in that area," Brinwathe was commenting to Anshwell, who was nodding pensively. Seeing Dreythan enter, he creaked into a bow. "My lord."

"I apologize for arriving so late, Master Brinwathe, Marden Anshwell," he said with a sigh, sinking into a chair. "Many citizens required my ear today."

Anshwell's smile was immediate and genuine. "Think nothing of it. We are here to serve, whenever you might require us."

"And I thank you for it," Dreythan said. The tightness between his shoulder blades eased a bit as the two scholars also took their seats, their chairs scraping against the stone floor. "Were you able to locate any pertinent information?"

Brinwathe nodded. "Indeed. After reviewing land deeds and

other records, I confirmed that Darman Lollma owns nearly one quarter of the forest surrounding Limbwood. Only half the forest is owned, my lord, so Lollma has quite the footing in the lumber trade." Unfurling a scroll, he pointed to a section halfway down. "Here he has claimed two hundred and thirteen men and women working in his employ. There are roughly three hundred and seventy adults living in Limbwood. Lollma practically owns the town."

"Hmm. The fact that so many voted against him speaks volumes." Dreythan met Anshwell's eye, frowning deeply. "How many testified to being threatened out of employment if they refused to vote for him? At least twenty?"

"Thirty-seven so far," Anshwell replied. "Although Captain Norland did mention that many were too frightened to speak with his agents. 'Tis clear Lollma would not have been elected had he not coerced those under his employ."

Drawing a deep breath, Dreythan closed his eyes, exhaling for several seconds. When his eyes opened, the pervasive weight that followed him had settled even more deeply than before. "I shall have to consider what is to be done," he said quietly. "Please do not speak of this to anyone yet. I feel it is a matter that must be handled delicately."

"Of course, my lord," Anshwell agreed as Brinwathe bobbed his cloud of white hair. "Other than the situation in Limbwood, the new system of taxation is off to an excellent start." Their graceful hand indicated a small stack of scrolls to one side of the table. "There have been murmurs of opposition to the change of taxation in some areas, but all townships have supported their chosen representative. Although the votes were close in Ingling and Herstshire, none have made protests over those chosen."

"These are the missives from the elected representatives?" Dreythan asked, already reaching for the scrolls.

"They are, my lord, as well as my personal notes."

Anshwell waited patiently, hands folded inside their sleeves, and Brinwathe puttered around, straightening this book and that scroll on the surrounding shelves as Dreythan scanned each of the scrolls.

When the king re-rolled up the last one and placed it on top of the pile, he met Anshwell's expectant gaze with a weary smile. "These are all in order," he said, relief trickling through him. He couldn't have selected a better candidate if he had spent moons searching: Anshwell's notes were succinct, accurate, and insightful. "You shall do well as Treasurer. I shall ask Matron Gulden to allocate a location for the office of the Treasury." Scooping the scrolls from the table, he stood, placing them in the Royal Treasurer's hands. "As soon as I have made a determination regarding the situation in Limbwood, I shall let you know."

"Of course, my lord." They bowed. "Pleasant day to you."

As they exited the study, their smoke-purple robes billowing behind them, Brinwathe stepped forward, a small bundle of materials in his withered hands.

"My lord, Fletch Wyndshaper requested that I give these to you when next I saw you." He shuffled to the king's side and set them carefully before him. "She purchased them from a traveling merchant in Verenshire some weeks past."

The king stared down at the written materials. Wonderingly, he ran one hand over them, his fingers tracing the worn, chapped binding. "*Unbreathing*," he muttered.

Guilt pricked him, a hot poker stirring his conscience. Several times over the last fortnight, he had glanced up from his dining table to see Fletch seated at hers, starkly alone in the bustling hall. Her head was always bent to her plate, as if trying to block out the sympathetic stares and pitying whispers from those who dined around her.

Something inside him widened, empty and aching whenever he saw her. He'd nearly summoned her to his table twice or thrice. But that would only bring more eyes to her, more stares for her to avoid.

To think that she hadn't forgotten him in her time of pain and loneliness... He was ashamed.

For Ivere's sake, he hadn't even found the courage to ask after her while she was recovering from the Unbreathing ambush.

"Thank you, Brinwathe," he muttered, avoiding the old librarian's keen eye. His gaze skimmed over the lectern in the corner of the study, then stopped. Had he imagined it? Crossing the room without thinking, he peered at the scroll tucked into the upper ledge.

"Ah," Brinwathe exclaimed, one hand smacking his forehead. "And she was here only hours earlier!" He plucked the scroll from the podium, his liver-spotted face flushing with embarrassment. "Thank you for the reminder, my lord. I shall have a messenger deliver this immediately."

Before he could change his mind, Dreythan tucked his bundle under his arm, holding out his hand. "That shall not be necessary," he said. "I shall take it."

Brinwathe bowed, placing the scroll in the king's hands.

"Thank you for your assistance, Master Brinwathe. Pleasant day to you."

The little man bowed. "Of course, my lord, and to you."

Fletch clambered down from her perch in the top of the library, frowning to herself. The royal archer's post was too high to overhear conversation. Though Harrild often reminded her not to listen to words the king exchanged with others, she just as often wondered what he could be discussing with such darkness shadowing his angular face.

Still, she had seen Brinwathe hand what looked like her books to the king. Why hadn't he stayed and begun to read?

She didn't have time to dwell on it. As soon as her foot met the cobbled street of Iventorr, a flat voice said, "Took your time. Come on then, we'll have to catch up. Looks like the king's headed for the garden."

Before she could nod, Parfeln Holden turned on his heel and stalked off.

She followed, her teeth gritting. The day she'd dreaded had arrived; Captain Norland had assigned her to shadow the sour Sentinel for the first time. Thus far, it had gone about as well as Fletch had expected; he'd ignored her completely, other than to snarl at her if she put a toe out of line.

Somehow his scowls seemed pleased. As if he found pleasure in finding fault in her.

As they trotted to the top of the Garden Wall, they were just in time to see Harrild Hammerfist slip into the shadows between two large trees. Dreythan proceeded down the path to his usual place, a stone bench in the shade of a sycamore tree. When he sat and deposited two books and a scroll onto the seat beside him, a smile curled onto Fletch's face.

Parfeln's fingers snapped, drawing her attention. Pointing at his eyes, he nodded down to the garden-less side of the wall. Pointing at Fletch, he then transferred his finger to the king.

She nodded her understanding. Turning her back to him, she hugged the edge of the wall and peered down, taking note of each detail.

As usual, the king was the royal garden's only occupant. It was a shame that only the royal family, Sentinels, their captain, and gardeners were allowed inside. The garden was a lush wonderland, filled with blooming roses, water lilies, climbing honeysuckle vines, morning glories, sun bells, and thickly leaved trees. There was even an odd shrub that changed color through the day; its light blue foliage in the morning shifted gradually to a deep, dark purple at sunset.

It was the sort of place to bring one's family, to sit and converse, enjoying the perfumed air and the gentle wisps of cool yellow Wynd that rustled through. But Dreythan always wandered in solitude, sitting or pacing in the green prison of loneliness.

As the sun began to dip toward the horizon, the king set down the book he'd been reading and switched to another. Only a few minutes later, he looked up sharply, glancing about the garden.

Instantly alert, Fletch stiffened. Had he heard something she hadn't?

"Fletch Wyndshaper?" his voice called. "If you are present, please come hither. I wish to speak with you."

She glanced at Parfeln. He shrugged, pointing to the oak tree that grew near the wall. Taking his cue, she used its limbs as a ladder to climb down, passing her quarters on the way. Once her feet reached the ground, she approached the stone bench and bowed. "Yes, my lord."

To her surprise, he stood, shifting the books to the center of the bench so there was room for them both to sit, one on either side. "Thank you for these most thoughtful gifts," he said. "Would you join me for a while?"

"Of course," she responded, giving a slight nervous dip as Petrecia had taught her.

They settled onto opposite ends of the bench. Before the quiet could become uncomfortable, Dreythan asked, "Have you read each of these?" He held up the book he was reading, thumb wedged between the pages.

Fletch blinked at *A History of Ivenhence*. "Er, yes," she blurted, realizing he'd asked her a question. "I'm sorry, my lord. Yes, I did read them." Glancing to where *Unbreathing* lay beside the small scroll, she heard herself ask, "Did you not find it to your liking?"

An eager light dawned in the king's black eyes. "I found it fascinating," he said. "To discover so much of the Unbreathing I did not know, and to realize how much there is that we still do not understand... I shall have to re-read it to ensure retention of all the information within."

He had read the entire *Unbreathing* volume in the span of two hours. She stared at him, her brows rising.

"But first I must ask," Dreythan continued blithely, opening the *History* book to the spot his thumb marked. "This passage troubles me, though I know not why. 'They blocked the chasm with this silver-laden stone, and Lady Luminia surrounded it with water to further prevent any attempt at escape.'" Raising his head from the page, he met her eye with a slight frown. "Why is this so maddeningly familiar?"

Fletch's eyes dropped to her clasped hands, her throat tightening. Of course Dreythan would be confused by the same passage she'd been. He didn't have the key to unlocking the puzzle: Kell Wyndshaper's journal.

Every night since Klep's death, she'd seen it lying on her desk, and every night, she'd pushed it to the back of her mind and picked up the history book instead. She told herself she needed to finish the history book first for the king's sake. But she knew it was partially a lie. She was avoiding her father's next entry. In it, she was certain he would recount the events that took place during his and Dreythas's enslavement under the Unbreathing. In it, he would recount the many horrors he'd witnessed.

Horrors that were too near and raw.

Swallowing, Fletch managed, "My lord, the merchant who sold me these materials gave me another book — my father's personal record. I beg your pardon for not presenting it to you as well." Swallowing, she continued, "It recounts our fathers' exploration of old Ivereland and their discovery of this island. They saw men and women enslaved, dumping mined ore across the bridge on the mainland. When they realized the slavers were Unbreathing and the ore being discarded was silver, they concluded this island is, in fact, the giant stone Ohnaedris used to imprison Kazael."

"I see," Dreythan murmured, staring intently at the page. "The Unbreathing enslaved humans to mine and remove the silver because the monsters could not do it themselves." Slowly, his head raised to gaze absently into the distance. "That must mean the Unbreathing were attempting to free Kazael. They wished to extract the silver that bound their god in place."

"Exactly our fathers' thoughts, my lord. 'Tis why they allowed themselves to be enslaved by the Unbreathing, and why they so carefully built a rebellion over the course of several years. They couldn't allow Kazael to be freed."

"Hmm." Eyes clearing, he glanced back at her. "This opens many new doors of thought. Perhaps this is the reason the Unbreathing are acting as assassins. They share the end goal of whomever wants me — us — dead. The downfall of Iventorr."

Fletch nodded. "I did wonder, my lord, if this could be the purpose behind the attacks. Perhaps the Unbreathing wish to continue their quest to free their master." She paused, then inquired, "About that, my lord. I am curious — was Captain Norland ever able to compare the arrow I presented him with the ones that... slew our fathers?"

Abruptly, Dreythan's expression darkened. "No," he replied soberly. "The arrows from the assassinations fifteen years ago are missing, though they were locked securely in the royal vault. There is no knowing when they were stolen."

"I see," she murmured, though her mind reeled from the blow. "So... still no clues as to the identity of the ones who want us dead." Fletch looked down at her boot toes. "I'm sorry," she offered after a few awkward seconds. "I ought not to have asked."

"Nonsense." The king's reply was firm, accompanied by a shake of the head. "If anyone ought to ask after such a matter, it would be you."

She looked up sharply, startled by the softness of his tone. His eyes, though still plagued by worried shadows, crinkled in a smile.

From the folds of his cloak, Dreythan drew out a small scroll. "Master Pruden sent this inside his census report for Herstshire. It is addressed to you."

She stared at the rolled parchment for a moment. Jon and Missy's faces blurred her vision, beaming. "Thank you, my lord," she finally murmured, tucking it into her belt.

"Speaking of census reports, there is another matter I wish to discuss with you." Dreythan's brow furrowed, and Fletch instantly recognized his intense frown. Over the past two weeks, it had been the visible symptom of an invisible weight hanging from his shoulders. "There is a situation in Limbwood," he continued. "A man named Darman Lollma won the election for tax representative by five votes. He employs many of Limbwood's residents. However, it has been confirmed he threatened to end townspeoples' employment and remove them from their homes unless they cast their vote for him." Dreythan paused, casting a glance at Fletch. "There are also rumors he has been sending messenger sun jays into Thissa. Head Forester Felwin has had difficulty confirming this, however."

"I see," Fletch mused. "If Thissa is indeed behind the assassinations and recent attacks, perhaps he's conspiring with them — feeding them information."

"Precisely. But since we do not yet know if Thissa is responsible, or if he is communicating with them at all, I am forced to give him the benefit of the doubt on that topic." Standing, Dreythan began absently pacing. His face was taut, his jaw clenched. "However, I cannot allow him to act as representative for Limbwood. Coercing those under one's employ is simply unacceptable. How then would we move forward with selecting the correct representative? Should it be Lollma's runner-up? If so, how ought it be announced? How can a man with that much power over a small town be punished for something that is not strictly against Ivenhence's laws?"

"Respectfully, my lord," Fletch interjected bluntly, "You are Ivenhence's law."

Halting, Dreythan turned on one heel towards her, his startled eyes crashing into hers. "How do you mean?"

She also stood. Something crackled inside her, bubbling to the surface of carefully numbed emotions. "How can you punish a man with that much power? Show him he's nothing without those under him."

"Remove his employees from him?" The king shook his head. "How I should like to, but it would be too drastic of a punishment. Removing his livelihood would be akin to dictatorship."

"No, my lord." Fletch bit her lip, mind racing. "I meant something a bit more subtle. What if you were to send a messenger back to Limbwood to proclaim for all to hear that Darman Lollma shan't be tax representative, and those who voted for him must vote for another? Hold a second election. Not only will everyone know his dishonesty, they'll know you care enough to expose it. That shall in turn bolster their faith in you. They'll remember your attention to their plight. If Lollma gives them trouble in the future, they'll know to bring their grievance to the throne."

For a moment, Dreythan stared at her. "By Ivere," he drawled, a grin breaking over his face. "You have the truth of it. Public humiliation and a reminder to the people — the power lies within their hands. I knew asking you would yield answers. Thank you, Fletch! I shall speak of this with Captain Norland and Brinwathe. Perhaps we could also spread word of this to the other towns, not only to increase the effectiveness of Lollma's punishment, but also to dissuade others from similar dishonesty."

Fletch shifted, then dropped a hesitant half-bow. "Of course, my lord. I'm at your service." Glancing down at the scroll in her belt, she paused. "Might I also ask how the changes to Ivenhence's taxes are progressing? Outside of Limbwood, that is."

"It has been instituted in Herstshire with nary an issue," Dreythan replied, a true smile softening his angular face. "Master Pruden is doing admirably in his post." The light fading slightly from his eyes, he lowered himself back into the stone bench. "Most of Ivenhence's other townships are also faring well, but there has been a... complication with the Merchants Guild of Aden. The tariffs of trade are having to be renegotiated as a result."

Ah. There it was. Fletch watched as Dreythan visibly deflated under the invisible weight again. She frowned. "I take it that's been difficult."

The bridge of his straight nose wrinkled. "Nay," he dissented, "not truly. Frustrating, I would call it. It has been frustrating. The ambassador for the merchants seemed to take my proposal well, but she did not believe the Guild would." Running a hand through his raven hair, he exhaled sharply. "And I cannot seem to discover why. Apparently the Isles of Aden have experienced poor relations with Ilumence as of late. I have been waiting for a missive from my cousin, hoping to glean insight, but nothing has arrived."

His cousin? Fletch squinted up at the trees as yellow Wynd stirred the branches, carrying the scent of lilacs through the garden. He must have meant King Morthan, ruler of Ilumence. "I'm afraid I don't know much about tariffs or trade negotiations," she confessed. "Is it a bit like haggling?"

"Haggling?" Dreythan repeated, giving her a curious glance.

"Yes, for example, a merchant has a certain price they wish to sell an item for, but they have it priced higher in the hopes it will bring in more coin. You, the buyer, start low and work up, trying to guess at a fair price while also avoiding insulting the merchant." Her cheeks stung as Dreythan's eyes twinkled. "I sound foolish, don't I?"

"No, not at all," he replied. "You are exactly right, though I wish the back and forth were as quick as haggling. The ambassador left for the Isles three weeks ago and is due to return any day according to her last missive." Wincing, he rubbed the back of his neck. "It has been nerve-racking."

She inspected his face: the fine creases that always seemed present on his forehead, the speckles of silver hair around his temples, the pale, blue-tinged skin. "I'm certain Ivenhence and the Isles will come to an agreement," she said, gently nudging his arm with her elbow. "You've always had an eye for structures and balances, my lord. The ambassador likely already appreciates that. You said yourself she viewed your proposal favorably."

The king blinked, his hand rising to close over his arm. "Indeed," he finally agreed, some color rising to his cheekbones. "Structures and balances. Hmm."

There was a brief moment of quiet, broken only by the soft whisper of Wynd through leaves and petals and the burbling of birds in the trees.

Dreythan's expression faded into solemn concern. "How fare you, Fletch?" When she raised a puzzled brow, he explained softly, "Norland told me of Klep Ironshod."

"Ah." Heart dropping into her stomach, Fletch looked away. As she blinked, she saw her hands clenched around the hilt of a knife, plunged into her friend's chest. Klep's boyish face, ghastly grey-white, flesh stretched over his bones as he screamed. "Don't worry after me, my lord," she managed. "I'll be all right."

The king's eyes lingered on her face, and he said, "You are not currently all right, then."

Fletch didn't reply, her bottom lip tucking between her teeth as her chest tightened.

"I am sorry for your loss," Dreythan offered gently. "Klep seemed a good man, and a good friend."

"An excellent friend," she agreed, her voice unsteady. With a raw chuckle, she added, "The best I ever had, if you can believe it. Though I suppose living in the Snowshod Mountains isn't conducive to a social lifestyle." She laughed again, trying to force herself to be cheerful as she struggled to swallow tears. "Once you have a friend and lose them, it becomes all too clear how isolated you truly are."

There was another pause, in which Fletch sniffed roughly and wiped her eyes with the back of her hand.

"I'm sorry, my lord," she mumbled. "Ought I to return to my post?"

"If you wish," Dreythan replied quietly. "But before you depart —" he paused, his jaw working as if feeling out the words before he uttered them "—I… I simply wished to say… I often find solace in my own father's writings." Fletch's eyes met his as he continued, "Although they mainly account past dealings with merchants and trade with Ilumence, Thissa, and Aden, the sight of his writ hand on parchment is some comfort. I am glad you have that same comfort in your father's journal."

It was a beautiful sentiment. They shared a comfortable, close silence, and Fletch smiled. "Thank you, my lord."

"My lord!" a voice called. One hand clutching his sword to keep it from clinking at his side, a guard hurried down the green-shadowed path toward them, gasping, "My lord, Ambassador Alicianna Kekona approaches the bridge." Pausing a few feet away, he wiped perspiration from his forehead. "Treasurer Anshwell is being notified per your request."

"Excellent," Dreythan replied, though anxiety instantly swelled within his eyes. "I shall meet her in the lower level of the guest tower. Please escort her there once she arrives."

The guard saluted and trotted away, chainmail cuirass jingling.

"I am sorry to cut our conversation short," the king said, turning to Fletch. "Will you accompany me to the guest tower, since you are on duty?"

Parfeln would undoubtedly scold her later, but she shoved the thought away with a nod. "Of course."

With Fletch a few paces behind, Dreythan exited the royal garden, heading directly to the guest tower. Her footfalls didn't make a sound as they brushed lightly over the cobblestone, no doubt an unconscious habit she'd learned in her years as Forester. He had to glance back once or twice to reassure himself she was still there, her green eyes flitting from side to side as her long legs swallowed the road in easy strides.

There was something about her that put his mind at ease, he reflected as they passed the throne hall. The way her gaze met his without hidden thoughts or reservation, how she inspected his face as if it could tell her more than his words could. When they spoke, she addressed him with respect, but it wasn't the same sort of respect most others offered. He slowed as they approached the welcome hall, picturing her expression. Something about it felt familiar, but he couldn't quite place it.

The mental image shifted to the moment she'd struggled to swallow tears, her fingers twisting on her knees as her face shadowed at the memory of her friend's death.

Dreythan's stomach hollowed.

Entering the welcome hall, they proceeded through the high-ceilinged chamber to the walled-in lower level of the guest tower within. The room was much the same as it had been three weeks ago. A polished mahogany table waited in the center, with well-cushioned chairs spread around it.

"My lord," Anshwell greeted as they bustled in, arms laden with writing supplies. "I have brought copies of the original and secondary proposals. Thank Ivere for the advanced notice." Setting their burden on the table, they began placing scrolls, clean parchment, quills, and inkwells in a tidy pattern where each chair rested.

"Indeed," Dreythan agreed as Fletch stationed herself beside the door. "Hopefully the second shall not be needed."

Self-consciously, he adjusted the crown and his robes, checking to ensure the brooch of his collar was perfectly centered under his collarbone. Though Ambassador Kekona was not royalty, she may as well have been with all her finery.

"Are you certain this is what the ambassador meant?" Anshwell shot a doubtful glance at him.

"Not entirely," Dreythan admitted. "Her missive did state, 'I shall wish to speak with Your Grace upon my return'. Being prepared as though her statement were a literal one is better than the alternative. In any case," he added, "Ambassador Kekona does not strike me as the sort of individual who speaks in figurative terms."

"I shall take that as a compliment, Your Grace," a melodious voice said from the doorway.

Dreythan turned as Alicianna Kekona entered, the road-stained hem of her amethyst robes drifting behind her. She paused to dip in a curtsey, the simple gold chain over her brow catching the lamplight. Shadows marred the dark skin under her eyes, but her gaze was steady and her smile firm as she rose, inclining her head toward the table.

"It is unusual for my messages to be interpreted exactly as stated," she said. "But greatly appreciated. As the Guild is ever so fond of saying, 'Time is the greatest of all currencies.'" Settling into the chair Dreythan offered, she removed weathered gloves from her hands, folding her fingers atop the table.

"I hope your journey was not an arduous one," Dreythan offered, taking a seat of his own.

The ambassador shook her head. "The sea and rivers were calm, thankfully."

Perhaps it was not her finery that made the diminutive, rounded woman so intimidating. Even in dirt-smudged, understated travel garb, the ambassador exuded power.

"Refreshments shall be brought shortly," Anshwell said, hands disappearing inside their sleeves. "Shall we wait until they arrive to begin?"

Kekona's dark cheeks dimpled. "The thought is appreciated, Marden Anshwell, but I fear I have kept His Grace waiting long enough for the Merchants' Guild's response to his proposal." Leaning back in her chair, she surveyed Dreythan as she added, "The Guild bid me convey their gratitude to you. It has been some time since a trade partner has been so thorough and conscientious in negotiations."

"Of course," he replied, careful to maintain his level tone. "But unless I am gravely mistaken, you are not here merely to thank me." It was a delicate game, showing he had given thought to the matter without revealing how consumed by it he had been. "Given the amount of time the Guild required from you, I take it they wish to decline my initial proposal."

The ambassador nodded. "I'm afraid you are correct," she admitted, glancing down at her hands. "While they understand the need to balance your citizens' taxes with trade customs, the Guild is opposed to such rigorous bookkeeping. None of our other trade partners have placed such a requirement upon the merchants within the their lands, and they are loathe to make such indulgences for Ivenhence without further incentive."

That was a rather harsh word, Dreythan thought with a frown. Indulgences. "But such bookkeeping would be manageable, given the frequency of the required reports. Is the opportunity to cross the border freely without taxation not incentive enough?"

"I do not disagree with you, Your Grace," Kekona said, raising a cautioning hand. "Such an argument was not lost on the Guild. Simply put, they do see how your proposal could be beneficial to both parties. However, the benefit weighs in your favor."

She paused as three servants entered, each of them carrying a tray or platter with a pitcher of water, cups, plates, and an array of sliced cured meats, cheeses, and fruits.

It truly was like haggling, Dreythan thought with a wry smile, glancing over Kekona's head at Fletch. She stood at stiff attention, her eyes fixed in a distant stare, but something about her posture told him she was listening intently to every word.

Once the servants had made their circle, deposited their burdens and quietly exited, Dreythan plucked a scroll from the table and turned it over in his hands. "Word has reached me that the Isles of Aden found their recent commerce interactions with Ilumence and Thissa to be... disappointing," he mused. "Is it because their offers also benefited their own nations more heavily than the Isles?"

"I cannot say for certain, as I am only ambassador to Ivenhence." Kekona hesitated, eyeing the roll of parchment as she took a sip from her cup. "But I believe that to be an accurate assessment, yes."

Nodding to Anshwell, Dreythan passed them the scroll, which they then offered to the ambassador. She accepted it, raising a questioning brow.

"Perhaps the Guild of Merchants would consider a more balanced proposal," Dreythan said. "One that would benefit Ivenhence and the Isles of Aden equally."

When he'd finally acknowledged he would have to rely on his own judgement rather than Morthan's insights for the second proposal, the realization had suddenly dawned on him. The simple, straightforward solution.

"I believe the Isles do not have access to iron or steel of their own, correct?" he asked. "The ore your craftsfolk use is entirely imported."

Kekona nodded, unfurling the scroll. "Correct, Your Grace."

"A new trade route has recently been established to Herstshire, a hamlet at the base of Mount Valer and Mount Norst," Anshwell told her. "Not only does it already possess a rich iron mine, but a safe route to Northcrag could easily be forged."

"Interesting," she murmured, scanning the parchment. "Several of our merchants frequently pass through Northcrag on their routes to or from Ilumence. Adding an ore stop to that route would certainly be worthwhile."

"It would also give the Isles a reliable source of iron." Dreythan suppressed a smile as the ambassador's eyes froze near the bottom of the page. "An exclusive source."

Aliciana Kekona slowly looked up at him, her full lips slightly agape. "This is far too generous an offer, Your Grace," she managed finally, blinking. "To provide access to an iron mine only days out of the way of a current route is one matter. But to give sole admittance to Adenite merchants?"

"Do not mistake me," Dreythan interjected. "This arrangement shall also greatly benefit Ivenhence. Herstshire withered when trade with Thissa failed. It is my hope that this agreement with the Guild can cause it to flourish again."

The ambassador was silent for several moments, looking from the scroll to Dreythan and back down again. Her eyes were as turbulent as the ocean during a storm, thoughts flashing through them like lightning.

"On behalf of the Merchants' Guild of the Republic of the Isles of Aden," she said, deliberately rising from her chair, "I tentatively accept your proposal." Meeting Dreythan's startled stare, she chuckled. "I do possess the power to do so. Your proposition is an excellent one. The Guild would be foolish to even think of declining it." Examining his face, she commented, "You are a skilled negotiator, Your Grace. Ivenhence is fortunate to have a ruler so invested in her well-being."

"You are too kind, Ambassador," Dreythan replied, allowing himself a rare grin. "But, thank you."

"Come, my lady," Anshwell said, ushering the ambassador to the tower's winding stairs. "You must be weary from your travels."

But at the foot of the steps, Kekona paused. Her dark eyes fixed to the right, she took a step back, then glided forward, one hand extended. "I apologize for being so forward," she said with a graceful smile. "But you are familiar to my eyes. Have we previously met?"

Freckled cheeks flushing, Fletch's distant stare shifted and focused to the ambassador. Confusion creased her forehead as she took the ambassador's small hand, giving a sharp bow. "I... I don't believe so, my lady," she stumbled, her green eyes flickering towards Dreythan. "I've only recently been transferred to Iventorr, and previously resided in the Valer-Norst Pass."

"Ah, I see." She chuckled, the melodious sound smoothing the room's sudden discomfort. "I am Aliciannna Kekona. And you are?"

"Fletch Wyndshaper," she replied, the wrinkle between her brows deepening. "'Tis an honor to make your acquaintance, my lady."

The ambassador's eyes glinted. "And yours," she said with a nod. "It is heartening to see women trusted with the protection of the kingdom. Would that Ilumence and Thissa take note."

With a final smile, she turned and made her way up the stairs, Anshwell shooting a puzzled glance over their shoulder at Fletch's equally confused face.

Chapter 14

The rest of Fletch's shift passed in an unfocused, bustling blur, despite receiving the expected scolding from Parfeln Holden. She couldn't seem to shake the Ambassador of the Merchants Guild of Aden from her mind. Her deep blue-green eyes, the color of eldergreen needles. Her long braided locks, woven with silk ribbon. The grace and fluidity with which she moved, despite the ample curves of her frame. The way her full lips had parted slightly, her eyes widening when Fletch had told her her name.

Worse, she kept remembering the way Dreythan had adjusted his crown and clothes before the ambassador's entry, how he'd bowed more deeply than she had ever seen. It caused her to feel both hot and cold inside, like a blizzard and an inferno were waging war.

But thankfully, a distraction waited for her. As soon as she had finished her evening meal and returned to her room, Fletch eagerly drew Jon and Missy Pruden's message from her belt and spread it over her table.

Dearest Fletch,

Jon was unsure how to start a letter, so there. I've started it for him. We hope you are well, and are finding Iventorr to your liking! I imagine you'll have your pick of prospects in the castle. Would you humor me sometime and try a dress with a bodice over the top such as the fancy castle women wear? You have such a lovely figure dear, if you'd only use it to your advantage.

An image sprang to her mind of Alicianna Kekona's fitted dress, and she wondered how something alike might fit her. What Dreythan would think if he saw her in it. Fletch's cheeks burned, and to her relief, the handwriting changed.

Sorry about Missy, lass. She knows you don't need a fancy dress to be fetching, she's just all in a tizzy picturing you living in Iventorr.

I'm certain you've heard, but the new tax representative for Herstshire is me. 'Tis an honor, and I'll do my best. The first trade caravan should be arriving soon, so keep an eye out for barrels of my ale in Iventorr!

Also, we have a new Forester. I am pleased with him. His name is Arnuld Wyntersoul, somehow a relative of the Captain of the Guard in Iventorr. He is an older man who has served on the border between Ivenhence and the Wynterhead for many years. In some ways, this post is retirement for him. He has a massive bow, longer than he is tall, and his arrows are as thick as his fingers.

A troubling thing happened two days ago now. Arnuld Wyntersoul found the body of a man in the Pass. 'Twas an Ilumencian messenger bringing a missive across the border to Ivenhence. He wasn't frozen, as it has been warmer here and some of the snow has melted, but there were bite marks on his neck and wrists, and his skin was pallid. There was no message found on his body. Arnuld believes that more Unbreathing have snuck into the mountains, and has cautioned all to remain inside while 'tis dark. He also requested silver-tipped arrows from the Foresters' Head. Given his history with the Foresters, I'm sure they'll fulfill his request quickly.

However intimidating his reputation and appearance are, I know he shall not defend our little village as stoutly as you have, Fletch. Your presence is already missed here. But don't you go feeling homesick. Your duties there are many times of greater importance than they were here.

We miss you, lass. Write us a reply when you can. Wishing you all the best.

The latter part of Master Pruden's letter worried her. Another nest of Unbreathing in the Pass... it might take weeks for Arnuld Wyntersoul's request to be processed, and even then, who would transport the arrows to Herstshire? How long would they have to wait? How many more of the villagers would be snatched away, never to be seen alive again?

She wondered if she ought to say something to Dreythan. But, no... Surely the Head Forester would recognize the situation and send the arrows without delay. Surely there was no need for worry.

But perhaps there was. The image of stark bite marks in chalky grey flesh flashed before her eyes. She shuddered.

Re-rolling the scroll, Fletch rose and placed it lovingly atop her chest of drawers. She would need to return to the library tomorrow. Perhaps Brinwathe would allow her to use a piece of parchment and a pen.

Still frowning to herself, she turned back to the desk. Her eyes fell on her father's journal.

She stood there in the center of the room, frozen. Several seconds passed as her mind raced for excuses. It was too soon after sundown to retire; were she to do so this early, she would wake exhausted the next morning. And she had given the other books in her possession to the king, so there was nothing else to prioritize.

There could be no avoiding it.

Reluctantly, Fletch sat back down, perching in the chair with stockinged feet tucked beneath her. Pouring herself a cup of a water from her pitcher, she took a long gulp, wishing it was ale. Then she unwrapped the leather strip and flipped slowly forward until she found the next entry.

The sixty-third year of Ohnaedris, nearing the end of autumn
I know not how to begin this entry. So much has occurred in these past years, it surpasses my ability to express it, even as I pen these faltering words. I suppose I ought to begin at the beginning, but to speak truth, I remember very little of it.

Pretending to be simple woodsmen from Ilumence, Dreythas and I approached the island's bridge. We were accosted by Unbreathing before we could set foot on the giant suspended planks. We didn't resist and were dragged through the streets of some form of castle, chiseled from the very stone of the island, past statues of leering gargoyles and grotesquely proportioned winged men until we entered a mockery of a throne room. Two Unbreathing sat on intricately carved stone thrones. We quickly learned one was named Vvalk, the other Sliv. Together they ruled the hive of Unbreathing they called the Crimson Horde.

Gods, but I still do not have the strength to remember it all. I do not know if I ever shall. Seasons we spent underground, panting and toiling by lantern light as sweat poured from our backs. Or above ground, chiseling the stone into whatever forms suited the monsters' fancies. Even so, Dreythas and I were fortunate. Yes, we worked ourselves to the bone and received beatings for it at the end of the day. Yes, we were starved; yes, we were used as cattle for the Unbreathing to slake their thirst from time to time. But we were not women. We did not have to hide in a dark silver-lined hole beneath the Hearth every moon, waiting to stop bleeding so the Unbreathing wouldn't rip us apart upon catching our scent. We were not raped repeatedly. We did not have to endure the horrid attentions the Unbreathing forced on others.

We did not survive the worst of it; the women of the Great Slaving did.

That is what they are calling it. The Great Slaving. From what Dreythas and I have been able to gather, it began shortly before Ilumence lost contact with old Ivereland. Very little is known of the past century; only by word of mouth did the history of old Ivereland stay alive, and most of that is tales of Hearth's beginning, of the goddesses.

Here there was a long paragraph that had been penned, then completely obscured. It was as if Kell had spilled several globs of ink onto the page and smeared them over his words with a finger.

Four weeks ago today was the Battle for Reclamation. The rebellion had been quietly, carefully simmering for three years. We excavated secret passages to key points in the castle. We hoarded silver and crafted makeshift weapons and binds. We planned, and hoped, and dreamed, and planned further. Now that it is over, now that so many of us were lost in claiming the freedom we sought, I cannot bring myself to savor it. The sweetness of liberty carries the bitter aftertaste of sorrow and profound loss.

Thankfully, there is little time to reflect on the torrent of memory and feeling within me. So much must be done to secure our future still: trade route negotiations, the re-settlement of long-abandoned towns, reconnecting with the rest of old Ivereland to spread the word of the defeat of the Crimson Horde, breaking ground for farms and tearing down the many horrid statues around the castle. It provides a most excellent distraction from the pain and joy that mingle in my soul.

The entry abruptly ended.

Fletch stared at the last paragraph, heart tight against her ribs. She had expected herself to feel relieved. Relieved that Kell had not gone into detail regarding the horror he'd endured, relieved that he hadn't named those he had lost or their relation to him. But instead, there was dawning realization. In the words of his journal, her father had shown her a tarnished mirror in which she could barely see her own reflection. He had buried his feelings deep down, preferring to focus on his work and duty rather than face the pain within.

She wondered if it was her imagination that tinged his words with guilt; was he ashamed of being alive and whole when those he had fought for were not?

Slowly, with numb fingers, Fletch closed the journal and tucked it close to her chest, eyes squeezing shut as tears rose unbidden.

It was strangely wonderful and terrible to realize, after all this time, how like her father she was.

When Fletch woke, it was difficult to guess the time. The sky was overcast and grey. Dark clouds hovered on the horizon, their towering hight threatening. Dressing hurriedly, Fletch paused at the door, snatched up her cloak, and rushed on.

Her footfalls pattered along the streets as she darted around a few carts and sleepy-eyed passersby. Ducking through the dining hall's main doors, she glanced at the mantle that held the day's ten hourglasses. One had been overturned, the sand equally distributed in both chambers.

"Half-past upfirst," she muttered to herself, slumping into her usual seat. There wouldn't be enough time to stop by the library until after her watch had ended... Hopefully the caravan to Herstshire wouldn't leave until the morrow. Lip tucked between her teeth, she peered around, wondering who she might ask. Her gaze fell on the king's table. Though he normally didn't appear until a quarter to upsec, Dreythan was already there. Left hand pinning something to the table, he leaned away from his plate as he chewed.

"I'm glad to see you've brought your cloak," Matteo Alwick said, grinning as he settled onto the bench across from her. "You'll likely need it this afternoon."

"You're to be my tutor today?" she asked.

Steel-blue eyes twinkling at the hope she couldn't keep from her voice, he nodded. "I know you've trained in the rain before, but those were simple showers. Looks like it's going to storm something fierce, so the king might retire to the royal tower hours earlier than usual. 'Tis the most troublesome place to guard him and remain hidden, especially for the archer, and especially during a storm." At the distant rumble of thunder, he raised a rueful brow. "I don't envy royal archers on days like this."

By the time they finished breakfast, a steady drizzle had begun to fall. It always fascinated Fletch to see water droplets falling from the sky, the colors of the Wynd within descending in muted sheets of turquoise which brightened to green, then yellow just before it reached the Hearth. Still, she was grateful for her cloak. Raindrops beaded on the coarse wool, rolling off and dropping around her feet. If only she could shape the water away like so many other Wynd-blood could. A memory flashed before her eyes: a woman with long hair and smiling brown eyes, rain cascading off a swirling barrier above her head. Throat tightening, Fletch shook the image away as she took her position beside Alwick, hidden behind the dining hall as they waited for the king to emerge.

"The Sentinels decided to hold your competency test next week," Alwick muttered out of the side of his mouth. "I oughtn't tell you, but I believe 'tis only fair since Parfeln Holden might play the part of judge."

Fletch's stomach twisted uneasily. "Why would Parfeln be the judge?" she asked. "Wouldn't it make more sense for Captain Norland to do so?"

"It would," he admitted. "But Parfeln has served as one of the royal guard for over thirty years, far longer than any other, including the Captain. His seniority carries weight. Not to mention he's judged the tests since before Captain Norland came to Iventorr."

Pulling her dismayed gaze away from Matteo's sober expression, she said bluntly, "He despises me."

"You have that right," he agreed with a grimace. "About as much as Darvick hates me, I'm afraid. He'll be looking for the most minute flaws, and will likely question you on the smallest details of our practices and schedules." He lent her a reassuring wink. "If it makes you feel any better, I like Parfeln about as much as he likes you. Harrild and I'll tell you all about it sometime."

The rear door of the dining hall opened. Captain Norland ducked out first, flipping his cloak hood over his helmet, and Dreythan followed shortly, hood already raised. As they set off down the street, their feet splashing through puddles, Fletch and Matteo fell in behind them at a casual distance.

It didn't take long for the king and captain to reach the throne hall's back door and slip inside. Glancing back at Fletch with a quick nod, Alwick waited thirty seconds, then they also entered the back door, closing it firmly behind them.

Fletch's mind churned as she climbed the stone steps up to her post. Harrild and Matteo were the most helpful and open of the Sentinels, but Darvick didn't seem to mind Fletch's presence. Aeda had only been assigned as her tutor once, likely because of their former relationship. Why, of all people, would the one person who wanted her to fail be chosen as the judge for her competency test?

No matter. As the king settled into the throne, the sound of drumming droplets close over Fletch's head, she began running over everything she had learned from the past few weeks.

In her mind, Fletch laid out a map of Iventorr Castle, pinpointing each of her hidden posts. The Garden Wall when the king paced the royal grounds. Her current perch when he sat on his throne. The hidden alcove in the top of the library. When Dreythan practiced his swordplay with the guards, out on the wide practice field, she had been told to observe from a distance.

Fletch frowned. The practice field didn't sit well with her. It was an ideal place for an assassin to loose a deadly arrow at the king. The instructed vantage point was insufficient for the king's protection. She pondered the problem as the king sentenced a young thief to three lashes in Verenshire's town square.

The issue with her designated vantage point from the grounds was this: she was on the same level with the king. If an assassin were to fire an arrow from the barracks or the armory, nothing could be done to stop them. She could attempt to fire an arrow in return, but the assassin would be protected by the narrow windows. Hitting such a target from so far away would be nigh impossible.

She decided to ask Aeda about it when next she saw her. She was a true master of her yew longbow, and if anyone could solve the issue, it would be her.

Thunder rolled overhead, building into a roaring boom as the pattering of rain grew to a rushing whisper. The king rose from his throne.

That was her signal. Swiftly descending the stone protrusions, Fletch reached the back door and ducked out, steeling herself.

A sudden gust of chill Wynd pushed against her, flattening her to the wall as stray raindrops splattered on her face.

That's when she smelled it.

Rust.

Blinking the rain from her eyes, Fletch yanked her bow out from beneath her cloak, stringing it with one quick tug. There was no doubt in her mind, though the scent had gone as quickly as it had come.

Unbreathing were in the castle, and close.

Fletch plucked a silver arrow from her quiver, nocking it to her bowstring as she slunk into the bushes. Crouching low, she scanned every shadow, every crevice she could see. No shapes shifted along the rooflines. No figures followed in the hedges.

For a moment, she hesitated, glancing over her shoulder as Matteo appeared at the back door of the throne hall. His hooded head turned from side to side, looking for her. Captain Norland and Dreythan appeared behind him, and he bowed, stepping aside.

Heart pounding in her mouth, Fletch padded through the wet underbrush, moving as swiftly as she dared. Another guard would only slow her down. She needed to act fast. An Unbreathing in Iventorr... what if it were the very one that had tried to Turn Klep? What if it had grown weary of waiting for another unwary soul, or was hunting the king?

Unaware of the danger, Dreythan and Captain Norland entered the southeastern door of the Sentinel tower and closed it behind them. They were cutting through; a shortcut. The perfect place to be caught off-guard.

Darting forward, Fletch skirted the Sentinel tower, reaching the other side just in time to see a shadow disappearing behind a tree. The sound of steel softly ringing barely made it to her ear over the pounding of the pouring rain. Or was that the pounding of her own heart?

There was no time to think. At any second Dreythan would emerge from the other side of the tower. At any second the Unbreathing could pounce.

Dropping to the right of the raised cobblestone path, Fletch dashed in a crouch toward the royal quarters tower. Whipping her bow up and over the path in one swift motion, she locked her knees.

Her boots plowed into soggy soil. The shadow behind the tree turned, yellow eyes flashing as it hissed, already running. Gods, it was fast. There was a flash of silver and a howl, gaunt hand raised like a claw to strike.

Fletch's fingers loosed the arrow.

The silver-capped missile met its mark. The shadow fell.

Then Matteo was standing over it, his sword at its throat. "'Ware!" he shouted, eyes fixed on the thing laying in front of him. "Guards! 'Ware to the king!"

Shaking, Fletch approached him and looked down. The Unbreathing's dilated, jaundiced eyes darted from Fletch to Matteo and back again, cracked lips stretched in pain over bared yellowed teeth. Her arrow had pierced its leg just above its right knee.

"By the gods," Matteo muttered. His silver blade arced upward.

"Wait," she cried. The creature stared at her through narrowed eyes. A chill crept down her spine. "We still don't know who's sending these monsters after the king. Perhaps the captain can squeeze some information out of it." Turning, she scanned the mud and grass around them, mind spinning. "I... I don't think it's here as an assassin."

Several guards swarmed in, surrounding the creature with their swords. Matteo shifted like a caged animal, eyes chained to the Unbreathing. "Be wary, lads. Even when injured, it has the strength of ten men."

"Not ten men, not now," interjected the king's voice. "Perhaps three or four. It is weakened by the wind and rain."

Eyeing the Unbreathing cautiously, Captain Norland interposed himself between Dreythan and it. "My lord," he rumbled, "You're not safe here. There may be more of 'em about."

Dreythan brushed past the captain to stand beside Fletch. Water dripped from his hood onto the Unbreathing's face, his face beneath eerily impassive. "Fletch. You believe he is not acting as an assassin. What led you to this conclusion?"

"My lord." She swallowed, heart still drumming in her ears. "He was careful to stay hidden, moving swiftly from one place to the next. A spy. If he were acting as an assassin, he would have chosen a hiding place and waited there for an opportune moment since he has no weapon."

"Indeed." Black eyes crackling with electric fire, Dreythan drew his own silver sword and pressed it to the Unbreathing's chest. The creature lay utterly still under the two blades that rested on him. It had been a man, once; a small, shriveled man with a weasel-like face. Dreythan leaned closer as the thunder rumbled overhead.

"You know who I am?"

It smirked, a grotesque twist of the mouth. "Yes."

"Who sent you here, and why?" The silver blade strayed lower, tracing across his belly.

"You shan't obtain answers from me."

"I see." Dreythan pointed the tip at the fork of the Unbreathing's legs. "I have heard your kind revel in the pleasures that your human Husks can afford you. Perhaps I shall confiscate that ability."

The creature did not stir. Its narrowed eyes fixed on the king's dangerously calm face.

"Or," he continued, the sword pointing to each of the monster's limbs, "I shall slice off your feet. Then your hands. You shall be trapped in that shell for eternity, unable to move, to act. To escape."

"My lord," Captain Norland said quietly. "Dreythan. Step away from him, I beg of you."

Fletch silently agreed with the Captain. Dreythan's tone sent a chill through her bones.

"Nay, Norland. This wretched thing has a master that has tried several times to kill me, to kill Fletch. A master that is responsible for the deaths of good men." The blade returned to the Unbreathing's throat. "Now, you shall answer me. Who is your master? What do they want with Ivenhence?"

Dreythan's black brows drew thunderously together. But before he could press the creature further, the Unbreathing's skin shrank back, collapsing and sagging. Seconds later, all that lay before their feet was wet, parchment-like skin, stretched over a thin bone frame.

"What in Luminia's name just happened?" Norland muttered. "Did it... die?"

"No," Dreythan said, drying his blade and sheathing it. "The Husk can only exist as long as the Devul occupies it."

"I didn't know they could do that," Fletch murmured. "Abandon their Husk." Feeling faint, she turned away from the skeleton and unstrung her bow, hands trembling as she wiped it down with one corner of her cloak.

"Alwick," Captain Norland barked. "Report. What happened here?"

"I'm not rightly sure, sir," came Matteo's hesitant response. His eyes met Fletch's for the briefest moment, then flickered back to the Captain. "Just as you and our lord entered the guard tower, Fletch ran past me with her bow ready. I followed, and she drew the thing out of its hiding place—" he pointed "—behind that tree. It began to flee away from her, towards me, and I raised my blade just as it reared to strike me. Fletch's arrow found it before it could land a blow."

Under the rim of his helm, Norland's eyes glinted. Turning to Fletch, he said, "Wyndshaper. What gave the thing away?"

Tucking her bow away beneath her cloak, she faced the Captain. "I smelled it, sir," she said numbly. "As I left the throne hall."

Red breath puffed from the Captain's nostrils, and though she couldn't hear it, Fletch knew he had sighed.

"You did well, Fletch," Matteo told her quietly. "Acting that quickly, thinking with such speed... Well done."

The praise fluttered with the nerves in Fletch's stomach. She turned to the Captain, startled when she met the stern gaze of a pair of sharp blue eyes.

Lightning flashed overhead, followed closely by a rolling, Hearth-trembling boom. "You'd best get inside, my lord," Captain Norland grunted. "Ye lot. Beland, Gorrin, Farrel. Take the remains to the infirmary and present them to Sytres Thrithinnis. Let 'im know that Fletch Wyndshaper sends a gift. Alwick, get the king to safety. I'll be there shortly." Swiveling his frown toward Fletch, he added, "Wyndshaper, wait a moment."

Fletch suppressed a shiver as Matteo escorted the king onward, casting a sympathetic glance over his shoulder. The other guards dispersed, leaving three to pick up the Unbreathing's cloak and carry it like a stretcher through the streets.

"Did I understand Alwick rightly, Wyndshaper?"

Cringing at the disappointment in Norland's voice, Fletch wiped her damp face with her soggy sleeve. She tried to return his flat stare, but couldn't. Lowering her head, she nodded. "He spoke the truth, sir."

"Ye didn't alert him to the danger? Ye acted on your own?"

Yes, that was exactly what she had done. Glad she hadn't raised her head to see the displeasure she could plainly hear, she nodded. "Yes, sir — that is, no, sir. That is, you're correct." This was worse than when her father had caught her pocketing shiny bits of silver. "I'm sorry."

A long pause followed, punctuated by a sudden clap of thunder and the brief blaze of lightning.

"Ye've got a good head on your shoulders, Wyndshaper," Norland said finally. His tone was so strange, Fletch's eyes were drawn magnetically to his face. The expression there was unlike any she'd seen before: thoughtful, frustrated, confused. "But ye've got to use it, lass. Especially in these situations. What if Alwick hadn't seen ye run by him? What if the Unbreathing had gotten to him? What if the Unbreathin'd decided to make a last-ditch effort to slay the king rather'n run?" He lifted one massive hand, roughly tugging his beard. "What's most important to the Sentinels, next to the king's safety and privacy?"

The Captain's words sank into Fletch like the rain soaking her clothes. Dismay and shame dragged her chin back down to her chest. It was the second lesson Harrild had ever taught her, and she had completely forgotten it. Or had she disregarded it? "Communication," she answered. "I know, sir. I ought to have alerted Matteo... I shan't make the same mistake again, sir. I'm sorry."

"I hope ye don't." Norland's hand fell back to his side, his gauntlet clinking against his belt. "If ye can't learn to communicate with your fellow guard, it shan't matter if ye can see the Unbreathing or not, lass. Because ye shan't be keepin' the king safe. You'll be endangering him and your fellow Sentinels. You'll be endangering Ivenhence."

With that, he turned and sloshed away, the rain pelting his wide shoulders as they stooped under the weight of dissatisfaction.

Dreythan shrugged off his soaked cloak, absently hanging it beside the fireplace as he turned to the crackling flames. Warmth pushed over his outstretched fingers, and he wondered what Fletch would see were she in his place. What did the heat of a fire look like?

"My lord," Norland said, appearing in the open doorway. "We need to talk."

Reluctantly, he nodded. "Come in."

Skirting around the king's desk, Norland flung his own cloak onto a peg and stood beside Dreythan, his back to the fire. The flickering light played across his hair, setting it aglow. "An Unbreathing spy," he grunted.

"Indeed." He tried to push it from his mind: the cold, malevolent fury that had risen within him at the sight of those lamp-like yellow eyes. But the embers of that frigid blaze still glowed in his stomach, biting and burning. He clasped his hands, hoping Norland hadn't seen them shake.

Behind him, the sound of rain suddenly grew louder. He turned just in time to see a slender female figure slipping through the door to the balcony, shutting it softly behind her.

"I don't like to think about why they've shifted their focus, my lord," the Captain was saying, "but we must ask ourselves why they're now trying to infiltrate the castle. Before, they wanted you and Fletch dead. 'Twas a simple goal, though their motivation's a mystery. This espionage troubles me."

"I wonder," Dreythan replied. "Perhaps their goal is the same, but they search for a new way to attain it. Perhaps Fletch's presence gives them cause to hesitate."

"I'm sure it does, since she has the ability to sniff 'em out." He snorted. "Quite literally, it happens." Swinging around to fully face Dreythan, he paused, his frown etched into his face by the fire's flickering shadows. "We need to know more. We should know more! But every time we get close to findin' an answer, to scraping up some clue, it's snatched away." His hand flailed through the air. "How long's the evidence from the assassinations been missing? I haven't got any leads. It could've been years. Or days. It could've been taken by a kitchen servant or a gardener." His head bowed as he added quietly, "And I've still no idea who the spy is, my lord. I doubt it was the Unbreathing Fletch just caught. She would've caught scent of them long before now if they'd remained in the castle."

It was the most defeated Dreythan had ever seen his friend look. "Your frustrations are my own, Norland," he assured him. "I had hoped to receive a response from Gorvannon regarding the establishment of a new trade route, but thus far, nothing. Still no word from our agent in Thissa?"

Norland shook his head. "None." Straightening, he pulled his still-damp cloak from the mantle. "I'm considering sending a messenger in after 'em. I'll give the matter more thought, my lord. But in the meantime, I'm increasing the guard around your person. And I request ev'ry guard be outfitted with a silvered weapon of some type, even if it's only a dagger."

"Your concerns are appreciated, Norland," Dreythan replied. "And I respect them. Inform Jorga Soothand to put aside stockpiling for the gypsies' visit and begin the production of silver weapons. She is to make them her priority."

"Aye, my lord." With a subdued salute and a nod, the Captain donned his cloak and exited the study.

Another streak of lightning, another roll of thunder. Through the glass of the balcony door, Dreythan could see the waters of the Emerald Basin churning uneasily, foam tossing atop the shifting waves. An especially vicious bolt of lightning split the clouds like roots splintering dirt, followed with a ground-shaking boom. The flash of light illuminated the silhouette of a shivering figure, their arms clamped around them.

Dreythan had long grown accustomed to the Sentinels' protective shadows following wherever he went. He hesitated, wondering how long it had been since he'd last noticed their comings and goings, or when he'd last thought about how cold or miserable they must be, guarding him from the places they did.

Crossing to the balcony door, Dreythan opened it, wincing against the instant rush of wind and rain. "Fletch?" he called, hoping she heard above the storm.

She turned slowly, unsuccessfully repressing a shiver. "My lord," she replied, her voice unsteady. "What do you require?"

"This is poor thanks for the service you have given," he said, giving her a bow and a little smile. "Come."

Obediently, she followed him in. When he closed the balcony door, she stood in front of it, her eyes darting over the room. Suddenly conscious of the rich carpet, velvet chairs, and silver-inlaid desk, Dreythan removed his crown, setting it aside. "You may hang your cloak in front of the fire," he said.

She unfastened the broach at her throat. Darting quickly across the room as if afraid to linger on the carpet, she hung the cloak from the mantle. Water droplets hissed softly on the stone hearth as they evaporated into steam. The fire lit Fletch's face from below, giving her an aura of power and mystery as she stretched her fingers towards it.

Dreythan wondered if he'd imagined the hearth brighten, crackling all the merrier as she peered absently down at it.

"Thank you for asking me in." She glanced over her shoulder, an uncertain smile wobbling to her lips.

Her green eyes held his for a moment, wide and questioning, hopeful and melancholy. There was something vulnerable in her expression. Something that made his hands shake.

Not in the same way they'd trembled as he stood over the yellow-eyed monster, his blade inches from the thing's flesh.

"You are most welcome," he replied, settling into the chair behind his desk. "You may wish to apply some fat to your armor so it does not crack when it dries. There is a jar and cloth on the mantle." Not knowing what else to say, or how to say it, he plucked Unbreathing from the desk and buried his nose in it.

Every so often he glanced up to check on Fletch's progress. She started on her vambraces, using just enough fat to cover the entire surface, and let it soak in for a while. While her vambraces waited, she removed her cuirass and covered that as well. Then, with the cloth, she polished the vambraces using small, circular motions.

He wondered if she'd had to teach herself how to maintain her own armor, out in the lonely Snowshod Mountains. Or perhaps her father had taught her before he'd died. Most of the castle guards took their armor to Jorga Soothand and her assistants to have their armor polished and suppled. Dreythan only kept the lard handy to polish his boots.

Leaning back in his chair, he peered below the desk at the black leather, caked in mud and... ash?

His gut twisted.

It wasn't ash, but disintegrated Unbreathing Husk. Shuddering, he pulled the boots off and crossed to the fireplace. With the hem of his cloak he wiped them clean, then paused, watching as Fletch buffed her armor.

"Have you ever frightened yourself?" he blurted.

She raised her head, blinking. "I'm sorry, my lord?"

Setting the boots down, he met Fletch's eye, his jaw tight. "Do you believe your father would have treated the Unbreathing in the same manner?" he asked hesitantly. "Or... or my father?"

"Hmm," she murmured, lowering her cuirass to gaze into the hearth. Her damp hair glinted like embers as the fire's red light danced across it. "I haven't confirmed this with my father's chronicle," she admitted slowly, "So I'm unsure if 'tis accurate. However, I've heard many stories of our fathers and their deeds during the Great Slaving and the Battle of Reclamation." Biting her lip for a thoughtful moment, she continued, "One of the Horde's generals was named Sliv, second-in-command to Vvalk. According to the tales, he was a despicable bastard, even for an Unbreathing. 'Tis said he preferred to drink the blood of women, because he relished torturing them in their weakened state.'Tis also said he ripped a young woman apart when she... when she unexpectedly began her moon's bleed. " She shuddered. "In any case. According to the stories, when the battle began your father's first target was Sliv. Dreythas stole into the monster's chambers, bound Sliv with silver rope, and severed his 'manhood.'" Fletch looked back into Dreythan's eyes as she finished, "At the end of the battle, when the carcasses were piled for burning, he threw Sliv into the fire, and didn't pale or turn away from the screams." Hesitantly, she smiled. "I think your father would've done more than threaten him, my lord." Smile fading, she added, "I'm glad you didn't. To answer your question, however — yes, I have frightened myself, but perhaps not in the same way."

He nodded, the knot in his stomach loosening. "I see." After a short pause, he said, "If it is not too personal a matter, may I ask how was it that you frightened yourself?"

The change in Fletch's face was instant. It were as if a barred gate slammed shut over her normally open eyes, the windows to her soul closing resolutely.

"It is personal, I'm afraid," she replied, forcing a little chuckle. "And something I'm quite ashamed of. But you're welcome to ask me something else if I can make an inquiry in exchange." She looked up, offering him the lard-laden cloth. "Did you need this?"

He took the rag, giving her a grateful nod. "A trade of questions, you say." Dreythan smiled at the idea, relieved she was still open to conversing. "Very well." He ran the cloth over the worn black boots, the movements deft from many years of habit. "Why did you choose to remain a Forester once your seven years had been served?"

Her eyes followed his hands, watching as he polished a heel to a high sheen. "Several reasons, I suppose," she replied after a few quiet minutes. "Jon and Missy Pruden. My cabin. The little trails and caverns, the familiar trees of the Pass. I couldn't bear the thought of leaving everything I'd grown to love."

"And now?" he asked. "How has that changed?"

To his surprise, a whimsical smile curled her pink lips. "I would have to tell you a story to properly explain," she said. "That wasn't part of our bargain. And you've asked a second question."

Before he could think of a witty response, she chuckled, pulling her cuirass on. "I suppose 'tis only fair, since you invited me in from the rain." The firelight danced across Fletch's face as she said, "I asked something similar of my father once. I might've asked why we lived in Iventorr, or why he was a servant of the king or the captain of the guard." Her smile softened, as if she could see her father's face, could hear his voice. "He said that the kingdom of Ivenhence was my sister."

Dreythan blinked. "Your sister?"

"Yes. He said he had helped give birth to this wonderful, beautiful, fragile nation, and he wanted to do everything in his power to protect it. Because he loved it." Her smile wavered. "Just as he wanted to protect me because he loved me." Glancing at Dreythan, she explained, "That memory is never far from my mind. Serving Ivenhence means protecting my sister. And if my sister is in danger, I'll do whatever I can to keep her safe."

Determination crackled in her eyes as another roll of thunder rattled the balcony door. The wind outside shifted abruptly, forcing rain to drum rapidly against the stained glass door. Fletch turned toward it as lightning lit the sky.

"What a marvelous storm," she said, and Dreythan wondered at the reverence in her voice. It reminded him of the eldergreen tree, the way she'd touched the bark and stared up into the distant needles as if worshipping at an altar.

"The trade caravan to Herstshire leaves Verenshire tomorrow morn," Dreythan told her, pulling his gaze away from her face. "Have you had the chance to write a reply to Master Pruden?"

She shook her head. "Nay, my lord. I didn't have time to visit the library today, even though I'd intended to. The rain caused me to rise late."

And she wouldn't have time after her shift. She wouldn't be able to write a letter before the caravan departed, not unless... Dreythan crossed to his desk. "It deceived me as well. I thought the hour much later." Lifting a blank square of parchment from a drawer, he slid it and an inkwell across his desk, then a jar filled with emerald green liquid and a quill pen. "Here, write your letter. I shall take it to the library when I return there this evening."

Eyeing the elaborate writing implements, Fletch hesitated, her stare settling onto the small stoppered jar. "But... only the royal family is permitted to use green ink."

"Only the royal family is permitted to use green ink for official matters." Dreythan smiled as her eyes lit from within. "But for personal documents and artistic pursuits, there is no such legislature."

He gestured to a chair in the corner of the room, which Fletch pulled to the desk and settled into as Dreythan sat across from her, picking up Unbreathing again.

Opening the jar of ink, she painstakingly poured several drops into the silver, leaf-shaped inkwell. Re-stoppering the jar, she pulled the parchment closer and picked up the quill. With a quick jab, the tip dipped into the verdant pool. Then, slowly, carefully, she penned word after word onto the parchment.

After several minutes, her fingers trembled with the effort. She set the pen down, flexing her hand, frowning distantly.

Glancing up, Dreythan glimpsed a paragraph:

Since coming to Iventorr, the only liquid I've imbibed is stale well-water. Not even so much a honeyed mead. 'Tis somewhat disheartening, now that I think of it. I look forward to the opportunity to taste your wonderful ale! The trade caravan cannot travel there and back again quickly enough.

He ducked his head to hide a smile, hoping she hadn't noticed. An impish voice whispered to him, telling him to look back up, to scan the rest of the laboriously neat script, to poke his nose into Fletch's words addressed to cherished friends.

But to do so would be a terrible breach of trust.

Eyes staring unseeing at the page gripped in his hands, Dreythan lowered the book. Did Fletch trust him? Did she... perceive him to be her friend? He looked sharply at Fletch's face as it bent down to the paper. Her dark lashes blinked, and he noticed how perfectly her eyes matched the brilliant green ink. Short, cinnamon-red hair escaped from behind her slightly pointed ear to hang over her cheek. An unspoken question echoed in her expression, her arched brows creased in a troubled frown.

Although I'm doing well here in Iventorr, I think of you and of Herstshire often. I miss your kind smiles and open hearts. I wish there were more people like you here in Iventorr. Many here in the castle look oddly at my trouser-clad legs and shorn hair. I think they see an outsider when they look at me. Perhaps they see a 'gypsy', and nothing else.

Heart settling in his chest like a stone in a murky pond, Dreythan's eyes lowered back to the book. Hadn't that been the first thought that came to his mind when he'd seen Fletch's hair? That she must have gypsy blood in her? It was likely that others in Iventorr thought the same. But why had she written the word 'gypsy' in quotations?

He flipped a page, the act a blatant lie.

"I've finished," Fletch said, capping the bottle of ink and pushing it back across the desk. "Thank you, my lord. Now Jon and Missy shan't worry."

A distant bell sounded, and she shot to her feet. "I fear I've overstayed my welcome," she gasped, already collecting her cloak. "Aeda and Matteo will be reporting for their shifts any moment."

Dreythan stood also, book dangling in his hand. A request for her to stay lingered on his lips. "You never did ask me your question," he told her as her fingers closed on the latch to the door.

She paused, throwing a glance over her shoulder. "Are those your father's boots?"

Throat tightening, he nodded wordlessly.

Fletch's expression mellowed. "They suit you," she said simply. "Good day, my lord."

"Good day, Fletch."

With that, she opened the door and was gone.

Sinking back into his chair, Dreythan stared at the flames. Why could he not think of the words he so desperately wanted to say?

Chapter 15

The morning dawned, though only just. Peeking through the still-dense cover of grey clouds, broken sunrays fell on Fletch's face as she stood at her window, debating whether she ought to bring her cloak. The rain had continued to steadily downpour after she'd left the royal tower, not letting up even after she had eaten supper. Imagining how she would have felt the day before without the thick wool garment, she shivered and shrugged it on.

Her boots splashed through puddles and squelched through patches of mud as she made her way to the dining hall, her mind far from her feet. She settled onto her usual bench and waited for a plate of whatever breakfast she would be served. When it settled in front of her, she began eating absently.

As water had pattered down her window the night before, she'd curled up in her bed with her father's journal. She'd expected to read stories of the Great Slaving. But rather than record memories of those lost or of the sacrifices that were made for the sake of freedom, Kell stuck to day-by-day entries. After the fall of the

Crimson Horde, the journal entries thinned out. Each one was shorter and further apart in time than the last. Years passed in as many pages, and Fletch's heart ached for her father. It was as if he was slipping away.

He mostly wrote about his service to King Dreythas and the duties he performed about the castle. It would seem that the captain of the guard held more responsibility then. In his records, Kell directly oversaw the Sentinels, the castle guard, and the Foresters and Fishers that patrolled their assigned areas around the Ivenhence border.

It had been difficult to sleep after closing the book and tucking it under her pillow. She'd lain awake, staring at the slow currents of persimmon Wynd moving across the ceiling. If she had trained for the Sentinels whilst her father was Captain, how would he have reacted to her mistake? Would he have demoted her to the castle guard? Would his face hold disappointment more bitter than Captain Norland's? Or would he have reprimanded her sternly, given her punishment for not following protocol, for endangering the lives of those around her?

The memory of that last thought sent a shudder of guilt and dread through her gut. With a deep, shaky breath, Fletch set her fork down, folding her fingers together. She swallowed, throat burning. Whatever punishment Captain Norland settled on, she deserved it. She wasn't in the forest mountains anymore, alone and independent. Here in Iventorr, her actions affected the people around her.

She wondered what Klep would have thought of it all. An image of his twinkling eyes rose before her, a burning band closing around her lungs. His cheerful voice was almost audible, saying something like, 'At least you knew the Unbreathing was there. More than any of the other guards can say' or 'Not to worry. Learn from your mistakes, as my pa always says. Just press through the embarrassment and let the experience make you better.'

"Wyndshaper."

Lifting her head from her hands, Fletch looked up into Captain

Norland's face. She yanked fully upright. "C-Captain."

He sat across from her, the long bench creaking under his weight. Propping his elbows on the edge of the table, he stated, "Ye made a mistake yesterday."

The red-hot band around her lungs slipped down to her stomach. She nodded, not trusting herself to speak.

"However, so has every guard during their training days. Even me." His whiskers shifted in a miraculous smile. "'Specially me. My error nearly burnt down an entire village. Considering your mistake only resulted in the capture and defeat of an Unbreathing spy, I'd say yours was a minor one." Sobering, he added, "But promise me this, lass — ye shan't make the same mistake again."

It took several seconds for the Captain's meaning to sink in. Brow furrowing, she slowly nodded. "You have my word, sir, but don't make light of my failure. Had Alwick not drawn his sword, he could've been gravely injured or killed because of me."

Norland's beard bushed in a scowl. "That's not how that works," he told her. "Ye can't judge one's actions based on what might've happened. There're endless realms of possibility, or so 'tis said. If all were judged by the possibility their actions might've triggered, we'd all be guilty of thousands of things that ne'er came to pass." Sword clinking against his side, he rose. "Stop dreading punishment. It isn't going to happen. But next time, make sure ye think before ye act, just as ye learned to think before you speak." Nodding down at her nearly-empty plate, he added, "If you're done, follow me."

She trailed him out the back door of the dining hall, her head light and wobbly. Past the kitchens they went, weaving between hurrying maids and manservants carrying baskets and platters to and fro. Trotting down a set of angled steps, they passed the statue of King Dreythas plunging his silver sword into Vvalk's heart. But instead of heading to the left and entering the throne hall, Captain Norland went right, entering the Sentinel tower.

Fletch followed, blinking as her eyes adjusted from bright sunlight to the comfortably dim interior of the tower. The low hubbub of voices quieted as she closed the door behind her. All the other royal guards had gathered in the main chamber. Waiting in a half-circle around the door, they each met her eye as she glanced around. Aeda Yewmaster, Harrild Hammerfist, and Matteo Alwick all wore bright, broad smiles. The picture of indifference, Darvick Hammerfist stood with arms crossed over his chest. And to one side, Parfeln Holden looked markedly ill, as if he had swallowed something foul.

"Fletch Wyndshaper," Captain Norland rumbled, "As the result of your quick, decisive actions yesterday, the members of the Sentinels have decided to bring ye into their fold as one of their own. By majority vote, no competency test shall be held."

At this, Parfeln spat out the open window.

"If you're willing and ready to become an archer of the Royal Sentinels of Ivenhence," Norland continued, ignoring the blatant hostility, "You'll repeat the oath after me."

Fletch swallowed. Though it had only been seven weeks since she'd left the forest for the first time, it had been the longest seven weeks of her life. "I'm ready, Captain."

Clenching her fist over her heart in a salute, Fletch echoed Norland as he intoned, "As a Sentinel of Iventorr, I hereby vow to guard Ivenhence and its royal family. I shall not suffer harm come to them and shall uphold the duties and codes of the Sentinels until my body make me unfit or until I am relieved of service. This, I, Fletch Wyndshaper, do swear."

"Hear, hear!" the others chorused heartily.

Heat rushed into Fletch's cheeks.

"Here you are," Harrild said, pressing something into her hand. "Your official badge. Wear it wherever you go. Those who reside in Iventorr will know you're a trusted servant of the throne."

It was a lovely green length of soft cloth. A swirling letter 'I' had been embroidered in the center with silver thread. Fletch scanned around; the others wore theirs around their upper arms. To avoid fumbling with it, she draped it around her neck and tied it in the back so the 'I' could be clearly seen over her collarbone.

Captain Norland clapped her on the back, beaming proudly. "You're one of us, now, lass," he said.

As she pressed her chin to her chest, peering down at the sash, warmth expanded in Fletch's heart. 'By majority vote', the Captain had said. At least three of them had banded together on her behalf. Seeing the warm faces of Aeda, Harrild, and Matteo, a grateful smile curved her lips. "Thank you," she said, looking at each of them in turn. "All of you."

"You deserve this honor," Aeda replied, a rare grin glimmering on her sharp face. "We simply recognize your hard word and devotion to the protection of Ivenhence."

"Couldn't have said it better," Matteo agreed.

Darvick shifted, shooting Matteo a dark glare. "If this ambitious young buck can be made a Sentinel, you certainly can," he grunted, then, abruptly, stuck out his hand. Meeting Fletch's eye, he added reluctantly, "Welcome, Wyndshaper. Glad to have you."

She shook, the strength of the hand that clasped hers pushing her smile even wider. Even Darvick had voted for her?

"One more thing." The Captain turned and glanced at Aeda, who nodded. "Since ye're now one of the Sentinels, ye're to have one day each week to yourself, as the others do. Your day of rest is today."

"But—"

"You are young," Aeda interrupted, "and you need your rest just as we do. I shall take your watch today. Go and enjoy the fresh air the storm brought to us."

"Right you are," Norland said. "Get you on your way, then, Wyndshaper."

Before she could duck out the door, Matteo took her hand in a hearty clasp, clean-shaven face beaming. "Well done, Fletch."

"Your trust in me shan't be wasted, I promise," she called past Norland's shoulder as he ushered her firmly out the door.

As it thudded shut behind her, Fletch stood before the door, allowing her eyes to re-adjust to the bright sunlight. Above, the clouds were clearing, fleeing across the azure blue expanse from the fiery sun which beamed warmly down upon the Hearth. Lifting her face to the gentle breeze that drifted over the castle wall, Fletch took a deep, full breath.

"Looks like you've pulled the wool over everyone's eyes."

As a pin to a bubble, the flat voice deflated the joy in Fletch's chest. She turned to meet the cold grey eyes of Parfeln Holden.

The displeasure in the aged man's wrinkled sallow face was all too clear. Her basest instinct wanted to taunt him, to throw her avoidance of his test at his feet like a challenge. But that would only bring her down to his level. So instead, she smiled blithely, commenting, "'Tis turning out to be a rather balmy morning, don't you think?"

He didn't reply. Arms crossed tight across his narrow chest, Parfeln's gaze narrowed into a glower.

"Right then." Shrugging, Fletch turned to leave. "Pleasant day to you."

"You can't trick me, gypsy-girl." The hiss halted her footsteps, drawing her eyes back to him. His lips were tight, jaw jutting as he spat, "I remember whose daughter you are."

It took Fletch several moments to process Parfeln's words. Upon the utterance of 'gypsy-girl' and 'whose daughter you are', the world had gone strangely still and quiet.

Before she could respond, he continued, "Norland may be fool enough to believe your tales of monsters and special powers, but he's always been a superstitious dolt. Were I captain, you'd be sent on your merry way back to the forest where you dreamed up these schemes."

A roiling ball of liquid fire ignited in her belly. Fists curling at her sides, the blaze spread through her entire being, tingling through her ears. "Were you captain," she heard herself say, her voice raw and low. "How long have you been a Sentinel, Parfeln? Thirty years, or longer? Certainly long enough to have been considered for the role of captain before Norland Wyntersoul was chosen, and yet here we are." Through gritted teeth, she growled, "Captain Norland is a good man — stern, smart, brave, and kind.

He's exactly the sort of man that makes an excellent leader. Unlike you. If you have some complaint against me, lodge it and be done. Don't hint like a spineless wyrm. And don't bring Captain Norland into it."

The watery eyes blinked, but otherwise there was no reaction. "You spread lies of the Unbreathing and your ability to see them to wheedle your way closer to the king," Parfeln said matter-of-factly. "Such a thing would never have been allowed in Ilumence, but then again, 'tis a nation of pride and tradition." His lips parted as if to add a final thought, but he bit the words off, teeth baring in a snarl. "And a castle guard died for the sake of your lie. Did Klep think he was doing you a service, pretending to be possessed? What payment did you promise him? Why did you decide to silence him? Couldn't risk the truth getting out?"

Fletch simply stared.

How in Luminia's name could she be expected to answer queries based on such a level of delusion? How could she begin to reason with someone so determined to hate her they'd convinced themselves every word she said was a lie?

Straightening, she frowned down at the slender man, realizing for the first time how much taller she was than he. "If you refuse to see the truth, I can't force you to," she told him, the molten lump in her gut slowly cooling into lead. "And if you haven't listened to my words before, you shan't now."

Astonished outrage surged to Parfeln's face as Fletch turned on her heel and strode quickly away.

That morning had been a busy one for the king. Although he'd quickly finished daily hearings in the throne hall, his attention had instantly been commanded. A messenger knelt before the throne, presenting three scrolls. One was from Verenshire; it announced the departure of the trade caravan to Herstshire. The second was far more elegant. Wrapped in wax-coated parchment and sapphire silk ribbon, it was sealed with the royal crest of Ilumence, a heart lit with flame.

A message from Morthan.

Dreythan didn't open it immediately. Tucking the messages into the folds of his cloak, he made his way to the library where Brinwathe ushered him into the private study. Throat tight, he sat and broke the blue seal.

To King Dreythan Dreythas-son, rightful ruler of Ivenhence and our cousin,

I thank you for your prompt and insightful reply to my plea for help. Your counsel was sound, and gave me such encouragement as I have not had since my father's death. So invigorated was I that I immediately set to work on dividing Ilumence into quarters on a map.

After several days of tireless research and scribbling in scrolls, I presented a proposal to my three advisors. They did not take kindly to my ideas, pointing out that my father had ruled successfully over Ilumence for thirty-seven years without having to make changes to the manner in which justice is done.

I do not understand what they want from me; I am not my father, and cannot rule Ilumence in this manner. I wish to be close to my people, not to see them through a veil of advisors. Why can I not make the law more malleable and approachable to the citizens of this kingdom?

To add to this, a missive arrived from Thissa days ago from its dictator Gorvannon. He demands that we reopen trade routes to and from Thissa, hinting at aggressive actions if I am to decline.

My vexation only equals my helplessness. Were the roads to and from Thissa more hospitable, were the danger of the route itself not so immense, I would consider re-opening a trade agreement with Thissa. But when an assigning a merchant to a trade route practically sentences them to death, I cannot begin to justify it.

This is our point of grievance with the Isles of Aden. The Merchants Guild wishes ready access to the resources unique to Thissa, and have been pressuring Ilumence to reopen the routes there. As a result of my declination, our relations have been less hospitable as of late.

As to the Merchants Guild, I find it concerning that they threaten to end trade routes through Ivenhence. This could greatly affect my own merchants' routes or expectations of trade in your kingdom as well. Will you also ask Ilumence for an adjusted trade agreement? With the current state of my reign, I am uncertain that trade negotiations would be successful.

If only you were here, my cousin. It would be simple to draft a system together that would convince even the shriveled hearts of the advisors to change, or plot a trade plan that would not risk the lives of brave merchants.

I shall await your reply.
Morthan Morthas-son

Several minutes passed, in which Dreythan stared unseeing down at the missive he'd just read. Eventually, he rolled it back up and set it aside, mind still whirling as his hand closed around the third scroll. He snapped the black seal and spread the parchment open. The words on the parchment were penned in a hand he'd never seen. Thick, blocky, and wide, the letters marched across the paper in perfect phalanxes.

King Dreythan of Ivenhence,

After fifteen years without a word regarding the trade routes Ivenhence closed, you ask to reopen them? I decline your offer. There are no advantages to developing relations with the kingdom of Ivenhence. You possess no unique resources and can't offer shorter passage to our current allies.

Unless this reality changes, amicable silence is expected.
-Gorvannon, High Commander of Thissa

Over time, Dreythan had come to learn that the best way to process difficult information was to allow it to settle in gradually. Tucking the scrolls under his arm, he frowned down at his boot tips as they carried him absently out of the library and down the cobblestone path.

Adjusting the heavy mass of cream cotton around her legs, Fletch took a deep breath. "Why must I torment myself so," she grumbled. Craning to peer over her shoulder, she cinched the cord lacing the back of the dress and tried her hardest to tie a neat bow. It ended up slightly lopsided. With a sigh and a shrug, she tied her Sentinel's sash around her neck and glanced once more in the mirror.

It had been a while since she'd seen Petrecia. Since beginning training with the Sentinels in earnest, she'd never gotten a chance to thank her for her patience and kindness. The most meaningful way to do so would be to wear a dress and speak properly, to show her that Fletch had taken her lessons to heart.

Resisting the urge to pick up her bow and quiver, Fletch let herself out of her quarters. The walk from the Garden Wall to the Wyntersoul home only took a few minutes. Even so, she passed a group of kitchen maids who were walking towards the servants quarters. She expected them to stare and perhaps giggle. But instead they met her eye and smiled. One of them even went to far as to say, "Pleasant day, Miss Wyndshaper."

"Pleasant day," Fletch replied, startled. The young woman's eyes strayed to the knife belted at Fletch's waist and the sash around her neck, but her smile didn't waver.

Realizing she was also smiling, Fletch allowed it to widen to a grin. Perhaps the people of Iventorr were growing used to her. Pausing outside the Wyntersoul home, she knocked thrice on the door.

A few moments passed and no one answered. Fletch decided against knocking again; the interior of the home was small enough that anyone could have heard.

Not knowing what else to do, she found her feet wandering

back towards her quarters. Were she in the forest, she would use any free day to visit Herstshire or explore new deer trails. Occasionally she used the time to observe the wildlife and their curious ways. But here in the castle, she was at a loss. How did one whittle a day away when surrounded by stone walls?

When she reached her room and saw the bare stone box filled with furniture, she grimaced. Snatching her father's journal from the table, she shut the door behind her once again and hurried down the hall and steps to the royal garden. Settling into the old rope swing, away from the sun's sweltering rays, she opened the book over her knees and found the entry where she'd left off.

The first two logs were much the same as the past twenty, the words a monotone of emotionless statements. Memories that were shadows of deeds with no flavor or feeling. But when Fletch turned the page, her heart already beginning to ache for her father, her eye fell on an unusually long entry. It filled several pages, front to back. Intrigued, Fletch bent closer, fingers pressed to her lips as she read;

The ninety-ninth year of Ohnaedris, the third week of autumn

It has now been nigh on thirty-three years since the defeat of the Crimson Horde and their master. Yesterday evening, the strangest thing occurred. Whilst waiting for the king in the garden, I heard someone approaching. The Wynd shifted with their footsteps, stirring the leaves in a whispering melody. When they appeared, I did not recognize the intruder, and so confronted them. It was a young woman, her brown eyes deep and wise beyond her years. Her name was Fiorelle.

Fletch's heart plummeted through her stomach. Swallowing hard, she forced herself to keep reading.

When I asked her why she trespassed in the royal garden, she replied that she was a stranger to the land, being of the Wyndarin and on her Wandering quest. She gracefully apologized for the intrusion, and allowed me to escort her to the Garden Wall. I have not seen her since, but word has drifted about the castle of a visiting gypsy woman in Verenshire. It has been many years indeed since I last saw another of the Wynd-blood, though I did not have the chance to tell her of my heritage.

My lord Dreythas took me aside today and instructed me to elect one of the Foresters as their leader. Apparently, I am stretching myself too thin. I admit that he is right; there is only so much one man can do. Thus, Norland Wyntersoul shall be made the Foresters' Head. He has proved his worth many times over to the village of Darmator, and will do well as a leader.

Whilst guarding the royal tower today, I watched Lady Ivy and young Dreythan cavort about the king's desk. He laughed, his greying hair glinting in the sun that shone through the window. It occurred to me how old the king is, and conversely, how old I am.

I had not thought of it until today. My mind has been devoted to serving and protecting the king. But now that it turns inward, in my heart I find an emptiness. Perhaps I am too old now to dream of it, but I wonder if 'tis still possible to be wed and to have love and a family of my own.

I left the royal family under the Sentinels' watch, finding my sudden burden too heavy. The garden called to me, a crisp, clear breeze pulling me to the trees and to the flowers. I followed it and now sit in the midst of the greenery. 'Tis soothing here. I can think more clearly.

How can I express this to the king? I know without any doubt that if I were to ask to leave the castle, he would grant it to me without hesitation if it meant my happiness. But I cannot leave Iventorr; I have sacrificed too much and fought too hard to leave now. However, none of the women in Iventorr have held any interest for me. They are pleasant and wonderful in their individual ways, but there is no one that I fancy, nor do I know of any who are unwed that would fancy a man of such age as myself.

One thing is for certain. I would rather spend my life in solitary service to the king than marry a woman who I do not truly care for, or one who does not feel anything for me.

It is strange. I feel as though I have been living asleep for many years. The pain of losing so many dear friends in the Battle of Reclamation dulled me. I never wished to experience that agony again, and I see now

that I shut myself off because of it.
The Wynd has awakened me, I believe.

Closing the book on one finger, Fletch frowned down at her pinched, perspiring feet. Mind far away, she removed her boots and stockings, burying her toes in the soft white flowers below the swing. She'd known the journal would contain mentions of her mother. Of course she had. But for Kell to write so clearly after first meeting her, after years of numbness and shadow…

She must have made an incredible impression on him.

The rising tide of nausea forced Fletch to shut her eyes tight, and she swallowed hard.

Chapter 16

Dreythan meandered aimlessly along the stone path, hands folded at his back as he gazed unseeing at the ground passing beneath his feet. How could he even begin to respond to such a missive? His cousin sounded at the edge of breaking. His reply would have to be carefully worded. Not only would he have to reassure Morthan of the stability of Ivenhence's agreement with Ilumence, but also of the same between Ivenhence and the Isles. And he would have to do so in such a way that sounded confident, but not condescending.

A blur of red fur flashed in front of his feet, nearly tripping him. Skittering up a tree trunk to pause on a branch, it chittered angrily down at him, bushy tail thrashing. Dreythan stared up at the fearless squirrel, his heart slowly settling back into its normal pace.

"You gave me quite the start," he told the creature, who promptly scurried away.

Shaking his head, he resumed his pace, this time with purpose.

It was a lovely day, despite the humidity. He entered the garden gates as a breeze drifted over the wall, carrying the sweet scent of apple blossoms. Ahead, the ancient oak tree spread its gnarled roots like an old man pushing fingers into the soil. Sitting in the worn rope swing in the shadows of the tree's canopy, surrounded by thousands of tiny white flowers, was Fletch.

At first glance he didn't recognize her. When he did, he started, then stared. He'd never seen her in a dress before. It was light blue, completely devoid of lace or frills, a thick cream petticoat peeking from beneath. A green sash was draped around her neck, and her hunting knife was belted around her waist. Her shoes had been discarded and sat at the base of the oak tree with her stockings inside them.

She hadn't noticed him. She wasn't swinging, but simply sitting in the swing with her bare toes touching the white buds. One hand clutched a worn leather-bound book, the other pressed to her temple.

He hesitated. She looked troubled, her expression pinched and pale. The sight made his throat tighten. Swallowing, Dreythan fought between turning on his heel and stepping forward, and nearly lost his balance. His heel rustled through the flowers.

Fletch's hand dropped from her face. Her startled gaze flashed to his. "My lord?"

Heat rushed to his ears. "I am sorry to disturb you, Fletch," he said, bowing stiffly. "I shall leave you be."

But Fletch stopped him with a smile. "To be honest, I'd be glad for the company."

"Ah. Then I am glad to have provided it." Suddenly unsure of how to hold his hands, Dreythan tucked them behind his back again as he took a few steps forward into comfortable conversing distance. "Might I ask what is troubling you?"

Fletch's forehead creased again. Her eyes dropping to the book in her lap, her head cocked to one side. "Something I've avoided thinking about for far too long," she replied. The sorrow and doubt in her voice surprised him. "I shan't be able to skirt it any longer, it seems. 'Tis as inevitable as the setting of the sun."

Meeting his eye, she smiled ruefully. "I'm sorry, my lord. That wasn't much of an explanation. I've been thinking about my mother."

"You've spoken of her before. She is a gypsy, is she not?"

"Indeed she is, though her people call themselves Wyndarin." Her gaze grew distant. "They don't usually correct those who call them gypsies because, in a sense, they are. But they take great pride in their identity as Wyndarin. According to their histories, just as Ivere and Ohnaedris created humans from the Hearth, so Luminia created Wyndarin from the Wynd. They believe 'tis why the vast majority of us have some form of affinity to the Wynd and seas."

Fletch had unconsciously excluded herself from her mother's people, Dreythan noted. "I see," he mused. "It must be difficult, only seeing your mother once every seven years."

Pain flashed across Fletch's face as sharp and sudden as if he'd stabbed her. "I haven't seen my mother since I was five years old, my lord." Not meeting his eye, she added, "I'm not certain I'll make myself known to her when the Wyndarin inevitably pass through on their septennial journey."

Stunned, Dreythan simply stared. Why would she wish to avoid her own mother? Why hadn't she seen her in over fifteen years? Not knowing what to say, he fumbled for comforting words and utterly failed to find them.

His expression must have shown his confusion. Fletch's cheeks flushed, tears springing to her eyes. "Surely you understand," she pleaded. "Don't you remember?"

"I must not, for I surely do not," he replied. It was foolish, but he'd never thought it was possible to see such raw emotion on Fletch's round face. She always presented herself with such confidence... It wrenched his heart to see her like this. Vulnerable.

Hand rising again to her brow, Fletch blinked hard, taking a long, deep breath. "My lord," she sighed finally. "My mother's name is Fiorelle. She left my father and I when I was five to ascend to her throne — the throne of the Wyndarin."

At those words, several puzzles at once fell into focus in Dreythan's mind. He blinked, disoriented by the sudden clarity. "Ah." He swallowed. "I... I do remember... how ignorant I have been. Twice the gypsies — that is, Wyndarin — have graced our land in their travels since I began my rule, and twice I have wondered why Queen Fiorelle appeared so familiar. Now I understand." After a brief hesitation, he asked quietly, "Why would she have left so young a child behind?"

"She didn't simply abandon me." Her slender hand brushed over her face, as if assuring herself she hadn't shed any tears. "'Tis a bit complicated, I suppose. Balance is of upmost importance to the Wyndarin. For each king in the royal line, there's a queen. A father's eldest daughter inherits his rule, and a mother's eldest son inherits hers. An a-gender child can inherit from either king or queen. If there's no daughter from the father, or son from the mother, or if the current ruler is a-gender, then the first-born child of the monarch becomes the next ruler.

"'Tis the Wyndarin coming-of-age passage to send the young king or queen-to-be out into the world at twenty-one years of age to make their own Wandering for seven years. At the end of the seventh year, they return to their people to rule. Such as it was with my mother. But during her time in Ivenhence, she met my father, wed him, and gave birth to me." She dipped her head, fingers twisting together. "When the time came for her to return to her people, I was asked to choose. I could leave with my mother and travel with the Wyndarin, or I could stay in Iventorr with my father."

"That is a heavy decision for anyone to make, let alone for a child so young," Dreythan said. "I take it you chose to stay with your father?"

She nodded. "After he died, I felt... forgotten," she admitted. "When I was young, I resented Mother for not returning to see Papa buried. Most of all, I was hurt she didn't come back for me." Ducking her head, she chuckled ruefully. "Sometimes, I still find myself asking, why did she never return? Why did she not seek me out when the Wyndarin passed through Ivenhence?" She shrugged. "Perhaps when I chose to remain with Father, she took it as a declination to have her in my life at all." Abruptly, something in her expression snapped. "But my actions did nothing but widen the already vast distance between us." Clearing her throat, Fletch looked up, her smile not quite reaching her eyes. "Forgive me, my lord. I fear I've overshared. Enough of my troubles. Does something trouble you as well?"

Remembering the scrolls tucked under his arm, Dreythan let them fall into his hand. His own uncertainty suddenly felt small and insignificant. He wanted to utter words of understanding and empathy, something that would bolster Fletch's spirits or help in some way. But the too-cheerful mask she'd donned told him she desperately wished to change the subject. "My cousin seems to be in some distress," he told her, handing her the blue-ribboned roll of parchment. "I wish to offer him some measure of help, but I know not how. He has realized the enormity of his ancestors' kingdom and feels the impossible weight of it on his shoulders. In addition—" He frowned, jerking his head at the missive. "Well, you shall see. Read it, please."

Fletch's startled eyes met his. Her lips parted to protest, then closed as she inspected the firm resolve on Dreythan's face. Slowly, she slid the parchment open. Her gaze flitted from side to side as she read, her expression gradually settling. When she re-rolled the letter and handed it back, her forehead held a pensive crease.

"What are your thoughts?" Dreythan prompted when she remained silent.

"'Tis difficult to say," she replied slowly. "It's rather odd that his advisors would be against—" She jolted to her feet, one hand flying to her mouth. "I have completely forgotten my manners," she said, eyes wide. "Wouldn't you like to sit down, my lord?"

Smiling, Dreythan picked up her shoes and stockings in one hand, gesturing to a nearby stone bench. "Certainly." They crossed to it, and Dreythan sat, setting the footwear in the grass between them. "Go on."

"Er, yes." Fletch peered at the shoes, a flush creeping over her ears. "As I was saying, I don't understand why his advisors would be opposed to testing change. Do they not understand that Morthan's effectiveness on the throne affects the well-being of the entire nation? One would think they'd support their new king, especially in a venture to possibly improve his reign." Finally transferring her gaze back to meet Dreythan's eye, she added quietly, "But the short paragraph regarding Thissa troubles me most."

The king nodded, his lips pressed in a sober line. "It troubles me as well. Especially considering this other scroll—" he tapped it on his knee "—is from Gorvannon, declining my offer to reopen trade between Thissa and Ivenhence."

Her eyes glinted. "Why in Luminia's name would they demand trade with Ilumence when they turned away Ivenhence?"

"Gorvannon's missive made his reasoning quite clear. He holds a grudge against us for severing trade routes with Thissa fifteen years ago."

"As did Ilumence, and yet he threatens them, not us." She tossed her hands in the air. "Why?"

"It is because Ivenhence injured his pride," Dreythan told her matter-of-factly. "We were and still are little more than an infant nation in comparison to Thissa, or to Ilumence, or even to the Isles of Aden. Cutting our trade routes with Thissa halved our export and import. It could have crippled us. Ilumence's trade routes were of little consequence to her. With such a well of resources at her disposal already, the loss of the trade routes would have been little more than an inconvenience to a handful of merchants and craftsmen." Stooping, he plucked a moss-speckled stone and a pebble from the dirt beneath the bench, holding one in each palm. "For example, removing this small patch of moss from this stone shan't effect it. However, if you removed the same amount of moss from the pebble, it would practically be naked."

"I see." Fletch took the pebble from his hand, exchanging it for the scroll. "Ilumence is the stone, and Ivenhence is the pebble?" Tapping her lips with one finger, she frowned thoughtfully down at the green fuzz-covered rock. "Thissa provided much more, proportionally, to Ivenhence than to Ilumence... and yet Ivenhence cut trade routes just as quickly. Perhaps... perhaps the Thissian dictator felt slighted."

"Precisely."

Fletch lifted her head, frown clearing as a twinkling smile rose to her cheeks. "That reminds me. I'm glad the ambassador accepted your trade proposal."

"As am I," Dreythan agreed. It struck him how perfectly Fletch's eyes matched the vivid moss in her palm and the emerald sash around her neck.

"You're now one of the Sentinels," Dreythan realized aloud, a foolish grin spreading itself across his face. "Congratulations!"

"Thank you." She smiled back, fingers absently straightening the silver embroidery. "I'm honored to be counted among them." Bending, she plucked the stockings from her shoes, cinnamon hair swinging over her reddened face.

"Wait, Fletch." A breeze rustled the tree limbs above them. Raising his head to watch the leaves stir, he added, "You need not cover your feet if you do not wish to. The gyp— that is, the Wyndarin do not wear boots at all, but open sandals."

Slowly, Fletch straightened, carefully avoiding his eye as she placed her shoes and stockings on the bench beside them. "I do savor the feel of the Wynd between my toes," she admitted. "Perhaps they feel the same."

Dreythan glanced at her, smiling as he realized she hadn't called him 'my lord' for several minutes. Seeing her face fall as she thought about the Wyndarin, and her mother, his heart clenched painfully. "Do not worry overmuch about your mother, Fletch," he told her gently. "It shall be a few more years before their next passage through Ivenhence."

A small smile softened her face, but it didn't quite reach her eyes. "You're right, of course. Thank you, my lord."

"Do not thank me, Fletch." It wasn't enough. His hands tightened around the scrolls, like they might on the reigns of a wild horse as he tried to slow his racing thoughts. "Your presence here in Iventorr has allowed me to be at such peace as I have not felt since my father's passing," he said, wishing he had more to offer her than words. "I have infinite cause to thank you." Standing, he brushed off the back of his cloak, then paused. "When the time comes, should you wish me speak to your mother on your behalf, it would be my honor. But if you prefer to maintain your distance, I shall not mention your presence. In any case, your wish shall be my command."

This time the smile rose, warm and bright, to her lips. "I truly appreciate that, my lord," she said quietly. "I'm not certain what that might look like... but I'll keep it in mind. Thank you."

"Of course. Pleasant day you, Fletch. I must take my leave."

"Pleasant day, my lord."

With that, he turned and strode away, already composing a reply to his cousin in his mind.

Heading directly to the library, Dreythan shut himself in the small study. Nearly breaking his nib with the fervor of his hand, he wrote:

To King Morthan Morthas-son, rightful ruler of Ilumence and our cousin,

Having never had advisors to council decisions or to broach subjects with, I am afraid I have little context to the frustration you must be experiencing. However, I find it unthinkable your counselors would be so out of touch with your kingdom as to oppose the possibility for positive change. To remain the same is to stagnate, and to stagnate is to wither. If they cannot understand this, perhaps it is time for them to retire and for more forward-thinking individuals to take their places.

As to Gorvannon and Thissa, the demand for renewed trade may be a result of our recent communication. In our attempts to revitalize the overlooked cities and hamlets of Ivenhence, I sent a missive to Thissa inquiring after the possibility of reopening trade routes. Gorvannon's reply was resounding: utter disdain. He pointed out Ivenhence's lack of consideration for the need of those routes a decade and a half ago. I believe he still holds a grudge against Ivenhence for the collapse of Thissa's trade. It is likely he demands renewed trade with Ilumence now to throw salt in the wound of his declination. For this, I am sorry. It was not my intent for Ilumence to be dragged into the spectacle of trade disputes between our nations. I can only hope that gifts and gentle diplomacy shall eventually soften Gorvannon's iron heart.

Thankfully, my news of the Merchants Guild is not so grim.

Penning a quick summary of the accepted proposal, Dreythan hurried on.

In the interest of fairness, both to my citizens and the merchants of the Guild, I believe Ilumence's current trade agreement should also be renegotiated in this manner. Perhaps not identical to the Isles of Aden's, but similar, especially in the regard of the frequency of reports, collection, and record-keeping. However, I understand your plight. Such a negotiation can take place once Ilumence is in a more stable position.

Do not despair, cousin. Though my words be the only assistance I can provide, know that I stand beside you in mind and in spirit. You are not alone. If I can provide further assistance, you have only to ask.

Dreythan Dreythas-son

Leaning back, Dreythan eyed the parchment critically, then nodded. Giving Morthan the choice to change the tax agreement now or later would assure him of Ivenhence's intentions. And learning the Merchants' Guild of Aden had accepted Ivenhence's proposal would likely go a long way towards assuaging Morthan's fears.

Picking aimlessly at the plate of food in front of her, Fletch eyed the cluster of guards that always sat one table over, the group Klep had invited her to join. It had been eleven days since she'd spoken with Dreythan in the garden, since she'd realized aloud how isolated and alone she felt. The thought had followed her since, like a storm cloud she couldn't shape away. If only she'd plucked up the courage to accept Klep's offer when he'd extended it. Were she to ask to join them now, his friends would feel obligated to say yes, and obligation was a burden. She had no wish to force her presence where it wasn't sought.

A shadow fell across the table. Heart leaping into her throat, Fletch looked up into a pair of brown eyes —

But they weren't brown. They were hazel. "Pleasant day, Fletch," Harrild said with a kind smile. "Might I sit here?"

"Of course," she replied. Gulping back the lump in her throat, she asked, "Anything I ought to be aware of before we begin our watch?"

"Not particularly." He paused, then chuckled. "Though there could be a bit of a stir this afternoon. You've heard that Ambassador Kekona is arranging the construction of a road between Herstshire and Northcrag. Well, the foreman of the project is apparently loathe to take direction from her and shall bring his complaint to the king. Can you imagine the expression on the king's face when he hears?"

She shook her head, but Harrild didn't seem to notice, already pleasantly droning on. Turning to her plate, Fletch frowned. Alicianna Kekona was everywhere. In the past ten days, Fletch had seen her twice as many times. Drifting through the streets to the guest tower, visiting the library to converse with Anshwell, conferring with Dreythan in the throne hall. No matter where she went, she carried a presence with her, an impressiveness that caused heads to turn. Perhaps it was the way she held her gold-braided, jewel-studded head, giving her an air of command. Or perhaps it was the grace with which she moved, her body shifting effortlessly like waves on the ocean. But then, it could be the rich clothing she wore, embroidered and gem-spangled velvets and silks that trailed behind her in a breeze that always seemed present.

Whatever it was, the presence made Fletch utterly aware of how tall and awkward she was, of how abrupt and disjointed her movement felt, of the trousers and cuirass that emphasized her skinny frame. She grimaced down at her cup, taking a large gulp.

"—and then," Harrild was laughing, "Parfeln says, 'Aeda, you ought to be ashamed. A young sprout of a Sentinel, and already more accurate with a bow than you?' and Aeda replies, 'You ought to be doubly ashamed! I did defeat you in last year's archery match!'"

Fletch managed a light-hearted grin before shoving a forkful of ham into her mouth.

"Fletch, you're not yourself this morning. Are you all right?"

Forcing her eyes to meet Harrild's concerned hazel ones, she replied honestly, "I didn't sleep well."

"Ah." He nodded, gaze dropping to the table. "The full moon. I understand."

Throat catching, she, too, looked down. One full moon after Klep's death, and she hadn't even realized. Her gut curled into a tight ball of jagged ice.

Harrild glanced up at the table where the king sat, pushing himself upright. "His Majesty is nearly finished," he said. "We'd best get into position."

Together they hid in their usual places behind the dining hall. When the king and Captain Norland emerged, they followed them to the throne hall, and Fletch climbed up into her loft.

As Dreythan settled into his throne, the Captain posted to one side, Fletch rubbed her eyes, pinching her cheeks to alertness. The previous night, she had lain in bed, staring upward as the bright moon had risen higher in the velvet sky. Though no defined thoughts had crossed her mind, no relaxation came. Only a sense of tension and uncertainty.

When she'd finally fallen asleep, there had been no peace. A pale face had hovered behind her in the darkness, accompanied by the stench of rust and salt. The hollow maw kept ravenously moaning her name, over and over.

Then there had been another face, one that looked a bit like hers, fuzzy and painfully familiar. She'd tried to reach out, to warn them away from the thing that haunted her, but the queenly visage had turned away from her, a cold blankness in her eyes.

Shuddering, Fletch shook herself and returned her attention below.

"Your crime, Harstan," Dreythan was saying, raising one hand to gesture to the man on his left, "was lying to your neighbor and to Kleft Ironshod regarding the amount of damage Thelnor's cow did to your crop. Your statement was clearly an exaggeration."

Fletch swallowed. Had Dreythan said... Ironshod? Was he kin to Klep?

Turning to the man on his right, Dreythan continued, "And your crime, Thelnor, was not realizing your animal had broken free and was roaming over the farmlands surrounding your village." His gaze leveled sternly to his left. "One of these crimes was an accident. One was not. Guards!"

The two guards who had ushered the men in stepped forward.

"Take Farmer Harstan to Verenshire town square stock. He shall receive three lashes for falsehood to Ingling's overseer." The guards saluted and promptly left, firmly escorting the man along between them. "Thelnor, you are free to go. There shall be no punishment for you at this time. However," he added, "Be sure that this does not happen again. If it does, you shall be held responsible for the lost crops."

Thelnor bowed his head gratefully, then hurried out.

A hushed conversation passed between Dreythan and Captain Norland as the guards ushered the next waiting petitioner down the aisle. The man between the guards was tall, brown-skinned, and well-built, dressed in brightly dyed embroidered robes without sleeves. His red-gold hair was gathered at the base of his neck in a beaded cord, and his face was clean-shaven. A wrapped parcel rested in his hands.

"My lord," one guard announced. "A messenger from Queen Fiorelle of the gyspy people."

Fletch's heart dropped into her toes.

"King Dreythan Dreythas-son." The man dropped to one knee. "My name is Ranar. My queen sends her greetings and good wishes, and presents this to your Majesty as an offering of peace."

A guard brought the package to the king. As he placed it in Dreythan's hands, the painted violet silk wrapping fell away like flower petals blooming open.

Within lay a silken silver-green garment of some kind. Dreythan inspected it silently for several moments, running his hand over the cloth. "Your queen has my deepest thanks," he murmured. "It is a most thoughtful and beautiful gift."

Ranar bowed his head. "I shall convey your words to my queen, King Dreythan. Our people have made landfall at Port Lunalin in Ilumence. Queen Fiorelle requests your assent to enter your kingdom in three weeks' time."

"Queen Fiorelle has it," Dreythan replied after only a moment's hesitation. "Please convey that she is welcome in Ivenhence, as are the rest of the Wyndarin people. If it please her, she is welcome to stay here in Iventorr's guest tower, as she has previously."

The messenger bowed even deeper before rising. "I thank you on behalf of my queen," he murmured, and was ushered out.

Fletch stared after him, her hands gripping the rail of her perch as the world went numb. Several minutes passed, the heightened wump wump of her heartbeat the only sound that reached her ears as her lungs compressed, so tight and filled with needles she could barely breathe without choking.

Surely she had fallen asleep at her post. Surely this was simply another nightmare, taunting her with its cruel semblance of reality. Any moment, she would wake in her quarters, cursing another night of little sleep.

But as the king finished with another citizen below, and as the quiet murmuring of the waiting crowd drifted up to her, as Wynd drifted lazily through the arches and arcades supporting the stone ceiling, it became clear she wasn't dreaming. It was too vivid to be anything but real.

The silver-green cloth bundle still rested on the king's knees.

A wave of nausea rushed up her throat, and she swallowed just in time.

The rest of the day passed in a hazy blur. As Fletch and Harrild trailed the king into the dining hall, Captain Norland intercepted them with a gauntleted hand. "Come," he said. "The rest of the royal guard await us in the tower."

Within minutes, they were ducking through the door of the Sentinels' tower. Removing his helm, the Captain tucked it under one arm and glanced around. "You're all here — good. I'm keepin' ye from your evening meals," he said shortly, "so I shan't dally words. Ye already heard of the surprise gypsy visit, expected to arrive in three weeks. Since this's off their usual schedule and we're unprepared, we'll need to rehearse our change of duties during the fourth afternoon hour each day when the king takes his supper, beginning tomorrow." His blue eyes pierced Fletch's for one brief moment. Turning away, he met each guards' eye before barking, "Dismissed! All except ye, Wyndshaper."

The others filed out slowly, quietly grumbling to each other. Fletch tugged her shoulders as straight as possible, trying not to let her eyelids droop. "Yes, Captain?"

"Over here, lass." He gestured to a table in the corner, upon which sat a cloth covering a large overturned basket. "Take a seat."

She slid uncertainly into a chair. Norland couldn't chastise her for looking tired, could he? Straightening even further, she did her best to look alert.

The Captain took the seat across from her, lifting the cloth and basket away to reveal two heaping plates of roast beef, potatoes, and carrots.

Fletch's stomach let out a painful gurgle. She cast a questioning glance at Norland, who was already picking up a fork.

"Tuck in," he grunted. "And quit thinking I'm going to

reprimand ye. Just eat, and we'll talk in a bit."

"Oh. Yes, sir."

Several minutes of near silence passed; the only sound was the gentle clinking of cups hitting tabletop and forks tapping plates.

"The caravan from Herstshire arrived in Verenshire today," Norland said finally. "A messenger asked for directions t' your quarters. I think there's a delivery waiting for ye."

"A delivery?" Fletch repeated hopefully. Perhaps the Prudens had written her another letter! "Do you know if the caravan did much business in Herstshire?"

He nodded, spearing a half potato on his knife. "Aye," he mumbled around a large bite. "They came back laden with casks of ale. And from what I understand, an elbecca farmer's planning to move out to Herstshire from Elmenger so's to be closer to the new trade route. That should bring a fair bit of business to the town, what with the milk and wool the creatures produce."

The thought brought a smile to Fletch's face. "The town would be glad for an elbecca farm," she said. "They've been hurting for a source of fiber and dairy for a good long while."

"Did I ever tell ye I visited Herstshire once?" When Fletch shook her head, Norland set his fork down to glance distantly out the tower window. "It reminded me of home, in a way," he said. "The snow everywhere, the biting cold and constant gusts of Wynd. A tight-knit village struggling as well as they knew how to get by. Thin bodies in patched clothes." His jaw twitched, blue eyes clouded and grey. "I wasn't there long... But I've often wished my father'd been able to see the town. Maybe then he'd realize that the Wynterhead Clan and those here in Ivenhence aren't so different." Shoulders heaving in a sigh, he added, "It's been twenty-five years since last I saw my family, lass. I... I can't imagine what I'd feel at the possibility of seeing my mother or father again." Turning back to Fletch, he soberly met her gaze, propping one elbow on the table. "How are ye holding up?"

It took several moments for the words to fully sink in. She stared at him, numb with shock. "How am I holding up," she repeated. Surely she hadn't understood correctly.

The Captain's eyes remained steady. "Aye," he said. "I'm worried about ye. What with the sudden announcement of a Wyndarin visit and the loss of your friend... It'd be a lot for anyone to handle. I want to make sure you're all right."

Fletch still didn't answer, too stunned to even attempt a stammer, but Norland didn't break eye contact. Concern was etched deep into each line of his face, even down to the set of his mouth beneath his bushing whiskers.

"I haven't thought much about... about my mother today," she heard herself murmur. Chest tightening, she forced herself to look away. "I don't think it's fully set in yet. It feels surreal. I've been reading my father's journal, and his memories of how he met her. I thought I was doing well, reading those passages despite the painful memories they stirred, but..." She tried to chuckle, but it died in her throat. "Now I don't know. And it's been difficult to sleep... My mind spins each time I try to rest. When I finally do fall asleep, my dreams are nightmares."

"I know what ye mean about it setting in," the Captain said. "It might take a few days, and that's all right."

Fetch straightened. "I don't have a few days. Every hour I'm distracted on duty, Dre— the king's safety decreases."

"Don't think that way," Norland interjected. One thick finger tapped the table, punctuating his words. "Don't be too hard on yourself, Fletch. Ye've been through more in one season than most endure in years."

"I know. But I can't allow that to detract from—"

The expression on Norland's face stopped her. He tugged a scarred hand through his massive bush of a beard. "You're allowed to be human, ye know," he told her. "You're allowed to feel, to think, to struggle, Fletch. We all do, whether we like to admit it or not."

The kindness in his rumbling voice was too much. She dropped her head, the tightness in her lungs claiming her throat. "It's easier to pretend I don't have time to feel," she said hoarsely. Her fingers ached from twisting so tightly together. "Less painful."

"No, it isn't, and ye know it."

She sensed him shift in his chair, but she didn't look up. Suddenly and uncomfortably aware of every fiber of her body, Fletch felt the droop of her eyelids and shoulders, the sting of tears her eyes wouldn't shed, the twinge of pain in her anxiously braided fingers. Too tense to breathe, her lungs drew short, shallow gasps, her throat burning. For the first time in her life, she felt old, as if she had seen too much.

"Have ye spoken to anyone about Klep?" Norland's voice asked gently.

The tension in her chest snapped, but rather than the rush of heat she expected, there was nothing. Just an aching, hollow emptiness. "No," she whispered. "I didn't even remember today was the full moon until Harrild mentioned it."

There was a pause, heavy and empty to match the void in Fletch's heart. "He's been gone as many days as I knew him," she said finally. "Yet I still think I hear his voice across the courtyard sometimes, or see his shadow cross the table in the dining hall."

"Ye were the closest friend he ever had in Iventorr, ye know." When she looked up, Norland met her eye with a melancholy smile. "He never got on well with most of the other guards. They teased 'im for being so young, called him an overgrown baby." He shook his head. "He always turned the joke back on the man bullying him, somehow. He was clever, quick-witted."

"And kind," Fletch agreed, thinking of his twinkling eyes and curly halo of hair. "He mistook me for a man at first, as many do. But when he realized his mistake, he... he didn't look at me strangely, or treat me any differently." The tiniest spark of warmth kindled inside her at the memory, and a wobbly smile curved her lips. "And he made sure I didn't eat alone. I think he understood that... that being alone around other people is the worst sort of loneliness."

Her words hung in the air a moment, and she blinked. There Captain Norland sat, one hand clenched around a tankard, eyes still focused carefully on her face. And she knew. He had intentionally arranged the little supper. He hadn't wanted her to eat in the dining hall, haunted by the absence of her friend on the one-moon anniversary of his death.

The warm spark sprang to life, spreading through her chest and up to her eyes. Blinking back tears, she beamed across the table.

It was another half hour before Fletch left the Sentinel tower, striding quickly across the cobbled paths and lush grass to avoid wasting any daylight. The sun had begun its majestic descent to the horizon, lighting the sparse clouds with golden edges and sending a muted rainbow of smoky blues, purples, pinks, and oranges across the sky as she and the Captain had shared memories of Klep Ironshod. Now the sun had nearly set, only shades of lavender and rose blurring into deepest navy near the distant tree line.

As Fletch headed toward her quarters, she remembered Norland's mention of a delivery. Careening up the iron staircase in the Garden Wall, she dashed to her door and flung it open, eye falling on a small keg and a wrapped bundle on her table. Throwing her unstrung bow and quiver onto the bed, she snatched up the parchment beside the bundle, fingers trembling as she carefully ripped it open.

Dearest Fletch,

Jon and I have been dashing about much alike to chickens on plucking day. The merchant caravan has been extremely generous with the good people of Herstshire, trading and buying left and right. We read your letter the first night the caravan arrived, and that has been two days ago now. They leave on the morrow.

I must say, Fletch, that while I am in a flutter to hear that you now have proper dresses to wear, I cannot picture you in one. Have you a bodice to wear over them? I hear that they are all the rage in Ilumence. You can also wear it beneath your armor, dear, so it does not chafe. I would imagine that it is better than binding up your breasts in cloth strips as you so often do.

Grimacing, Fletch hoped that Master Pruden hadn't read that last sentence, but knew it was futile. The handwriting shifted as Fletch kept reading.

'Twas good to read your letter, Fletch. I do wish we could do more to make you feel at home there in Iventorr, but all we can do is send you bits of Herstshire. Missy insisted on sewing a bodice for you, and stayed up last night so as to complete it before the merchants leave us. Also, there's a keg of my finest ale, the one you like best, with mulberry and spice in it, and a mug to—

The writing on the parchment blurred and swam, forcing Fletch to blink and wipe her eyes.

—and a mug to drink it from. I know you've watched me serve ale many a time, so I shan't waste the rest of the parchment telling you how to tap the keg.
We miss you, Fletch. Keep your chin up and your nose clean, and don't you mind what those castle-dwellers think. We here in Herstshire know your worth (which is more than words can possibly say), and they are lucky to have you. Please take care and give Roderick pats for us.

Fletch carefully refolded the letter and placed it with the scroll on top of her drawers, then sat down at her table and unwrapped the cloth parcel. A red clay mug with a slightly chipped handle rolled out into her hands. An image rose in her mind: Master Pruden standing at his counter, laughing and chatting. Smiling, she lifted the bodice out next. White linen lined the center underneath dove grey lacing, and the sides and back were deep blue, the color of storm-dark seas.

In a few moments, she had removed her cuirass and cloth strips and had slipped the odd article over her head. It took several attempts to cinch the cords correctly. Once she had pulled them tight and tied securely, she had to admit the bodice was actually quite comfortable. It was far too beautiful and well-made to bear the thought of staining it with perspiration. A snowball in Kazael's pit would have greater odds of survival than of her wearing the bodice under her armor. She would save it for rare days when she wore a dress.

Would Alicianna Kekona wear such an item? An image of the ambassador rose, swathed in rich fabrics that draped her curve-bestowed form. No, she reflected, her throat tightening. Her clothes were all perfectly fitted, and not of Ivenhence make. Finely crafted structured robes of velvet and silk were more likely to suit her.

What would Dreythan think if he saw Fletch in such a pretty item? The thought made her ears burn furiously. Removing the garment, she folded it and gently placed it in her chest.

"Thank you, Jon, Missy," she murmured to herself as she tapped the little keg. Tipping it over, clay cup in hand, she poured out some of the precious ale.

"You drink ale?" An incredulous voice echoed in the back of her mind, the words imbued with a grin. *"We ought to grab a pint in Verenshire sometime."*

She stared soberly down at the mug for a moment, then lifted it toward the window. With a nod to the full moon, she murmured, "Cheers, Klep."

Swirling the ale around in her cup, she threw it back and drained it in one gulp. The tangy, spice-infused liquid burned pleasantly on its way down her throat.

Chapter 17

The following weeks were a blur of frenzied activity as the castle began preparation for the approaching gypsy visit. Sun jays flocked to and from Iventorr's falconry tower in droves, their vermillion and crimson plumage flashing through the air as they bore messages to and from the Isles of Aden, Ilumence, and major cities within Ivenhence proclaiming the impromptu Wyndarin arrival. Merchants bustled to and from Iventorr and Verenshire, vying to secure spots to set up booths or tents as vendors.

Fights broke out between traders, a couple even coming to fisticuffs. The guards already had enough on their hands rehearsing new patrol routes and shifts and didn't take kindly to the interruptions. Neither did Captain Norland when the guards inevitably brought the quarreling, bruised merchants before him. He dealt with the miscreants swiftly and ruthlessly, banning them both from entering the castle until winter's arrival.

The Sentinels had begun escorting the king more closely, rehearsing the shift in operations during the Wyndarin's stay.

Rather than pattering unseen behind Dreythan, Fletch followed him and the Sentinel swordsman (usually Matteo Alwick) thirty paces behind. It was frequently difficult to track them through the crowds of people that bustled through the streets. A few times, she had no choice but to follow above along the edge of slanting slate roofs. As each day passed, excitement and anticipation grew on people's faces as they chatted and gossiped about what the next few weeks would hold.

"Do you remember the bounty of silks and laces the gypsies brought last time? My mum says there's no better time to buy the makings for a new dress!"

"Jorga Soothand's been stockpiling armor for years. Hopefully we'll get a chance to purchase some of her craftsmanship. It's wasted on the guards. They never see real danger, all nice and tidy within the castle walls."

"Papa, Papa! Benny said the gypsies make candies all the colors of the rainbow! Is that true?? Did you see them before?"

"As fascinating as the gypsies may be, I'm more lookin' forward to the vendors from the Isles o' Aden, m'self. Not the pearls or shells, mind you, but the barrels o' salted fish and strange fruits. A treat for yer mouth, near anythin' from Aden is."

As much as she tried to ignore them, snippets of conversation made their way into Fletch's ears as she wove through the castle, the hustle, bustle, and excitement flowing around her like a rapid river flowing around a lone protruding rock. The words she overheard invited unwanted thoughts to her mind's door. Even though she kept that door firmly locked and shut, the thoughts shouted from the other side, determined to make themselves heard.

Should she try to avoid her mother, or try to make contact with her? If she chose to avoid her, and her mother let her be, there would be no chance to mend things. But if Fletch did try to approach her, and her mother spurned her... things would be broken between them forever.

It was difficult to decide which was worse: eternal uncertainty or decisive division.

The closer the Wyndarin visit drew, the more frequent her nightmares became, filled with images of a face that looked like hers, a face that kept turning impassively away. With each day Fletch's dread built, stretching time into an agonizing eternity.

At last the day of the expected arrival dawned, but Fletch was already long awake, splashing cold water on her shadow-eyed face and staring hollowly into her reflection. After a quick bite of breakfast, she began her shift as usual, trailing Dreythan and Harrild to the throne hall.

Gradually, time inched by, the sky turning from gold to pink to amethyst to azure as the king patiently gave audience to the citizens who had gathered. Just as more people were crammed into Verenshire and Iventorr than usual, so were there more issues for Dreythan to attend to. Disputes over lodging and stable space, heated arguments over merchant licenses, and vendors accusing each other of bribery for favored display locations. Fletch listened to the proceedings as well as she could, keeping her eyes straight ahead as she stood at attention, the sound of her own heart hammering in her ears.

When the sun had fully risen, Torrin the gatekeeper pushed through the doors to announce that the gypsies were approaching the castle bridge.

That was Fletch's cue. Padding down the aisle, she slipped out the throne hall door and around the edge of the building to a set of narrow stone steps. Up she climbed, onto the steep roof of the throne hall itself. She trotted along the slanted surface to the front of the building above the hefty double-doors.

Just in time. They spread wide, an assortment of guards spilling out followed closely by Dreythan, Captain Norland, and Harrild Hammerfist. Immediately turning east, the retinue proceeded by the gardens that separated the throne hall from the welcome and dining halls.

Turning, Fletch sprinted to the other side of the roof where it joined seamlessly with the castle wall. Onto the top of the wall, then south-east she ran, passing guards on duty as she kept the king in sight. For a moment, the trees in the orchard blocked him from her vision. Then she reached the small section of wall over the castle gate, and they were visible again.

A lemon-colored breeze brushed past her ear, pushing her hair forward and carrying with it a light, sweet, strangely familiar scent. Chamomile? Curious, she turned.

Across the immense bridge, gathered on the large hilltop in a crowd of blinding hues, were the Wyndarin people. Fluttering robes of every imaginable color and pattern wrapped loosely around them like the plumage of tropical birds. Above them swirled an immense cylinder of slowly cycloning Wynd. Warm sunny yellows, brilliant orange, and even traces of streaming crimson bore aloft what she first thought were seagulls. But they weren't gulls; they were enormous puffs of white fluff, soft and delicate as whips of cloud. They drifted gently on the ever-flowing circular current of Wynd above the Wyndarin, the lowest fluffs a mere two to three meters above their heads. A few of the Wyndarin at the edges of the crowd lifted their vividly clothed arms, shaping the breeze that carried the strange but delightful things ever aloft.

There weren't as many of them as Fletch had thought there would be. She scanned the distant hill, counting, estimating. Three or four hundred adults? It was difficult to guess with the gaggles of small children running about between them. Men and women alike pulled carts with their bare, muscled arms, though the effort only guided the vehicles. Sails filled with Wynd billowed from the top of each horse-less wagon, propelling them forward.

Many of the Wyndarin had already begun setting up large tents, woven with thread just as bright as their clothing. Swirling lines and shapes danced across the cloth.

The breeze blew past Fletch's face again, calm and soothing. It came from one of the Wyndarin, she realized. They were shaping the Wynd, purposely passing it through the castle gates. Perhaps it was a manner of greeting. Perhaps the figure at their lead was the creator.

Dressed in a silken autumn-red robe, the graceful form seemed to drift rather than walk toward the castle, feet making no sound as she reached the planks of the Great Bridge. Her brown hair hung in loose waves past the small of her back, partly gathered on a golden crown fashioned in the shape of birds' wings. In her left hand was a staff of ash which she bore like a scepter.

It was Fiorelle, Queen of the Wyndarin. Fletch swallowed painfully.

Her mother had arrived.

Dreythan approached the gate with measured steps. Every man, woman and child of Iventorr had turned out to witness the arrival of the legendary gypsies. They lined the streets and castle walls, eyes alight with excitement. Hushed murmurs slowly grew in volume until it reached a mumbling clamor.

Across the bridge, a handful of Wyndarin broke away from the rest, the queen at their head, and began to approach, leaving the majority behind on the grass-clad hill. Bare feet flashed at the hems of their long robes as they walked, their strange clothes flowing and snapping in the breeze which grew stronger the closer they came.

A breeze had accompanied the Wyndarin arrival three years ago as well. Dreythan's lips pinched downward. He had known so little of the Wyndarin people at the time, it made him ashamed to think of it. He had not even acknowledged their culture as anything but a strange choice to live their lives wandering wherever the wind blew.

They reached the end of the bridge and stepped onto the island, now only a dozen paces away. The golden-crowned woman at their lead halted, bowing her head.

"King Dreythan Dreythas-son," she said, her voice clear and

warm. The breeze suddenly ceased. "These last three years wear well on you."

"Queen Fiorelle of the Wyndarin," he replied. "Your fairness never fades. You and your people are always welcome in Ivenhence."

She raised her head, smiling. It struck Dreythan how similar in appearance she and her daughter were. They had the same fair freckled skin and round, fine-featured faces. Fletch's chin was a little stronger than her mother's, Dreythan reflected, and her brow thicker and more slanted. But it could not be denied that they were blood.

"I thank you for your hospitality and graciousness, King Dreythan," Fiorelle said, dipping in the slightest bow. "I shall not burden your home with the presence of all my subjects. If it please you, they shall remain across the bridge and make camp there."

"Your thoughtfulness is appreciated. Iventorr is crowded with many who have anticipated your arrival." Dreythan turned, and gestured. "You are welcome to make your home in the guest tower, as well as your retainers."

"You have my thanks," the queen answered with a smile.

She turned to nod to her companions. Dreythan could have sworn that, for the briefest moment, her eyes flashed to the top of the wall where a certain royal archer stood.

The dining hall was abuzz with lively conversation as Dreythan lowered himself into his usual seat. He had barely even lifted his water goblet to his lips when Queen Fiorelle and her handservants appeared, accompanied by excited whispering and pointing from the tables below. A flurry of kitchen staff showed them to their seats: Queen Fiorelle to Dreythan's left at the head table, and her subjects just below her to the right.

He rose, standing until she had drifted down into the chair beside him, then returned to his seat. "We are humbled by your gracious presence, your majesty," he said. "How are you finding your accommodations?"

"You are far too kind, my lord," the queen replied, her rich brown eyes crinkling in a smile. "The guest tower's quarters are far more luxurious than any others I've had the pleasure of residing in. I thank you."

They paused as their cups and plates were filled, a moment of silence heavy with the tumult of other voices.

When the servants stepped aside, Fiorelle turned deliberately to Dreythan. "I am certain you must be wondering the same thing many others are, my lord. Why I and my people spring a visit upon Ivenhence outside our usual seven-year schedule?"

Her tone was solemn, strained, her gaze abruptly intense. Dreythan stared numbly back, the noise and motion from the room siphoning away until it were as if they were only two beings present. "You are not wrong," he heard himself say. "Many speculate that the winds have changed this year, and wonder if we ought to expect a harsh winter or other natural phenomenon."

"Our hurried arrival is not without cause." Fiorelle's eyes twinkled again, then faded. "Though the cause is not related to the Wynd. Fear not — your winter ought not vary from its usual pattern."

She hesitated, her eyes dropping to the laden plate before her. Clearly struggling to find words to convey her thoughts, her fine brow wrinkled, her chin dipping towards her chest.

Not wishing to pressure her words, Dreythan looked delicately away. His eyes wandered over the crowd until they rested on Fletch sitting with the other Sentinels. Her quiver was propped up between her knees, bow laid before her on the table as she ate and drank.

"Many in Iventorr may not recall this," Fiorelle finally said, her voice husky and halting, "but I was once a citizen of Iventorr, although it was only for a few short years." Her goblet trembled as she lifted it to her lips. When she set it down, swallowing hard, she continued, "Some weeks ago, one of my people met a young woman who had been transferred to Iventorr to train as a castle guard. They sent word to me, and I traveled here in the hopes that... Might I ask, my lord, if... if the young woman wearing the green sash... is she... What is her name?"

At the hope and desperation etched into every line of the queen's face, the tension in Dreythan's shoulders eased. Fiorelle had spoken plainly, as would he. "Her name is Fletch Wyndshaper, daughter of Kell Wyndshaper," he replied quietly. Pausing, he glanced at Fiorelle as she gazed at the tables below, tears pooling in her eyes. "She is brave, strong, kind, and thoughtful. She has saved my life on more than one occasion." After another brief hesitation, he added, "She would make her father proud."

"Indeed she would," Fiorelle agreed softly, whisking the moisture away with a finger. "You're already aware that she is my daughter. I can hear it in your voice."

Fletch must have sensed eyes on her. Her head rose to meet Dreythan's eye, an easy smile rising to her lips. But then her eyes wavered to Dreythan's left, and froze. The smile dropped, as did her gaze. Stiffly, abruptly, she pushed her plate away and rose, nearly knocking over her quiver. She snatched it and her bow up, shoulders high and head down, and stalked away.

"I feared this," Fiorelle whispered, her face white as cotton. "She does despise me, after all."

Remembering his conversation with Fletch only three weeks past, Dreythan shook his head firmly. "No, Your Majesty," he said. "She does not despise you. Surely she turned away from the shock of meeting your eye after these many years apart."

The queen smiled weakly. "Earlier, your tone might have convinced me, but Fletch's actions have just told me otherwise."

True, she had acted rather coldly, Dreythan admitted. "I cannot explain why she did so." His hand tightened around his goblet as he added, "But surely you shall not give up on something so precious so quickly."

"No," Fiorelle agreed. Taking a deep breath, she straightened, rearranging her features into a semblance of serenity, though her eyes were still clouded by doubt. "You're right, my lord. I... shall respect her choice should she make it clear she wishes nothing to do with me." The sureness of her tone wavered, but she kept on, "But I would like to speak with her first. With your permission, my lord, might I summon her to my chambers whilst in Iventorr?"

Dreythan stared down at his plate, stomach clenching. He hadn't spoken with Fletch, not more than a passing greeting since their encounter in the royal garden. Several times he had wondered if he should summon her, to ask her what she wished him to do should her mother ask after her. But both of them had been so preoccupied with preparations for the arrival... there had never been time.

"I cannot speak on Fletch's behalf, Your Majesty," he said slowly, calculating each word before it formed on his tongue. "But I know I would do near anything for a chance to speak with my mother. Perhaps that is all Fletch needs — a chance." Meeting the queen's eye, he gave a single, deliberate nod. "But it is her choice, not mine. You may extend an invitation to her, not a summons, and it must be after setfith, when her guard shift ends."

As if agreeing not to discuss the matter further, they both turned the conversation away from Fletch. Fiorelle inquired after the new taxation method she'd heard about, and commented that a few of the villages they'd passed through seemed more prosperous than they had on the Wyndarin's last pass through Ivenhence. This sparked a thread of earnest conversation; they discussed at length how the new system worked and how it might be improved upon.

After bidding Fiorelle a pleasant evening, Dreythan took his leave. The cacophony of the boisterous dining hall faded as he exited the north door and glanced back. Captain Norland and Matteo Alwick had fallen in several paces behind him and were conversing quietly.

When their discourse reached a lull, Dreythan said, "Captain, I should like to speak with you."

Norland gestured to Alwick, who paused, dropping out of earshot. When he caught up to the king, Norland asked, "Something amiss, my lord?"

"Not amiss, no. There is a matter you ought to be aware of, as it pertains to the royal guard." Dreythan hesitated, his forehead tensing as he watched the cobbles pass beneath his feet. "Queen Fiorelle shall request Fletch's presence in the guest tower. I have granted her my approval to do so, so long as the summons is issued after the fifth afternoon hour."

"Ah." The concern dissolved from Norland's scarred face, and he nodded. "Understood, my lord."

Dreythan shot a sharp glance at the captain. "You are not going to inquire as to the cause for the queen's interest in Fletch?"

To his astonishment, Norland's bushy red beard parted in a wide smile. "Nay, my lord," he replied.

"You knew," Dreythan realized aloud, staring in dismay at his captain's smug grin. "How long have you known, Norland? And why did you not inform me?"

"I was promoted t' Head of the Foresters when Kell Wyndshaper was still Captain," Norland replied easily. "I met him, his wife, an' his child. But I didn't know Fiorelle was royalty at the time. When the gypsies first came through while I was Captain, I was confused as t' why Kell Wyndshaper's wife would be their queen." He shook his head, chuckling.

"Why did you not see fit to tell me?"

Finally meeting Dreythan's eye, Norland's expression sobered. "My wife told me Fletch shut down at the mention of th' gypsy queen when she started training in th' castle. If it's painful for her to even hear about her mother, how much worse would it be if folks knew and asked her about it? People have no tact. It's Fletch's business if she wants her kinship known, my lord," he said quietly. "It's been clear she'd rather keep it secret, so secret I've kept it."

Abashed, Dreythan dropped his gaze. Norland was right; he'd had no right no know. But if Norland knew, how many others in the castle did? How many could recognize Queen Fiorelle as Kell Wyndshaper's widow?

"Although," Captain Norland said, giving the king a sly smile, "this means our best archer is a princess, my lord."

Heat rushed inexplicably into Dreythan's ears. "I am aware," he grunted. "That is all, Captain."

Obediently, Norland fell back to join Matteo Alwick, through Dreythan was sure the smile remained, hidden under the captain's red whiskers, for some time.

Dipping a cloth strip into the jar of lard on the table before her, Fletch dabbed the gelatinous goo onto her left vambrace, massaging it firmly into the leather. Another day had come and gone. She'd only just finished her guard shift, leaving Dreythan and Harrild at the dining hall. In lieu of the previous day's fiasco, she'd decided to avoid taking supper in the hall with the others, so she'd stopped by the kitchen to say hello to Matron Gulden and to pick up a hot potato and a few strips of jerky.

Ears burning, Fletch glared downward as she worked the fat into her armor. She'd nearly choked when her eyes had inadvertently met her mother's. As soon as she'd exited the dining hall door, she had stopped dead in her tracks, heart beating wildly in her ears. What had she been thinking?! It would've been the perfect chance to smile, to nod, to meet her mother's gaze openly. Instead, she'd turned tail and run like a whipped dog.

She bent her head, furiously buffing her vambrace as she wished she hadn't let instinct take control. What might have happened had she stayed? If she had been able to maintain eye contact?

There was no sense worrying about what might have been, or so she tried to tell herself. But the sentiment rang hollow.

Setting the vambrace aside, she drained the last drops from her mug of ale, then set to work on her cuirass. Just as she finished polishing the upper half, three heavy thuds pounded at her door.

"One moment," she called. Slipping her feet into a pair of

stockings, she stood and opened the door.

It was Captain Norland. For a moment, he simply stared down at her, face curiously blank, before announcing, "Queen Fiorelle of the gypsies has requested your presence in her chambers."

Fletch's heart leaped into her throat, then dove into her twisting stomach. "Y-yes, Captain," she stammered, but her loosely stockinged feet stayed glued to the stone floor.

"I did say 'request', lass, not 'require.'" Norland's blue eyes regarded her with concern. "If ye do want to see her, you'll need to be dressed a bit more presentable than that."

Right. Giving the rest of the cuirass a quick, shaky polish, Fletch pulled the armor on over her head, buckling its sides together. Tugging her vambraces on over her tunic sleeves, she tried to fasten them in place, but her trembling fingers wouldn't comply. Here was her chance. But what could she possibly say?

"Here," the captain said, his voice gentle. Pulling the straps just tight enough, he buckled them, soberly meeting her eye. "You don't have to do this," he said haltingly.

Nodding, she swallowed, the lingering taste of ale souring on her tongue. Stuffing her feet into her boots, she shoved the hem of her trouser legs down inside them. When she straightened, Captain Norland handed her the green sash.

"I'm ready," she said. The wobble in her voice said otherwise.

Norland hesitated, then squeezed her shoulder. "Follow me."

Together they exited the Garden Wall, striding past the vegetable gardens down roads that were lined with vendor booths and crowded with bustling people even so late in the day. Passing the kitchens, they entered the richly appointed welcome hall. Passing pillars of marble and hanging flowering vines, they proceeded to the grand carved staircase that led up into the guest tower and began their climb.

Heart pounding harder and faster with every step, Fletch found herself swallowing over and over, her stomach twisted into a painful knot. Questions spun through her head, too fast and dizzy to follow.

They reached the top of a flight of steps that emptied onto a cozy, brightly lit landing. A few Wyndarin stood nearby in a group, chatting quietly with one of the castle guards. Their conversation ceased as Fletch passed, their eyes wide and curious.

Leading Fletch through an open door into a room with an open, wide window, Captain Norland stepped aside, bowing.

"Queen Fiorelle," he said stiffly, removing his helmet. "May I present Fletch Wyndshaper."

Heartbeat thundering in her ears, Fletch realized she was in a sitting room. The newly setting sun's warm light illuminated vivid tapestries hung on the walls. A low ornate wooden table occupied the center, fluffy turquoise and yellow cushions lining the floor around it. Atop the table was a tray of fruits and cheeses and a crystal decanter. And in the corner, standing with her slender hands folded gracefully, was Queen Fiorelle.

"Thank you, Captain," she said.

He bowed and turned away. Fletch silently beseeched him to stay, staring at him, but he avoided her gaze and strode quickly out, shutting the door softly behind him.

Slowly, like a deer trying to gauge if the shadow behind a tree was a stalking wolf, Fletch turned and looked into her mother's brown eyes. "Hello," she heard her voice rasp.

Fiorelle stepped forward. In one swift motion, she took Fletch's hands in hers. "Fletch," she murmured, her gaze sweeping up and down Fletch's full height, then fixing on her face in a teary smile. "How you have grown."

Her hands were strong, desperate. Clutching. Fletch's shoulders shrugged awkwardly, and she looked down, pulling her fingers free of the tight grip and folding them behind her.

There was a long, painful silence.

Still feeling the heat of her mother's hands on hers, Fletch's stomach churned. She was making a mess of things already. Gulping down a hasty breath, she stammered, "I, er, I h-hope you're well."

"All the better for seeing you," Fiorelle replied huskily. "And you?"

At the emotion in her mother's tone, a wave of heat rushed up from Fletch's gut. "I think I'm going to be sick," she said. Swallowing hard, she managed to force some of it back.

"You do look quite pale. Here, sit down."

Fletch shook her head and stepped back. "I would only soil your pillows," she choked, and nearly retched.

"I shan't keep you if you are ill." Fiorelle brushed lightly past her, pushing open the door into the hall. "I... am glad you came."

Their gazes locked for a brief moment. Beyond any doubt, Fletch clearly saw grief and shame in Fiorelle's eyes.

Another wave of bile washed up from her stomach. She rushed out of the room, hand clapping over her mouth.

"Wyndshaper?" Standing at the spiral staircase, Norland straightened, scowling. "What's wrong?"

Snatching his helm, Fletch thrust her face into the leather and vomited. "That's what," she choked weakly, wiping her chin. "I'm sorry, Captain."

Straight-faced, he handed his helmet to the close-by guard and barked, "Take that to the nearest well and rinse it, then immediately to the armory to be cleaned."

The guard nodded briskly and hurried off without looking down.

Glancing at Fletch as they descended the first few steps, Norland fumbled, "I take it your reunion did not go smoothly."

"It surpassed my expectations," Fletch admitted, the tight knot in her stomach slowly uncoiling. "I... I'd feared she would want nothing of me."

Shooting her a strained glance, the Captain frowned. "That's clearly not the case," he said. "She did ask to see ye, Wyndshaper. And she obtained permission from the king."

"She asked the king," she murmured to herself, wondering if saying it would make it feel true. "Gods, but she seemed mournful. And lonely."

If only she hadn't let her stomach revolt, she would be sitting across from her mother, sharing a conversation for the first time in over fifteen years. Maybe they would be talking about small, silly things, like the weather or the pillows they sat on. But her nerves had gotten the better of her.

The chance had been wasted.

Her empty gut quivered. A weight fell more and more heavily on her shoulders with every step as she descended the long staircase, not even daring to hope that her mother could forgive her.

Chapter 18

When Fletch's eyes opened the next morning, the sun's light was already streaming bright white-gold through her window. She jerked upright, yanking her blankets aside in panic. Within minutes she was hopping toward the door, pulling her second boot on and snatching up her bow.

Sleep had eluded her for hours. She'd stared at the ceiling, wondering why she had felt so ill, why she hadn't been able to keep herself from fleeing. She'd wanted more than anything for her mother to simply acknowledge her, but when she had, she'd only wanted to escape. It just didn't make sense.

Once she'd finally found slumber, she'd tossed and turned, tortured by the vision of her mother's tearful brown eyes, soft and sorrowful, and her quiet voice.

Shrugging the shadow of the nightmares away, Fletch focused on her duties. Trailing Dreythan, Norland, and Harrild through the castle, dodging vendors and visitors. Climbing up into the loft above the throne hall and library. It was enough to keep her distracted, but the moment the fifth afternoon bell rang and she returned to the quiet of her quarters, the shadow descended over her again.

She had wasted another chance to let a spark catch and rekindle. The knowledge was a block of ice in her gut, tight and cold. Too angry and frustrated to even look at herself, she avoided glancing in the mirror as she plucked a comb off her chest of drawers and ran it quickly through her hair.

"I'm a fool and a coward," she muttered.

She knew she couldn't stay cooped up in her quarters the remainder of the day; she would surely go mad. Even though the thought of seeing her mother again sent shudders down her throat, it was worth the risk. Perhaps she could take such an opportunity to make amends.

Perking up slightly, she turned toward her window. Ever since the Wyndarin messenger had arrived three weeks ago, every soul in the castle had been abuzz about the magnificent wares the 'gypsies' would bring with them from all across the Hearth.

"You know, they sail the seas in giant ships," she'd overheard one of the kitchen maids gushing. "They go places that no one else has ever been, and bring strange fruits and spices back from mysterious lands! Last time they were here I was only a girl, but my mum bought a piece of dried fig for my brother and I to share. I've never had anything else like it."

"I cannot wait to look over their fine silks," another chimed in. "I hope to find some white silk to make a wedding dress from!"

"But you're not even betrothed," the first one laughed. "Better not let Torrin hear you speaking like that. You may scare him off, poor man!"

Fletch smiled at the memory of the cheerful exchange. Reaching beneath her chest of drawers, she pulled a jingling sack free of its hidden place wedged behind the last drawer. The reward Dreythan had given her for saving his life. Maybe she'd find something in the market worth spending it on. Not to mention, shopping could be just the distraction she needed.

The entire castle seemed to be overflowing with people. Not only Wyndarin and Ivenhencians, but also individuals hailing from the Isles of Aden, their open embroidered vests and sashes and tall curved caps making them easy to find in the crowds.

Many of the persons Fletch passed stared openly at her, confusion clearly etched in their faces. She had expected as much. With her red-brown hair and green eyes, most folk likely assumed she was a 'gyspy', but she wasn't wearing gypsy clothing. Glancing down at her armor, she silently thanked Jorga Soothand for the royal Ivenhencian crest emblazoned on it. No one could mistake her for a Wyndarin when she wore the ten towers of Iventorr.

She wove through the river of bodies, wondering how she could have thought that shopping would be a good idea. What she wouldn't give for a day in the forest... the only sounds the whisper of Wynd through the trees, bird calls, and distant troll and wolf howls. The soft shimmering streams of translucent mint green and buttercup yellow swirling between trunks and boulders, the bits of azure sky that could be seen through the leaves, limbs, and needles.

Reaching the kitchens, she cut sharply around the northwestern corner and nearly bowled over another figure. They both halted sharply, missing collision by inches.

"I'm so sorry," Fletch blurted. "Sorry. I'll... I'll just be on my way." Face burning, she ducked her head even lower and turned to hurry away.

"No, I ought to be the one apologizing," said a voice behind her, then, "Fletch? Are you alright?"

It was Dreythan. Gods, she had nearly crashed into and then brushed off the king. "Yes, my lord," she managed, smoothing her face into a cheerful grin as well as she could. "I was so eager to look at the merchants' wares I wasn't watching where I was going. I'm sorry."

"Not a worry." The king's smile was warm, genuine, crinkling the corners of his eyes. "I, too, was distracted, thinking of the many missives I have yet to write. My eyes were not on my path, either." He paused, expression falling as he examined her face. "How fare you these past few days? Since the Wyndarin arrival, that is."

Fletch blinked. He'd called them by their proper name. "As well as I can be," she lied. He'd been sitting beside her mother at dinner... He must have seen her run. "May I ask how the tax reformation in Limbwood is going?"

Though his smile didn't waver, his eyes sharpened. Fletch had no doubt he knew she'd deliberately changed the subject. But he nodded obligingly. "Ah, you refer to the situation with Darman Lollma. A second election was held, and his original runner-up, Roera Hiddle, was the clear winner." He hesitated. "I wished to thank you again for your sound insight. I would have approached you sooner, but... it seemed that I would distract you, were I to speak to you whilst you are on duty." As if to himself, he added, "It is strange to see you each day without ever conversing."

A warm hand closed around Fletch's heart as color rose to the highest points of Dreythan's cheekbones. "I understand your meaning," she said softly. "When we traveled from the Pass together, and each time we've seen each other since, we've exchanged words. We've become accustomed to it, and not to do so feels..."

"Wrong," Dreythan finished.

Just as the absence of a curly-haired head and a pair of smiling brown eyes across the dinning hall table felt wrong. "Precisely." She nodded. "I remember my father telling me once that the pains of distance or of absence are the most bitter pains of all."

Eyes softening, Dreythan asked, "You still remember your father's voice?"

"Well, no." She dropped her gaze to her boot toes. "But I do remember his words, and the feel of his calloused hand around mine."

"There was a melody my mother used to sing to me." Fletch looked up to find Dreythan turning toward the horizon, watching as the sun dipped below the glowing crimson skyline. "I cannot remember the words nor the tune. I cannot even remember her visage. But sometimes, in a dream, I hear a song and see a kind, gentle face I am certain is hers."

They stood together for a few moments, a wordless understanding passing between them; they had both experienced pain, loss, and loneliness. But they had also found purpose, and hope. Their eyes met, and they smiled simultaneously.

"I have kept you from your shopping long enough," Dreythan said with a tiny bow. "Forgive me, Fletch. Pleasant evening."

"Thank you, my lord," Fletch replied with a smile and a wink. "The same to you."

She watched as he strode away, followed at a distance by Aeda and Matteo. When they had gone, she turned and kept on toward the castle square.

It was even more packed with vendors, traders, onlookers, and oglers than the streets had been. Starting at one corner of the square, Fletch did her best to work her way through each vendor to the other side. Colors and scents bombarded her senses from every direction. Merchants called to any who passed nearby, urging them to approach and take a closer look at their wares. There were precious gemstones, gold and silver chains, pendants, crystals. One small cart was swathed in strands of gleaming pearls. Fletch paused; she had never known they existed in so many different shades. Many were glossy white, creamy yellow, or subtly pink. More fascinating were the black, purple, and blue pearls. She fingered a strand of the purple ones until the merchant spotted her and tried to badger her into purchasing. Across the cart, a familiar kitchen maid — Sariah? — giggled as Fletch ducked quickly away.

Just past the pearl vendor was a Wyndarin woman draped in robes of vivid violet silk. Her small wagon was stacked with bolts of cloth: silk, linen, cotton, wool, and other fabrics Fletch couldn't identify. The strange sheer material moved with even the slightest breath of Wynd. The clever saleswoman frequently swirled a breeze around her cart, causing her cloth to flutter like butterflies' wings, drawing oohs and aahs from the young women crowded about.

The next display was an open booth manned by four men, clearly from the Isles of Aden. Brown from the sun, they strode about, huge baskets filled with bizarre fruits nestled in their muscular arms. One of them split open a large green fruit with a wickedly sharp curved knife. He passed slivers of the fruit out to the crowd, beautiful white teeth flashing in a brilliant smile.

Fletch just managed to snag a piece. She blinked down at it, astonished to find the flesh of the fruit to be as rosy orange as the rising sun. Avoiding the rind, she bit down.

If sunshine had a flavor, she was certain it would taste just like the fruit. Light and sweet like honeysuckle, with an acidic punch and a hint of tartness. She swallowed, flagging down the man who'd given her the sample.

"Beg pardon," she said, pointing to the basket of green fruits. "What are those called?"

"It is called pawpaw in the Isles." He grinned, his umber eyes sparkling. "You find it to your liking?"

"It's delicious," she replied, feeling her cheeks burn. His smile was quite handsome. Taking a coin from her belt pouch, she held it out. "I'd like one, please."

Eyes widening at the sight of the gold, the man turned and called to the others in an unfamiliar language. In short order, they collected one of each fruit they were selling, piling them all into a woven rush basket with the pawpaw atop. "Here," the merchant said, transferring the basket carefully into Fletch's hands. "You are far too generous."

Her mouth watered as the light, sweet scent of the ripe goodies teased her nostrils. "I can't possibly eat all this," she protested.

"I am certain one as giving as yourself can find others to share our goods with." He winked, turning back to the crowd. "Tell your friends about our wares!"

The next cart couldn't be reached. Children of all ages crowded around, craning to get a better look at the rainbow of delectable candies on display. Towering among their midst was Captain Norland, beaming at his two sons as they leaned from the secure cradle of his arms to ogle the sweets. Beside him, Petrecia pointed at candies that looked like gems as the merchant smiled and bobbed, sliding them into parchment pouches. Not wanting to disturb the family in their happy delirium, Fletch turned away.

Covered in patchwork materials that had long-since faded to shades of grey, the next wagon was startlingly familiar. Very few passersby actually stopped to take a look at the drab-by-comparison setup. Those who did pause merely looked puzzled before hurrying on.

Fletch wove through the crowd, peering expectantly around the tied-back canvas flap. Sure enough, there sat Naraan the Nomad, surrounded by his scrolls and books.

He raised his head as Fletch hopped up into the wagon, his weathered face breaking into a wide smile. "Fletch Wyndshaper," he said, rising smoothly. "I had hoped our paths would cross again."

Remembering her manners, Fletch held out her basket. "The same to you! Please, take one. I can't hope to eat these before they over-ripen."

The laugh lines around his eyes deepened. "If you insist." He selected a yellow star-shaped fruit covered in spikes. "You wear a Sentinel's badge, I see. Congratulations. But it appears you have been lax in practicing your Wyndcalling. I would encourage you to rectify that. It could prove a useful weapon against the Unbreathing."

She cocked a puzzled brow at him.

"Your blood," he smiled in answer to her unspoken question. "A few of us can see the Wynd flowing through others' veins. Fewer still are able to see the effect the Wynd has on the being it flows through." Inclining his head toward her hands, he continued, "It flows through each of us differently, but I have only seen the Wynd stream through one other as it does through you.

Tell me, are there elements of Wyndcalling that resist you?"

Remembering how she'd shivered furiously in the rain outside Dreythan's study, Fletch nodded sheepishly. "Water is difficult to manipulate," she admitted. "And I can't create flame. I can heat water easily if it's contained and stagnant, but otherwise—" Trailing off, she shrugged.

"As I thought." Naraan nodded sagely. "In that case, you must take this."

She took the scroll he offered, unfurling it curiously. It was covered in drawings of human figures dressed in flowing robes. In each sketch, they appeared to be dancing. Lines of ink flowed from the figures' mouths and hands to stream across the parchment.

"What is it?" Fletch asked.

"'Tis a Wyndcalling primer scroll," Naraan replied. "It cannot compare to having someone teach you, but the form of Wyndcalling which flows through your veins is an unusual one. It would be a shame to squander it. Should you need guidance, you are always welcome to ask."

Murmuring her thanks, Fletch placed the scroll atop her basket, then paused. "Also, I must thank you for the books you provided at our last meeting. Especially," she added, watching his face carefully, "my father's journal."

"Ah." His grey eyes twinkled, creases multiplying at their corners. "To the point, I see. You have not completed reading it, correct?"

Cheeks flushing at his keen glance, she nodded.

"Hmm." Brow wrinkling, Naraan turned thoughtfully away, fingers combing his trimmed beard. "Well, t'would be unfair to leave the question in your eyes unanswered. How did I come by Kell Wyndshaper's journal?" Deliberately swiveling back to face her, he folded his hands into the sleeves of his robe. "Our father was Wyndarin," he said matter-of-factly. "And Kell's mother a citizen of Ilumence. Our father was unaware of Kell's conception, and so moved on with the Wyndarin when it was time to continue Wandering. Several years later, he was Chosen by a Wyndarin woman, and together they bore me."

"Your father," Fletch repeated, her mind numb with shock. The words swirled into a crescendo as her face broke into a stupidly wide smile.

"You might call me your uncle, if you would like," he said, and for a moment, his calm exterior wobbled, as if he refrained from speaking further.

It was all starting to make sense. "And my father's journal?" Fletch asked.

Naraan paused, his eyes shifting past her to stare out the back of the open wagon. She could nearly see the hundreds of clouded thoughts swirling in his storm-colored eyes. "After Fiorelle was forced to return to our people, Kell sent word to me by messenger. His letter was vague, perhaps intentionally so. He suspected a plot was forming to bring Ivenhence to its knees. In his message, he told me where he would hide his journal in his quarters, and requested I retrieve it were anything ill to befall him." Meeting her gaze, his countenance softened. "He also asked that I see you safely to your mother, but by the time I had returned to Iventorr, you had already enlisted to train with the Foresters."

It was all Fletch could do to stare at her uncle — her uncle! For several moments, all she could hear or see were the man standing in front of her and her own spinning thoughts. "That must be why you were so familiar to me," she heard herself say. "You reminded me of Papa." As questions began to settle slowly into focus, she asked, "Did he say why he suspected a plot against Ivenhence?"

"No," Naraan said, shaking his head. "He did not. But 'tis clear he feared his journal would fall into the wrong hands. You shall understand once you have finished reading it."

Her cheeks flushed under his keen gaze. It was as if he saw the hesitation, the reasons she kept feeding herself to postpone reading.

"What did you mean, 'when Fiorelle was forced to return'?" she blurted.

Face instantly darkening, Naraan looked away. "'Tis not a

matter I ought to speak of," he replied after a long, heavy pause. "Your mother should be the one to explain the events that took place. You ought to ask her while she is here, not I."

"I don't know if I'll be able to ask her anything after how horribly our last two interactions have gone," Fletch mumbled. "That is, after how awful my reactions were... I can't blame her if she never meets my eye again."

"What do you mean?" Naraan's voice was sharp. "What happened?"

Reluctantly, she recounted the past two interactions with her mother, and how badly she's handled them. As she finished, hot anger swelled in her stomach. She clenched her fists, growling, "I've been so stupid."

Naraan's sandaled feet shifted. "Your reactions were understandable," he told her solemnly. "Your mother knows this, Fletch, as painful as it might be for her."

Startled, Fletch looked up, the heat frozen in her face. "What?"

"You have been without your mother three quarters of your life. You feel in some way that you have rejected her. Or perhaps you fear that is how she feels. You wish to draw close to her, but you are afraid. Of hurting her, of being hurt yourself." He leaned forward, hands sweeping earnestly forth. "But understand, Fletch, that by running, you are already hurting the both of you. You are annulling the chance for a new relationship. Face your fear of pain, or there shall be no chance of spanning the bridge between you."

Fletch stared at him, heart thudding fast and hard against her ribs. "But how?" she asked desperately. "What can I do?"

"I cannot advise you there," Naraan said quietly. "But you ought to make your decision soon. The Wyndarin shall only remain for a few days. Once that has passed, another chance may never come."

Fletch nodded, then paused. "May I visit you again?"

Gray eyes softening, he nodded. "You may. Now go, and think."

"I will. Thank you, Uncle," she added, and Naraan's face lit up.

She had already begun to hop down out of the wagon when she stopped, hand straying to her coin pouch. Turning back to Naraan, she cleared her throat. "Ah, I, er, nearly forgot. Do you have any books regarding Wyndarin history, culture, or traditions? I have a friend who is an avid reader, and I believe he would value learning about us."

Dreythan settled into the worn chair in the library's study, silently thanking Ivere for the peace and quiet. His day had been filled with a whirl of bustling color. From his usual time in the throne hall, to his meeting with Treasurer Anshwell and Ambassador Kekona, to the short hearing with the Adenite merchants who had questions regarding the records they were required to keep. It was a relief to finally sit down in a small, cozy room by himself.

Pulling a scroll from his robe, he inspected it, apprehensive hope rising within him. A messenger had delivered it hours before, but he'd been too busy to open it. Wrapped in waxed parchment, the scroll was sealed with blue wax pressed with the insignia of a burning heart. Another reply from Morthan. Breaking the wax disc, Dreythan rolled out the parchment to read;

To King Dreythan Dreythas-son, rightful ruler of Ivenhence,
I am afraid an impasse has been reached with the royal advisors. During our most recent meeting, they expressed their concern over my desire to change Ilumence's system of law. My response was firm, yet simple; I explained the need for improvement, and suggested that their opposition was the result of fear. Fear of how change might affect them, and fear that they would lose the little power they currently hold.
It wasn't meant as a challenge, only as a statement. I wished them to examine themselves, to look at their reasoning and question their motives, but they retaliated instantly and with such heat as I have never seen.

They threatened to revolt, promising that were they to do so, they could practically strip me of power. Posing as if carrying out my will, they instead would rule Ilumence, rendering me a helpless puppet.

'Tis only natural they would question my ability to lead after the debacle with Thissa last week.

Gorvannon sent a trade caravan to our border in the northern foothills of the Snowshod Mountains. With them were two scores of armed soldiers. Though no threatening words were uttered, it was strongly hinted that the post (manned by a mere ten men) would be attacked unless the trade caravan were allowed to pass. I could not, in good conscience, refuse their entry. To do so would have sentenced those ten men to death. But I have now set a precedent; Gorvannon shall expect me to be lenient and soft-willed in the future, as shall my advisors.

I am at a loss. Not only are those who pledged their service to my father betraying me, promising to practically dethrone me, but the nation with which Ilumence has maintained fragile peace is bullying us into submission. I confess that I cannot see an end to this madness, and I know not what can be done, or indeed, if anything can be done at all.

I cannot in good conscience allow you to believe that trade negotiations will take place between our nations in the near future. There is simply too much at stake at the moment to consider it.

Although, if you were to come to Ilumence, perhaps you could make the advisors see reason. You have always been more eloquent than myself, cousin. Will you not come to Ohnaedris's Hold? Not only to review the system I have pieced together and to speak with my cabinet, but to pay your respects to my father Morthas? I know it would please him if you did, but I shall understand if it is not possible.

I pray you, do not obligate yourself to me, cousin. Your council has already been of more assurance and aid than you can possibly know.

Morthan Morthas-son

For a moment, Dreythan simply stared at the letter, his stomach cold and hollow. If only he could drop everything and run to his cousin's aid. He knew all too well the struggles of being newly crowned... even though he'd never had to stand against such opposition as Morthan was.

But traveling to Ilumence simply wasn't possible. Ivenhence would be without a ruler in his absence. Had he died during his brush with the Unbreathing in the Pass, what would have happened? He'd asked himself the question over and over. Ivenhence would have been annexed by Ilumence, though not before Thissa attempted to invade. The land would have been ravaged by war. Pain, suffering, starvation, and bloodshed would tear the fair land apart, and eventually, Ivenhence would be no more. The kingdom that so many had given their lives for would be lost, their sacrifices in vain.

Dreythas the Reclaimer's legacy would be no more.

If Dreythan left Iventorr again, the Unbreathing would strive to complete their task and claim his life. His father's kingdom would be reduced to ash.

He straightened, pulling a fresh sheet of parchment toward him. He couldn't sit by and allow a similarly horrible fate to befall his cousin. There had to be a way to convince Thissa, Ilumence, and Aden to unite, to put aside their differences. To show Morthan's advisors how foolish, even blind, they were. Bending his head over the paper, he carefully began to write, measuring each sentence before it flowed out of his quill.

To King Morthan Morthas-son, rightful ruler of Ilumence and our cousin,

It is with greatest regret that I must decline your invitation to visit Ohnaedris's Hold. I cannot leave my kingdom for an extended period of time when there is none to govern in my absence. The attempt on my life three moons past has made that painfully apparent.

Even though I cannot leave Iventorr, I feel certain we could find solutions, given time together. You are always welcome here in Ivenhence, cousin. Were you to leave Ilumence for a short time, your advisors would likely gain a false sense of security, believing you to have conceded to their will. Such confidence can be used against them. Not to mention, once they have a taste of what a burden rule truly is, they shall likely discover they do not possess the stomach for it.

As to Gorvannon, your dilemma was an impossible one, yet the decision you made was sound and saved the lives of your citizens. Had you denied Gorvannon's demand, it is possible he would have ordered an assault on your border. He is a proud man and does not accept rejection well, as shown by his continued disdain for Ivenhence.

If Gorvannon has indirectly threatened violence, it is possible direct threats may be issued in the near future. We must be prepared for the worst scenario while attempting to guide all parties involved down the path of peace.

Ambassador Alicianna Kekona of the Merchants Guild of Aden currently resides within Iventorr. Word could also be sent to Gorvannon of Thissa. Were he to accept and were you to attend, I would consider it an honor to hold a trade and relations summit here in Ivenhence. This could give our nations the opportunity to renew our relationships and strengthen, or even develop, bonds.

I anticipate your reply, cousin. Do not give up hope; the possibility for peace yet remains.

Dreythan Dreythas-son

As he signed his name and leaned back, waiting for the ink to dry, a smile tugged at Dreythan's lips. For the first time in many years, he didn't wonder if his father would have been proud of him.

He knew.

As Fletch left Naraan's wagon, the sun's setting rays flooded Iventorr's streets with amber-gold light and shifting shadows. The hubbub of the square clanged in her ears, drowning out each thought that rose in her mind. Irritably, she held her basket close, pushing townsfolk, visitors, and merchants alike aside as she tried to escape the noise. Was there anywhere peaceful left in the castle?

Not even her quarters were quiet. Shrill calls from the traders lined up along the outside of the Garden Wall pierced the stone. Pausing, she turned to the west. Perhaps the noise couldn't reach the Garden itself.

She charged through the alleyways and cobbled streets, resolutely wading through the waves of people until she reached the southern Garden gate. The guards on duty shifted as if to block the way. Then one's eyes widened, and he muttered to the other. Both stepped smartly aside.

As Fletch entered the green sanctuary, her feet slowed, the racket of the castle faded to be replaced with the sleepy buzzing of bees and the trill of birdsong. Late-blooming crimson and violet irises nodded from the flowerbeds beside orange and yellow sunbells, interrupted here and there with heavily laden rosebushes. The blossoms swayed in a gentle yellow breeze, their delicate perfume filling the air.

Her shoulders slowly unclenching, Fletch crossed to the old oak tree. She was just about to set her basket down and remove her boots when the rustling of footsteps reached her ears. Expecting to see Dreythan, she straightened, smiling, and found herself staring into an equally shocked pair of brown eyes.

It was the queen.

They gaped at each other for a moment. Then, turning away as if with great effort, Fiorelle said quietly, "I must be disturbing—"

"No," Fletch blurted. "You're not! Er, disturbing me. You're not disturbing me."

Fiorelle halted mid-turn, looking back at Fletch as relief washed over her face. There was a moment of uncomfortable silence before she asked, "How did you know to find me here?"

Fletch blinked. "I didn't," she heard herself say, then quickly added, "But... I'm glad I found you."

The uncertain sorrow in Fiorelle's brown eyes faded, faint hope glimmering in its place. "I am not so innocent," she admitted with a small laugh. "I had hoped to cross your path, though I did not think to do so here." Eyes straying to the ancient oak tree, then falling on the old rope swing, a melancholic smile curled her lips. "This place was special to Kell and I. We met for the first time on this very spot."

Swallowing the nerves that rankled in her throat, Fletch gestured to the stone bench. "Will you... tell me?"

They sat together, the distance between both far too great and far too little. Fletch peered at her mother cautiously, watching as Fiorelle's fingers twisted tightly in her lap. So that was where she had learned that tick from.

"It was my second moon of Wandering," she began quietly, furtively glancing at her daughter. "I had heard of Castle Iventorr many times over the years. Tales of human slaves rising up against their Unbreathing masters and overthrowing them, tales of loss and bravery, of oppression and freedom. I felt strangely drawn to Iventorr and Ivenhence. Thus, I found myself crossing the Great Bridge, agog at the craftsmanship of such a monstrous undertaking. Every step I took, every stone of every building, told a story. Crumbled statues covered in moss, stone structures added onto with lumber and thatch. I was so engrossed by the architecture, engravings and stone stumps that I followed the castle wall, admiring the skilled masonry. Before long I found myself in a large garden, and sat below an oak tree to rest a bit."

A wistful smile crossed her face, and for a moment, Fletch saw her mother as she must have looked twenty years ago: fresh and beautiful, her wide eyes filled with thoughts too deep to discern.

"A deep voice startled me near out of my skin. A soldier was standing before me suddenly, his silver-streaked hair and beard ruffling in the breeze. Even to an utter stranger, to a 'gypsy woman' trespassing on royal property, he was courteous and kind. I was afraid I would be taken to the king and accused of being a Thissian spy. But he simply escorted me out of the Garden Gate and bid me a pleasant day."

It was strange to have heard the same tale from two different perspectives, and to hear such a vast difference and yet such similarity in both. Seeing the distant gleam in her mother's eye,

Fletch felt herself smile. "What happened then?"

"I visited Verenshire to observe the harvesting of apples from the orchards. The following day, Kell approached me under the trees and asked if I should like to take supper with him. He revealed that he was a Wynd-blood himself, and we spoke at length of our lives and... and of our hopes and dreams, the things we wanted to change." Her cheeks pinked, dimpling. "We... met each evening for supper for the following fortnight, and by the end, I realized I had no desire to leave Iventorr. I approached King Dreythas whilst he was in the throne hall and asked him if I could find a place to live and work. Kell must have told him who I was, for he only asked that, when I became the Wyndarin queen, I would bring the Wandering of my people through Ivenhence for trade."

Raising one brow, Fletch commented, "That was rather generous and trusting of him."

"Indeed." Fiorelle smiled, the corners of her eyes and mouth crinkling. "King Dreythas was a wise man. Though I still earned my keep in the castle gardens, I have kept my word. Our trade has only helped Ivenhence grow. Far across the sea to the east, in the empire of Thindle, Ivenhence is renowned for its smithery and leather goods. In Ilumence, few still view this kingdom as a newborn or as a dissident. Most Ilumencian citizens now see it as its own entity."

"It amazes me the impact good trade relations can make," Fletch said. "A relationship between two distant points or peoples can nourish even the most impoverished place."

"Precisely," Fiorelle agreed softly.

Silence hovered between them for a few moments, calm and smooth as a still pond. Recognizing her opportunity, her stomach jittered against her ribs. Fletch clasped her hands together to keep them from trembling. "I'm sorry. That I ran from you," she managed, stumbling over the words. "In the dining hall."

"Do not apologize," came the gentle reply. "I believe I understand."

"No," Fletch insisted, frustrated with the heat of her face, with the sticky mess of her words. "I didn't know how to react. I didn't mean to run, I was caught off guard. It frightened me. I didn't mean to hurt you."

A slender hand covered hers. It was warm, and kind, and wrapped Fletch's heart in a comforting embrace. Slowly, Fletch unclenched her fingers and took her mother's hand, certain she was dreaming and would soon awaken.

"To speak truthfully," Fiorelle said, her voice thick, "The Wyndarin have broken their cycle of Wandering on my command. When I heard you were no longer stationed as a Forester, but assigned to Iventorr, I couldn't delay. I had to see you, to speak with you." Brushing her eyes with one finger, she gave a small, choked laugh. "To meet you, Fletch. But tell me — how did you come to be part of the castle guard? King Dreythan mentioned you have saved his life several times, but I merely thought it a manner of expression. Yet others have mentioned it as well. Was the king's life truly in danger?"

"It was." Fletch nodded. "'Tis the reason I transferred from the Foresters to the Sentinels."

As she apprised her mother of the Unbreathing in the Pass, the narrow escape, and the return to Iventorr, Fiorelle shifted, her expression strangely thoughtful. "You said the Unbreathing arrows were entirely black, made of ebonite and black goose feathers?" she asked. "Is there one here in Iventorr?"

Fletch nodded. "I believe Captain Norland has it in safekeeping."

Fiorelle's lips parted, but her reply was cut off by the echoing bong of a ringing bell, signaling sundown. Her face fell. "I must go to my people," she said, rising. "I am already late. I must arrange tomorrow's traders." She hesitated. "Will you... come with me?"

Fletch shook her head. "No," she replied, noting the steadiness of her own voice. The flutter was gone from her chest, the weight gone from her shoulders. "I would only get underfoot." Before Fiorelle's face could fall, she added, "But perhaps you could come to my quarters tomorrow, after the fourth afternoon hour?"

Her mother nodded, eyes sparkling. "I shall," she said, and the force of her joy caused the oak leaves above them to stir in a vigorous burst of Wynd. "Until tomorrow, my daughter."

Staring down at his plate without seeing the venison and roast vegetables steaming there, Dreythan poked at the food with a fork. The image of Fletch's troubled face wouldn't leave him, nor would the quiver of her voice as she abruptly switched the conversation away from herself. Surely things had gone poorly with —

"A pleasant evening to you, Your Grace," said a rich velvet voice.

He glanced up as Queen Fiorelle gracefully lowered into the chair beside him. "A pleasant evening," he replied quickly. "Your pardon, my lady. I was deep in thought and did not realize your arrival."

It instantly struck him how vastly different her demeanor was than it had been during their previous shared supper. Her eyes, formerly clouded and filled with melancholy, were now hopeful, focused. Where the skin around her mouth had been pinched and worried, it was curved in a soft smile.

"I thank you for encouraging me to speak with Fletch," Fiorelle said after several quiet minutes had passed. "I would not have had the courage to do so otherwise."

Dreythan nearly choked on his bite of potato. Swallowing hard, he managed, "I take it you were able to meet with her?"

Her smile faltered, then widened, cheerful lines crinkling her face. "I was," she replied, her voice light with restrained delight. "Though it did not go as I had hoped at first, we were able to connect a little this evening. The few moments we have already had are more precious to me than all the riches in this world."

"I am glad to hear it."

"I must also thank you for treating her according to her station," she added, watching his face closely. "It is fitting, I think, for the Wyndarin princess to serve as part of Iventorr's Sentinels."

Heat swept up from below the collar of the king's tunic, flooding his cheeks and ears.

"But I had noticed that she dines with the other guards on the main floor, and that she does not have a chamberservant of her own. Is this by choice?"

"Nay," Dreythan replied haltingly. "That is, yes? No one knows that she is of royal blood. She only informed me of your kinship weeks past."

Chuckling lightly, Fiorelle laid her hand on his arm. "I understand," she said. "Do not trouble yourself over this matter, my lord. I shall inquire with Fletch. Before I take my leave for the evening, there is another matter I wished to discuss with you, if I may." Her visage became somber. "Might I request an audience with you tomorrow in the throne hall? It is not a casual matter, I'm afraid. You may wish the captain of your guard to be present."

The king nodded, still doing his best to gather his scattered wits. "Of course, my lady," he said, smoothing his face into calm. "A quarter bell before noon, I ought to have finished with the citizens of Ivenhence. My guards shall be prepared to receive you."

Rising with one fluid motion from her chair, Fiorelle bent in a slight bow, one hand sweeping behind her. "Thank you again, my lord. Until tomorrow."

The following day passed much the same as any other. Dreythan rose, broke his fast in the dining hall, and shortly arrived at the throne hall to see to his citizens. Thankfully, few of them occupied the pews, and he had finished with those present just after the fourth morning bell rang.

As the final citizen left, Dreythan turned to Captain Norland, motioning him closer. "Let us prepare for Queen Fiorelle's audience, Captain," he said quietly. "Dismiss the guard. Instruct them to remain outside until the queen has departed."

"As ye wish, my lord," the Captain said with a nod. "But the Sentinels'll remain. Have ye any idea what she might wish to discuss?"

For one brief second, Dreythan's mind flashed to their dinner conversation from the previous evening. Heart in his throat, he shook his head. "None. But I suppose we shall find out soon enough."

Captain Norland quietly did as instructed, and the guards filed neatly down the aisle and out the doors. Only Fletch remained, her eyes bright and curious as she stood beside a pillar halfway down the aisle, and unseen Harrild, swathed in shadow behind the throne.

At exactly one quarter bell before noon, the double doors of the throne hall swung wide, sunlight spilling across the emerald carpet, illuminating Queen Fiorelle's silhouette and glinting off a simple gold crown adorning her brown hair. A flowing rich blue robe trailed behind her, as did a man Dreythan did not recognize. Tall and lean, his skin red-brown from the sun, he sauntered down the aisle, broad shoulders swiveling.

The guard who escorted them in halted at the steps with a low bow. "My lord, I present Queen Fiorelle of the gypsies. Accompanying her is Tradesman Whendor."

"Queen Fiorelle," Dreythan greeted with a nod. "Tradesman."

"My lord," the queen said clearly, dropping into a bow. "Thank you for giving me your ear. My daughter made mention that an attempt on your life was made, three moons past."

Three moons, Dreythan mused. It seemed both too long and too short a time span. "Indeed," he replied. "Unbreathing ambushed my guards and I in the Pass between Mount Valer and Mount Norst. Might I ask why this is of interest to you?"

"Of course, my lord," Fiorelle said, ignoring her companion as he shifted, face darkening. "Judging by the description of the weapons your assailants used, it would sound as though they are the work of a master craftsman. Given that my people trade with craftsmen across the Hearth, 'tis possible we may be able to direct you to their maker."

Captain Norland's beard bristled. "By Luminia," he muttered. "That's not a half-bad idea. If we could discover who's making the arrows, we might track down whoever's controlling the Unbreathing."

And whomever was trying to kill him. "Retrieve it," Dreythan said.

When the Captain returned, broken black arrow in his hands, Fiorelle took it from him. Instead of looking at it herself, as Dreythan had expected, she handed it to the man behind her and murmured, "Well, Whendor? What say you?"

Lifting the arrow into the beam of light filtering in through a high window, Whendor peered closely at the fletchings. His blue eyes narrowed. "'Tis as you had asked, my queen," he said reluctantly. "This arrow is undoubtedly the work of Purveyn."

"Purveyn?" Norland growled. "Who is he?"

Returning the missile to the Captain, Whendor replied cooly, "Purveyn the Fletcher is a renowned weaponsmith in the southern reaches of Ilumence. He and I have an arrangement; I trade ebonite from the grovers of Thissa, and he pays me well for it. As a return favor, he provides me with arrows for my quiver. I do not use ebonite arrows. I prefer poplar. But his craftsmanship has earned him a fair bit of renown amongst our people. We've never found another who uses silk thread to secure the fletchings, nor does any other craftsman hand-carve grooves for the feathers to rest in."

"You are certain that this arrow was crafted by Purveyn the Fletcher?" Dreythan asked.

The Wyndarin scowled, as if resenting being questioned. "I am certain."

"You said that he resides in southern Ilumence. Were the Captain to present you with a map, could you point out his location?"

Whendor nodded wordlessly, still scowling until Fiorelle gave him a quelling look. "You have only to show me the map," he said reluctantly.

Dreythan stood, turning to Captain Norland. "Take Whendor to the library. Once he has shown us where this Purveyn lives, organize a small group to travel to Ilumence to find and question him."

Though one of the Captain's brows rose, he only said, "Understood, my lord."

"I shall compose a message to King Morthan for you to bear to the Ilumencian border, as well as an advance letter to be carried by sun jay," Dreythan added, knowing what Norland was thinking. "I have no doubt he shall allow you passage."

"As ye wish, my lord. Come, Whendor," Norland rumbled to the Wyndarin man. "Let's make haste — Brinwathe may've already left the library for his mid-day meal."

As they departed, Dreythan inclined his head toward the queen. "I must thank you, my lady, for coming to us with this information."

Fiorelle only smiled and returned the bow. "You are most welcome, my lord," she replied, her eyes twinkling in a smile. "I do have one other query. As an expression of gratitude to Ivenhence and its citizens for welcoming our unexpected visit, would you allow us to throw a banquet in three days' time?"

"It would be an honor," Dreythan replied. "Where would this banquet be held?"

"If it pleases you, my lord, we should like to host it in your dining hall."

"You may also utilize our kitchens, if you so choose. Would you need assistance with preparations from Iventorr's staff?"

Fiorelle shook her head. "The offer is a thoughtful one, Your Majesty, but no. I should like to speak with the head of the kitchens to ensure mutual goodwill, but I believe that should suffice."

The king nodded. "Of course. I shall send word to Matron Gulden on your behalf."

The queen smiled, dipping in an elegant bow. "Thank you, my lord. Once the banquet has finished, my people and I shall be on our way, following the Wynd and its Wandering."

"You are leaving so quickly?" The question spilled from him before he could stop it. "But you have only just arrived."

"Indeed." Straightening to her full regal height, she said, "For any time spent away from the Wynd's path wrenches my peoples' hearts. Once we've departed here, we shall resupply in the Isles and in Port Oasa of Thissa, but after that, we must return to our original course. Thank you again for your ear, my lord. Please do not hesitate to call should you require me." With that, Fiorelle turned and gracefully glided down the aisle toward the door.

Within minutes, Dreythan was seated in the small library office. Fletch and Harrild had, to his great surprise, led him atop the outer wall of Iventorr Castle, high above the bustling, jostling crowds. Though many heads turned toward them and many fingers pointed, they reached the library faster than Dreythan would have thought possible.

Setting the scroll weights in place, the king jabbed his quill into the inkwell, wiped, and scribbled:

To King Morthan Morthas-son, rightful ruler of Ilumence and our cousin,

The captain of my guard, Norland Wyntersoul, has sent a small group of our most trusted men to Ilumence's southern border. If it please you, we request passage to obtain some information from a weaponsmith in southern Ilumence. We suspect this arms craftsman might have created the very arrows meant to end my life; thus, our mission is an urgent one. Your acquiescence would be most deeply appreciated.

Dreythan Dreythas-son

Once he had signed the scroll and leaned back to examine it, it seemed short, even abrupt. Ah, well. It couldn't be helped. Perhaps it would convey to Morthan that the guards' errand was an important one.

He was just rolling up the scroll and sealing it when a knock came at the study door. The sound of Captain Norland's anvil-like fist was unmistakable. "Enter," he said without looking up.

The door shifted open. "I've got it arranged, my lord." The captain's heavy boots thudded into the room, his sheath and armor clinking as he leaned against the wall. "Matteo Alwick'll be leading three of my best men to Ilumence's southern border. They leave within the hour. Is the missive written for Alwick to carry?"

"Nearly," Dreythan replied shortly, handing the first scroll to Norland and pulling a smaller blank one towards him. "This must be taken to the falconry. Tell Master Belland to send the fastest sun jay. This message must reach Ohnaedris's Hold before your men reach the southern border."

The captain poked his head out the door and held a hushed conversation with someone outside. When he closed the door again and returned to his position against the wall, Dreythan was already wiping off his quill and setting it aside. "You said you are sending Matteo Alwick?" he said curiously. "Is he not the youngest of the Sentinels? Aside from Fletch, that is."

"He is," Captain Norland admitted, "but he's proven himself trustworthy many a time, my lord. Our most seasoned Sentinel, Parfeln, did volunteer to lead the expedition." A shadow passed through his eyes, then was gone. "But he's growing old. Not t' mention, Alwick's an experienced rider."

Rolled parchment in hand, Dreythan rose. Rather than turning to exit, he stood where he was, frowning down at the scratched wood grain surface of the table.

"You're asking yourself the same question, I'd wager, my lord," Norland said grimly. "What if it's true?"

The king slowly nodded. "What if this Ilumencian weaponsmith did create those arrows? Was he commissioned to craft them? If so, by whom?"

He stopped, not wanting to continue his train of thought, but Norland finished, "What if Thissa hasn't been behind the attacks at all?" He rubbed his ginger beard, scowling. "We can't get ahead of ourselves, my lord. We need to keep our focus clear, not make assumptions. With any luck, we'll finally get some answers."

Chapter 19

Seizing the edge of her table, Fletch dragged it into the center of her quarters, glancing quickly at the door, expecting a knock at every moment. She had dashed back to her quarters only moments before, stomach in her throat. The Wyndarin were leaving in only three days. It was precious little time, especially for something so important and so impossible as reconnecting with her mother. She couldn't make a mess of things again.

She jumped at a soft knock behind her. Wiping nervous, clammy hands on her tunic, Fletch pulled the door open to find Fiorelle standing outside, two handmaidens flanking her. The queen was dressed in a simple robe of light blue cotton, a hood secured over her hair with the weight of a curious pearl-colored circlet.

"Fletch," Fiorelle greeted, smiling tentatively. She stepped lightly aside. "These are my handmaidens, Miara and Noelle. May we enter?"

The two women, carrying a cylindrical item between them,

curtsied as well as they could, murmuring polite greetings.

"'Tis a pleasure to make your acquaintance," Fletch said, glancing at their burden. "That looks heavy. Would you like help?"

Smiling, they shook their heads and brushed quietly past her into the room, depositing the mystery item on the floor beside the table. Without a word, they curtsied again, and left.

"Thank you both," Fiorelle called after them. Turning to her daughter, she gestured at the object they'd left behind. "I hope you do not mind," she said hesitantly. "'Tis a gift."

"Oh." Fletch's cheeks flared. A gift? "Should I open it?"

"If you would like," she said. Though Fiorelle's expression was carefully neutral, her eyes couldn't hide a hopeful glimmer.

Kneeling beside the burlap-wrapped package, Fletch tugged at the rough cloth, wondering what could possibly be inside. As the wrapping pulled free, something suddenly loosened and unfurled like a large scroll across the floor. It reminded Fletch of the tapestries hanging in the guest tower's sitting room, though with a more muted color palette and woven much more thickly.

"Tis a rug," Fiorelle said, a bit sheepishly.

Rather than the patterns and fanciful swirls most Wyndarin cloth or art carried, the fiber was grouped in small rounded mounds or pointed peaks of many different shades of green. Dark forest shadow, olive, emerald, lime, pea, grass, running river. The multitude of different hues formed the shapes of trees as perceived from a distance. Above the green, outlining the forest horizon, were dusky violet mountain peaks dusted with white blankets of snow.

"When word reached me you had left the forest," Fiorelle was saying, "I thought perhaps you would miss it. And... I was unsure if you would find use for anything else I might have crafted."

"'Tis beautiful," Fletch whispered, running her hand over the ever-so-soft loops of fiber. "I don't think I could dare to walk on this. Perhaps I could hang it up, as if looking out of a window over the Pass." Meeting her mother's anxious gaze, she smiled, warmth closing around her heart. "I love it," she said frankly. "It does remind me of my old post, of my home. Thank you."

Spots of color rose on Fiorelle's cheeks as her eyes crinkled into a wide, joyful beam. Her slender fingers traced over the surface of the rug, outlining the multitude of tiny trees which had clearly been dyed and woven with great care.

Fletch's heart thudded against her ribs.

"That scroll," Fiorelle said suddenly. "Is it possible?"

Startled, she looked up to see her mother staring over her shoulder, her expression stunned. Puzzled, she turned, her eye falling on the Wyndcalling scroll sitting atop her table. "It was given to me yesterday by a book merchant, Naraan the Nomad." Pulling out one of the chairs, she sat as her mother did the same.

"Naraan," Fiorelle repeated, her tone low and unreadable. "Did he... say anything to you? About me?"

"He did," Fletch admitted, curiosity bubbling within her at the sudden fragility in her mother's serene face. "He mentioned you were forced to return to the Wyndarin. When I asked him to elaborate, he said it was a matter he ought not discuss. What did he mean?"

For several moments, she was silent, her forehead creasing and smoothing as her lips pinched. "It is not a simple matter," she finally said. "When I left on my Wandering, Naraan was a messenger in the service of my father, King Farwhyn." Her shoulders heaved in a deep sigh. "During my father's reign, the Wyndarin people... withdrew from the rest of the world. King Farwhyn was proud, even haughty. He believed in the superiority of Wyndarin blood, and would only allow us to Wander through lands in which we were treated with the respect and decorum he expected. His attitude toward the nations of men greatly hindered our prosperity. Many nations grew reluctant to trade with us or even allow us passage through their lands." Eyes glazed and distant, she turned absently to gaze out the open window. "Nearly seven years after I left my people on my Wandering," she finally continued, "a messenger brought word from my father."

"Naraan?" Fletch guessed quietly, and her mother nodded.

"In the message, my father announced that he had grown ill and weak. Though it was not quite time to return to my people, and though there is no limit to the time spent in one's personal Wandering, he demanded I return and take my place as the Wyndarin queen."

Fiorelle's face hardened, and she fell silent.

Chest twisting tightly, Fletch shifted in her seat. "Did he know?" she asked. "About Father? About me?"

"Oh, yes," her mother replied, her words as bitter as wyrmroot tea. "He knew. I had written him before to inform him of my betrothal, and then of my marriage, and then of your birth. Never once did he bother to reply, although Naraan assured me my messages had been delivered safely into his hands. I wrote him again, informing him that I would return to my people as soon as I may, but that my husband first had to find a suitable replacement as Captain of Iventorr's Guard, and that such a process was an arduous one and could take some time."

"I take it he didn't react well," Fletch observed, watching Fiorelle's eyes narrow.

"No, he didn't. He threatened to make my brother king." She half-laughed, half-snorted, chin squaring. "He would have broken our most sacred tradition. And why? So the Wyndarin people could continue to dwindle under an even more vain and arrogant ruler?"

"Your brother was even worse than your father?"

Fiorelle nodded. "Farnen is not a good man. I was forced to exile him from our people some years ago after he… Hm. But that is beside the point." She sighed, one hand rising to rub across her brow. "Yes, he would have been even worse for the Wyndarin people than my father was." Lips parting as if to speak again, she stopped. Blinking, she took a deep, shaky breath. "Your father and I discussed it at great length," she said huskily. "At last we decided that I would return to my people, and that he would join the Wyndarin once he had found a suitable successor for the

Captain of the Guard. But we could not decide what would be best for you, Fletch. To stay in Iventorr with your papa, or to come with me and live with the Wyndarin, never settling in one place?" Tears springing suddenly to her eyes, her lips wobbled in an unsteady smile. "So we asked you what you wished to do."

"And I chose to stay with Papa," Fletch whispered.

This must've been the part of the reason Naraan left the Wyndarin. But something in Fiorelle's eyes told Fletch there was another part of the story, something that involved Naraan that she'd shut away and locked tight.

She swallowed, the lump in her throat swollen and painful as she absorbed her mother's words. The raw pain and bitterness in her mother's eyes made it difficult to even consider her words as falsehood.

Fiorelle and Kell had never intended to remain apart.

Dizzy, Fletch put her elbows on the table, cupping her head in her hands.

"Even though whispers of conspiracy floated through the castle, even though unrest had begun to stir, I left you and Kell," her mother was saying. "And when your father was slain, I did not make it back to Iventorr before you had pledged yourself to the Foresters."

Fletch glanced up sharply. *You didn't come back at all* sprang to her lips, but she bit it back. Something in Fiorelle's voice, in the way she'd said it, gave her pause.

Her mother's eyes were deep pools of crystal emotion swirling with regret. "Because of me, you have lived a life far more harsh and isolated than any child should have to endure."

"Wait." Fletch shook her head. "You said you didn't make it back before I joined. You... you returned?" She'd based her entire perspective of her mother on... a misconception? "When? Why did I not hear of it?"

"I came to Iventorr on my own, leaving my people at Port Lunalin in Ilumence. No one knew I was here. Young King Dreythan was still mourning the loss of his father, struggling to find purpose as ruler. I could not bring myself to disturb him. I asked around the castle with those I had been close to. Matron Jaida and others in the kitchens and gardens told me that little Fletch had asked to be trained as a Forester, and had been granted her request by the king himself." She looked down at her clasped hands, her knuckles white. "I was too late, Fletch. Forgive me. If only our ships had been faster—"

For a brief moment, it were as if Fletch sat in her mother's place. She saw before herself the impossible choice: her people, or her family. Though the events thereafter weren't connected directly to the decision she had made, she still saw threads woven between them and blamed herself for the aftermath. Even after all those years, she still bore the weight of that blame on her shoulders.

"I should be the one begging you for forgiveness," Fletch said, her voice husky as it strained past the lump in her throat. "I'm the one who took the Lonely Vow when I renewed my tenure with the Foresters." She tried to swallow, but heat prickled behind her eyes, blurring her vision. "I was angry, bitter. I... I wanted to hurt you. And preventing you from making any contact with me... it seemed like the best way to do that."

But Fiorelle was already shaking her head. "It did hurt," she admitted, "but I knew you were punishing me for abandoning you."

Reaching across the table, Fletch clasped her mother's fingers firmly. "You didn't abandon me," she said, the words as much a reassurance for herself as they were for her mother. "You didn't. No amount of regret will change what happened, and even if it could, I wouldn't change my past." She paused, stunned. Even though she'd never thought it possible, the phrase rang with truth. "It has shaped me into who I am today," she continued, the conviction growing with each syllable. "Had I not become a Forester, I wouldn't have come to know and love Jon and Missy Pruden, or the little town of Herstshire. I wouldn't have learned to hunt and survive on my own. I would not have slain a den of Unbreathing and gained the experience needed to save the king's life." Squeezing her mother's hands, she met her eye steadily as she said, "But I'm glad you're here now. Will you forgive me for shutting you out?"

The tears spilled from Fiorelle's eyes as her hands circled her daughter's. Head bowing, her shoulders trembling, she returned the squeeze with a fierceness that startled Fletch. For several minutes, they simply sat that way, elbows planted on the wooden table, basket of fruit pushed idly to one side as their hands folded warmly into each other.

"How I wish Kell could see us," Fiorelle whispered finally, heaving a great shuddering breath.

Fletch smiled, remembering the feeling of a large pair of calloused hands enveloping hers. "I believe he can," she said quietly. "I believe it brings him peace." Shifting, she gently withdrew and folded her fingers together in her lap.

"I do hope so." Her mother gave a little hiccuping laugh, wiping her eyes. "I like to imagine he had a hand in sending word to me of your new post."

"How did word reach you?"

"Naraan sent word by wyrm several weeks past, but his missive was less a message and more a hint." Giving an extremely un-queenlike roll of the eyes, Fiorelle shook her head. "Meddlesome man that he is. It was enough to stoke the flames of hope within me, and I directed my people to begin the journey across the seas to Ivenhence. But only a fortnight past, I received another message, this time from Ambassador Kekona of the Isles of Aden."

"The ambassador?" Fletch gaped.

"Indeed. She sent word in the hopes I would arrange future trade relations with the Isles in exchange for the knowledge of my daughter's post and wellbeing."

It was all Fletch could do to lower her head, hoping doing so would hide her face.

No wonder the ambassador's eyes had widened when she'd heard Fletch's name.

"I have arranged to meet with her this evening," Fiorelle said, turning to look out the darkened window. "It is already close to our agreed time." Her face falling, she slowly stood. "I'm afraid I must be going."

Fletch lurched to her feet. There was still so much she wanted to say, so many questions she wanted to ask. "My day of rest is tomorrow," she blurted. "Perhaps… we could see each other again?"

"But of course!" Her mother's reply was immediate. "It would be my great pleasure to introduce you to my people and show you about our camp. Shall we meet in the dining hall to break fast tomorrow morn?"

She nodded, her heart swelling at the joy in Fiorelle's brown eyes. "I look forward to it."

Before Fletch could react, Fiorelle wrapped her arms around her shoulders, pulling her into a hesitant but warm embrace. Fletch stiffened, shocked. Then she melted, her arms circling her mother as she returned the hug.

Though minutes passed, it felt like mere moments as they held each other, their arms tightening until they were fiercely close. Fletch smiled over her mother's head, realizing how much taller she was. When she'd been a child, she'd always thought her mother towered above her.

When they finally pulled away, tears again brimmed Fiorelle's eyes, but they were full of joy and wonder. Smiling, she ducked her head, wiping them away. "Goodnight, Fletch. And… thank you."

When the door closed softly behind Fiorelle's departing footsteps, Fletch stared at the iron-fitted oak, wondering if she had dreamed the last two hours. But no, her mother's tapestry still lay unrolled on the floor. Stooping, she traced the mountain range with one finger, a little smile curving her lips.

"If only you could see us," she said quietly. Glancing over at her chest of drawers, she straightened. Atop it sat Jon and Missy Pruden's last letter, and beside that, Kell's journal, leather strip tying it neatly shut.

'Tis clear he feared his journal would fall into the wrong hands. You shall understand once you have finished reading it.

Naraan's words echoed in Fletch's mind. Crossing to the drawers, she picked up the book and settled onto her bed.

Hurrying across the thoroughfare, Fletch flipped her hood up, her boots splashing through puddles as she clamped her precious burden against her side. Her day of rest had dawned grey and drizzling. Green and yellow Wynd advanced sluggishly across the sky, driving storm clouds ever closer. The muggy air was heavy with the promise of constant rain.

Reaching the arched oak door of the library, she tugged it open and ducked inside, pausing to shed her dripping cloak.

"Sentinel Wyndshaper," Brinwathe's aged voice croaked. He peered over the top of his desk, white brows disappearing into his halo of wild hair. "Can I be of assistance?"

"I hope so," Fletch replied with a quick smile. "I should like to write a letter, but I'm afraid I have no parchment or ink of my own."

The little man rose creakily from his chair, nodding as he gathered a few things from various drawers and shelves. "Easily remedied, my dear, easily remedied. Come, I shall set up a desk for you. Right this way."

He shuffled down an aisle between shelves before Fletch could ask, "Would you like help carrying—"

"No, no," he interrupted cheerfully. "I am here to assist you, not the other way 'round." He halted beside a large table, setting objects down in rapid succession. "Parchment, ink, quills, blotter, wiping cloth. Ah, yes, and inkwell. There you are, Sentinel. If you require your letter be taken to the falconry, I shall have one of the apprentices do so. You have only to ask."

Fletch blinked. "The falconry tower? 'Tis a personal missive, Master Brinwathe... I thought the employ of sun jays was reserved for urgent or important matters."

The old codger lent her a grin, tapping the side of his long, pointed nose. "And royalty." With that, he retreated down the aisle, humming as if immensely pleased with himself.

Word was somehow spreading of her kinship with the Wyndarin queen, Fletch reflected as she turned to her parchment, pulling a book out from under her cloak. She wasn't quite sure how to feel about that.

Dipping a quill into the inkwell, she bent over her letter. For a while, the only sounds to be heard were the pitter-patter of rain on the shale roof high above and the scratch of her pen against paper. Unlike the last letter she had written to the Prudens, the words came easily. She thanked them for their thoughtfulness and kindness (probably a few too many times), proclaiming how beautiful the bodice was Missy had made, how delicious Master Pruden's ale, and how she had missed its taste and how she missed them both.

There were good people in Iventorr, she wrote, not to worry. Matron Gulden, Captain Norland, Petrecia Wyntersoul, Klep Ironshod. Her quill hesitated for only a moment, then feverishly sped on, recounting what a good friend Klep had been and how welcome he had made her feel before his death.

Fletch had just begun to write about the Wyndarin when a startled voice said, "Oh. Er, pleasant day."

Glancing up, she met Dreythan's surprised eyes. "My lord." She smiled, then remembered and snapped to her feet. "A pleasant day to you."

His gaze strayed to the letter, then back to her face, clearly puzzled. "I am surprised you are here before the dining hall has even opened for breakfast. That is," he added, "I assumed you were partially covering Matteo Alwick's shifts while he's away."

Fletch shook her head. "Captain Norland has assumed his duties," she explained.

The king's confusion dissolved. "Ah. It is no wonder the Captain has been following me so closely these past days. I feel as though I am a chick being shadowed by a mother hen."

"He clucks like one, too," Fletch added with a grin, and

Dreythan laughed. It was a beautiful sound, deep and pure.

When his chuckle subsided, he dipped in a little bow. "I shan't keep you from your letter."

"You weren't," she told him, still smiling. "You're welcome to interrupt me any time."

"Unless you're saving my life again, I should think," he jested, then hesitated. "Might I join you? Sharing the quiet with a like mind is the best form of peace."

"Of course," she replied firmly. "Please, sit."

Brinwathe doddered to the table, carefully setting a stack of tomes atop. As Fletch returned to her writing, he and Dreythan exchanged a few quiet words, picking up a couple of the books and thumbing quickly through them. The librarian shuffled off again as Dreythan sat across the table from Fletch and began to read.

The soft scritch-scratch of quill and parchment, the gentle dripping of steady rain, and the occasional swish of a turning page all combined to form the loveliest of melodies. It was a song of peace and refreshing quiet. Fletch paused to listen, raising her head from her letter to glance around. Down the aisle, Brinwathe sat at his desk, vigorously scribbling away in an enormous scroll. One of his apprentices stood nearby, sorting through books and scrolls and muttering quietly to herself. Dim grey light filtered through the windows, colliding with the warm illumination of lit lanterns and lamps to cast sepia tones across the scattered shelves and tables.

Across the table, Dreythan turned another page, brow furrowed. One hand held the book he scanned. The other hand's thumb was planted under his square chin, the index finger over his lips which were pressed into a thoughtful crease. His black hair hung over his eyes, but he didn't seem to notice. Muted lamplight flickered across the sharp angle of his high cheekbone and temple.

Fletch's stomach fluttered. Gaze dropping back to her letter, she continued to write, though her thoughts weren't on the words.

For the first time, she realized how comfortable she felt around

Dreythan. Most people made her skin prickle or her fingers twitch, as though they expected something of her that she couldn't give. She could count on two hands the number of people she had known that had never made her feel so: Jon and Missy Pruden, Klep, Captain Norland, Naraan, and Dreythan. But Dreythan's presence was even different amongst those. Around him, she felt she could be entirely herself, without fear of judgment or disappointment. He understood that she was odd, even strange, but he didn't seem to fault her for it.

Remembering how he'd smiled at her bare feet, trying to dissuade her embarrassment, she ducked her head, ears burning.

Finishing the letter took some doing after that, but she eventually managed it. As she set her quill aside and poured the leftover ink back into its pot, Dreythan looked up. "I'll be going as soon as the ink has dried," she explained to his quizzical glance. "My mother and I arranged to meet in the dining hall this morn... hopefully the rain shan't force us to change our plans."

The king nodded. "Might I ask how... how you and your mother are getting along?"

At the evident anxious hope in his dark eyes, warmth rushed through her chest. "We're getting along well, my lord. I'm sure there are many questions we yet have for each other, and there are hundreds of topics yet to discuss. But it feels as though the beginning phases of mending are nearly done." With two quick motions, she folded her letter, then stood. An instinct to slide her fingers into Dreythan's hand flashed through her mind.

"It gladdens my heart to hear it," the king said, also rising.

They stood there for a few moments, smiling companionably at each other.

Fletch hesitated, reluctant to break the cozy silence. "That day in the gardens," she offered finally. "I hadn't spoken of my mother in many years. I think that perhaps speaking of difficult things makes them easier to bear. 'Tis a lesson I've only recently learned, in part thanks to you."

Dreythan's smile widened, then suddenly faded. "Do not thank me," he said quietly. "That is what friends do, is it not? Listen to each other?"

When he didn't continue, Fletch swallowed. "I suppose it is, my lord." After a brief pause, she added quickly, "I nearly forgot." Plucking the book she'd brought with her off the table, she held it out to him, peering hopefully at his face. "The Wyndarin merchant I previously purchased from is also visiting, so... I picked this up for you."

The king's hands closed around the hard-bound volume, his expression softening as he read the title. "The Culture and History of the Wyndarin." His throat bobbed. When he looked up and met her gaze, there was something in his eyes that turned her insides to jelly. "You are exceedingly kind. I am in your debt, Fletch. Thank you."

"Of course," she replied with a little wink, hoping her cheeks weren't as red as they felt. "I hope you find it useful. A pleasant day to you, my lord."

As soon as Fletch took her seat in the dining hall with the other Sentinels, Sariah set a plate in front of her with a timid smile and a curtsey. Nodding her thanks, Fletch shoveled food into her face as quickly as possible, hoping to finish before her mother arrived.

Just as she gulped down the last of her stale water, a voice behind her said, "Are you still available today, my daughter?"

She gulped too sharply, shooting to her feet as she gasped, "Mother! Yes! Yes, I am."

"Wonderful." Fiorelle smiled sunnily. "Shall we be off?"

As Fletch swung her leg over the bench and plucked her quiver and bow from the table, she glanced up to find Harrild and Darvick openly staring.

"Did she just call her 'Mother'?" Harrild whispered, his hazel eyes as round as grapes.

"You missed the part where the queen called her 'daughter'," his brother said with a smirk.

Heat rushing to her cheeks, Fletch turned and trailed after her mother. The other Sentinels weren't the only ones gaping. Many other pairs of eyes from all corners of the dining hall followed her out.

Once they exited the dining hall, Fiorelle stepped aside and waited for Fletch, a dome of dense citrine Wynd swirling to life above her, scattering falling raindrops in a perfect circle. "Should you like to step closer, my Everbreeze can shelter you as well," she offered.

As she obligingly shifted under the spiraling canopy, Fletch squinted up at the translucent yellow-green. If only she'd been able to make one that miserable day the Unbreathing spy had been caught... "I've never liked rain," she admitted, scowling at the water falling all around as their feet clunked across the boards of the enormous bridge. "It feels as though it's taunting me. All that falling Wynd, and me unable to do anything about it."

"Perhaps 'tis the perfect day to visit our camp, then." Fiorelle chuckled. "Several of our watchfolk must maintain a much larger Everbreeze when it rains." Pointing, she added, "The flutterwisps cannot survive a storm."

Ahead, the multitude of brightly-colored tents and wagons waited on a grassy distant hill. The gentle vortex of Wynd still swirled above the Wyndarin camp, bearing aloft pure white spheres of fluff in a never-ending circular stream. But above that, just as Fiorelle had said, spun a far larger, far more dense disk of compact Wynd.

"You're protecting the white puffs?" Fletch glanced curiously at her. "Flutterwisps. What are they?"

"They are seeds," the queen replied. The dim light bathed her cheeks in a gentle glow, illuminating a tender smile as Fiorelle gazed upward. "Seeds to a breed of flower that was nearly lost. Far across the seas, there is a land that few have traveled called Markal. 'Tis a land of stone and stand, filled with deadly creatures and poisonous plants. Yet, at an oasis in the desert, we found them — plants we had never seen any other place on Hearth." Her eyes glimmered, widening with wonder. "Imagine it. A spray of yellow and orange petals like the noon sun, the bud as wide as a man is tall. Each time the Wynd led us to the oasis in the desert, the sunwisp flowers began producing these seeds. The yellow petals would wither and shrivel, leaving behind the white puffs you see above us. But one year when we arrived at the oasis, we discovered the flower grove decimated. A swarm of locusts or some other such insect had swept through, leaving only three of the plants barely alive."

Fiorelle's brow smoothed, her eyes clearing. "That was my second year as queen," she said softly. "I couldn't bear the thought that something so beautiful might be lost to the world forever. Thus, we have been transporting the seeds across the Hearth, planting a few each place we go in the hope that they might survive."

Fletch watched the puff balls circle for a moment, a pang echoing through her chest. "The seeds — flutterwisps," she said. "They live on the Wynd?"

"They do," Fiorelle replied, smiling up at them fondly. "Our herbnurse, Master Relman, discovered so through trial and error."

"Have any of the seeds sprouted? In the years since?"

"They have, in the most unusual of places. For example, along the coastline of the Isles of Aden, and in one of Thissa's oases."

Eyeing the multitude of shades in the slowly spinning cyclone, Fletch asked, "Did Master Relman also discover the seeds need varying temperatures?"

The queen's smile broadened as her eyes met Fletch's. "That he did. He's an extraordinary man with unusual Wyndcalling skill. I hope you're able to meet him before we depart."

Remembering the roll of parchment in her quiver, Fletch tugged it free and held it out. "Speaking of Wyndcalling, could you help me decipher this? T'was a gift from Naraan."

"Certainly." A shadow crossed Fiorelle's brown eyes as the scroll unfurled in her fingers. "I am surprised he held onto it for so many years."

Puzzled, Fletch glanced from her mother's troubled face to scroll and back again. "This was yours once?"

When her mother didn't answer, her lips pinching into a thin line, she looked down. It was impossible to guess Fiorelle's expression. Irritation? Pain? Anger?

"Not precisely," the queen said finally. "But... 'tis difficult to speak of." Swiveling, she paused to allow Fletch to follow, leading her back toward the octagonal tent as she continued, "I believe my father hoped I would Choose Naraan when I returned from my Wandering."

"Choose him?" Fletch echoed.

"Yes. Marriage is a serious commitment among the Wyndarin, and is only entered after two people have borne or raised a child together. And before that, one must Choose their mate." Her glance met Fletch's frankly. "I believe my father wished for Naraan and I to bear a child together. He often gave him gifts like this scroll, and bestowed favors on him such as appointing him as messenger of the Wyndarin."

"Oh. I... I see."

Face clearing, Fiorelle glanced back down at the scroll in her hand. "But no matter. This particular Wyndscroll is meant for those who call the Wynd with their motions. There are many ways to call the Wynd. Your father Kell was best suited to whistling, coaxing the Wynd with his lips. My father drew the Wynd with his voice, singing and speaking. My brother called it with an instrument. And I summon it with my mind." Pointing to the first figure on the parchment, Fiorelle continued, "There are also many different Wyndcalling skills. Shaping a breeze is one matter, but moving water, raising and lowering temperatures, and manipulating the weather are all vastly different. Some Wyndarin are able to perform most of these, and some only possess one or two abilities. Your father was skilled in shaping the free air, thus his surname. I am able to shape air, water, and weather. I cannot produce freeze or flame. This scroll will help you determine which skills you possess." Handing the scroll back, she added with a smile, "Do not be discouraged when a form eludes you. No Wynd-blood is able to manipulate every aspect of Luminia's breath. T'would make us no less than the goddess, and that is something we can never be."

Fletch slipped the scroll back into her quiver, glancing ahead. They were only a few hundred feet from the edge of the Wyndarin camp. "I've never been able to produce fire either," she admitted. "And I have difficulty shaping moving water. But I always assumed it was because I was going about it the wrong way."

Her mother chuckled. "It is possible! Once we have made our tour, I can guide you through the Wyndcalling forms on the scroll. But until then, come! I have much to show you."

For a brief moment, Fiorelle's hand fluttered towards Fletch's as her sparkling eyes smiled. A silent question lingered there, hesitant, almost timid.

Summoning her courage, Fletch sucked in a quick breath and slipped her fingers into her mother's palm.

As they stepped between the first sets of elaborate tents, the green swirl above Fiorelle's head dissipated. A few passing Wyndarin in beautifully tooled leather armor froze, saluting sharply as they passed. With a regal nod, Fiorelle continued on, weaving between tents and wagons, sidestepping adults and children who stopped to gaze at Fletch with wide, curious eyes.

"Forgive them," Fiorelle told her apologetically. "They only wish to catch a glimpse of the princess they've heard so much about."

Princess... it jangled in Fletch's ears, and she shook her head. It was a title for someone else, someone graceful and well-appointed. Not someone who'd served as a Forester over half her life, someone who could barely wear a dress without tripping over the hem.

"Our camp is divided into sections when we travel by land," the queen was saying, guiding her down a row of vermillion and magenta tents. "These are the quarters for the Wyndarin who are around your age, young adults who must soon depart on their separate Wandering. Here they practice living on their own, away from their family, for a span of time of their own choosing."

Several youths were gathered around a map, pointing at various regions and conversing earnestly. They paused as Fiorelle and Fletch passed by, their faces open and curious. Fletch bobbed her head at them. A few waved, grinning.

"Over here," Fiorelle continued, "the green and turquoise patterned tents are the traveling homes of families and those with children. The violet and blue tents across from them are the storage and trading stations for merchants."

They continued through the camp for over an hour, stopping to visit families, craftfolk, merchants, and elders alike. At one point, they passed a weaving tent, where many baskets of raw and dyed fibers were stacked neatly in corners away from huge copper vats filled with steaming liquid. A young woman with hair as bright as ripe wheat raised her head from a spinning wheel to beam at them.

Fletch followed reluctantly as her mother stepped lightly onward, watching over her shoulder as the young woman's hands fed the fiber steadily into the wheel, pulling, stretching, sliding. It was mesmerizing to watch.

But there were too many wonderful things to see to look backwards for long.

The queen led her daughter past several more vendor storage tents, pointing out the owners and greeting them if they were near. Cloth, pearls, exotic fruits. Fletch recognized each of the merchants from Iventorr Castle's square. And only minutes later, they stopped at a tent where two women sorted through shelves and piles of precious and semi-precious stone. From raw gems and polished round crystals to cut rubies and even diamonds, the tiniest spark of light sent a rainbow of colors flashing along the cloth walls.

Fiorelle exclaimed over the beauty of a freshly polished opal as Fletch examined a vibrant purple stone, her reflection refracting in its surface. It was the same beautiful shade as the brooch Ambassador Kekona wore with her travel cloak. The sort of color royalty wore.

"It was good to see you again, Relman," a familiar voice said, cutting through her reverie. "May the Wynd carry you ever onward."

Plopping the gem down on its shelf, Fletch ducked out of the tent just in time to see a brown burlap robe disappearing around the corner.

"Naraan?"

Sure enough, the book peddler paused as she trotted up behind him, a smile breaking over his leathered face as he turned towards her. "Well," he said with a chuckle. "We keep running into each other, young Wyndshaper. What brings you to the Wyndarin encampment?"

Fletch hesitated. Should she speak of her mother? Every time Fiorelle spoke of Naraan, her expression was tense, sharp. As if she wished she could forget.

She was thankfully spared a decision when Naraan glanced past her, folding into a deep bow. "Queen Fiorelle."

Spinning slowly on her heel, Fletch found her mother behind her, slender hands folded majestically. Her face was a taut, blank mask, she intoned, "Naraan."

A too-long, awkward moment passed, in which Fletch glanced from her mother to her uncle and back again, her stomach flopping nervously. An invisible force crackled between them, both repelling and attracting. It blazed in Naraan's grey eyes and the line of Fiorelle's lips, both of them poised as if ready to run.

"Mother and I have been... reconnecting," Fletch interjected. "And she's been introducing me to her — er, your — that is, our people."

"I see." Naraan nodded, the energy dissipating from him as he folded his large hands within his sleeves. "I am glad to hear it. But I see the Wynd still moves sluggishly within you. Have you not been able to use the scroll I gave?"

"I haven't had the chance to practice it with it yet," she confessed, pulling it from her quiver.

"Ah. Well, since I am here, would you like to go over a few of the—"

"I have already offered to assist her," Fiorelle interrupted, her voice too sharp. Cheeks reddening, she added, "Though... there are forms I cannot aid her with, as I am unable to create them myself."

Sensing the tension building again, Fletch swallowed. "Your Unbreathing book mentioned the monsters are weak to Wynd, Naraan. Do you think that flame or ice could be used as weapons against them?"

"I do." Gesturing to Fletch's quiver, he said, "If you are creative with your applications of Wyndcalling, you can even combine it with skills you already possess, such as your father did. You could create ice shards for arrowheads, or light your missiles aflame as you loose them."

"I wonder if an ice arrowhead would be as effective as a silver one," she muttered, imagining how differently the Unbreathing ambush might have gone.

"There is only one way to find out. I offer my assistance in training, should you be interested." When Fletch looked up, Naraan smiled. "I have no other place to be currently, and can remain in Verenshire for a fortnight or so until you have mastered the basics."

"You are not rejoining the Wandering?" Fiorelle asked.

Naraan's gaze flicked to meet hers. "I had not intended to."

"I... I see." To Fletch's puzzlement, Fiorelle ducked her head.

Pulling her eyes away from her mother, Fletch nodded to Naraan. "I'll take all the training I can get. Thank you. Both of you," she added, and Fiorelle smiled.

"Excellent," Naraan said, his teeth glinting in a rare grin. "The pursuit of knowledge is never in vain. Seeing as you already have the scroll with you, shall we get started?"

Fletch wove her way through the emptying streets as the echoes of the fifth afternoon bell rang. The Wyndarin departure feast was to be held on the morrow. As if in protest, the castle had been a swarming hive of activity all day, the square and market packed with shouting vendors and shoppers alike. Wyndarin had hurried here and there, pulling carts and carrying armfuls of ribbons or vegetables. In the past twelve hours alone, they had transformed Iventorr, hanging bright streamers and cords from every nook and cranny and stringing them between buildings so they dangled high above the streets.

But now, with the Wyndarin preparing to leave, so too were the merchants from the Isles of Aden and from Ilumence. The last of them were packing up their wagons, humming or whistling to themselves with the cheer of a profitable week. A few were gathered around Ambassador Kekona in the square, showing her notes and books as they conversed earnestly. As if sensing Fletch's glance, the ambassador looked up, meeting her eye with a smile and a graceful nod.

Throat tightening, she returned the nod and hurried on. Where on Hearth could her mother have gone?

"Sentinel Fletch?" a soft voice called, accompanied by the clip-clopping of hooves. "Are you looking for Queen Fiorelle?"

She turned just as a large shape lowered near her face, braying, "Heeeeerich?"

"Hello, Roderick!" She grinned as the elbecca nuzzled her cheek. She scratched his forelock, peering around his neck at the small cart hitched behind him. "Hello, Sariah. Yes, have you seen her?"

The maid pushed a strand of curls away from her eyes, nodding. "She was headed to the kitchens last I saw. I think she said something about needing to make arrangements with Matron Gulden for dessert." Clucking her tongue to Roderick, she lent Fletch an apologetic shrug. "I'd best get back to work. Those vegetables shan't cart themselves!"

"Right." She stepped aside, giving the elbecca one last vigorous pat as he fluttered his long, white lashes at her. "Thank you!"

Continuing onward toward the kitchens, Fletch's stomach tightened. Only one full day was left before her mother would leave. And there still remained the banquet... there was no telling how much time they would actually be able to spend together. She swallowed, shifting her quiver higher on her shoulder. After tomorrow, she likely wouldn't see Fiorelle for four years, until the next septennial Wyndarin trade visit.

The thought weighted her footsteps, slowing her path. It didn't seem right that they were... separating again. After only just beginning to reconcile, to become acquainted with each other. The last few days felt fragile, as if the things they had overcome and the progress they'd made could be erased with time and distance.

Squaring her jaw, Fletch straightened. Their new relationship might be fragile, but it was worth nourishing. She would do whatever she could to keep it alive.

Breaking into a trot, she hurried past the welcome hall entrance just as a group of Wyndarin emerged from the kitchen doors, followed by Matron Gulden and Fiorelle.

"I look forward to seeing the children's faces when they see the mango blossoms," the kitchen head was saying, her normally set face wreathed in a rare smile. "And I know my staff is anticipating learning new recipes and cooking techniques from your people. We shall wrap up breakfast at the upsec bell. Afterwards, we shall be at your disposal, Your Grace."

"You are too gracious," Fiorelle replied. "Thank you, Matron. Rest well, for tomorrow shall be long."

Turning, the queen's eyes met Fletch's. She lifted a hand, a wide smile breaking over her face. With a quick murmur to her attendants, they bowed and hurried away, leaving Fletch and Fiorelle alone in the nearly-deserted courtyard.

"Would you like any help with preparations?" Fletch asked, twisting her fingers together behind her back. A sudden paranoia crept into the back of her mind, whispering that she was being a nuisance.

"No," her mother replied quickly. "Our preparations are complete for the evening. What I would like is to spend the little time I have left here with you." Her smile faltered. "Would you accompany me to the garden?"

In response, Fletch threaded her arm through her mother's. They fell into step side by side, their feet tapping a light rhythm on the cobblestone as they turned the corner and made their way down the quieting street.

"Is something troubling you?" she asked, casting a quick glance at the small frown lines around Fiorelle's tight lips.

Several moments of tense quiet passed.

"Yes," she finally admitted, her chin dipping toward her chest. "There is something I must ask you, but I feel it is far too soon. But if I do not ask now, it shall be too late when next I see you." Her narrow shoulders heaved a sigh. "I do not know what to do, I'm afraid."

Teeth clamping on her lip, Fletch hesitated. "I think I understand," she offered haltingly. "Questions... they're easy to think, but hard to voice, sometimes. What if... What if I asked you a difficult question first?"

"An exchange of information?" Fiorelle raised her head, chuckling. "You sound like Naraan. Has he used that trick on you?"

"He has," she replied, warmth blossoming in her chest as she watched the anxiety dissolve from her mother's face.

"Very well, then. Perhaps I shall have the courage to ask my question after answering yours."

All too aware of her mother's eyes fixed on her visage, Fletch shook away her growing doubt and asked, "Why did you marry Papa?" Before Fiorelle's expression fell, she rushed on, "It wasn't your custom to marry before bearing children, and you knew you would have to leave Iventorr to become heir to the Wyndarin throne. I'm... I'm merely curious, is all."

Her mother nodded, understanding and relief dawning. "I have told you of how we met, and of how I came to live in Iventorr. Soon after we grew acquainted, I fell in love. He was so kind, and loyal, and wise. It did not matter to me that he was thrice my age. I loved him with my entire being. Of course," she added, her face reddening, "I could not show him my feelings. I was heir to the Wyndarin throne. I had a duty to my people that could not be denied. But the love I harbored for him would not fade, no matter how I tried to push it down and conceal it." She paused as they entered the royal garden, settling onto one of the benches. "I even tried to ward him off by telling him that I would have to return to my people in less than seven years, but he only laughed and said, 'But you have those years to live freely! 'Tis more time and freedom than some are given.'"

Heat prickled behind Fletch's eyes. For a moment, she could almost remember her father's voice, picture his face. "What happened then?"

"After a time, he asked me to marry him. He said that he cared not that I would have to leave him. His words were, 'I would rather love you for six years than not at all.'" She threw her hands up, laughing even as her eyes filled with tears. "How could I refuse him? We wed, and a year later, I bore you into the world. It was the happiest time of our lives, and we knew that one day it would end, but we lived each moment as it came. That is," she added, smiling sadly, "until it became apparent that our time would end prematurely. Then, it felt that every day was filled with a desperation to show our love for each other, to create memories that would never fade."

"I hadn't realized his age was so far beyond yours." Fletch smiled, trying to picture them together. "You were twenty-two? How old was he?"

"Your father Kell was sixty-three years old," she smiled. "He did not look a day over thirty-five. Those of the Wynd-blood age more slowly than those of Hearth. But come, Fletch." Fiorelle took her hands. "You asked your question. And it is now time that I asked mine." A stream of Wynd rushed into her nostrils, then exited in a long, slow, exhale. "But... my question is one that I must ask you not to answer. 'Tis a matter that I would beg you give long, careful consideration to, unless you are absolutely and immediately certain of the answer."

Hope and apprehension battled in Fiorelle's brown eyes. Heart in her throat, Fletch nodded. "I understand."

"Thank you, daughter." Her fingers tightened briefly, then withdrew. "As you know," she said slowly, as if carefully picking each word, "the eldest borne of the Wyndarin royal line must take the throne if there is no son to secede a mother or a daughter to follow a father. You are my only child, and I did not wish to consider bearing another until I had spoken with you." She swallowed, the curve of her throat bobbing unsteadily. "When the Wyndarin next pass through Ivenhence, would you join the Wandering Way and become queen of our people? If you have no wish to do so, I will absolutely understand. But I need to know for the sake of the royal line. If you do not wish to ascend to rule, I shall need to Choose and bear another child."

Queen. That word felt even more unsuited to her than 'princess' had. She stared down at her intertwined fingers, knowing that a queen's should be neatly folded in her lap, that a queen would sit regally straight rather than propping her ankle on her opposite knee. Ambassador Kekona fit the words 'queen' and 'princess' far better than she ever would.

Aside from that, it would be unfair to the Wyndarin. She'd never lived among them, didn't see their culture as her own. She wasn't even fully aware of her own Wyndcalling abilities. How could she command others to use theirs on her behalf?

Her mother was waiting for her to say something, her eyes fixed on her face. "I shall think on it." It was difficult to say, to make that promise not only to her mother, but to herself. To tell herself to consider the burden and responsibility of rule.

"I know it might be alien to think of," Fiorelle told her gently. "Leaving the nation you've dedicated your life to protecting. All I ask is that you give me your answer in four years. Whatever choice you make, whichever path you deem best, I shall not dissuade you." Her hand rose and rested on Fletch's arm, warm and comforting. "But come, daughter. Let us speak of more cheerful matters. I met a lovely maid in the kitchens today — Sariah, I believe her name is. She mentioned you've become friends because of her elbecca?"

Chapter 20

A cool breeze swept past Dreythan as he strode down the street. A few leaves, just turning yellow and orange, trembled loose from shifting branches to drift through the air. Strung from every roof peak, buttress, and balustrade, streamers of red, amber, and gold fluttered overhead, casting criss-crossing shadows on the crowded alleys and thoroughfares below. Even the main courtyard had not been spared this extravagant treatment. At the top of the central fountain, a bundle of ribbons had been tied, then draped in every direction in a delightful explosion of color.

Every possible corner and cranny was filled with people. They lined the street, waving streamers and cheering as Dreythan proceeded past them, flanked by Captain Norland and Harrild Hammerfist.

"Look at how many have come for the feast," he said, shooting a quick glance over his shoulder at the Captain. "I do not believe I have ever seen Iventorr this… lively."

"They're just here for the free food and drink," Norland

growled morosely. "Greedy bastards."

Hiding a smile, Dreythan quickened his pace. The banquet could not start until he arrived, and he had no wish to keep his citizens and visitors waiting.

The crowd parted at his approach. At the landing to the dining hall doors, three feminine figures waited. One was Queen Fiorelle, her dazzlingly white robes and winged gold crown seeming to glow in the afternoon light. With her stood Ambassador Kekona, who had toned down her usual bejeweled presentation for an azure blue velvet gown, silver lotuses embroidered into the edge of the skirt and the tips of her bell-shaped sleeves.

Not recognizing the third figure, Dreythan squinted. She was taller than either of the other women, her slender form accented by a long dress of soft dove grey and a sapphire blue bodice. Her auburn hair had been braided into a wreath that encircled her head, woven with cornflowers and silver pins in the shape of simple leaves.

His heart leapt into his throat, and for a moment, his feet faltered. Queen Fiorelle had asked permission for her daughter to join them at the banquet, but it hadn't occurred to him until now what that might mean.

"May I say how lovely you look, my lady," Ambassador Kekona was commenting. "That color blue suits you quite nicely."

"Thank you," Fletch replied. Her tone was genuine, but her smile was hesitant. "As do you. That stone in your hair — I've never seen its like before. 'Tis beautiful."

"Turquoise," Fiorelle interjected with a wide smile. "It comes from across the ocean, from a country called Monhein."

Pausing in front of them, Dreythan dropped in a bow as they did the same. As he straightened, his eyes met Fletch's. Her lips curved in a smile, and the sounds of the crowd dimmed as Dreythan's blood thundered in his ears.

"Queen Fiorelle," he greeted, his voice thankfully steady. "Lady Fletch, Ambassador Kekona. Please, join me."

They parted to let him pass. As he entered the dining hall and his eyes adjusted to the dimmed light, they were met with wonder. Ribbons had been tied from the rafters, weaving in and out in a dizzying geometric pattern. The cloth-draped walls were lined with kegs, a few tapped and ready to be drained, many more waiting. Food of delightful colors and varieties piled the tables, filling the air with a plethora of scents. Butter, garlic, roasted meats and vegetables, cinnamon, and clove all mingled, teasing a growl from Dreythan's stomach as he walked past. At the table where he normally sat alone, four chairs waited.

As he lowered himself into his usual seat and the three women chose theirs, townsfolk, merchants, and travelers alike began filtering in, already conversing and laughing as they took their seats, gasping at the intricate decor and gaping at the piles of prepared foods.

When the hall was full, and those seated at the tables fell silent and turned expectantly toward the nobles' table, Dreythan deliberately rose.

"All thanks to Queen Fiorelle of the Wyndarin and to her people for this bountiful banquet," he intoned, his voice echoing into the far corners of the room. "Let us begin."

He sat as servants swarmed around him, whistles and applause bursting from the multitude below.

Several minutes passed in a bright, happy, noisy blur. Drethan's plate was filled with dishes; some that he recognized, some he didn't. There was venison, buttered herbed potatoes, stewed greens, and candied beets, as well as a strange red seeded fruit that had been cut into the shape of a blossoming flower. Next came a goblet of ale, which he instantly recognized as Master Pruden's, and a mix of colorful vegetables he couldn't quite place.

"Ambassador Kekona, I believe you have previously met my daughter, Fletch?" Fiorelle was saying lightly as a servant filled her wine glass.

The ambassador nodded, the jewel on her forehead flashing. "Indeed, though only briefly." Her dark eyes flitting to Fletch, she added, "I regret that I have not had the pleasure of speaking with you since. Your duties keep you busy, my lady."

"They do," Fletch conceded. "But your responsibilities far outweigh mine, Ambassador."

"I am not so certain." Alicianna smiled. "From the rumors that flit about Ivenhence, I understand that you have saved His Grace's life multiple times. What duty could be more weighty than the wellbeing of a king?"

Her gaze traced Fletch's cheekbones, the curve of her ear peeking out from the woven crown of hair. Throat suddenly tightening, Dreythan looked down, pretending to be highly interested in his plate.

"I do take your point," Fletch's voice replied. "But I simply meant that your position as ambassador is an important one to the Isles of Aden and to the Merchants' Guild, and 'tis clear it consumes much of your time. Meeting with merchants and monarchs, arranging negotiations and trade routes. It must require great attention to detail."

"That it does. Though I do occasionally find myself with time for leisure, it does not happen often." After a brief pause, the ambassador added, "It would seem the same is true for you. I frequently see you about Iventorr accompanying His Grace, but rarely otherwise."

Sneaking a quick glance at Fletch's face, Dreythan instantly wished he hadn't. She was leaning forward, her emerald eyes sparkling as she replied, "I do receive one day of rest per week, but I often spend it in the library or exploring the area surrounding the Basin. 'Tis likely why you don't see me. What of you, ambassador? How do you occupy your free time?"

"I prefer to spend it in the company of remarkable women such as yourself."

Nearly choking on his ale, Dreythan spluttered it back, resolving not to drink again until the conversation had ended.

"It is fascinating," Ambassador Kekona continued, "how vastly different our views, backgrounds, and personalities are, and how they clash or meld. I am deeply curious to know how we might match together, my lady."

Heat surging into his ears, Dreythan couldn't look away from Fletch's face. She stared at the ambassador, her lips parting slightly as realization struck.

"But alas, I am afraid I must save my curiosity for another time." Folding her napkin, the ambassador placed it over her empty plate, turning to Fiorelle and Dreythan. "I must beg your pardon. The Guild sent a missive this morn bidding my return to finalize our trade agreement. I'm loathe to leave this—" her hand swept the hall "—but their instructions were clear."

"I am glad you were able to join us," Fiorelle smiled, "even if it was only for a short time."

She was leaving? Shoving his relief under a regretful nod, Dreythan lifted his glass. "No offense is taken, Ambassador. Iventorr shall welcome you back upon your return."

"You are too kind."

Before she could stand, Fletch said, "Ambassador?" Kekona paused as she hurried on, "If you hadn't sent word to my mother when you realized my identity, I — well — it's likely the Wyndarin wouldn't have deviated from their Wandering. My mother and I wouldn't have been given the opportunities to reconnect that we have." Ducking her head, she finished quietly, "So, thank you."

"Yes, thank you again, Ambassador," Fiorelle agreed, tucking her hand into her daughter's elbow. "Safe travels to you."

As Ambassador Kekona rose and made her way out of the hall, Dreythan inspected his plate, his appetite mysteriously gone. Tension he hadn't been aware of drained away from his body, leaving behind a sense of prickliness. Casting another glance at Fletch, he swallowed as she grinned, her freckled cheeks dimpling.

"I don't believe I've ever seen so much food in my entire life," she was commenting to her mother. "You must have been hard at work all day! However did you manage it all?"

"Matron Gulden and her workers are quite efficient." Fiorelle smiled around her daughter at Dreythan. "Not to mention, they are fast learners. Even though I assured them we could prepare the feast on our own, they insisted on helping."

Swallowing his bite of venison, Dreythan said, "I shall be certain to tell her you said so. Your kind words honor her." He glanced down at his plate. "I shall also need to ask her if this root vegetable dish can be recreated from memory. Is it a traditional Wyndarin recipe?"

The queen blinked. "It is."

"Was there a chapter about food? In the book, that is?"

He turned to Fletch as she raised a curious brow. Suddenly hyperconscious of his hands, he clasped the arms of his chair. "There is, though it is considerably shorter than the other chapters, and duly so. It seemed the author wished to pay homage to the many fascinating aspects of Wyndarin culture."

"You enjoyed it, then?" Fletch asked.

"That is an understatement. I have read it thrice already." Her eyes widened, drawing a smile he couldn't suppress. "Did you know that the tents the Wyndarin use when camped also double as sails? Not only for their carts and wagons, but for their ships when they travel by sea?"

She shook her head. "I didn't."

"There are many parts of our culture that other peoples rarely notice," Fiorelle commented, smiling sadly. "Such as our practice of making all our equipment multifunctional. Did Naraan also mention that our carts and wagons double as rafts for forging rivers, or that they can be broken down and easily reassembled into merchants' booths?"

"He did. I never knew how incredibly resourceful your people are, Your Grace." To Fletch, he added, "There was also a chapter regarding Wyndcalling. Though, I have grown so used to thinking of it as Wyndshaping, the alternate term felt strange to read. It mentioned that all Wynd-blood lack at least one of the calling forms."

Fletch nodded. "Indeed, though I only discovered that a few days ago. I thought I couldn't shape moving water or create fire simply because I was going about it the wrong way, but it turns out I was only half right." She glanced up, her eyes meeting Dreythan's, and his heart thudded hard in his chest.

Leaning back in her chair, her stomach already comfortably full, Fletch took another sip of Master Pruden's ale. There were five large barrels marked with the Grubby Mug sign stacked against a far wall, and two of them had already been tapped. She tried to picture Jon's reaction to his ale being served at a royal banquet. The resulting image made her chuckle.

Seeing the empty chair beside her mother, Fletch lowered her eyes to her plate. It was clear that Ambassador Kekona had intended to leave, given her travel robes and relatively simple jewelry. But there was a heaviness in the back of Fletch's mind, a sadness. The ambassador, the most graceful, poised, powerful woman she'd ever met had fancied her. Her. The more she allowed herself to think about it, the more foolish she felt.

Swallowing hard, Fletch set her fork down, stomach twisting. Instead of seeing the ambassador as her own person, she had instead perceived her as a mirror, something to measure herself against, a comparison in which Fletch could only fall short. Because Alicianna Kekona was everything Fletch thought she herself should be, but wasn't. Her own insecurity had cast the ambassador in a negative light.

A light laugh interrupted this train of thought. Dreythan must have said something amusing, for Fiorelle's crowned head was thrown back, her brown eyes squeezed shut to contain their mirth. At her infectious laughter, Dreythan chuckled.

A warm hand closed around Fletch's heart as she watched his face crinkle merrily. She again wondered what it would be like to slip her hand into his, for the warmth of his breath to be close enough to feel.

Remembering how Dreythan had straightened his robes before the ambassador's arrival, Fletch carefully looked away, heat rising up her neck. Dreythan had seemed nervous before meeting with Ambassador Kekona. She'd been jealous because of it, and she hadn't even known. Perhaps that was the reason she'd compared herself to the ambassador.

Fiorelle's infectious chuckle pealed out again. "Did you hear, Fletch?" she gasped. "His Grace said—" Seeing Fletch's expression, she stopped, excused herself to the king, and turned back. "Something troubles you?" she asked softly.

"No," she replied, donning a cheerful smile. "Merely thinking about how different my life is than I thought it would be, even two seasons ago."

The hall was so noisy, so crowded and boisterous, that it was a wonder they could distinguish each other's voices. Random bits of songs burst forth from various tables, sweeping across the hall until nearly every soul present was belting the tune. Dishes clattered on tables, cups clinking in toasts. Children tooted happily on horns and flutes from vendors's booths, troupes of them weaving through the tables in chaotic makeshift parades.

As Fletch glanced over the tables below, her eye fell on a familiar head of silver-streaked copper hair. Naraan was seated with Aeda Yewmaster and Harrild Hammerfist. The three of them were leaning toward each other, conversing intently. Even Aeda, her dark lips moving far more rapidly than Fletch had ever seen. As she wondered what they could be discussing, Naraan looked up and met her eye. A smile rose easily to his weathered face. He raised a hand in greeting, then glanced at Fiorelle. The smile and the hand both fell, and he looked deliberately away.

Confused, Fletch turned to her mother, who was staring down at her plate, her entire face bright red.

The morning after the banquet, the sun's first rays reached warmly over the horizon, casting rosy hues over the whole of Iventorr. All traces of the night's frivolities were gone. The streamers had been taken down, the cloths and tapestries rolled up, the hundreds and thousands of cups and plates had been washed and tidied away, and the leftover vegetables simmered in Matron Gulden's enormous soup cauldron.

Fletch had woken an hour before. Though her puffy eyes and aching head begged her for more sleep, she dragged herself out of bed and dressed, then made her way toward the guest tower. Fiorelle was already awake, giving various instructions to a flock of handservants. Her eyes met Fletch's across the room. With a tiny smile and a nod, Fiorelle turned to the attentive Wyndarin. "Do you understand your assigned tasks?"

"We do, my lady," a few murmured, the rest nodding.

"Very well. I shall meet you all at the gates at dawn."

The Wyndarin hurried out, leaving Fletch and Fiorelle alone. Fiorelle tried to smile, her eyes filling.

"'Tis strange to think we shall not see each other again for four years," she whispered hoarsely. "It seems an eternity."

Fletch slipped her fingers into her mother's. "It'll pass," she told her, fighting back tears of her own. "Just as the last fifteen years did." Swallowing hard, she added, "I'm simply grateful for the time we've had together, Mother. Papa would be so glad to see us as we are now."

Her mother's only response was a slight squeeze of her hand. They proceeded down the winding stairs of the tower together, the only sound the soft tapping of feet against stone.

"I'm sorry," Fiorelle burst out. She halted on the stair, her hand pressing to her forehead.

Startled, Fletch paused. "Mother?"

"I am sorry that I made you choose so long ago, Fletch," she said haltingly, her shoulders hunched. "Between your father and I. It was wrong of me to do so. You were too young to make such a decision... It was unfair." Hand dropping from her face, she raised her head to hesitantly meet Fletch's eye. "It has weighted my soul since the day I left you. I was afraid to say so before now, but I cannot allow another four years to pass before— before I ask your forgiveness."

Fletch shook her head firmly. "Don't fret so, Mother," she said, putting her hand through Fiorelle's arm and helping her continue down the steps. "There's nothing to forgive. I'd thought that when I chose Papa, you believed I'd cast you out of my life. If you hadn't offered me any choice at all, I would have firmly believed you'd abandoned us both." She squeezed Fiorelle's hand, forcing her to look into her eyes. "You've made difficult choices, and so have I. Did we choose correctly? Had we chosen differently, where would we be today? No one can know. I wouldn't chose differently, given the chance, and I don't think you should, either."

The conviction that clenched in her chest must have shown in her expression, for Fiorelle wiped away her tears, smiling unsteadily. "You are a strong woman, Fletch," she said quietly. "Words cannot express how proud I am of you. Thank you."

They proceeded through the silent castle streets, clutching each other as if afraid to let go. The ground beneath them passed too quickly. Within minutes, they approached the castle gate where the king, Captain Norland, and a group of Wyndarin waited.

They came to a halt before the two men, who bowed ceremoniously. With one final squeeze, Fletch reluctantly released Fiorelle's hand and stepped back to stand beside the Captain.

"Your Majesty Queen Fiorelle," Dreythan greeted, glancing curiously at Fletch. "It pains me to say farewell to you and your people. You have brought wondrous goods and gifts to Ivenhence and to its people. The Wyndarin shall always be welcome, so long as I reign."

"I thank you for your generosity and hospitality, opening your home to us and trusting us to provide fair trade," Queen Fiorelle replied. "I consider Ivenhence a valuable ally, not only in commerce but also in friendship. Should you require anything from us, you have only to send word."

Dreythan nodded at Captain Norland, who turned and barked, "Open the gates!"

The heavy, iron-reinforced oak doors swung outward, pushed

by two guards on each side.

Atop the hill across the bridge, the Wyndarin people stood silent. Hundreds of vividly dyed, sail-topped wagons and carts waited in rows upon the green grass. The sun's first rays shone over the horizon, turning the sky from lavender to pink.

"My people do not believe in saying good-bye." Fiorelle smiled, eyes shining as she bowed to the king. "For the Wynd returns many times, often leaving but never abandoning. Just as we shall return many times to you."

"Then I wish you and your people a good journey, and fair Wynds to fill your sails," Dreythan replied courteously. "May the seas carry you wherever the Wynd shall take you."

Fletch smiled at the honorary farewell, heat sparking to life in her chest.

"May your lands prosper, and your crops flourish, and your people grow in kindness and wisdom," Fiorelle replied, cheeks rosy with pleased surprise. "No child of Hearth has ever given such a farewell, Dreythan Dreythas-son. Luminia's blessings upon you."

The sun's crimson edge peered over the horizon. A distant sound grew, tingling in the air, carried by a gentle yellow-green breeze that smelled of chamomile.

The Wyndarin were singing, Fletch realized as the wordless melody grew louder. It rose and fell with the Wynd, rhythmically pulling at her feet and shoulders. A sudden desire surged within her; to sail the seas, to feel the Wynd all around her and to follow it to the ends of the Hearth. To ride the storm and chopping waves like a knight upon a wild horse. To shape the Wynd with others, to speak of the colors that danced, swirling, all about.

Fiorelle and her handservants were already halfway across the bridge when Fletch shook herself out of this train of thought. Her duty, her future, was here. In Iventorr. It was strange to be so sure of something. But it was a certainty that she felt in the very pit of her stomach.

As the singing reached a crescendo, Fiorelle turned and lifted her hand. Fletch knew it was meant for her. Blinking, she waved back, one arm milling wildly.

As the Wyndarin tribe slowly crested the hills, Dreythan glanced down at Fletch. Her hand drifted back to her side, her cheeks flush with the sun's rosy light as her eyes glimmered with moisture.

"Why did you not go with them?" he asked.

She turned sharply. "My lord?"

"Why did you not go with them?" he repeated, surveying her solemnly. "You are heir to their throne. They possess the same ability to see and shape the Wynd that you do. Do you not feel more at ease, more at home with the Wyndarin?"

Captain Norland stepped out onto the ledge that connected the bridge to the island, clearly pretending to be deaf.

"It isn't a question of being at ease, my lord," Fletch replied slowly. "Nor is it a question of where my home is. My duty, my livelihood, is here in Iventorr." Gesturing at the wagons that had begun their retreat over the horizon like a flock of birds migrating across the sky, she added, "With the Wyndarin, I'd be depended on, looked up to." Ducking her head, she smiled. "I'd prefer being an oddity here in Iventorr than lead a people whose lifestyle I've not shared, whose culture would feel borrowed."

"You would be distinguished as royalty, as their future leader." He shifted closer, also facing the horizon. A magnetism had taken him, pulling him closer to Fletch. To her bright eyes and honest face. "As you were born to do."

"My answer is unchanged, my lord," Fletch said firmly. "My duty is here. My life is here." She paused, then chuckled. "My friends are here. The Sentinels, Captain Norland and Petrecia, Roderick and Sariah. Iventorr is my home now."

Dreythan nodded, relief draining through him. "It makes my

heart glad to hear it. But," he added quickly, "for what it might be worth, I believe you would make an excellent queen."

Heat closed around his heart as Fletch's expression softened. "Thank you, my lord," she said softly. "'Tis a great honor to hear you say so."

They were silent then, watching the caravan. The sun rose higher, growing brighter, into a full dawn. A few fluffy clouds appeared in the east, floating easily across the rosy horizon.

Dreythan glanced down at Fletch. She stared up at the sky, bright emerald eyes flitting back and forth as if watching something. He looked up also but saw only the sky as it turned from coral to yellow to lightest blue. "Tell me," he said bemusedly. "What do you see?"

She glanced at him, puzzled. "My lord?"

"In the sky. What is it that fascinates you so?"

Cheeks pinking, she replied, "The Wynd currents, my lord. As the sun rises, the sky warms."

"Tell me."

He watched her face as her brows drew together, her lips working as she formed the right words in her mind. It reminded him of the time she'd told him the children's story on their return from the Pass. How her hands animatedly illustrated her every word.

"Well," she ruminated, returning her gaze upwards, "you can see the sunrise, the wash of colors that the sun's arrival spreads. Imagine another layer of hues over it. Translucent, shimmering, always moving."

"Like the cloth the Wyndarin merchants sell," Dreythan murmured.

"Yes! Precisely. But the shades you see also hold meaning." She paused, her bottom lip tucking thoughtfully between her teeth. "Warmth comes in many shades. Red, orange, maroon. Even darker purples, and sometimes a lovely cinnamon color. The cold is usually green, blue, or light violet. Imagine that this translucent layer blends and dances with the colors that you can see. Swirling, swooping. Sweeping!" Raising her arms, she traced the wind's movements with her fingers as Dreythan listened intently. The way her eyes danced and sparkled made his heart thud in his throat. "But," she said ruefully, arms falling to her sides, "I can't describe such a thing, my lord. I should like to learn to paint. Perhaps one day, I might show those born of Hearth what the Wynd-blood see."

"You say you cannot describe it, but you have," Dreythan said quietly. "For a moment, I could see the Wynd in all its hues and majesty."

Cinnamon was a shade of warmth, then. It seemed only fitting, as the sight of Fletch and her auburn hair was enough to kindle a spark within him. Before he could stop it, his hand shifted—

His knuckles brushed something warm. Startled, he glanced down to see Fletch's hand also reaching for his.

They both froze. Slowly, their gazes rose to each other, their shoulders only inches apart. Dreythan scarcely dared breathe as he stared into Fletch's eyes, hoping against hope that she understood his unuttered question. Her fingers brushed his. His heartbeat buzzed in his ears as their fingers intertwined. The touch was gentle, but it ignited a tingling inferno through his entire body. Fletch's hand tightened, and he savored the feeling of her warmth as they shifted ever so slightly closer.

He couldn't look away, and never wanted to. She was only inches away, but he longed for her to draw near. Every fiber of his being hummed with brightness, ready to spark and to blaze.

"My lord," Captain Norland's voice rumbled. "The upfirst bell has already rung. Fletch has only a few minutes to eat before she must meet the rest of the guard in the tower."

Their hands sprang apart as if stung.

"Of course," Dreythan said reluctantly. "You may go, Fletch. Pleasant day."

Her face flushing bright red, Fletch saluted Captain Norland, bowed to Dreythan with a hesitant smile, and darted away.

Dreythan stared after her, his hand hanging limply as if it could no longer find purpose. Chest tight, he turned toward the dining hall.

"She's a fine young woman, my lord," Captain Norland said. The gentle prodding in his voice surprised Dreythan. It made him wonder how much of his thoughts the Captain had guessed. "And would indeed make a fine queen, as you said."

They strode together toward the hall, Dreythan contemplating Norland's words. Did he mean a queen of the Wyndarin, or a queen of Ivenhence?

"She shows capabilities for leadership," the Captain continued. "She's kind, thoughtful. Generous. And she's got a sharp mind."

"You are telling me things of which I am already aware, Captain," Dreythan replied irritably. "I assume you have a point. It is unlike you to chatter needlessly."

"I'm not chattering, my lord," Norland growled, his blue eyes piercing Dreythan's keenly. "I'm trying t' make ye see that ye need not force yourself to live in loneliness." With that, he turned his gaze stubbornly forward and set his bearded jaw.

Wincing, Dreythan hurried his step, trying to catch his friend's eye. "Norland, I did not mean offense."

"None was taken, my lord," the Captain replied, but he did not slow his tramping gait or turn to meet the king's eye.

A week passed, though to Dreythan, it felt longer. Since the Wyndarin departure, Iventorr had fallen under a sleepy quiet. But tension itched beneath the surface.

No word had arrived from Matteo Alwick or his company, and Norland was beginning to worry. Even though he tried to hide it, it was reflected in the deep blue pools of his eyes and etched into the series of lines between his brows. Fletch was also concerned, though her anxiety was far more evident. She hovered around Harrild and sat with him at each meal, laughing and making light conversation. Dreythan's chest tightened each time he saw them together, even though he knew she was trying to distract Harrild from his partner's absence.

Lowering himself his chair, he peered over the tables that were slowly filling for breakfast, his heart jittering at the sight of a bright chestnut head of hair. They hadn't spoken more than in passing since the Wyndarin departure. Since their fingers had intertwined.

Every time he remembered it, the hand which had held hers tingled as if aflame. He wondered if Fletch experienced the same sensation, if she had felt the same desire to draw closer, to share more.

How long had he cared for her? Had it begun when he'd run into her in the garden, when she'd spoke to him of her mother? No, before that. Perhaps when he'd spoken to her over the Unbreathing book. It had to be prior to that, even, he admitted, remembering his irrational anger when Klep Ironshod had asked permission to court her.

And when Fletch had returned from collecting the ballots in Herstshire. He'd been worried sick to learn about the riderless elbecca, had paced in the throne hall for hours.

The more he pondered the matter, the more it dawned on him. Once Fletch had escorted him safely back to Iventorr three moons ago, he had been loathe to bid her leave to return to her post in the Pass.

Was it possible? Had he come to care for Fletch as they walked and conversed together through the forest and over the plains of Ivenhence?

A servant appeared to his right, interrupting his dazed train of thought. "A missive for you from the falconry, my lord," he said with a bow. "From the looks of it, King Morthan sent his fastest sun jay."

It was a small scroll, sealed with a sapphire ribbon and matching wax. Morthan's reply missive. Snapping the wax seal, Dreythan rolled the parchment out on the table.

To King Dreythan Dreythas-son, rightful ruler of Ivenhence and our cousin,

Your urgent missive was received before your royal guard and his company reached our border. I have granted them entrance to Ilumence, and pray they find the information they seek.

The idea of a trade summit intrigues me. Were it to go smoothly, relations with Thissa might be patched over. While I am a realist and cannot hope for re-established trade, I acknowledge the chance to avoid further conflict. This, at the very least, would make this summit worthwhile. I hope Gorvannon sees the same possibility. Given our recent interactions, I shall not hold my expectations too high.

Upon discussing your proposal with Ilumence's advisors, they have agreed that a visit to your kingdom may be of benefit (much to my consternation). However, given the recent attempt on your life, they demand I travel with a score of guards. I hope this will not burden you, cousin. You are already putting yourself out on my account, and I have no wish to become an inconvenience.

If agreeable, I plan to arrive before the end of the second week of autumn. This shall allow us some time to look over Ilumence's current state and evaluate potential change before the summit. With your help, I am certain solutions can be found.

I anticipate our time together, cousin. Such hope has not filled my soul since I ascended Ilumence's throne. Together, we shall forge a bright future for our sister-nations.

Morthan Morthas-son

Dreythan stared at the parchment for a moment, then turned. "Captain."

Norland was instantly at his elbow. "Yes, my lord."

"My cousin Morthan plans to visit Iventorr in two weeks' time. A score of guards shall accompany him on the road. Accommodations must be made for his men, perhaps in the barracks."

The Captain frowned. "That should be simple enough, my lord. Do ye know how long he'll remain?"

Dreythan shook his head, glancing over the missive once more. "He does not say. It depends largely on the trade summit, and whether Gorvannon accepts our invitation."

"Gorvannon?" Norland grunted, eyes glinting. "Inviting the man who might want ye dead? Who could've killed your father an' Kell Wyndshaper?"

"Indeed." His glance fell on the first sentence, relief trickling through him as he showed the penned words to the Captain. "It is my hope we shall have a report from our scouting party by the time the invitations must be sent. Look here, Norland. Alwick should return any day now."

For the first time in over a week, Norland's expression relaxed, a smile curling his fiery whiskers. "I'm glad to hear it. I'll tell the guard to keep an eye out for 'is return. As soon as they see him, I'll send word." With that, he bowed and clinked away.

The king had half-risen, ready to make his way to the library and pen a quick reply, when his eyes fell on his untouched plate. He fell back into his chair with a sigh. Picking up his fork, his eye fell on a particular empty place at a table, the fingers of his right hand burning.

Chapter 21

That afternoon, just as Dreythan rose to take his leave of the throne, the doors to hall swung sharply inward. A guard trotted down the aisle, panting.

"My lord," she gasped. "Sentinel Alwick returns!"

"Thank Luminia," Captain Norland muttered.

Stomach twisting, Dreythan paused. Finally, they would have some answers. At long last they would have a clue as to who wanted Ivenhence to end. "Thank you," he managed. "You may return to your post."

The guard nodded and hurried to the doors of the throne hall. Just before she reached them, a limping and stone-faced Matteo Alwick entered. The young Sentinel gave the guard a strangely nervous look as she passed him on the emerald carpet.

Dreythan settled into his throne as Captain Norland stepped forward, arm extended. "Alwick," he grunted. "Glad to see ye back."

"I'm glad to be back, Captain," the Sentinel replied, raising eyes that were wreathed in heavy shadows as the two men clasped forearms. "My lord." Alwick dropped into a bow before the throne, wobbling forward before straightening.

When he didn't continue, Dreythan's gut tightened. The only occupants of the throne hall remaining were posted guards, but the Sentinel glanced about as if seeing ghosts in every corner. "I take it you wish to speak more privately," he said, lowering his voice to a whisper.

Alwick jerked his head in a nod.

Heart sinking, Dreythan turned to Captain Norland. "Dismiss the guard."

Though his brow furrowed thunderously and his mouth pressed into a scowl under his beard, Norland did so without question. Within moments, the only souls remaining in the enormous arched hall were Dreythan, Norland, Alwick, and Fletch.

Norland hadn't dismissed her when she'd descended from the archer post high above. Her eyes met Dreythan's briefly, confusion swirling within.

"I'm sorry for my crypticness, my lord," Alwick said, pulling a gauntlet off to rub his eyes. "I've reason to believe there's a traitor in our midst."

Silence met his stark words, echoing through the throne hall.

Dreythan nodded grimly. "Tell us what happened."

He removed his helmet, running a hand through flattened short brown hair. "I'd better start from the beginning," he said. "The first portion of our venture went smoothly. We arrived in Herstshire on the third day to meet with the local Forester. Then we were delayed."

"Delayed?" Norland interrupted. "Wyndshaper, listen closely." As Fletch obediently approached, the captain nodded at Alwick. "Go on. What manner of delay was this?"

"When we reached Herstshire, the townspeople were barricaded within. The Forester and other brave souls had already slain one Unbreathing, but another two were skulking about, attacking at random. It took us several hours to track down and kill the other monsters."

Dreythan cast a quick glance at Fletch. Her wide eyes were fixed on Alwick's face, her expression tense.

"A few villagers were wounded, but none seriously," the Sentinel continued. "The next day, with the Forester's aid, we finally reached the Pass and then the Ilumencian border. King Morthan had already sent word to allow us to enter his kingdom, so we had merely to present your letter to the border guard to gain passage to Ilumence.

"The location Whendor provided was accurate. We found Purveyn's residence without any trouble, in a little village called Wuthera. But when we arrived, everything crumbled to Kazael's Pit." Alwick swallowed hard, the apple of his throat bobbing. "The villagers were too afraid to say much. They'd heard screams and a horrible commotion in the dark of the night. Purveyn's workshop and home had been torn down. Brick scattered from brick as if struck with immense force. We sorted through the ruins to be thorough." Folding his hands behind his back to hide their trembling, he ducked his head. "Two bodies were found. The townsfolk identified them as Purveyn's wife and son. No sign was found of the fletcher." He paused, his sun-browned face pallid, eyes staring blankly at the carpet under his feet. "The son had been drained of blood, my lord, but the woman... her body was broken. Bite wounds on her neck, wrists, the crooks of her knees... Her dress was torn and bloody. She died horribly."

Dreythan shook his head, struggling to absorb the implications of Alwick's tale. "What of the workshop?" he asked gently.

Alwick looked up, living nightmares fading from his steel-blue eyes. "We did find black feathers and a spool of black silk thread, my lord. In spite of the wreckage, there were signs of a struggle. A broken lantern had started a fire on the floor, which was smothered before it had a chance to spread. It almost appeared as though Purveyn had been abducted."

Dreythan carefully looked away, willing his face into neutrality.

He couldn't let Alwick see how disappointed, how frustrated he felt. Not after the Sentinel had witnessed such horrors to bring him this information.

"Only hours before ye were able to reach him," Norland growled. He glanced at Fletch, who had been listening quietly, her green eyes dark and turbulent. "There've been Unbreathing in the Pass before, haven't there? Did ye have word of this?"

"There was a nest of Unbreathing in the Pass, yes," she replied slowly. "But they were all slain several years ago. I did receive word from Master Pruden some weeks past that an Ilumencian messenger was found drained of blood in the Pass, but he didn't mention that any of the townsfolk had been attacked." Raising her gaze to meet Dreythan's, she said, "'Tis exceedingly strange. Unbreathing don't simply 'attack at random', especially not whilst the sun is up. When hungry, they prefer to stalk their prey, picking off a lone soul here or there to feed from."

"Unless their intention was not to feed at all," Dreythan finished for her with a nod. "They knew of our goal and intentionally delayed the journey. What other explanation can there be? How else would our only lead in years have disappeared without a trace mere hours before we reached him?"

Captain Norland's clenched fist crashed into his open palm. The thud echoed through the chamber. They all turned to stare as he lowered his head, glowering at the floor.

"The Unbreathing knew. Again." His low growl echoed through the nearly-empty hall. "Before we could even get there. They couldn't've intercepted the sun jay bearing the king's letter... King Morthan had already sent word to the border with his blessing when Alwick arrived, which means he got the letter without delay. Even if there were spies in Luminhold, reading Morthan's missives before or after 'im, they couldn't've reached a southern border town before our party's arrival. Not to mention, only a handful of people even knew about this venture... which means... which means..." His shoulders slumped. "There must be a traitor among the guard," he admitted, avoiding the king's eye.

"A traitor among the guard?" Fletch echoed, doubt flitting across her face.

Norland nodded, head bowed. "It shames me to say it. I've trained each of them myself, put time and effort into choosing the right individuals to protect this castle. I can't stand the thought that a soldier I trained harbors ill intent toward you, my lord."

"That's what I was afraid of as well," Alwick agreed softly.

"It is somewhat encouraging, in a strange way," Dreythan mused. "By taking such drastic action as to abduct a weapons smith and kill his family, our enemy has revealed much. We know now that Purveyn the Fletcher held information that would have aided us. And we know they were so desperate to keep that information from us as to put their informant at risk."

"You're right," the Captain said, his jaw and shoulders squaring. "I'm not wasting this chance. It's only the four of us that know about this. Perfect opportunity to plant red herrings and see where the false information leads."

Alwick glanced from Dreythan to Norland, then back again, some color returning to his face. "Do you mean... this wasn't for nothing?"

"You are correct," Dreythan affirmed. Though it felt strange to do so, he placed a hand on the weary Sentinel's armored shoulder, lending his his most reassuring nod. "Have heart, Alwick. You did well." He turned to Norland. "Is there any way to verify if this Purveyn crafted the arrows which were used for the assassinations fifteen years ago, or for the recent attacks on my person? It must be at least one of the two, given our enemy's silencing tactic."

"I wasn't a part of the castle retinue when the assassinations took place," the captain grunted. "With the original arrows gone, 'tis difficult to say."

"Parfeln was a guard back then," Alwick said.

"I suppose I was here, too," Fletch murmured, her voice barely audible. Her freckles were stark against her cheeks as she stared down at the floor, the color evaporating from her face. Shadows passed behind her eyes, the memory of horror of pain.

Dreythan's chest tightened. He was about to reach for her hand when Norland asked, "Fletch? You all right?"

"Y-yes, Captain," she replied, blinking.

Dreythan's hand fell to his side, his ears stinging as she continued, "The arrow that killed King Dreythas was black, but... I don't recall anything more."

"As was the arrow that was meant for me," Dreythan agreed, hoping Fletch hadn't noticed his movement.

Alwick glanced between the three of them, clearly puzzled. "Was there not evidence kept from King Dreythas's assassination?"

"There was," Dreythan replied. "But it disappeared, and we are not certain when."

Again, Fletch's expression darkened. "In the same manner as the library's books on Unbreathing."

"We ought to ask," Norland interjected. "What if the arrows which slew King Dreythas and Kell Wyndshaper had been crafted by Purveyn? What difference would it make? He's gone now, and we can't know who employed him or why."

"You have a point," Alwick nodded.

As if answering his own questions, Norland straightened, folding his arms across his broad chest. "No matter. I'll increase the guard around ye in the throne hall and other public areas, my lord, but I'll pick the men doing it myself. I'll also plant threads of false information and see where they lead."

"I believe that is wise, Captain," Dreythan said. He hesitated, peering at Fletch. There was no doubt she'd been too absorbed in troubling thoughts to see his hand reach for hers. Her eyes were still fixed on the floor, a frown etched into the curves around her mouth.

Before he could ask her what was amiss, Norland turned. "Alwick, go get some rest. And for Luminia's sake, find Harrild first. Wyndshaper, have one of the guards summon Brinwathe and Anshwell. I've got an idea."

Fletch snapped into a salute. "Yes, Captain." Turning on her heel, she hurried away, auburn hair whipping around her ears with the speed of her steps.

Fletch scowled down at the whirling ball of Wynd shimmering red between her fingers. Every day since the Wyndarin departure, she'd met with Naraan on the sparring grounds to practice Wyndshaping. And every day, he had her move through the exercises for creating flame, then shifting water, then back to flame, then water again. The best she'd been able to manage was a small spark that had sputtered briefly to life and promptly died, and lifting the liquid contents of a cup into the air before it lost form and splattered across the dirt.

But today, she couldn't even reproduce the spark. Or lift the water from the cup. Releasing the hot air with a huff, she scrubbed her forehead with the back of her hand.

"Your mind is not on the forms we practice," Naraan told her with a knowing look. "Flame requires complete control, for it is a fickle thing." He gestured her closer. "Tell me what is on your mind while I demonstrate."

Shifting uncomfortably, Fletch shrugged, remembering too late how Petrecia had scolded her for doing so. "There are many things I've been asking myself recently," she said slowly, watching as Naraan cupped his hands, "but... they are unanswerable. Or, at least, they seem so. Others have been seeking such answers since my father's death. And when we finally came close to finding answers, they slipped through our fingers."

He nodded keenly. Between his palms, crimson air condensed to cinnamon, then flashed. A tiny flame wavered between his fingers. "Answers regarding the assassinations?"

"Yes. I shouldn't say more, though."

There were so many things she wished she knew. How had word of Matteo Alwick's mission reached their enemy so quickly?

Even with the knowledge that there was a traitor amongst the guard, it was inexplicable. Word could not have traveled that quickly to the Unbreathing in the Pass, not unless it had been sent by sun jay directly from Iventorr. But sun jays were only trained to be sent to cities, and select ones at that. She scowled. It also wasn't possible that a messenger could have reached the Pass before Alwick and his party reached Herstshire. No horse was that fast.

Naraan extinguished the fire with a puff of his breath. Squaring his feet, he settled into a lower stance, his hands wider apart.

"Uncle," Fletch said, "have you traveled the Pass between Mount Valer and Mount Norst?"

"I have," he replied. "Several times. Why do you ask?"

"If you were given three days to travel from Iventorr, then to the Pass, then to Herstshire, would you think such a thing possible?"

Naraan was already shaking his head, then stopped. "Do you mean Iventorr, then Herstshire, then the Pass?"

"No. The Pass second, Herstshire last. Would you think it possible?"

There was no hesitation as he replied, "Not unless I took no rest and drove the very finest Roanite stallion every second of the journey. But that would kill the horse." He inspected her face closely, clearly intrigued. "Why would one pass by Herstshire, only to turn around upon reaching the Pass? T'would be faster and easier to travel onward to Wuthera, not to mention safer."

"To deliver a message." Absently, Fletch tapped a finger to her lips, then froze. Deliver a message. Slowly turning toward Naraan, she met his eyes as her own widened. "You deliver messages," she said stupidly. "You're a messenger."

One corner of his whiskered mouth turned up slightly. "I am." He again kindled a fire between his hands, this time shaping it into a crackling ball the size of an apple. A sphere of yellow Wynd coated its exterior, keeping it contained, protecting Naraan's palms.

Wuthera... Wuthera. Why did that name sound so familiar? She pushed the thought aside. "Have you ever delivered messages in Thissa?"

"On occasion. None of them were of much import, usually a quick one or two-line missive to fishers along the coasts, or ebonite farmers along the edge of the desert." Chuckling, he raised a brow, dousing the flame as he met her eye. "I do hope you shall answer some of my questions once you have finished peppering me with yours."

Wuthera. She had nearly shoved the name away again when she remembered. It was the name of the town in Ilumence, the one Purveyn the Fletcher had lived in.

"You've been to Wuthera as well, I take it?" she asked, her voice strange and high in her own ears.

"Indeed I have. Several times. Though a sleepy little hamlet, it maintains a steady flow of coin and makes an excellent stop for any traveling the Pass."

"Would you—" she swallowed. "You wouldn't have met the arms smith there?"

This time, Naraan blinked. He stared at Fletch for several moments before responding hesitantly, "I have, as a matter of fact. Do you refer to Master Stormold or Purveyn?"

"Purveyn the Fletcher. What can you tell me of him?"

"Very little," he said, still giving Fletch a rather odd look. "I imagine his younger sibling could tell you far more. I've borne messages between them in the past, but it was long ago, and only twice."

"Where does his brother reside? What is his name?"

"He resides here in Iventorr," Naraan said. "Though I cannot remember his name... he was the sort of man one easily forgets. A nondescript face. As I said, it has been many, many years since I last bore a message between the Holden brothers."

Holden. The name echoed in Fletch's mind like the noon bell, pealing over and over again. She shook her head, dazed. "The brother's name... surely it wasn't Parfeln."

"That does sound familiar," he muttered thoughtfully, running a calloused hand over his beard. "I believe he left Ilumence when King Dreythas was near his twentieth year of reign. From what I recall, he became one of the castle guard, or perhaps a smith." He smiled ruefully. "But I am speaking of the wrong brother. It is Purveyn you were inquiring after.

"Purveyn Holden took over his father's armory business when his brother departed for Ivenhence. He has a unique manner of craftsmanship, and a keen mind. His fletching art had been perfected the first time I met him, perhaps forty years ago, when the Wyndarin passed through on their Wandering. He told me that the design was his father's, though he had made his own changes."

Fletch's heart pounded in her ears. "Did you ever see black feathers, spools of black silk, or rods of ebonite in his workshop?"

"Your questions begin to hold the tone of interrogation." Naraan frowned. "But yes. Once, upon entering his shop, his workbench was littered with goose feathers and ebonite. I still remember how ill at ease he seemed until he had cleared his workbench of those materials."

"How long ago was this?" Fletch leaned forward eagerly.

"Perhaps fifteen, sixteen years?"

Frown deepening, etching itself into his leathery face, he nodded. "T'would seem so." Giving her a long, intense stare, he finally straightened. "I shall not receive any answers regarding this line of queries, shall I."

The pounding in her ears beginning to settle, she shook her head ruefully. "I'm afraid not. It is a matter of importance, and secrecy."

For a moment, Naraan's head lowered like a bull readying to charge, his brows furrowing in a glower. Then his shoulders relaxed. "Very well," he said with a sigh. "If you refuse to exchange information, at least commit yourself to practice."

Relieved, she raised her hands, picturing the swirl of hot Wynd she wished to summon.

"Remember the sphere," her uncle said, his grey eyes critical as they watched the air take shape. "Tighten it, else the flame shan't hold."

Twisting her arms, she molded the Wynd into a ball, gradually shrinking it, forcing the air to condense. Her right hand twitched, and the sphere winked out.

"I was too tense," she said as his lips parted.

He nodded. "Give it another try."

Gritting her teeth, Fletch narrowed her eyes, squinting at the space between her hands as another dense ruby globe blossomed to life.

Freshly bathed and dressed in a nightshirt, Fletch flopped onto her bed, spreading her father's journal open on the midnight blue coverlet.

Though the initial shock of Naraan's words was wearing away, her stomach still twisted. What if Parfeln was Purveyn Holden's younger brother? Was that why he had volunteered himself to travel to Ilumence? She chewed her lip, wincing. If so, he didn't even know his brother was dead.

Remembering Matteo's shadow-wreathed, haunted eyes, she stared down at the leather book cover, running her hand over the worn surface. The emptiness in his expression made her think of the time she'd discovered the missing townsfolk of Herstshire, their bodies frozen chalky grey and covered in snow. She was sure her own expression couldn't have been much different.

"He and I have only seen hints of the horrors you did," Fletch quietly told her father's journal. "I wonder what you would have to say, were you here."

Slowly but surely, she had been making her way through the worn, weather-stained pages. She'd made it a point to read an entry or two each night before laying down to rest. Now only a few bits of paper in the very back of the book remained.

Kell's entries had become far more frequent, more personal, since meeting Fiorelle. He wrote of the kindness he saw in her, and the way her eyes inspected his face as if wondering. She awoke things in him, he said. For many long years he had buried all feeling and memory in a deep, dark corner where it would not distract him. But spending time with Fiorelle, or 'Relle, as he called her, made him realize he longer wanted to live in numb forgetfulness. Haltingly, with many a word or line scratched out and many a wobbly pen stroke, he began to open up.

It was clearly difficult for him to think of the savagery he'd witnessed as a slave of the Unbreathing. At first, he penned these memories bluntly, stating facts. A woman who had begun her moonly bleed unexpectedly had been torn apart in the courtyard, Unbreathing sucking the blood from her dismembered limbs. Emaciated, too weak to work let alone stand, a man collapsed in the mines. When brought to the surface, rather than allow him to be fed or given water, the Unbreathing Turned him.

But the more he wrote, the more he began to show how these events had affected him. He confessed to questioning whether resisting was worth the fight, if it would one day be worth the price they paid.

Seven years we spent, building the rebellion. Seven years of constant paranoia, digging tunnels in short, frenzied shifts, forging weapons in secret with stolen scraps of silver. And when all of our plans and pain finally grew ripe, the fruit of freedom came at a terrible cost. So many of the fine people I had come to know as my friends and comrades died fighting the horror they had so long survived.

I ought to have spoken of this long ago. The wound of my memories is now so old and scarred that many details have faded. How many brave souls have I forgotten? How many abominations that we swore to forever stand against? Have I grown complacent in my willful ignorance of the past?

The Battle of Reclamation, they call it now. The end of the Great Slaving. A heroic name for a frenzied bloodbath. Starving miners wielding pickaxes and shovels sharpened and tipped with silver. Women who'd endured rape and barbarity, stabbing their tormentors in the heart with shivs made from sharpened silvered nails. And Unbreathing mowing through their former slaves before being whelmed to the ground.

I spoke of it to 'Relle yesterday. Halfway through the telling, I realized it had all occurred before she was born. I had not even spoken of it to anyone during the years she'd been alive. The thought caused me to stumble. Even though she encouraged me to keep going, I could not, but I feel I must now.

When the battle wound to a close, Dreythas gathered the survivors. Together, we built a fire, into which we cast Sliv, bound as he was by silver-dipped rope. But Vvalk was given to the people. They formed a line, each with a blade in hand, and cut the flesh of his shell as they passed. I shall never forget the words he screamed in his agony. They howled through the castle, shaking the stones beneath our feet, but no one cowered. No one stopped the cutting line.

"Relish this victory whilst you can, Corwynter and Wyndshaper. When I rise again, both your lives shall be forfeit. Your offspring shall Turn to Kazael. No matter how you strive to stem it, the Crimson Horde shall rise as a tide of blood to sweep across the land. Man will grovel before me like a snake on his belly. Your daughters shall be my slaves, my cattle. I shall slake my thirst by their blood, a river which shall never run dry! Nothing can turn back the hands of fate. Nothing!!!"

The manner with which his eyes lit, glowing with a sickly yellow light, and with which the ground itself trembled, causes me to wonder if Vvalk somehow channeled the power of Kazael in that moment. The air itself thrummed with tension until Dreythas plunged his knife into Vvalk's heart. His husk crumbled into ashes around our feet.

There was a long gap on the paper.

'Tis strange how writing these things stirs memory and feeling. I had long believed I had forgotten half the things I experienced, but now, it is as though it only happened yesterday.

Perhaps it is foolish, but certain recent events have made me uneasy. Many of the survivors of the battle from forty years ago are dying. Though many of these occurrences seem to be of natural causes, there have been several that cause me to question whether these deaths are truly nature's course or something far more sinister.

Old Daggin Gulden was one of them. He served as a guard in Verenshire all this time, though rheumatism had begun to slow him down. He was still hale and hearty, and could wield a spear better than any. But his body was found at the edge of the wheat fields one week past, torn as if set upon by wolves.

Another was Loren Pendlewood, found foaming at the mouth by another librarian. Though they tried to save her, it was too late.

Is there a reason the survivors of the Great Slaving are being snuffed out, one by one? Is there an enemy that wishes to extinguish the knowledge we hold?

It causes me to wonder if Dreythas and I are next.

Something foul approaches; I can feel it in my gut. I cannot shake the feeling that preparations must be made, should the worst come to pass. I have already written to Naraan, disclosing the hiding place for my journal. The knowledge the survivors hold must not be lost, but it must not fall into the wrong hands.

Fletch quickly turned the page, expecting to find a continuation of the same entry. But her eyes fell not on words, but on drawings. Maps. She leaned closer, her nose almost touching the paper. They were schematics of tunnels beneath Iventorr, the tunnels the slaves had made in secret. Small lines wound in and around each of the major points in the castle. The barracks, dining hall, throne hall, library, prison. Even the royal quarters and guest quarters towers had lines spidering to and from them.

This must have been what Kell was so eager to keep secret. This must have been why he'd hidden his journal for Naraan's retrieval. Had the wrong person found it, had someone who wished harm to the kingdom found it, they could have easily assassinated the king while he slept.

The king, sleeping. A vision rose in Fletch's mind of black hair against a white linen pillowcase, moonlight playing over a high cheekbone—

She shook her head. There were far more important things to occupy her mind. Swiveling to dangle her arms off the bed, Fletch studied the maps, heart thudding against her ribs.

It has been many, many years since I bore messages between the Holden brothers.

Pushing her hair back from her face, she took a long, shaky breath. Her father had listened to the voice of warning that whispered in the back of his mind. But what could it mean for the Sentinels, for the king, if Fletch did the same? Staring down at one map, her eyes traced a tunnel directly from the royal tower to the one where the Sentinels resided.

It couldn't be a coincidence. Parfeln had to be Purveyn the Fletcher's younger brother. Holden wasn't a common last name, and Naraan remembered the brother being part of the guard. Or a smith.

Fletch pushed the journal aside with a grimace. Cradling her head in her hands, she stared between her knees at the floor. She had to tell someone, had to ask someone if they knew whether Parfeln had a brother. Matteo didn't know, that much was sure. He disliked Parfeln as strongly as Parfeln disliked Fletch. If he had reason to suspect Parfeln of treason, he would have given voice to it.

One by one, she considered Aeda, Darvick, and Harrild, but decided against it. Aeda, though a stoic individual, hid a fiery passion. She would capture or kill first and ask questions after. Darvick wouldn't take kindly to the loyalty of his old friend being questioned. And Harrild... well, he was already numbed to complaints against Parfeln from having to listen to his lover.

Captain Norland, then? Or perhaps... Dreythan? She shook her head. Going directly to Dreythan would undermine Captain Norland's authority. No, this was a matter the Captain needed to know about, and the Captain alone.

The following day, most of Fletch's guard shift passed with her carefully considering how to approach the captain. Though her stomach bubbled with anxiety every moment she let herself realize what she was thinking, the cautious voice in the back of her mind reassured her that she was doing the right thing.

Especially when she raised her head to find Parfeln staring intently at Dreythan's table during breakfast.

When the fifth afternoon bell rang and Aeda relieved her of her duties, Fletch had decided on a plan. She would intercept Norland in the garden on his way home.

It occurred to her as soon as she found a spot to wait that she might have made a terrible mistake. What if Parfeln found her standing there? What if Dreythan did? What would anyone think, should they find her standing outside the Wyntersoul home?

Just as she was about to turn and scurry off, the captain appeared at the gate. Her anxiety must have shown on her face, for Norland raised a bushy red brow, his customary scowl absent.

"Wyndshaper."

She swallowed. "Captain."

"I take it ye've a reason for ambushing me in front of my home?"

"I'm sorry, sir." It did look like an ambush, she realized sheepishly. "There's a matter that's been troubling me, and I need to bring it to your ear. Is there a— a better time, perhaps?"

His head shook slowly. "No better time'n the present. Tell me what's on your mind, lass."

Right. Taking a deep breath, Fletch began, "Did you know that my father, Kell Wyndshaper, had a half-brother?"

She quickly explained who Naraan was, how he'd traveled the lands as a messenger, how he'd met Purveyn the Fletcher and borne messages between the Holden brothers, the youngest of whom lived in Iventorr. How Naraan remembered black arrows on Purveyn's workbench, and that his brother might have been a guard, or a smith.

The entire time she spoke, Norland's eyes didn't leave her face. His arms didn't cross, and his weight didn't shift. He simply stood there, listening intently.

"I wasn't certain if I should say anything, since Naraan can't remember the younger brother's first name or even what he looked like," Fletch finished lamely, embarrassment creeping up her spine. She looked down as her fingers twisted instinctively together. "But I thought I ought to inform you at the very least."

A long pause hovered between them before Fletch finally looked up. To her surprise, Norland didn't look vexed. Rather, his expression was distant, troubled.

"Ye haven't spoken of this to anyone else?"

She shook her head. "No, Captain."

"Hmm," he grunted. "I've said it before, Wyndshaper, and I'll say it again. Ye've a good head on your shoulders, and it seems ye've learned to use it. Ye were wise to bring this to me." His forehead creased, gaze sharpening. "Don't speak of this again. I don't want anyone t' think ye have it out for a fellow Sentinel."

Too stunned to vocalize a response, she could only nod.

"Right. Anythin' else ye wished to discuss?"

"Y-yes, captain." Shoving aside her confusion, Fletch held out a few pieces of rolled parchment. "My father's journal contained maps of hidden tunnels and passages throughout Iventorr. I made rubbings of the maps for you to review, if you wish."

Norland did scowl then, his beard shifting like a roiling storm cloud. His enormous fingers closed around the makeshift scroll, gaze meeting hers for a moment before it transferred to parchment in his hands. "Ye know this knowledge'd be deadly in the wrong person's hands," he said after a long, tense moment. It wasn't a question.

"Yes, I know, sir."

"I'll look them over, then burn them. Ye have my word." He raised his head. Though his lips were bent in a deep frown beneath his bushing whiskers, there was a softness in his eyes as he inspected Fletch's face. "G'night, Fletch."

With that, he escaped quietly inside his home and closed the door.

Fletch stared at the door for a few bewildered seconds, then turned, her feet carrying her absently back to her quarters. A cyclone of apprehension swept within her. What had the captain meant when he'd said he didn't want anyone to think she had it out for a fellow Sentinel? Did he think that about her?

Perhaps he already knew who Purveyn's brother was, and it wasn't Parfeln Holden.

She cringed at the thought.

Dreythan shifted in the wooden throne, his back and neck aching. This time he could scarcely blame his discomfort on the stiff chair. Even though the throne hall had been completely empty when he'd arrived, he'd chosen to stay in the hopes that a citizen would need his ear, providing a much-needed distraction. Since the arrival of Morthan's last missive, a tension he couldn't shrug had settled into his shoulders.

He'd written missives to Ambassador Kekona and to Gorvannon the same day, issuing invitations to the trade and relations summit. Ambassador Kekona's reply had arrived by sun jay only three days later, graciously accepting the invitation. But nothing had arrived from Thissa. Not even so much as a briskly scrawled, flat-out 'no', even though ten days had passed.

The more he allowed himself to dwell on it, the more worried Dreythan became. What if the spy Norland had sent into Thissa moons ago hadn't returned because he'd been caught? If Gorvannon wasn't behind the assassination attempts, he would surely take offense to spies in his lands. But if he was behind them, the discovery of a spy could cause him to become overly cautious, paranoid, even. There was also the possibility that Gorvannon had been the cause of Purveyn the Fletcher's disappearance. If he had been, the invitation to a trade summit would look more like a dagger poised to strike than a flag of truce.

Casting a quick glance to the right, Dreythan straightened. Rather than sitting high above the empty pews in her hidden archer's perch, Fletch stood before one of the columns, her bow readied in one hand. Her head held high, she stared at the opposite column.

In preparation for the arrival of royal guests, Captain Norland had tightened security in Iventorr. The guard rotations had increased, as had the Sentinels' shifts. And rather than staying hidden at a distance, the Sentinels were now ever-present and visible.

He wondered what else Norland was requiring of those under his command. Many of them bore signs of weariness, their shoulders drooping as if under invisible weights. Others rubbed puffy eyes, stifling yawns. Even Fletch's eyes were wreathed with shadow.

As if sensing his gaze, her head turned toward him. He looked quickly away before their eyes could meet, heat prickling up his neck into his ears.

The door to the throne hall creaked open. Expecting to see the guards usher in a townsperson, he leaned forward attentively. But instead, it was Captain Norland who entered. Sword clinking against his side, his legs swallowed the green carpeted aisle in huge strides.

When he reached the bottom of the steps up to the throne, the captain paused, jerking in a brief bow. "My lord. I've urgent news." Straightening, he ascended two more steps, then stopped. "Good, bad, and unknown."

At the steely glint in Norland's eye, Dreythan's heart dropped. "You have my ear," he said.

"The good news is, our agent returned from Thissa in th' dead of the night," Norland told him quietly. "The one we haven't heard from in moons. He said he couldn't risk sendin' a message for fear it'd be intercepted. The bad new is, only days ago, Gorvannon commanded th' Thissian navy be mobilized. An armada of warships now barricades the sea around Port Oasa. There's also whispers of unrest with Ilumence, and fear in Thissa that it'll spread to us." Stepping closer, he dipped to one knee, extending one hand. "And here's th' unknown."

It was a scroll, sealed with black wax and a strip of ebonite shaving. A missive from Gorvannon. With numb fingers, Dreythan took the parchment and snapped the seal.

King Dreythan of Ivenhence,

First you ask to reopen trade routes after fifteen years of silence, without mentioning your intent to revise taxation in Ivenhence. Then you renegotiate your agreement with the Isles of Aden to include ore, the one resource we can offer which they value. On top of which, you welcome the gypsies with open arms, not requiring a single coin or bolt of silk as tariff. Yet after all this, you have the gall to invite me to a 'trade and relations summit' held within your borders with the nations you've stolen our trade from?

Such insolence cannot be ignored. Keep your new trade partners. Should a merchant of the Isles, Ilumence, Ivenhence, or the gypsy clan so much as approach our borders, they shall be met with the ire which their betrayal deserves.

Do not contact me again unless you desire to further stoke my wrath.

-Gorvannon, High Commander of Thissa

Dreythan stared at the parchment, at the heavy-handed square letters which had been penned with brutal precision. The first time he'd seen Gorvannon's handwriting, he'd thought the style militaristic, but now it looked threatening.

"Norland," he said slowly, "where did Queen Fiorelle say she intended to go after leaving Ivenhence?"

The captain frowned, his scars puckering. "I'm not sure," he grunted. Turning, he motioned to Fletch. "Wyndshaper, approach."

Stepping briskly forward, Fletch dipped in a bow, then saluted. "Yes, Captain?"

"Where were your mother and her people headed after leaving here?"

One brow arched sharply, but she simply replied, "To the Isles to negotiate future trade visits, then to Port Oasa to resupply." Her eyes flicked between Dreythan and Norland's faces, darkening.

Port Oasa. "They could be in great danger," Dreythan told her, his stomach thudding dully. "Thissa has barricaded the port with their navy, and Gorvannon promises retribution."

"Retribution?" Fletch repeated, stunned. "Why? What have the Wyndarin done to anger him?"

"Nothing, except to trade with Ivenhence without taxation."

He handed the scroll to Norland who scanned it, scowling. "This doesn't make any sense," the captain growled. "Why would he take such offense to such simple actions?"

"He has always been a prideful man," Dreythan said, but even as the words left his mouth, doubt stirred. "I do agree, it makes no sense. But given the movement of the armada, I fear for the safety of the Wyndarin people. Gorvannon could simply be seeking a chance to instigate a war." His jaw clenching, he grated, "Attacking an innocent ally of Ivenhence could be the spark needed to start the blaze."

The statement hung in the air, suspended by the tension that suddenly filled the room. Fletch blinked, the color fading from her cheeks.

"They've likely left the Isles by now," she whispered, her voice hollow with dread. "Is there any chance to warn them?"

Warn them, yes. Absently, Dreythan rose from the throne to pace before it. "Perhaps," he said, jumping through quick calculations. "In Ambassador Kekona's missive one week ago, she mentioned the negotiations with Queen Fiorelle were going well. It is likely at least two or three days more were needed to finalize an agreement, perhaps longer."

"That letter would've taken two days to reach us. That means they've likely been sailing south for five to six days." Norland tugged a hand through his beard, inspecting Fletch's face. "They might be rounding our southeastern coast right about now. If a messenger took a fast steed and headed directly t' Port Liarin, they might could catch 'em."

Dreythan hesitated. "It is risky, though. If the messenger were not fast enough to intercept them at Port Liarin…"

"They could cross the foothills of the Snowshod Mountains into Thissa and try to catch up." Fletch's voice was quiet, steady. "I can do it."

"What if you were caught at the border, lass?" Norland shook his head. "Gorvannon'd have even more reason to breed ill will against Ivenhence."

"No, he wouldn't," she insisted, her hands clenching at her sides. "I wouldn't get caught. Even if I were, I would tell my captors I was working independently. That Fiorelle is my mother." Turning to Dreythan, she added softly, "No blame would fall on Ivenhence. Please, my lord. I can't knowingly chance that my mother might come to harm."

His feet faltered. For a moment, he stared down at Fletch. At her brilliant green eyes filled with anxiety. At the fingers which twisted absently at her waist, at the careful line of her lips which she'd pressed together, as if keeping more words at bay. He hated the thought of her crossing into Thissa, of her evading or being caught by Thissian border patrols. But… he couldn't forbid her from going. Not when it meant warning an ally of the kingdom.

When it meant saving her mother.

Gut churning, he descended the steps. When he reached the bottom, he whispered, "May I take your hand, Fletch?"

Her cheeks instantly flared, but she offered hers in silent reply.

Taking her fingers in his, Dreythan swallowed hard. This time, there was no buzz, no fire that wakened every fiber of his being. This time, he simply wanted to hold her, to comfort her, to ease the darkness and the worry that swirled in her eyes. And all he could do was take her hand.

"Please be careful," he told her.

"I shall," she promised, giving him a gentle squeeze.

Norland joined them at the base of the steps, his blue eyes troubled. "I don't like any of this," he said, his gravelly voice unusually muted. "Stay alert out there, Wyndshaper. And take the elbecca. His long legs an' stamina will get ye to your destination more quickly'n a horse can."

"Yes, Captain." She started to turn away, then hesitated, her cheeks still pink. Abruptly, she threw an arm around Norland in a brief, awkward embrace.

A smile broke the captain's worried visage, and he returned the hug. "Go on, lass," he said, giving her a gentle push. "Hurry back."

Her head ducked, Fletch hurried out of the throne hall, the doors thudding behind her.

Chapter 22

"My lord?"

Dreythan glanced up from his desk, the weight of his head barely allowing the simple movement. "Enter," he intoned. Setting his quill aside, he tried to straighten. Sleep had been hard to obtain. Hours had passed as he stared at the canopy over his bed, suppressing images of Fletch running from Thissian soldiers, of her being captured. Tortured.

When he'd finally fallen asleep, he'd dreamed of her finding her mother, and leaving forever.

The door to his study creaked open, and a guard poked their head in. "My lord, a party approaches the castle gates on horseback. They bear the banner of Ilumence."

He stared for a moment, uncomprehending. His chair skidded backward as he lurched to his feet. "Morthan," he murmured, automatically reaching for his crown. "Very well. Has Captain Norland been notified?"

"Aye, sir, er, my lord," the guard stammered, bobbing. "He's on his way now."

Shrugging on his ceremonial cloak, Dreythan paused to clasp the silver brooch and straighten his tunic. Hurrying into the spiraling stairway down, he found Matteo Alwick and Harrild Hammerfist waiting for him. They flanked him silently as he brushed past, their footfalls echoing in sync.

Exiting the royal tower, he rushed through the garden gates. In the street ahead, a broad-shouldered frame topped with red hair skirted a cart, muttering a quick apology.

"Norland!" Dreythan called.

The captain paused long enough for the king to join him. "My lord," he greeted with a brisk nod. "I'm guessing this arrival's a surprise to ye."

"It is," he admitted. "I wonder why Morthan did not send a messenger ahead of him."

Norland's beard shifted, his forehead creasing, but all he said was, "Perhaps he's in a hurry."

They turned onto the street in front of the welcome hall, slowing to a more sedated pace. In the courtyard before them, twenty men bearing steel pikes sat atop gleaming Roanite stallions. Polished blue-enameled plate armor glinted even in the muted daylight as the soldiers remained still as statues, indistinguishable from each other in their visored helmets. Even the horses looked nearly identical, their soft grey coloration fading to white at their manes, tails, and feet.

Beside the fountain, a single man stood. Though his horse was larger than the others, his sapphire-cloaked shoulders were level with the stallion's charcoal withers. His ebony hair was cut short, his angular face clean-shaven and regal.

As Dreythan approached, the man's black eyes flashed to Dreythan's, his tight, thin mouth relaxing. "Cousin," he said, bowing deeply. "King Dreythan Dreythas-son. My heartfelt thanks for inviting me to your home."

A subtle spark in Morthan's eyes belied the sober tone of his words, and Dreythan found himself smiling in return. He swung his hand forward as Morthan did the same. Their hands met each other's forearms with a satisfying smack, and Dreythan gripped as hard as he dared, matching Morthan's strength. "I am glad you could come," he replied, his heart swelling as he stared into the face that resembled his so closely. "King Morthan Morthas-son." He tilted his head over his shoulder. "This is the captain of my guard, Norland."

Morthan's horse lifted its muzzle from the fountain. A clang rang sharply as the creature chomped the bit in its mouth, shaking its neck.

"Flighty creature," Morthan said as he chuckled, giving the reins a slight tug. "I shall be glad to be free of you the next few weeks." He nodded to the silent soldiers around him, then at Norland. "Captain. Might my men find a place to rest? What with the recent attacks on His Majesty, and with the hostility from Thissa, I thought it best to arrive as swiftly as possible. We traveled through the night."

"Aye, Your Majesty," Norland replied, bowing. "We've prepared comfortable quarters in the barracks. Allow me to take your steed and lead your men to the stables. Our grooms'll make sure your mounts're well cared for."

For the briefest moment, the captain's eyes flashed to Dreythan's. Then he took Morthan's stallion's reins, clucking his tongue as he led the creature down the street. In pairs, the guards dismounted their own horses and followed, their footfalls in sync as they marched behind.

Dreythan stared after the captain, confusion muddling his already clouded thoughts. Had he imagined the cold glare in his old friend's eyes?

"I do apologize for arriving unannounced," Morthan was saying, rubbing the back of his neck ruefully. "But since a messenger would have arrived only moments before my company, I did not think it wise."

He turned back to his cousin, confusion fading. "Of course," he replied, smiling. "You must also be weary from your travels.

Come, let me show you to the guest tower."

"You seem to forget that I have visited Iventorr previously." Morthan chuckled, then hesitated. "I am loathe to retire so soon after arriving, but... I fear I shall not be much of a conversationalist until I receive some rest."

As they turned toward the guest tower, a low mutter from Matteo Alwick reached Dreythan's ears.

"Parfeln's going to love this. Look at them in all their pomp and circumstance."

"Mind yourself," came Harrild's whispered retort. "Don't do anything that would cause our lord grief."

Matteo grumbled back, too low for Dreythan to hear.

Thankfully, Morthan hadn't seemed to notice.

Fletch leaned forward in the saddle, the Wynd whipping past her face with the speed of her passage. She wanted to urge the elbecca to go faster, to bump his ribs with her heels, but instead, she patted his wooly neck. "Keep going, Roderick," she muttered. "Keep going!"

They'd left Iventorr at noon the previous day, immediately after Dreythan had given his leave. Seeming to sense the frantic anxiety Fletch was trying to suppress, Roderick had wasted no time. He'd broken into a gallop as soon as his hooves had reached the other side of the great bridge. His speed only slowed when Fletch reined him in to rest for the night.

Wiping sweat from her stinging eyes, Fletch swallowed hard. She'd left so abruptly, she hadn't even left a message for Naraan. He would be wondering where she had gone, why she'd skipped training.

But it was just as well. She had no idea how he would react to being told his queen's life, his entire race's wellbeing, was in danger.

A dagger of ice throbbed in her stomach. So many unknowns lined the path ahead that she could scarcely focus. She wanted to believe that a nation of Wynd-bloods could defend themselves against any threat on the seas. But Norland's and Dreythan's expressions had said otherwise. Genuine fear had hollowed their faces at the mention of Thissa's navy. Did Thissian ships possess deadly weapons? Weapons that the Wyndarin had no defense against?

Fletch's fingers tightened on Roderick's reigns. Hopefully when she reached Port Liarin, the Wyndarin would not have passed by. Hopefully she would be able to simply wait for them, and intercept their ships with a signal. But she knew better than to count on it. If they had already passed, matters could become entangled quite rapidly.

Still… she frowned at the grassy plains ahead. None of it made any sense. Why would Gorvannon attack the Wyndarin? Because they had done free trade with—

Two black shadows darted into the path. Roderick reared, screeching. Fletch lunged for his neck, her fingers burying in his wool as the saddle slipped beneath her. The elbecca's front hooves flayed the air, then came down hard.

Fletch kicked her feet from the stirrups and threw herself backwards. There wasn't time to string her bow. She yanked her hunting knife from its sheath just as the tang of salt stung her nostrils.

Unbreathing. As she spun to face the path, they were already charging. Two of them, their black hoods falling away from their faces with their unnatural speed.

She couldn't defeat both with just a knife. It fell from her hands as a sphere of crimson Wynd sprang to life in her fingertips. At the spark of fear and fury that lit in Fletch's gut, the ball blackened, imploded. Light curled within her palms.

A quick exhale, a flick of her wrists. The fire divided in two. The Unbreathing were feet away, their feet plowing into the dirt as they tried to stop. Raising her palms, Fletch pushed, jets of flame bursting forward. She squinted against the heat, pain searing her hands as the two Unbreathing ignited like dry parchment. They tried to run, but their bodies crumbled into embers, scattering in the grass.

Another scream rent the air. Fletch whirled. A red-hot poker of dread jabbed her ribs. Five more Unbreathing were already closing in. Two of them were raising bows towards her.

The flames were gone. Her palms felt as though she'd thrust them into a furnace. Snatching up her knife, Fletch dove to the side as two arrows whistled toward her. "Roderick, run!" she screamed.

But the elbecca wasn't running. His long neck arched as he reared again. He plunged forward, his horn thrusting at the Unbreathing in front of him. But before the deadly spiral could gore the creature's chest, it slid off an invisible force, missing the Unbreathing completely. The monster laughed. Saliva dripped from its elongated fangs, fingertips lengthening into claws as it reached back—

"NO!"

The knife flew from Fletch's fingers, burying in the Unbreathing's neck. It gurgled, its flesh dissolving as its compatriots raised their weapons.

There was no time to think. Dropping to one knee, Fletch swirled her arms around her head. The Wynd sprang to her call. A wall of current swirled around her and Roderick, snatching the black arrows in its stream, tossing them off course.

But the Unbreathing were caught in it too. They leaned against the building torrent, raising their hands to their faces as it yanked at their cloaks, their hair, their flesh.

Wobbling to her feet, Fletch threw a frantic glance at the elbecca. "Roderick, come!"

This time the creature listened. He backed up to her side, huddling into a ball as she redoubled the Wynd's speed. The cyclone moaned around her, vengeful voices quaking the air as her hair whipped her cheeks, her cloak snapping from her shoulders.

One of the Unbreathing was lifted from its feet, then another, spinning inside the wall that encircled Fletch. The others tried to throw themselves to the ground, but the furious tornado still tore at them, ripping shreds of clothing from their bodies.

Hands trembling, Fletch snatched her bow from her back and strung it, nocking an arrow to the ready. Taking a deep breath, she raised her weapon, waiting for the Wynd to fade.

But the cyclone didn't waver. Heart pounding in her throat, Fletch watched as the tornado's green, yellow, and orange fingers slashed the Unbreathing apart. The monsters' husks failed one after the other, exploding into puffs of ash and bone like whispers of smoke strung away by a storm.

Still the Wynd howled around her, baleful, cautioning. Hesitantly, she lowered her bow. Thrusting out a stinging hand, she focused on one point, willing the current to decelerate.

At her command, it faded, but gradually. When the last bit of Wynd finally died away, a shower of bones clattered to the ground in a perfect circle around her.

A few seconds of shocked silence passed before Roderick raised his head, giving Fletch a quivering, "Heeeerich?"

"I know," she agreed, her voice shaking. "That was a close one."

She glanced down at her palms. The skin was bright red and swollen, pale blisters already rising to the surface. Her hands needed to be bandaged, but that would take time she didn't have to spare.

Roderick heaved to his hooves, panting as he backed away.

"What's wrong?"

Vice-like hands clamped around her windpipe.

She thrashed against the crushing pressure, panic rising like a tidal wave. Her limbs flailed uselessly. Remembering her bow, she swung it behind.

Nothing. She reached for the Wynd, but it didn't respond. Roderick's screeching distantly reached her ears, warped, muted.

The hands squeezed even tighter, lifting her to dangle convulsing over the grass. Her lungs were turning into raging infernos, her heart fluttering weakly against her ribs. Black specks swam in her vision. The bow dropped from her hand.

But not the arrow.

As the dark spots threatened to swallow her sight, she gripped the missile, jabbing it next to her throat.

There was a flash of movement, a burst of bright stars and pain. She coughed violently, rolling to her feet. An Unbreathing crouched only feet away, hissing as it gripped its forearm. He'd thrown her, she realized dazedly. The arrow was still in her hand, the wood behind the silver head blackened and steaming.

The monster's head jerked up. Jaundiced eyes pierced Fletch's for a fractioned moment before he launched himself toward her, lips stretched back over gleaming fangs.

She thrust the arrow up and out. There was a sick cracking squish, then weight. Trembling, Fletch released the missile as the monster collapsed to the ground, arrow buried under its chin. She could only stare, trying to catch her ragged breath as the flesh moldered into grey powder.

Fletch snatched her bow from the grass and whipped another arrow to the ready. She spun, her eyes darting over the hills and fields that surrounded her, heart thundering in her skull. But nothing else moved.

Her lungs burned, her eyes and hands stung, and her head was swimming. She pushed all that aside. Turning to Roderick, she buried her face in his neck, gingerly touching her throat. She had to keep going. She had to warn her mother.

But the Unbreathing... they had ambushed her. They had known where she was going, what she was doing. Even though she'd left Iventorr before anyone had known she had.

Fletch froze.

They'd lain in wait, even though she'd left Iventorr before word of her errand could have spread. Which meant... She slumped to the grass, all sound fading but the wheeze of her own labored breath.

Her mission to warn her mother had been a trap.

She stared numbly down at her blistering fingers. It couldn't be coincidence. Whoever had set the trap had meant it for her, just as surely as the Unbreathing had waited for her outside of Herstshire.

Roderick gently nudged her shoulder, fluttering his lips. "I'm all right," she tried to tell him, but it came out as a croak.

If the mission to warn the Wyndarin had been a trap, did that mean her mother was safe? That the Wyndarin weren't in danger? Fletch scowled, absently chewing her lip. No. If Gorvannon were behind the attacks, it was possible he still meant harm to the Wyndarin. It was possible to have two goals for one plot.

Pulling herself to her feet, Fletch straightened Roderick's saddle. She'd already swung herself onto his back and pointed him southward when it suddenly occurred to her.

The orchestrator of the attacks had lured her out of Iventorr, and had tried to kill her. Again. Were more Unbreathing heading to Iventorr?

She reined Roderick in, her stomach twisting. There was no other reason for someone to want her gone. Dreythan was in danger.

Turning, Fletch stared north, then south, then north again. A weight settled over her, leaden and cold. It couldn't be coincidence that Gorvannon's message arrived mere days before King Morthan's expected appearance. If the Thissian dictator were behind it all, she didn't doubt he meant to kill both kings in one fell swoop.

Still, she didn't move. Tears squeezed to her eyes, and she blinked them back, raising her head to the sky.

To the south lay the sea, and the chance that her mother and the Wyndarin might be headed toward danger.

To the north, Iventorr, and the certainty her king's life was at stake.

Swallowing around the burning ember that had settled into her throat, Fletch gritted her teeth. Fiorelle's smile, the feel of her soft, warm hand in hers. She despised the thought that she might lose the relationship she'd never even hoped to have. And simply knowing someone might wish harm to the peaceful, nomadic Wyndarin was enough to make her stomach roil and her vision turn red.

But her kingdom was in danger. The kingdom she'd sworn to protect, that her father had given everything for, was on the precipice of destruction. Ivenhence, her sister, needed her.

And Dreythan. Fletch's chest tightened. She looked down at the hand he'd held so tenderly, now prickling with blisters. An image flashed through her mind, of his body broken and bloody, Iventorr's stone stained crimson with his blood.

A shudder caressed her spine. Her hand clenched into an agonized fist. Tugging Roderick's reigns, she turned him northward, urging him into a gallop.

They traveled through the night, only stopping for water and to let Roderick's breathing slow. When they reached Iventorr the following morning, the elbecca galloped past the gatehouse and across the bridge. Fletch half expected the iron gates to be hanging off their hinges, smoke rising from the castle's towers. But the gate guards simply saluted as she rushed past, townsfolk trundling here and there with carts and armfuls of baskets or crates as usual. The normalcy of it all was frightening, off-putting.

Tugging Roderick to a stop at the fountain, she slipped from the saddle, giving his neck an absent pat. She had to find Dreythan. Where would he be?

Across the courtyard, three figures exited the guest tower. The sun's pale light glinted blue off the raven-dark hair and high cheekbones of the leading man. Fletch's heart leaped. Her feet started to carry her toward him, then slowed.

The man wasn't wearing a green cloak or a silver crown, but sapphire blue robes trimmed with gold. The two guards flanking him clinked inside their cobalt enameled plate armor.

None of them drew breath.

As if sensing Fletch's stunned gaze, the black-haired man turned, his eyes meeting hers. A chill traced her skin as she took an instinctive step back. The malice of his glance clenched cold in her stomach. It bored into her, narrowing, before the man's nostrils flared. He turned, muttering to his guards.

Tearing herself from the spot she'd been rooted, Fletch ran. Unbreathing were in the castle. Why did one of them look like Dreythan? She had to warn him, had to keep herself from being caught.

Her eyes flitted to the sky. The sun was high, not quite to its apex. It was still before noon, then. Slender legs pumping as fast as they would go, she sprinted toward the throne hall. Her lungs burned, her eyes stung, and her head was swimming, but she pushed all that aside. Teeth gritted, she ran as she'd never run before. Maids and gardeners stared as she passed. A couple of people jumped out of her frenzied path, shouting reprimands, but she barely heard them.

Skidding around the corner of the throne hall, she slipped through the door as quickly as the guards could push them open. To her dismay, the hall was empty.

"You there," she choked, pointing to one of the guards. "The king. Where — where's the king?"

"In his quarters, awaiting King Morthan," the dumbfounded man stammered. "He said they were to discuss... Sentinel Wyndshaper, wait!"

But Fletch was already gone. This time her flying feet carried her toward the royal tower. King Morthan? Dreythan's cousin. That's why he looked like him. The king of Ilumence was Unbreathing.

Fletch hurtled down the steps between courtyards, taking two at a time. Darting past the Sentinel tower, she fixed her eyes straight ahead on the tall, stout stone column of the royal quarters. Not swerving from her beeline, she leaped over garden walls, bushes, and more stairs, her long legs swallowing the ground in desperate strides. She reached the oaken door at the base of the royal tower. At her vicious shove, it whipped open with a boom.

Two figures within spun towards her, hands springing to their weapons. She hadn't realized her hand had done the same until Captain Norland's voice said, "Lady Luminia, Wyndshaper. What's the meaning of this?!"

"Captain," she said, but it came out as a croak. Black spots swam again in her vision. Pain burst in her knees. As the shadows cleared, she found herself kneeling on the floor, gasping for air. "Dreythan," she wheezed, the fire in her lungs squeezing tears to her eyes. "Where?"

"The king's in his study at the moment, awaiting his cousin." A strong hand pulled her back to her feet, bright blue eyes fixing on her neck. "What—"

It hurt to speak, to swallow. To breathe. "Unbreathing." She pointed to her neck, trying to blink away the pain. "Ambushed me halfway to Port Liarin. Morthan's guard, Morthan, they're—"

The second figure stepped forward, arrow still nocked to his bowstring. Parfeln Holden's sour grey eyes inspected her coolly.

Norland's gaze narrowed. He turned, still grasping Fletch's shoulder.

The arrow rose to point at his face, Parfeln staring down the shaft. "Don't move," the elder man hissed. "I shall kill you if you do."

For a moment, time seemed to freeze. The captain's blue eyes sharpened dangerously, his face dropping into a blank mask as his hand stilled on Fletch's arm. Parfeln didn't blink, his stare fixed flatly between the both of them as the arrow swiveled steadily back and forth.

Fletch swallowed, biting back a wince. Her knife hung at her side, her fingers only inches away. She had to do something. With every passing second, Morthan and his 'guards' drew closer. Within minutes, she and Norland would surely be dead, and the king would soon follow.

"How, Holden?" Norland rumbled, his question echoing starkly off the stone walls.

The arrow paused on the captain, as did Parfeln Holden's narrow gaze. "That's your question?" He spat, jowls curling with a sneer. "Not 'what have you done', but 'how'?"

"I know what ye've done." Still not moving, Norland raised one brow at the Sentinel in front of him.

The sneer dissolved into a scowl. Parfeln shifted uneasily, glancing out the open door. "Do you, now?"

The arrow still hadn't wavered from Norland's forehead. Fletch nearly reached for her blade, but stilled that thought. Foolhardy action would only make a dire situation worse.

He shrugged. "Likely not all of it. But I know someone removed the evidence from the assassination fifteen years ago, as well as the library's records of the Great Slaving and the Unbreathing. I know someone's been sending missives to Ilumence frequently over the past two decades. I know your brother crafted th' arrows that slew Kell Wyndshaper and King Dreythas." A muscle in his red-bearded jaw twitched, a vein pulsing in his temple. "But what I don't know is how, or why."

It was nearly more than she could stand. Surely the captain understood that every moment they delayed, Dreythan's life was closer to a perilous edge. Not to mention their own lives. Her fingers itched to close around the hilt of her dagger. But as if sensing her thoughts, Norland's hand squeezed around her arm, followed by a barely perceptible shake of the head.

Not yet.

"Ye couldn't've managed it all on your own," Norland continued, a dry smile curling one corner of his mouth. "You're not patient enough, or smart enough. So who was it? And why?"

"Why?" Parfeln repeated, rolling the word around in his mouth. "Why. Because I serve Ilumence, that is why, Norland Wyntersoul. Your ancestors couldn't protect old Ivereland from invaders. They fled to their precious mountain, shut themselves off from the suffering of the people below. Ilumence didn't ignore the plight of Ivereland's people. Ilumence sent aid. But when the youngest of the Corwynter royal bloodline freed the inhabitants of the land from oppression and slavery, what did he do?" His lip curled back from his yellowed teeth as he snarled, "Rather than honor his word and return old Ivereland to the fold of great Ilumence, Dreythas the Usurper claimed the land as his own. And the people who had been freed mindlessly supported his rebellion. Instead of joining and supporting the nation who assisted in their relief and recovery, in their power-drunk state, newly liberated, the former slaves chose isolation." Muddy eyes flashing, he drew back even further on the bowstring. "Ivenhence should not even exist."

Fletch stared at Parfeln, knife temporarily forgotten. Words he'd spat at her moons ago suddenly echoed through her mind.

He hadn't believed the Unbreathing were real, or that she could shape the Wynd. It suddenly made sense.

"You weren't part of the Great Slaving," she rasped. Parfeln whipped toward her, missile aimed at her chest. "You didn't witness the horrors that took place in this very castle. How can you judge those who survived for valuing their freedom?"

Norland's fingers tightened again below her shoulder, but this time, he didn't shake his head.

"How can I not?" Parfeln hissed. "They were crazed, spinning wild tales of their captors to justify their prolonged imprisonment. Monsters who drink human blood? We call them 'wights' in Ilumence. Tales to frighten small children into obeying their elders. Nothing more."

Unable to comprehend the depth of his willful ignorance, Fletch simply stared. He stood, arrow leveled against the captain of his guard and against a fellow Sentinel, having betrayed two kings and an entire kingdom, simply because he believed he was right. Never mind the eyewitness accounts of hundreds of survivors. Or the scars borne by those who yet lived. Or the many elderly women who had never been able to bear children because of the horrors they'd endured.

Her father had survived, had helped so many others survive, as had Dreythan's father. And here this arrogant cock was, telling her that her father was a delusional, rebellious fool. Molten heat bubbled up from her gut, rising slowly through her chest to consume her.

Her lips parted just as Norland's hand squeezed sharply, twice.

"You're a fucking imbecile, Holden," the captain said, a wide smirk flashing across his face. "Aid? Ilumence sent two men to scout the land to the south, not an army. Assisted in relief and recovery? Your 'great nation' sent wagons of blankets and food, sure. But they didn't nurse Ivenhence back t' health. And they certainly didn't earn the right to make Ivenhence part of their nation." He shook his head, grin broadening. "Ye moron. Ye've been duped. Ye've been serving the monsters all along. But I'll wager whoever's been pulling your strings didn't see fit to tell you. So who's the puppet master? Who's smart enough so see what's going on and cover it all up?" He peered up the ceiling, as if thinking. "Hmm. Someone who has access to the library, someone who came here from Ilumence during Dreythas's reign. Let me guess. Brinwathe?"

Doubt flashed across Parfeln's sallow face, his arrow hovering over Norland's heart. "Talk all you wish, Captain," he snapped. "The Ilumencian men you're so sure are monsters will kill you soon enough."

"Oh, they're monsters, all right." Norland chuckled. "Why don't ye try stabbing one of Morthan's guards with a silver blade? Or, better yet, Morthan himself. Not like ye'd have the stones to try it." His hand squeezed once more, then dropped to the hilt of his sword.

The bowstring sang.

Parfeln was already nocking another arrow. The heat within Fletch erupted into a livid fury she'd never known. Twitching both hands to the open door, she yanked. Wynd blasted into the corridor as Parfeln's second arrow loosed, barreling into him like a falling boulder. It flung him into the wall, a hollow crack echoing as his skull collided with unyielding stone. Limbs splaying, he slumped to the floor. A long, slow stream of Wynd escaped his nostrils, then faded.

Dead. He was dead. The inferno in Fletch's sternum was suddenly a spike of ice. Trembling, she turned to Captain Norland.

His hand was clamped over his neck. Crimson spurted between his fingers. It was trickling down his tunic, down his cuirass, down his arm. It was pooling in front of his feet.

She reached him just as he staggered. Her hands slipped on the blood-coated armor to catch under his armpits as she helped him sit against the red-splattered wall. Fingers shaking, she yanked the Sentinel's green sash from her neck and shoved it over his fingers. He only lifted the pressure for a moment, but blood gushed out, drenching the sash before his hand could close over it.

"Fletch," he grunted.

"Don't move, sir," she said without taking her eyes off the wound, clamping her fingers down atop the captain's. "You'll only speed the bleeding."

"The king. Ye've got to warn the king, lass."

He didn't need to remind her. "I know. We must stop the bleeding first."

His other hand rose to gently lay on hers, forcing her to meet his eye. "It's not going to stop bleeding, lass," he told her, smiling weakly.

Fletch's heart plummeted to her stomach.

"Help me to my feet," he grunted, the twinkle in his kindly blue eyes slowly dulling as his skin turned a sickly shade of yellow-white. "In those maps your father drew, there's a passage to the king's office. Hit the left sconce and get him out of there. I'll hold 'em off here as long as I can."

There wasn't time for tears. Grasping the captain's clammy, bloody hand, she put her shoulders under his arm and hoisted him to his feet. As he leaned heavily against the wall, his breath slow and ragged, she met his dying gaze.

"I've wondered a few times what I would've said to my father, had I been with him in his last moments," she whispered hoarsely. "Your family loves you, Norland. As do I. I'll look after them. You have my word."

There was a subtle shift in the fading light behind Norland Wyntersoul's eyes. Heaving himself straight, he drew his sword.

"Go," was all he said, and he turned away.

There was no time to waste. As Norland slid the door shut and wedged his blade between it and the doorframe, Fletch forced her heartsick, weary, beaten, bruised body up the flights of curving stairs at a dash.

Every bone in her body screamed at her not to leave her friend, her captain, in his last moments. In his dying moments. Was this his last breath? Or the next? Had he already collapsed on the floor in a pool of his own—

She couldn't think about it. Dreythan's life would also be lost if she didn't keep going.

Hit the left sconce, hit the left sconce. Get him out of there.

The words played over and over in her head as she sped haphazardly upward. One toe caught the lip of a step and she stumbled, catching herself just in time. Her hands left wet red prints on the cool grey stone. Choking back vomit and tears, she jerked upright and hurtled on.

Reaching the second floor, she cast a wild glance around. Nothing.

Faint thuds echoed from below, punctuated by shouts. The Unbreathing were trying to force the door. Her footfalls accelerated. Something warm trickled down her face. Eyes blurred, throat throbbing, Fletch wiped the moisture roughly from her cheek, hardly noticing the resulting sting as she pushed her rubbery legs as fast as they would go.

A distant boom. The rushed stomping of running feet. The sounds reached Fletch's ears just as she burst into the third floor.

Dreythan scanned the mess of parchment and books that littered his desk, setting his quill aside with a satisfied nod. It had taken him most of the previous day and much of the morning, but with Anshwell's help, he had finished compiling reference materials he thought would be most beneficial to his cousin. Records of trade with Thissa and the Isles, Anshwell's personal journals of their travels and trade negotiations, treatises of law and government. All of them had been carefully marked with dyed strips of parchment, a method of categorizing information that Brinwathe had recently introduced.

Checking the title of each tome and the color of each paper slip, Dreythan began stacking them in neat piles, his jaw clenching. It had been a welcome diversion from Fletch's absence. Now that the task was nearly done, he found himself dreading the empty time where anxiety usually nestled.

A sudden gust of wind rushed through the room, lifting loose papers and scattering them across the floor. Rising, he absently scooped the sheets of parchment back onto the desk. Fletch ought to have reached Port Liarin. He hoped she'd made it there before the Wyndarin.

Glancing toward the balcony, he straightened with a frown. The door was closed... Where had the wind come from?

There was a muffled thud. Seconds of eerie quiet passed.

The door to Dreythan's study crashed open. His hand jumped to his sword, heart in his throat until he realized.

It was Fletch.

He started to smile, to ask her why she'd returned so quickly, but the words died on his lips. Crimson trickled down her cheek to a ring of mottled bruises around her neck. One of her eyes was bloodshot and swollen, but they both snapped with frenzy.

Her chest and hands were covered in blood.

"Fletch?"

"No time, my lord," she snapped, her voice a horse croak. Dashing to his left, she slammed her palm into the candelabra that hung from the wall. It shuddered, shaking the single brick it was embedded in. Grunting "Gods damn it," she grabbed the wax-coated brass in both hands and yanked.

Behind Dreythan's desk, a thin panel of stone slid dustily to one side.

He gaped at her, at the blood covering her hands and the chest-high passage to his office he'd never known existed. "Fletch, what —"

"Forgive me," she interrupted. Gripping his shoulders with startling force, she shoved him toward the opening. "Get in. Stay quiet. Your life is in danger."

Dreythan started to spin back towards her, to demand answers. But his eyes crashed onto the handprints around her throat, and the blood dripping from her face. Without a word or a sound, he slipped into the black tunnel.

The sound of heavy armored feet thundered towards them. Ducking into the opening behind Dreythan, Fletch turned, twisting her arms and fingers toward the balcony door. Another rush of wind sent papers flying. The balcony door flew open. Her hands clamped around the edge of the stone panel and slid it back into place, plunging them into darkness. Dreythan's heart hammered louder than the approaching footsteps as Fletch's side pressed against his.

"Stay silent," she breathed.

He barely heard over the pounding in his ears.

The tramping avalanche outside trembled to a crescendo, then halted.

"WHERE HAVE THEY GONE?"

Dreythan flinched. Morthan?

"Search the tower. He was here only moments ago. His scent is still fresh."

Crashing feet dashed back into the hall. This time the sound branched, traveling both above and below. Dreythan's gut twisted. What did he mean, 'his scent'?

"Find him! Him and his precious Wyndshaper. She's wounded. Do not allow yourself to be tempted by the beguiling scent of her blood. She. Is. Dangerous."

Fletch shifted beside him, a cautioning hand drifting onto his arm. His fingers closed over hers. Together they crouched in silence for what seemed like hours. Finally, the sound of trotting feet returned and a flat voice reported, "They're not within the tower. We have searched high and low. They must have escaped by the balustrade."

"ESCAPED?!" Morthan thundered. "TRACK THEM! Search the castle. They cannot have raised the alarm yet. Find them before they do. Kill the Wyndshaper. Bring the king to the terrace. If they are not found within the hour, I shall rip you from your Husks myself."

They left just as suddenly as they came, and after only a few seconds, all was silent.

Chapter 23

Inhaling shakily, Fletch focused and exhaled into cupped hands. She tried to summon the spark that had sprang so easily to life on the fields of Ivenhence, but her fingers trembled, and the sphere wouldn't hold its shape. Turning, she pushed a current of Wynd down the pitch-black corridor. The little breeze corkscrewed down and around, then disappeared from sight. Taking Dreythan's hand, she whispered, "This way."

It was slow going. Shaping the Wynd around the steady spiral of the tight passage was difficult enough without bumping into walls. Dreythan stumbled into her several times, nearly causing her to lose her footing. As they went, the passage seemed to narrow and shorten until they were nearly on hands and knees, their backs inches from the stone above. The air grew hot and heavy. Damp, stale soil mingled with the tang of blood and perspiration in her nostrils.

Suddenly, there was a soft light. It grew as they descended, ever brightening until they found themselves in a rounded stone chamber. Three windows the width of Fletch's hand sliced through the stone to allow daylight to filter in, gently illuminating the small space.

Releasing Dreythan's hand, Fletch rubbed her neck. Her thoughts could barely string together into a uniform idea, the shock slowing them, weighting them. Gods, what was she supposed to do next?

"Fletch." A hand on her arm slowly turned her. She found Dreythan staring at the blood that was crusting red-brown on her blistered fingers and the bruises that were surely rising on her throat. "For Ivere's sake, please. Tell me what is happening. That voice that commanded others to find me and to kill you... Was that my cousin I heard?" The angle of his throat bobbed as he swallowed, black eyes darting over her face. "Your cheek is wounded, but nowhere else. Why is there so much blood?"

Think. She needed to think. Legs turning into jelly, she slumped against the wall, Dreythan's words slowly sinking in. Her cheek? "Parfeln's second arrow," she realized dazedly. "I didn't even feel it."

Dreythan's hand didn't lift from her arm. Just as Captain Norland's hadn't. Not until he forced Parfeln to shoot, giving Fletch a window to act.

"Fletch." Another hand descended on her other shoulder with a hesitant shake. "I need to know what has happened. Please."

A furious sting in her cheek brought her crashing back into focus. Tears were streaming down her face, trickling into the gash Parfeln's arrow had left. Gulping in a deep breath, she managed, "Unbreathing ambushed me halfway to Port Liarin. I returned here, knowing you must be in danger. Morthan and his guards were in the courtyard—" she swallowed painfully "—and they don't breathe. I tried to find you, but we were betrayed. By Parfeln Holden. He's an Old Ilumence Loyalist." Blank grey eyes flashed through her vision, and she shuddered. "Was." Her hands instinctively tried to twist together. At the crunch of dried blood and the stinging squish of blisters, they yanked apart. "We must keep moving, my lord," she heard herself say. "While Morthan's Unbreathing search the castle for you, we've no choice but to keep using these tunnels. We must find our way to the Sentinel tower, or to the barracks. The guard must be rallied. We've got to drive them out."

She tried to heave herself upright, but Dreythan's hands didn't move. He met her eye, his expression scribed with quiet insistence. "Is that Parfeln Holden's blood, then?" he asked.

"No," she whispered. "It's Captain Norland's."

A multitude of emotions battered across his face. Horror, fear, anger. Then, the heartbreaking descent of disbelief.

Wobbling to her feet, she pulled Dreythan to his. "He commanded me to get you to safety," she told him hoarsely. "And that's what I'll do. Come, my lord. We must keep moving."

Taking Dreythan's arm, she led him again into the darkness. They hadn't come across any forks or branches in the tunnel, but that was just as well. If they had, she wouldn't have known which direction to take. She cursed herself for not memorizing the tunnels in her father's maps, for not finishing his journal sooner.

"It begins to fall into place," Dreythan's voice said absently. "Parfeln... he was one of the castle guard when your father was captain and my father king. He must have allowed the assassin to enter Iventorr, or given him weapons upon entry. You said he was an Old Ilumence Loyalist... he must have believed he was serving Ilumence by sabotaging Ivenhence."

"That makes sense," Fletch muttered, her throat throbbing with every syllable. "Parfeln's brother, Purveyn, would have supplied the arrows. Possibly sent them directly to Parfeln."

"And the black arrows," Dreythan droned on, seeming not to hear. "The ebonite arrows were a simple distraction. Why suspect Ilumence of the attack when Thissa bore us ill-will? Use arrows made of wood only grown in Thissa, and the red herring is cast."

Their footsteps padded softly for a time before he added, "My uncle Morthas would never have organized such a heinous plan. He supported my father, and after him, me. Morthan was the one behind it all. My father's assassination. The attempt on my life as I traveled to Ilumence. The spy, the rumors of war with Thissa. The disappearance of the fletcher, Purveyn. It all makes sense. He would have gained an entire kingdom from it." He shook his head. "Perhaps my uncle Morthas died before his time. Who can say?"

Fletch remained silent. Dreythan's quiet pondering was drawing uncomfortably close to a question she could only pray he wouldn't ask.

"That note," he continued. "The Unbreathing that attacked you on your return from Herstshire. The note was written by Morthan. How could I not have seen it? For Ivere's sake, it was written in blue ink. I ought to have seen it." There was a brief pause. "But... you said that Purveyn the Fletcher was Parfeln's brother?"

There it was. She cringed, hurrying onward as if it would allow her to escape.

"How did you know? Why did you not say anything?" Dreythan stopped, his hand slipping from hers.

"I suspected, my lord," Fletch replied miserably, glad the darkness hid the flare of shame in her face. "But I wasn't sure. My uncle bore messages between the Holden brothers many years ago. But he couldn't remember the younger brother's name."

The king didn't immediately respond. For several moments, the only sound in their ears was the quiet echo of their careful footsteps.

"You did not bring this to my attention because you feared I would disregard you?" he asked finally. "Or perhaps because you wished to be certain before making such an accusation?"

The thoughtful understanding in Dreythan's voice curled softly in Fletch's chest. Finding his hand again in the darkness, she insistently tugged him forward. "A bit of both," she admitted. "I knew you would hear me, but... even if Parfeln were Purveyn's brother, that in itself wasn't evidence of his betrayal. I needed proof. Even so, I told Captain Norland." The name caught in her throat, burning, and she swallowed hard.

Dreythan's fingers tightened in hers.

It was difficult to guess how long they walked. Dreythan could see nothing in the utter darkness. His only guide was the steady pull of Fletch's hand and the whisper of her boots across stone.

A thousand thoughts and questions gushed through his mind. But they were like the ocean during a storm, uniform in their overwhelming crushing power. He couldn't pull a singular drop from it to focus on, and so allowed the waves to crash against him numbly.

Ahead, a hint of light. It grew gradually stronger until they found themselves in another small octagonal chamber. Dropping his hand, Fletch crossed to one of the three slitted windows and peered out.

"We're on the north side of the island," she told him hoarsely, swallowing. "Judging by the shadows. We should be close to the barracks, perhaps directly under the armory."

Red and purple bruises mottled her pale neck. One of her eyelids drooped as if she'd been struck, the eye beneath bloodshot and swollen. The cut on her cheek had stopped bleeding, but the trail of drying crimson had trickled down her neck to disappear under her cuirass, interrupted by tear-stains. And Norland Wyntersoul's blood covered her clenched fists.

She turned toward him, shoulders hunched as she did her best to conceal her pain. "Come, my lord," she said, nodding at two passages which branched off into the darkness. "Which should we take?"

From the agony in her eyes, the way her voice had caught when she said Norland's name, he already knew. Norland was dead. The knowledge echoed dully though his gut. He couldn't comprehend it. His mind shut it off from him, closing him away from the pain he desperately needed to feel.

But the Unbreathing had tried to kill Fletch, too. He stared at her, his hands limp at his sides. Of the torrent of thoughts pounding through his head, one halted, crystal clear.

He had very nearly lost her.

"Fletch," he said quietly. "I should like to hold you for a moment."

Her green eyes met his, startled and questioning. Then, bowing her head, she nodded. "I would like that too," she whispered. "But only for a moment, my lord. We have precious little time."

Dreythan's arms circled her ribs as she looped hers around his neck, pressing her cheek into his shoulder. He could feel the warmth of her hair against his neck, feel the rise and fall of her chest as she breathed. Her hand brushed absently through his hair, sending a tremor through his entire being. Though she smelled of blood and sweat and damp dirt, he wanted to keep her in his embrace forever.

Suddenly, Fletch stiffened. "They're following us." Pushing away, she whirled to the two passages. "Hurry. Which way?"

"Left."

"You first. I'll guard the rear."

She whipped an arrow from her quiver as they plunged again into darkness. Without Fletch guiding him, Dreythan trotted as quickly as he dared, his hands tracing the stone wall, fingernails and skin scraping over the rough surface.

"They're gaining on us," Fletch's voice gasped, barely audible over the scraping of their feet against stone. "Keep going, Dreythan."

Muffled trotting, echoing down the tunnel. It was impossible to guess if the sounds were from their own feet or from pursuers. The sound of their breath, heavy and painful. Oppressive, complete darkness. The pounding and tingling rush of blood in his ears. Under his feet, he could feel the tunnel descending. A tunnel to the barracks would have taken them upward. His pounding heart sank. They had gone the wrong way.

Suddenly, his hand met something cold.

"Wait." Fletch's hand found his arm. "The Unbreathing have

stopped. I... I can try to give us some light."

A small globe of fire swirled to life, illuminating the burns in the palms of her hands. The light from the tiny fire danced in her eyes and cast mesmerizing shadows over her cheeks. For a moment, she seemed mysterious, unfathomable. Then she winced, and a sharp pang pierced Dreythan's chest.

"Don't overexert yourself," he said. His sword rang as he pulled it from its sheath. Slicing a swath from the bottom of his cloak, he wrapped the cloth around the blade and knotted it in place. "Light this."

A tiny smile curved her lips. She touched the crackling ball to the cloak, which reluctantly caught. The flickering light danced brilliant blue over streaks in the stone walls, and Dreythan suddenly knew why the Unbreathing had stopped.

"We've reached the mines," he breathed.

They were surrounded by silver ore. It flowed in streaks and streams through the rough walls. In places, the stone had been chiseled roughly away, leaving jutting clefts sticking awkwardly out.

"The very top of them, at least," Fletch added, pointing where the passage dove sharply out of the light. "It leads further down."

Dreythan hesitated. "If we keep going, we might not reach the surface for some time. Can we double back to the other passage? To the barracks?"

She was already shaking her head. "They're too close, at least five of them. And they shan't stop for long. We need to keep going or they'll catch up." Drawing her bow and arrow again, she nodded down the passage. "Go on. I'll watch behind."

Sword-torch held carefully aloft, he obeyed.

Minutes passed, the only sounds the gentle crackle of the flame consuming cloth and the tap tap of their footsteps. The silver veins in the tunnel walls thickened and twisted around them like metal vines through the rock and Hearth.

Suddenly, Fletch paused. "Do you feel that?"

Dreythan peered over his shoulder, the torchlight revealing

Fletch's pale, battered, worried face. He opened his mouth to ask her what she meant. A tremor beneath his feet stopped him.

Lowering her bow, Fletch pressed an ear to the tunnel wall. "Listen."

He copied her, the chill of the rock seeping into his flesh as he strained, waiting.

Thrum thrum. Thrum thrum.

The vibrations hummed through Dreythan's bones. Yanking away from the stone, he had only to glance at Fletch's face to know she'd felt it too.

"It sounds like a pulse," she said, eyes widening. "An enormous, ancient heart. You don't think...?"

They turned in unison, staring down the passage that kept diving into the darkness.

"We can't go back," Fletch muttered. "Gods, but I hope we don't have to go down much further."

Fingers tightening around his blade, Dreythan swallowed. Together, they continued down the tunnel, unconsciously keeping close. The thrumming gradually grew, the air itself throbbing, pulsing.

"I... I suppose some part of me still believed the tale of Kazael's prison was simply that," Dreythan said, his voice hollow in his own ears. "A tale. But... but this sound..."

"It makes it all feel real." Fletch lent him a rueful smile. "Hearing a fallen god's heart beating." Her frame stiffened. "They're after us again. Let's hurry."

Their feet pattered along the stone as they rushed, still downward, the pulse strengthening until the earthen walls around them seemed to tremble. A few thoughts managed to crystalize in Dreythan's shock-fogged mind as his feet limped into a run. First, they had no idea where they were going. Second, the Unbreathing could see far better in the dark and would inevitably catch up to them.

Third, Morthan had ordered Fletch killed.

Abruptly, the light split, illuminating a fork in the tunnel.

"We have to find a way up," Dreythan panted, holding the torch toward one, then the other.

"They're gaining on us, but slowly." Fletch slung her bow across her back, cupping her hands as the little flame sprang to life again. "I'll scout this passage, you scout the other. Meet back in sixty seconds?"

He nodded. "Go."

She disappeared down the tunnel she'd chosen, the glow from her globe quickly fading. But rather than follow his designated passage, Dreythan turned and dashed back the way they had come.

Morthan had commanded Dreythan be brought to him alive. He could buy Fletch the time she needed to find a way out of the tunnels. She would find Norland who would rally the guard and the Sentinels, and…

Norland.

He stumbled, the hand holding his blade shaking. His oldest and most loyal friend, gone? It didn't feel real.

He couldn't bear the thought of losing Fletch too.

A clammy hand crept along his back. Heart hammering in his throat, he straightened.

"Here I am," he said quietly into the inky dark. "Let us not delay any longer. Come. Take me to your master."

Six Unbreathing materialized out of the darkness, yellowed eyes squinting against the flickering fire. Wordlessly, soundlessly, they surrounded him.

Pit pat pit pat pit pat.

The soft echo of footsteps flooded Fletch's ears. It was the only thing she could hear other than the soft whisper of her own breath and the thrumming of her heart. Or was it Kazael's? Dropping the globe of heat that stung her prickling fingers, she guided a breeze along the passage. The stream of Wynd sloped gradually upwards. For the first time in what felt like days, her heart fluttered hopefully.

Scuttling back to the fork in the passages, she peered down the one Dreythan was scouting. "This passage leads upward," she said. "And the Unbreathing's scent has faded. I think we might be safe."

There was no answer. The tunnel was dark.

"My lord?" She took a few steps down the passage, waiting, listening.

Still, no answer.

Stomach turning to lead, Fletch rushed down the passage, passing numerous branching tunnels and alleys. Still no light, no voice. No Dreythan. She stood rigid in the center of passage, swallowing rising panic. She had to find him.

Sprinting upwards, she blasted the Wynd in front of her. Surely his torch had just gone out, and he was simply waiting for her ahead, unsure of the path in the darkness.

Still no Dreythan.

If he had taken this tunnel at all, she would have caught up with him by now. Which meant... he hadn't taken the passage.

But why? Had he retraced their steps?

A shard of ice jabbed her gut.

He must have, otherwise she would have found him. But if he had backtracked, the Unbreathing must have captured him.

Terror's clammy fingers tried to close around her. Her mind flashed to her mother, to the unknown that lurked where the Wyndarin were headed, to the possibility she might be dead. Had she made the wrong choice? Why had Dreythan left her behind?

Her hands clenched into blister-popping fists as her teeth clamped on her bottom lip. She couldn't let Captain Norland's sacrifice be for nothing. Even if Dreythan had turned himself over, she wouldn't give up. She couldn't.

The tunnel was finally leading upwards. By moving forward she would emerge at the island's surface sooner than by going back. Shoving her pain, weariness, hunger, and thirst from her mind, she shifted her quiver higher on her shoulder.

Her thoughts sped as quickly as her feet as she set off at a run yet again. Where would the Unbreathing have taken Dreythan? Morthan had mentioned a terrace, but which one? There were several throughout the castle. How many of the monsters lurked across Iventorr? Should she alert the Sentinels and trust them to spread the word through the guard? Or should she try to find Dreythan before—

A faint light gleamed off the stone wall ahead. Choking back the instinct to cry out, she doubled her speed.

But when she rounded the corner, Fletch skidded abruptly to a halt, hand flying to her dagger.

Leaning against the wall was a man. He was clothed entirely in steel-studded leather armor stained the color of evening shadows. His form seemed to bleed into the tunnel wall behind him, as if he were carved from the stone itself. She might not have seen him at all had he not held a beacon of pure white light in his hand.

The light swiveled to her face. She grimaced, hands flying to her eyes.

"There you are, Your Majesty." The beam of light lowered slightly. "I was beginning to wonder if I had the wrong corridor after all."

"I'm not the king," Fletch growled, squinting through her fingers. The stranger's head was covered in a black cowl, the lower half of his face concealed behind a bit of cloth attached to the hood. Translucent persimmon escaped through the cloth; an impatient sigh. Not Unbreathing, then. "Who are you?" she demanded.

"Not important. Drink." He thrust a hard, oddly-shaped container into her hands.

Her numb brain struggled to collect itself, but her hands clasped instinctively around the object and lifted it to her lips. Sweet, cool water washed down her throat. She hadn't realized how parched she'd been.

Accepting the container back, the man slung it over his

shoulder and began to stride off, the light in his hand bobbing with his steps. "Come. We must find Dreythan Corwynter before they Turn him."

Though the man was tall and his strides long, Fletch kept pace, following close on his heels. His words stuck a jangling chord in Fletch's mind, and its reverberations shook her to her core.

"They mean to Turn Dreythan," she repeated. The man didn't slow. "Holy Luminia. Morthan's plan wasn't to take Iventorr by force, but to Turn Dreythan and... and..."

Despite the pounding in her skull, she urged her feet into a trot.

"Indeed," agreed the stranger, his voice oddly empathetic. "Morthan's intent was to kill you first, then Turn the king. Over time, the Unbreathing would have Turned more of the Iventorr guard. In a matter of a few years, the silver mine would be reopened under the ruse of expanding Ivenhence's trade routes."

"And Kazael would be set free," Fletch finished. There was a ring to his statements, as if he knew beyond the shadow of a doubt. As if he had seen it with his own eyes. She hesitated. "Are you Wyndarin?"

"No."

The passage curved up and to the right.

Fletch's head pounded behind her eyes. She raised a hand to her brow. Morthan had commanded she be killed because she would've noticed the change in Dreythan. He must have wished it done outside of Iventorr so no one would know she'd been murdered. It would have been assumed she'd left to follow the Wyndarin. All of Iventorr would have had fleece pulled over their eyes. They would have been oblivious to the fact that they were being slowly turned into Unbreathing.

She shivered. It was a near flawless plan. Had they succeeded in killing her, Morthan would have won.

And despite her survival thus far, he still might.

It was difficult for Dreythan to guess how long it took his captors to find their way out of the tunnels. They had wrenched his sword from his hands, tossing it aside as if touching it burned them. Without the makeshift torch, he stumbled in the darkness, the vicious grips on his arms not allowing him to slow. A couple of times, the Unbreathing paused. He wondered if they were at forks in the path, questioning which way to go.

When Dreythan emerged from the tunnels, firmly escorted by the Unbreathing, he found himself in a place he didn't recognize. The wall of Iventorr jutted behind him. Over it, he could just see the eave of a tower. So little of it could be seen, he didn't recognize it. Before him lay a semi-circular stone terrace, littered with aged, papery leaves and crumbled rock. A cracked shoulder-high wall separated him and the Unbreathing from open air and the long drop to the Emerald Basin. And there, standing with his feet shoulder-width apart, staring out over the Basin, was Morthan.

"Sir," one of the Unbreathing said, snapping to attention. "We've found him."

Morthan turned, white teeth baring in an unnerving smile. "As I can see. What of the Wyndshaper?"

"She wasn't with him when we captured him, sir."

They kept addressing him as 'sir' and not 'my lord', Dreythan noted. Odd. 'Sir' was a title used to address captains and other military officials, not kings.

Morthan's eyes narrowed into coal-dark slits. "That is interesting," he growled. "Tell me, cousin, what happened to your precious Sentinel?"

"She tried to lead me out of Iventorr by way of the tunnels," Dreythan replied. "But... she had taken an arrow to her chest."

"Sir," another one of the Unbreathing interjected, "we were able to track them through the tunnels by the scent of blood. However, the deepest section of the tunnels is lined with light-metal—"

Morthan shuddered.

"—and we lost them there."

"Fletch died there," Dreythan snarled. It was a lie, but an easy one. The anger, the disbelief, that was real. His best friend and most trusted ally, Norland Wyntersoul... He couldn't bring himself to believe he was truly gone. "I tucked her body beneath a silver vein so you monsters would not find her." He shifted, intentionally drawing Morthan's gaze to his. He held that black stare, letting the fury roll over him in a wave of roiling heat. "Tell me, Morthan," he said, glaring into his eyes, "what do you plan to do now? Norland Wyntersoul's blood shall be discovered in the royal tower. The alarm shall be raised any moment. Was this what you were aiming for?"

But the man before him didn't flinch or blink. Instead, he stepped closer, leaning in. Holding Dreythan's stare, a slow smile curled his lips, deliberate and cruel. "I confess I am rather weary of answering to a Corwynter's name," he purred. The black in his irises morphed, changing hue and saturation before Dreythan's horrified stare. In seconds, Morthan's eyes weren't black, but sickly gold. "The pathetic man you knew as Morthan hasn't possessed this body for quite some time. My name is Vvalk, and I have claimed this husk to fulfill the oath I made to your ancestor a half-century ago. I have come to gift your soul to Kazael."

Dreythan couldn't look into those yellow eyes for long. The livid malice within them forced him to break contact. "I see," he muttered. "I understand. You came here with the sole purpose of using my body as one of your husks. You mean to Turn me."

"Such hubris does not become a Corwynter," Vvalk replied with a grin, taking a step back. "Nay, Dreythan Dreythas-son. My sole purpose in coming here is to take this island, this prison, from the hands of the humans who do not even comprehend its purpose, and to free my Master. As to my plan, I shall improvise, as I have been forced to do many times over the past years."

"As you did when Kell Wyndshaper defended me with his life?" Leaning forward in the unyielding grasp of his captors, he snarled, "Or was it part of your plan to slay him all along?"

He had to keep him talking. Surely Fletch would find her way out of the tunnels any moment. Surely she would gather the guard and launch an attack.

He could only hope she would forgive him for leaving her.

Chapter 24

Fletch hurried close on the stranger's heels, each footfall stamping a new question in her mind. Why had she not seen Harrild and Matteo at the royal tower? They should have been posted outside Dreythan's door. What if they returned to their posts and found Captain Norland's body?

The thought sent a thrill of hope and terror through her. Perhaps Harrild and Matteo could raise the alarm... But if Unbreathing still lingered, they would kill the Sentinels before they could leave.

"How did you know?" she blurted.

The man slowed slightly, head swiveling to meet her gaze. "How did I know where to find you? Or how did I know the Unbreathing mean to Turn King Dreythan?"

"Neither," she responded, then hesitated. "That is, both. But I meant, how did you know there were Unbreathing in the castle at all? If you're not a Wynd-blood, how did you know they're Unbreathing?"

He sighed again, his hazel eyes fixed ahead as he resumed his trotting pace. "Asking me questions will yield nothing," he said, his voice heavy and monotone as if tired of answering. "I can't and won't give you answers."

"'Won't'?" Fletch repeated curiously.

"Will not."

Abruptly, he halted, raising his light. The white beam shone on a tangle of knotted roots above which engulfed a small square door.

"This leads to the orchard," he told her. "We have to find the king. Where might they have taken him?"

"Morthan commanded his Unbreathing to bring Dreythan to a 'terrace' when they found him. But," she added, heart sinking, "there are many terraces throughout Iventorr. I don't know which one he meant."

"It would be out of sight of the rest of Iventorr. If Morthan means to Turn the king, he wouldn't do it where he might be caught." The stranger folded his arms across his chest, gazing up through the roots. "I've already passed through most of the underground tunnels. They aren't down here. Likely on the side of the island, outside the wall."

Fletch conjured up images in her mind from Kell's maps, foggy through her pounding head. But it was no use. She simply hadn't studied them closely enough to remember. "My father's journal," she muttered, frustration with herself bubbling in the pit of her stomach. "It has maps of Iventorr, even the secret passages. It might show us a hidden terrace."

"Perfect." Climbing up between the roots, he thrust his shoulder against the ancient door. It groaned open, dust showering them. "To your quarters, then."

She followed the stranger up the ladder, into bright, blinding sunlight. Drawing a long, painful breath of fresh air, she blinked furiously, turning to her surroundings.

They had emerged just in front of the library. At the sight of familiar vegetable gardens and rooftops, the tension in Fletch's shoulders eased.

Distant shouts and screams echoed through the air.

"Fletch!" the stranger hissed. "What are you doing? Fletch!"

But she was already limping into a run, bow and arrow drawn with her heart in her throat.

On the barren grounds before the barracks, chaos reigned. Bodies littered the soil, a dozen at least, their blood seeping across the dirt. The guards of Iventorr were hard-pressed. Silvered weapons drawn, they struggled to force back the blue-armored fiends that spun amongst them. Several of the Unbreathing had thrown aside their helmets and spears, their fangs bared, crimson smeared on their lips as they threw themselves at any who dared approach.

Skidding to a stop, Fletch took a deep breath. Leveling her bow at one of the helmet-less monsters, she waited. The Unbreathing knocked aside a guard's sword and reared back, fingertips stretching into claws. Before its strike could land, her arrow found the center of its ear. It tumbled backward. Armor clanked to the ground, ash and bones spilling out.

To the left, an Unbreathing swung their spear, smashing the haft into the chest of a guard. She went flying, crashing to her back. Weapon lost, she tried to rise, to elbow away from the Devul that approached, eyes and teeth gleaming. Fletch's next arrow found the monster's eye socket.

A figure in studded leather armor whirled like a deadly cyclone across the field, two short blades flashing as he ducked an Unbreathing's strike. The stranger?

Another bowstring sang over the cries and shouts of the battle. Another helmetless Unbreathing fell. Spinning, Fletch spotted her old mentor, Aeda Yewmaster, across the field. Her dark skin glowing in the sun, her hand flashed to her quiver, drawing and releasing in the same breath. Their eyes met. The relief that flashed through hers was unmistakable.

"Sentinel, watch out!"

Fletch threw herself to the side, the whistle of a blade slicing the air where she'd stood. The blood-soaked ground slowed her roll. As she struggled to her feet, the Unbreathing who'd swung at her grunted, whirling its spear. This one wore a helmet. She fired at his neck, but it pinged off the cobalt-enameled metal. Snarling, it cleaved downward.

Its blade slowed, arcing directly at Fletch's forehead. Time yawned to a near-stop, everything sticky and deliberate as molasses. Cries warbled through the air, distorted and buckling.

Her toes dug into the blood and mud. Clenching her fist, she thrust up and out, punching out a gust of Wynd with a wild uppercut. The burst of air slammed into the Unbreathing like a battering ram. It flew back, tumbling over the fallen corpse of a guard. A snarl escaped the grille of its helmet. It tried to rise, but a silvered blade pierced under its chin. Breathing heavily, the guard who'd finished the monster straightened, wiping blood from his forehead. A green sash around his forearm shimmered in the sun.

"Harrild?"

At her shout, the Sentinel turned, blinking. "Fletch? Where's the king?"

A nasty wound opened his scalp, his eye shut against the flow of blood that streamed down his face. Yanking her eyes away from the gash, Fletch nocked another arrow. "Morthan has him. I don't know where."

There. Two guards back to back, beset by three Unbreathing. Her bowstring twanged, her arrow finding the back of one monster's knee. Seizing the opening, one of the guards jammed his blade through the blue-enameled helmet.

His companion parried a strike from another Unbreathing, yelling, "You're not bad in a fight, old man!"

Relief flooded through Fletch. That was Matteo's voice. So the guard fighting with him—

"The same to you," came the grunted reply from Darvick. "I underestimated you, it seems."

They were all right then, the rest of the Sentinels. Her friends. Her knees nearly buckled from relief.

One of the Unbreathing behind them fell, its killer turning to new prey before the armor could clank to the ground. It was the stranger, his twin blades whistling as they struck.

"Go!" Harrild turned back to the fray, blade wobbling to the ready. "Find Dreythan. Hurry! We can handle the rest."

More of the guard had fallen, but the Unbreathing's numbers were rapidly dwindling. Swallowing hard, Fletch turned away, her boots slurping in the gore-stained dirt.

The stranger appeared by her side, matching her step for step. "Let's hurry. We've lost precious time."

"At least we shan't have to worry about hiding," Fletch panted.

The adrenaline that had coursed through her was beginning to run thin. Her feet were growing heavy, her stomach hollow. Every swivel of her shoulders, every running step sent a stiff twinge through her. Around her, the stone and lumber amalgam buildings of Iventorr blurred and swam. She could barely see out of her right eye; it had swollen nearly shut. Her head throbbed.

But she kept going, pushing herself into a dash.

She had to save Dreythan.

Up the stairs, into the Garden Wall, and down the hallway they thundered, Fletch throwing her door open with a boom. Snatching the journal from her bed, she thumbed to the back, her trembling hands nearly losing their grip on the faded leather and parchment. Crusted blood from her fingers flaked onto the journal, burying themselves between the pages.

There. She pulled the book open wider, angling it toward the strange man who glanced curiously around her barren quarters. "Look," she said, pointing. "A group of three terraces along the outer wall."

He was already shaking his head. "Near the Sentinel tower and throne hall? It can be seen from the tower. They'd be somewhere secluded, unknown."

Fletch swallowed, forcing her darting eyes to slow, to focus. But the maps spun in her vision. She looked down, blinking hard. As her vision wavered back to clarity, it fixed on the mud-caked, blood-smeared toes of her boots.

The stranger's boots were spotlessly clean.

"Here, next to the armory." His gloved finger jabbed the parchment. "Is that hidden?"

Yanking her eyes back to the book, she shook her head. "No. It joins with the courtyard by an arch beneath the wall. Clearly visible from the practice field."

This was taking too long. Every second that passed was another Dreythan could be dead. Or worse. She glanced desperately at the royal tower. Where could he possibly be?

Heart flopping in her stomach, she pointed. "It's there."

On Kell's map, below the royal tower and to the west, was outlined a semi-circular structure. A footpath wound around the island from the castle gates and connected to it, as did the series of tunnels that spidered underneath Iventorr.

"You're sure," the stranger said. It wasn't a question.

She nodded. "I've never seen that terrace. It must be built into the side of the island, below the outer wall."

Already heading for the door, he called over his shoulder, "To the royal tower, then. Let's keep low. There may still be Unbreathing keeping watch."

Chapter 25

Morthan — no, Vvalk — turned away, shoulders hunched. "Indeed," he replied, his tone dangerously casual. "I had planned for Kell Wyndshaper to meet his end that night, but not in that manner. The Ilumence Loyalist, Parfeln, wisely improvised. He slew our assassin before the other guards reached him, ensuring his silence."

"I see." The Unbreathing's grip on Dreythan's upper arms was merciless. His fingers had lost all sensation. "What of the incident in the Pass? Did you kill Morthas to achieve another opportunity to end me?"

"Nay. The old man met his death naturally. I would have hastened it, but that would have thrown scrutiny upon me," he explained, chuckling darkly. "After all, I had to remain Morthan to Ilumence's eyes. When your uncle did finally draw his last breath, it was time to spring our second ploy."

He needed more time. Fletch needed more time. Damn it all, he should have told her his plan, should have ordered her to leave him, not tricked her into separating. "It must have infuriated you when you discovered a Wyndshaper had thwarted you once again," Dreythan taunted. "Is that why you sent your minions after her on the road from Herstshire?"

Vvalk's hands clenched into fists.

Sensing the sudden turn in his mood, Dreythan said, "You had originally planned to take over the rule of Ivenhence as Morthan, once my father and I were dead. Was it Parfeln who removed the Unbreathing books from the library? Did he also destroy the evidence from the assassination?"

"Not quite," came the low answer. "I see that you are putting the pieces together. I did not wish for any to suspect my true nature, but knew that some would. Destroying records of the Slaving would delay the eventual revelation." He smirked. "No, Dreythan Dreythas-son. You have more than one traitor within Iventorr's walls."

More than one traitor. Dreythan lowered his head as it spun, his core wrenching from the vicious kick of those words. "Another Loyalist," he said, mostly to himself. "I assume."

Vvalk turned back, once again smiling. "You have a brilliant mind. 'Tis a pity Kell Wyndshaper slew my compatriot, Sliv. He would have been quite at home in your Shell."

Leveling his gaze at that sly, slitted smile, Dreythan knew Vvalk was trying to unsettle him. But his chest still tightened nonetheless. "The elders who survived the Great Slaving. Were their deaths also part of your plan?"

Vvalk hesitated, brows drawing sharply together. "Perhaps you are too brilliant for your own good, Corwynter," he said finally. "Yet, you could not have noticed this on your own. You were a mere child. Tell me, who brought this to your attention?"

"A Wyndarin traveler."

"Gah," Vvalk spat. "The Wynd-blood. One day they shall be wiped from the face of this Hearth and rejoin their beloved Luminia in spirit. Then the world shall be without Wynd, and Kazael shall roam free." Golden eyes glinting, he bared his teeth as they stretched, elongating into jagged fangs. "Enough talk," he snarled. "It is time you surrendered your soul to my Master."

It didn't take Fletch and her odd companion long to reach the wall near the royal tower. To Fletch, every second took ages. Thousands of questions whirled through her mind, throbbing to the beating rhythm of pain behind her eyes. There wasn't time to ponder any single one. Even if there were, the adrenaline and nerves spiking within her wouldn't have allowed her to focus.

Together they crept silently into the garden, their feet whispering through grass, moss, and fallen leaves. Fletch motioned the stranger back, then peered out from behind a hedge.

Two guards in blue-enameled plate mail waited outside the entrance to the royal tower. They twitched uneasily, jerking at every small sound or puff of Wynd.

"They're under bloodlust," the stranger muttered. "If we get any closer, they'll smell us and alert V— Morthan."

"Easily remedied," Fletch whispered back. She pulled a gentle breeze toward them that rustled through the leaves of the bushes. "We're now downwind."

"Well done." He flicked his wrists, two identical silver knives springing into his hands from hidden sheaths on his thighs. They were only as long as his hand, strangely narrow and small. Rearing back his left arm, he threw twice in the blink of an eye. The Unbreathing crumpled to their faces. "Almost there. Let's go."

She followed him to the wall that overlooked the Basin, curiosity burning like a torch within her. Who was this man? How did he know so much about Morthan's plans?

Reaching the wall, the stranger knelt. Clasping his hands palms-up, he jerked his head at the wall. "Too high to scale," he whispered. "I'll help you up."

The smooth wall was taller than Fletch by at least four feet. She had no choice but to obey. Placing her foot in the stranger's hands, she stood. The stranger grunted, heaving himself upright and throwing his hands over his head, vaulting Fletch into the air. Slinging her head and shoulders over the edge of the wall, she elbowed her way to the top.

Atop the wall, a four-foot-wide flat walkway was separated from the steep cliff overlooking the Basin by shoulder-high blocks of stone. Crawling to a gap between the blocks, Fletch poked her head between them and peered down.

There, thirty feet below her, was a small terrace, jutting precariously from the side of the island. Four men stood upon it. Three of them didn't draw breath.

"We found them," Fletch breathed, relief draining through her. "They haven't Turned him yet."

There was no reply.

Scrabbling back to the edge of the wall, she leaned down, ready to extend a hand and help the stranger up.

He was nowhere to be seen.

There was no time to look for him. No time to panic. Whirling back to the gap, she was just in time to see Morthan spin and stride swiftly toward Dreythan.

For a brief moment, time seemed to slow. The instinct to draw and fire an arrow flashed through her. But the angle was impossible. She risked hitting the king rather than Morthan. Without time to think or plan Fletch drew her silver knife and threw herself over the wall.

The Wynd gushed around her as she plunged downward. Grasping it with her free hand, she tugged, spinning toward Morthan.

As Vvalk whirled and strode purposefully, deliberately toward him, something in Dreythan wanted to close his eyes and shrink away.

Instead, he gulped down his quivering gut and steeled himself. If this was to be his end, he would meet it with as much courage as he could muster. Not cowering away from the horror and fear.

He wondered if Norland would be proud. Or his father.

A dark shape suddenly hurtled from above. There was a thud and a crash, and Vvalk was sprawled on his back, another figure stumbling to their feet beside him.

In one frozen instant, he realized it was Fletch. White as a sheet, blood streaking down her face and caked on her boots, fist clenched white-knuckled around the hilt of a dagger, she was the most beautiful sight he had ever laid eyes on.

There was a blur of movement. Vvalk gripped her by the throat, lifting her off her feet as she thrashed. He leaned in, eyes glinting cruelly.

"A valiant try, Wyndshaper," he purred in her ear. "But I smelled you coming."

"NO!" The scream tore from Dreythan's mouth. Pain seared his arms as he struggled wildly in the Unbreathing's grasp. "NO! FLETCH!!"

Fletch's hand flashed through the air, slashing once, twice, thrice. The dagger streaked through Vvalk's forearm. He hissed, arms flailing. Fletch went flying, her body meeting the stone wall with a crunch. Bouncing limply to the ground, she lay face down, still and silent.

"FLETCH!!!"

"Save your cries." Striding casually to where Fletch's bow had fallen, Vvalk picked it up and snapped it with a single flex. "Your precious Wyndshaper cannot hear you. Sadly, you shall not be joining her or your captain in the abyss."

Seizing Dreythan by the hair, Vvalk yanked his head to one side.

There was a moment of blinding, jarring pain. Then everything went dark, empty, and cold.

The first sensation to return to her was agony. It coursed through her shoulder and ribs like a raging fire, singeing her very bones within her flesh. With each pulse, she heard her own heartbeat gushing in her ears, blocking out all other sound.

Fletch's eyes lolled open. She was sprawled face-down on the stone, her arm pinned beneath at an awkward angle.

She was alive, she marveled, blinking. Her eyes felt like splintery wooden spheres in her head, dry and prickly. Something bright glinted on the stone beside her nose, swimming gradually into focus.

A silver-tipped arrow.

In one fractured moment, her senses came flooding back. Gulping in a deep, bracing breath, Fletch's good arm flashed out. Fingers closing around the arrow shaft, she heaved herself upright. Brilliant dots burst in her vision, her breath hitching as the pain abruptly crescendoed.

Before her, two Unbreathing held Dreythan upright. The monsters' eyes were fixed intently, ravenously, on the king's deathly pale face. His head was pulled to one side by a fist clenched in his hair. Morthan's back was to Fletch as his face pressed into Dreythan's neck.

There was a sickening slurp.

Left arm dangling uselessly, Fletch lurched forward. At the sound of her shuffling footfall, the two Unbreathing stirred, their eyes finally darting towards her.

"Vvalk," one of them grunted.

This was her final chance. Funneling every last ounce of strength in her battered body, pulling desperation from her pain, she thrust the arrow out and up, straight through Morthan's back.

He reared, swinging a clawed hand wildly. His lips and elongated teeth were smeared bright red, eyes glittering with cruelty and malice. She shoved the arrow deeper. Morthan's frame went rigid, stiffening as if turned to stone as his flesh turned to sand and fell from his bones, sifting between the folds of his clothes.

His frame collapsed in a pile of white bone, sand, and cloth, his skull falling neatly atop.

Dreythan slumped to the ground as the remaining two Unbreathing released his arms. They turned deliberately, disbelieving gazes rising from Morthan's remains.

Fletch stumbled back. With her right hand, she swung upward, trying to summon the Wynd in another forceful burst. But her arm was like jelly, weak and trembling, and the result was a puny gust, little more than a breeze.

"You bitch," one of them spat, fingertips growing into deadly points as he advanced toward her. "We were so close. Why can you not die?!"

"Oh, she'll die." The other one darted forward, yellow eyes glittering. "After we ruin her."

The terrace swam around her as the Unbreathing's hand rose, claws curving to rend her flesh.

A silver blade impaled it from behind, cleaving through the spine and throat to stick out of its neck.

It crumbled away as its companion whirled, striking blindly. Its claw pinged off a parrying sword. The blade swiveled up and around, cleaving into the monster's neck.

It dropped without a sound.

A moment of tense silence passed before Matteo Alwick and Harrild Hammerfist stepped forward from the shadow of the cliff.

At the sight of their faces, relief such as she'd never known flooded through Fletch. She wobbled, her strength gone with her desperation.

Matteo rushed to her, slipping her good arm over his shoulders. "Fletch," he gasped. "Are you alright?"

"No," she admitted. "Dreythan?"

"He still breathes, though just barely," Harrild said, his hand already over the king's throat. "He needs a healer."

Hugging her limp arm to her side, Fletch tried to cross to him, but her toe snagged on the rough stone and she stumbled. Matteo caught her, helping her up to cross the terrace.

"Dreythan," she whispered. All other thought and feeling was a distant echo. Pulling his head and shoulders onto her lap, she held him as close as she could, tears streaming down her cheeks. He was alive. How much of Dreythan's blood had Morthan drained? Her fingers brushed his pale forehead, glad to find it still warm.

Harrild and Matteo exchanged a significant glance. "I'll fetch the physician," Matteo said. "Will you guard them?"

"You haven't any idea where those passages lead. Where has that stranger gone? You shall only get lost in there without him to guide you."

"There should be a footpath," Fletch said hoarsely, not lifting her eyes from Dreythan's face. "On the side of the island. It should lead to just below the gates."

Matteo trotted to a narrow gap in the corner wall of the terrace. "There is, albeit a dangerous one," he told her. "I shall return quickly." With that, he was gone.

Fletch watched Dreythan's chest rise and fall in shallow, ragged breaths. With careful shifts of her wrist, she shaped warm Wynd into his nostrils with each inhale. It seemed to help, just as it had Klep. After a few moments, some color returned to his skin.

Hesitantly, she peered at his neck. An oval series of red punctures ringed with stark white flesh was surrounded with a quickly flowering purple bruise. The sight churned her empty, prickling stomach.

"I wish you had been here for Morthan's arrival, Fletch," Harrild said quietly. "Every single one of Morthan's soldiers was Unbreathing. And we wouldn't have known until it was too late, were it not for that stranger."

His words registered distantly in Fletch's ears. "A stranger, you say. There must have been two of them," she murmured. "A man I'd never seen before helped me out of the tunnels, helped me find Dreythan."

The Sentinel shifted. "They must have been working together. Ours wore strange leather armor, studded with metal. A cowl and mask covered his face, and he carried a light that he could hold in his hand."

Fletch frowned. "That sounds exactly like my stranger, but the man who assisted me had hazel eyes. And he had hidden throwing knives in his armor, each exactly alike."

"So did ours," Harrild said after a slight pause. "And he spoke oddly, and would tell us nothing of himself."

"Where did he find you?"

"In the Sentinel tower. The king had dismissed us when he had returned to his quarters from the throne hall, saying he didn't wish Morthan to feel uneasy." Harrild shook his head. "Matteo didn't like it, but we obeyed. We were playing Ivere's Favor when a dagger flew through the window with a message attached, saying there were Unbreathing in the barracks. So we naturally went there, and the odd man appeared out of nowhere, startling the wits out of us. He told us both your lives were in mortal danger.

"We didn't take him at his word," he admitted. "So he cut his thumb with one of his daggers, and every one of Morthan's men turned and stared at the same time. One of them rushed forward, teeth bared, and the stranger threw a dagger between his eyes. The supposed Ilumencian guard crumbled into dust. The others attacked, and... Well, you saw part of the battle. The stranger was... a blur. Most of the Unbreathing fell by his hand.

"We spread the word through the rest of our ranks to track down and kill the other Unbreathing and followed the stranger underground. He led us here just in time."

It didn't make any sense. Their descriptions matched perfectly, but... "He couldn't have been the same man," Fletch said, her mind trying and failing to focus on the puzzle. "The stranger who helped me led me above as the other was leading you below."

"It was strange," Harrild muttered to himself. "Strange that he knew so much, but made such mistakes. He called me 'Captain', once."

They were silent for a few minutes until Dreythan stirred slightly, his face close to its usual color. The cold, tight coil of anxiety slowly relaxed in Fletch's chest as she held him, wishing she could run her other hand through his raven hair.

"Fletch." Harrild knelt beside her. "We need to find the Captain. He wasn't in his home, or in the barracks or the Sentinel tower. Was he... was he present when Morthan—?"

She looked up into his hazel eyes. Numbness was settling in. The pain was drifting away, or perhaps she was drowning in it. "Parfeln betrayed us. Captain Norland was dying as he barred the door to the royal tower," she replied quietly. "He gave me enough time to get Dreythan into the tunnels."

His brown brows drew sharply together, and he looked away. "I... wish I could say I was surprised," he murmured. "Parfeln Holden was a sour, bitter man. Ah, Norland. I'll send word for guards to locate him in the royal tower as soon as we've returned to Iventorr proper."

At the sound of approaching footsteps, he leaped to his feet, drawing his blade. Appearing from the footpath was Matteo Alwick, followed closely by Sytres Trithinnis. The physician knelt beside the king, inspecting the oval of punctures.

"We must get him to the infirmary," he said, and glanced up at Fletch. His eyes traveled over her limp arm and misshapen shoulder, to her bruised, mottled neck, and finally to her cheek. "You need attention far more urgently." He raised one of her eyelids with a thumb. "You have taken quite a beating today, young woman. Come, let us find you some rest."

Chapter 26

Fletch woke slowly, a soft sound she couldn't quite identify stirring her to consciousness.

Her right eye wouldn't open. Pain radiated up her shoulder and down her spine, drumming steadily in her head. Swallowing a groan, she gingerly, deliberately pushed herself halfway upright.

The low stone walls and neatly dressed cots of the infirmary surrounded her, soft moonlight falling through the windows. Some of the beds held guards, bandages swathing their red-seeping wounds. Survivors from the Unbreathing attack, she mused foggily.

The thought sparked her mind into alertness. She jolted straight, glancing wildly around.

In the cot directly beside hers, in the corner of the room, lay Dreythan. His chest rose and fell rhythmically, each exhale releasing a steady stream of persimmon-colored Wynd. White bandages were wrapped around the base of his neck. Though his cheeks weren't devoid of color, his black lashes were stark against his skin.

Fletch's chest tightened. Slipping from her cot, her bare feet whispering across the stone floor, she crossed to his bedside, slipping her fingers into his palm. The warmth of his hand swept up her arm, wrapping around her heart.

There it was again, the sound that had woken her. She turned, her eye falling on a white curtain which partitioned off the opposite end of the room.

Behind it, someone was sobbing.

Everything inside her slowly sinking, Fletch left Dreythan sleeping. The cold of the smooth floor drained into her stomach as she made her way across the room.

When she lifted the curtain aside, she found Petrecia Wyntersoul weeping over a long, narrow table. A shape draped in white cloth rested atop. Her fingers clutched the hem of the shroud as if she had set it back in place but hadn't the strength to let go.

She raised red-rimmed brown eyes to meet Fletch's. The brokenness there was shattering to see.

"Would you like me to leave?" Fletch whispered.

Petrecia's only response was to shake her head, trembling.

Not knowing what else to do, she swallowed the lump of fire in her throat, crossed the cold stone floor, and put her good arm around Petrecia as the golden-haired woman pressed her face into Fletch's shoulder.

They stayed that way for what felt like hours, Petrecia's body wracking with silent, anguished sobs, Fletch holding her as tightly as she could, staring over her friend's shoulder at the shrouded body of Captain Norland Wyntersoul.

Thoughts and questions cascaded over her. The tangle of emotions woven through them were as abrasive as burlap over an open wound.

It was only by Ivere's luck that Dreythan had not joined Norland on the embalming table. Or, worse, Turned, his body used as a puppet for a Devul. Fletch's arm clenched around Petrecia as tears rose to her own eyes. Thank the gods that hadn't happened to Norland. She couldn't bear the thought of having to slay a monster that wore her friend and mentor's face.

Dreythan had taken a horrible risk, leaving her behind in the passages. Backtracking the way they had come. She wanted to believe it had simply been a mistake, but it wasn't possible. For Dreythan to get as far away from her as he had in the short minute she'd been gone, he would have had to sprint down the chamber only moments after she'd left. It had been intentional.

Her hand started to clench into a fist, but stopped at the stiff crackle of her scab-coated palm. Had he not trusted her to keep him safe? To find a way out of the tunnels? But that didn't make sense. If he didn't believe in her, he wouldn't have abandoned her and dashed toward danger. What could have possibly possessed him to run headlong toward the very creatures who sought him?

Gradually, Petrecia's weeping slowed. Her chest heaved in long, slow, shuddering gasps, and she pulled away, pressing her hands to her swollen face. "I don't know what I am going to do," she said. Her voice was as hollow as her eyes, broken and empty. "How am I going to raise our sons without him? How can I show them what it means to be a good man, a good father?"

A good man. A good father. Remembering her own father's journal, Fletch smiled, tears pricking her eyes as she took Petrecia's hand. "Norland has already shown them," she told her hoarsely. "Just as my father did for me. All you must do is keep his memory alive." Swallowing the ember that burned in her throat, she added, "Before Norland... passed, I told him how much his family loved him. How much you loved him. And I swore to him I would look after you."

Petrecia's eyes filled again, tears spilling silently down her cheeks, gazing at Fletch as she stumbled on, "I'm here for you. You needn't even ask. Anything I can do, simply say it, and it'll be done. I promise."

Dropping her gaze to the floor, Petrecia reached for Fletch's hand, squeezing tight. "Thank you," she choked. "I was afraid... well, I thought perhaps Norland had died alone, without any hope. But... I am glad you were there, Fletch." Wiping her eyes, she managed a fragmented smile. Her glance traveled over Fletch's broken arm, bound to her in a sling, her eye, and her neck. "But look at the state of you. Come, let us get you back to bed."

Fletch tried to protest, but the little woman wouldn't hear it. She walked her back to her cot and helped her lie back, fluffing her pillow and pulling her coverlet up to her shoulders.

"I overheard Harrild Hammerfist speaking to a man named Naraan this afternoon," she said as she gave Fletch's blanket a gentle tuck. "Naraan was asking after you. When Harrild told him everything that happened, the man went deathly pale and left without saying a word. The guards say they saw him leave not a quarter bell later, riding a bizarre single-wheeled contraption with a sail fixed atop. The guards said they'd never seen a man move so quickly, not even on horseback."

"Where was he headed?" Fletch asked, hope stirring in her chest.

"Harrild believes he travels to Port Liarin to intercept the Wyndarin." Her cool fingers brushed Fletch's hair from her forehead. "So rest easy, Fletch. Your mother and her people are being warned."

Through the darkness came a voice, muffled and distant, as if the sound couldn't quite penetrate a heavy curtain or a wall. It was warm and soft, its sound forcing the heavy darkness back. The scents of freshly baked bread, hot stew, and medicinal herbs mingled in the comfortably cozy air. As Fletch's eye fluttered open, she realized the voice was Dreythan's.

"I feel all right," he was saying, as if in response to a question. "Weak, dizzy. But otherwise well. How long have I been asleep? How is Fletch? Where is—what happened to Vvalk? That is, Morthan?"

"You've been asleep a little over a day now," Harrild Hammerfist's voice replied quietly. "As has Fletch."

She prickled guiltily. Was it more proper to sit up or to pretend to be asleep?

"As for Morthan," Harrild continued, "well..."

"I surrendered myself to the Unbreathing without Fletch's knowledge," Dreythan interjected. "I did not come into their hands from any fault of hers. I had hoped to buy her enough time to warn the Sentinels, the guard. But Vvalk — that is, Morthan — was eager to get on with his purpose. He did not give me as much time as I had hoped."

Vvalk. Easing herself upright, Fletch pushed her hair away from her face. "You've said that twice now, my lord," she said sleepily. In the daylight, she realized her cot was much closer to Dreythan's than she'd thought. Close enough to intertwine her fingers with his. "When you say 'Vvalk', you correct yourself with 'Morthan'."

He turned toward her, his eyes meeting hers like a crashing wave on the shore. Warmth washed over her as a smile curled his lips, softening his angular face.

"Indeed," he agreed.

"But Vvalk was Kazael's general, one of the Unbreathing who presided over the Great Slaving. The monster the freed slaves stabbed one by one with silvered weapons."

"And he was also the Devul who possessed Morthan's Husk." He glanced down, swallowing. "Vvalk claimed Morthan's soul and body many years ago, even before our fathers were slain." He glanced over Fletch to Harrild. "But I do not understand how Captain Wyndshaper would not have..." The words died on his lips.

Turning, Fletch glanced where his eyes had fallen, to where the far end of the room was closed off by white curtain.

"Norland is being prepared for burial," Harrild said quietly. "We found him in the royal tower, my lord. His sword was wedged between the door and its frame, the door itself splintered inward. I don't know why or how, but his body was unspoiled." He ducked his head, swallowing hard. "We believe he must have bled out before the Unbreathing broke through the door."

"The monsters don't hunger for cold blood," Fletch whispered.

"A small mercy."

A long, hollow silence filled the room, heavy in its emptiness.

Dreythan's face tightened, his black eyes strained as they stared unseeing at the curtained corner.

Fletch could only guess what was passing through his mind. His cousin? A monster, the shadowy entity behind the attempts on his life. The most experienced and senior Sentinel? A traitor, only serving Ivenhence with the intent to make her fall. His oldest friend and most trusted ally?

Gone.

Steeling herself, Fletch pushed herself upright, wincing as pain seared through her ribs and shoulder. It was oddly comforting, the pain. Simple, straightforward. Uncomplicated. Unlike the confusion and shock that echoed in her, mirrored on Dreythan's face.

Dreythan blinked, glancing down at his empty hand, then at Fletch's, then up into her eyes. He turned his hand upright, his wordless question plain.

"It doesn't feel real," she said, slipping her hand into his.

His head bowed as he folded his fingers warmly around hers.

"I can't bear to speak of it longer," Harrild told them quietly, his eyes carefully fixed on the floor between his feet. "Forgive me, my lord. The Unbreathing were defeated, at great cost to our guard. Since then, everyone has been on edge. The remaining guard has cleaned up the Unbreathing remains for Sytres to study. But it somehow feels as though our work is incomplete. The other Sentinels and I have organized heightened guard shifts across the castle, and a group has been assigned to Verenshire as well to ensure the safety of our citizens."

"That is enough talk for now." Sytres Trithinnis appeared from around the corner, carrying a pitcher and two cups. "My patients still need rest, Sentinel Hammerfist, as well as food and drink."

Harrild had already nodded and risen when Dreythan stopped him.

"Wait. Has... has Petrecia been informed?"

Fletch looked down, her throat tightening.

"She shall bring her sons tomorrow to pay their respects," Sytres told them, his normally sharp face softening somberly. "Once you have taken your fill of eat and drink, you may do so as well, but not before."

"He died protecting Iventorr." Dreythan's voice was low, whether with the weight of emotion or the lack of it, it was difficult to tell. "He died protecting me. Should his family wish it, he shall be buried in the royal garden."

Harrild bowed deeply, hand clenching over his heart. "As you wish, my lord."

"If Petrecia and her sons need anything — anything at all — be sure that need is met."

"Of course, my lord," the Sentinel replied, bowing again.

"Thank you, Harrild. You may go." Dreythan turned to the physician, eyeing the glass that was held out to him. "Is this another tincture?"

"No, merely water, my lord. Matron Gulden shall scold me something fierce if she discovers I allowed the two of you to be awake this long without taking your meal." The thin man lifted a laden tray from a nearby table, setting it between the two beds like a bridge.

Something in the physician had changed, Fletch observed as she plucked a slice of bread from the tray. His shoulders were more relaxed, his nose not so high in the air. Rather than tilting his head back to look down at others, he met their eyes directly.

"You have my word we shall eat and drink our fill," Dreythan told him. "I should like a moment to speak with Sentinel Wyndshaper. Alone."

"Of course, my lord."

As he turned to walk away, Fletch frowned. He truly had changed. "Thank you, Master Trithinnis," she said.

Though he didn't look back, she knew he had smiled.

When the door closed behind him, Dreythan turned to her, sliding his feet over the edge into the small gap between their beds.

It didn't take them long to polish off the stew and bread. Glancing at the last slice left, she hesitated.

"We could split it, if you would like," Dreythan offered, the smallest twinkle appearing in his black eyes.

She allowed herself a smile, folding the piece in half and offering him one side to tug on.

"The wound on your cheek," Dreythan said. "Was it from Parfeln?"

Her fingers rose automatically to brush the grooved scab. "Yes." Full stomach giving an uncomfortable jolt, she forced her smile to widen, feeling the skin tighten and pull around her wound. "'Twill heal in time, I am certain."

"You should not worry over it," he told her quietly, his gaze tracing the gash. "Even if it does not heal, your loveliness shall only be punctuated. It gives your appearance a fierceness that matches your spirit." Lifting the tray, he shifted it to his bed, then paused in the middle of rising. "May I... may I sit beside you?" he asked. "I should like to hold you."

Not trusting herself to speak, she nodded, heart thudding in her throat. Dreythan settled onto the bed beside her, carefully looping one arm behind her back and taking her hand with his other. Hoping he couldn't hear the pounding that gushed in her ears, Fletch let herself relax against his warmth, pressing her cheek to his collarbone as she inhaled the scent of sage soap drifting off his white tunic. His chest rose and fell in a silent sigh, his hand finding her waist to shift her slightly closer.

"I am sorry, Fletch," Dreythan said. His deep voice reverberated through her chest. "For not giving you a choice."

She shifted to look up at him, though his jaw and the line of his throat consumed her field of vision. It was a strangely intoxicating sight. "Do you mean in the tunnels?"

"Yes." A muscle in his jaw twitched. "I knew you could not willingly leave me without breaking your oath, and you would likely refuse to do so even were I to ask." He sighed again, head bowing. "Did it anger you when you realized I was gone?"

Remembering the surge of panic that had crashed over her, Fletch hesitated. "I wasn't angry. I was too terrified for your wellbeing to care that you'd tricked me into leaving you."

His hand squeezed hers, head bowing further. "Just as I was worried for yours. When you seemingly dove out of the sky and Vvalk had you by the throat…. When he threw you against the wall…"

The bright tightness in her chest blossomed, spreading molten fire through her core.

Dreythan pulled slightly away. Raising her head from his shoulder, her eyes met his. He stared at her, the same intensity burning in his gaze. "I care for you," he told her, his face so close she could feel the Wynd of his breath on her skin. "Your life is as precious to me as my own." Color flooded his high cheekbones, though his eyes never left hers as he said, "Should you wish to take it, I offer you my hand in courtship."

"Should I wish to take it," Fletch repeated dizzily. Dreythan's lips were very close. Lifting her hand, she brushed her fingers along his jawline, watching embers roar to life in his eyes. "My lord, I can't think that I have ever desired anything more."

His hand slipped more snugly into the curve above her hip as they leaned into each other, lips closing together in their own embrace. Fletch's hand found the back of Dreythan's neck as he tenderly caressed her mouth with his. Exquisite bursts of heat pulsed through her entire being at his touch. He hesitated, pulling back to cast a quick glance over her face as if to ask permission, but she tugged him back in, brushing the angle of his throat with a kiss.

Something in his face shifted. Brushing her hair back from her forehead, he cupped the back of her head, pressing his lips to her cheek, her forehead, the tip of her nose, and finally, her mouth. She returned the kiss, though this one was different from the first. Longer, slower. Deeper, gentler. It was an entire conversation without a single word, one of long-burning passion, of familiarity, of something stronger and wilder than attraction or affection. The bloom in Fletch's chest was now a tree, rooted bottomlessly in her soul, its leaves fluttering like flame at Dreythan's every breath, every look, every touch.

When they finally, reluctantly, broke apart, Dreythan's hand drifted back to Fletch's. She looped her fingers with his, feeling her cheeks ache with the width of her smile.

"May I call you by your given name, my lord?" she asked, and Dreythan answered with a delighted chuckle.

A breeze strayed through the open window above them, its daffodil-yellow stream ruffling Dreythan's black hair and stirring the white curtain in the corner of the room.

As the smile faded abruptly from Fletch's face, Dreythan turned to glance where she looked, and his expression instantly fell. For several minutes, they sat together, staring at the corner.

Finally, Dreythan rose. Circling to the other side of Fletch's bed, he offered his hand.

"Together?" he asked soberly.

She nodded. "Together."

A chill Wynd drifted between the silent citizens gathered in Iventorr Castle's courtyard. It pushed and carried fallen autumn leaves which rustled across the ground or spun through the air under an overcast sky. A thick covering of dreary milky grey clouds hovered low to the Hearth, obscuring the uppermost points of Iventorr's towers.

Suppressing a shiver, Fletch wrapped her arm around herself, glancing behind as more and more people filtered in from streets and buildings to fill the square. They had all dressed in muted colors, from black to grey, to slate blue and walnut brown. Seeing their heavy eyes and desolate faces, she dropped her gaze, fingers clenching in the charcoal folds of her own simple dress.

An empty raised platform waited in front of the gathering congregation. Four figures stood below it facing the courtyard, their hands folded, heads bowed. The remaining Sentinels of

Iventorr. Each had donned a ceremonial set of silver-inlaid armor, though the weapons they carried were their own. Their silver-embroidered sashes were missing from their forearms. Instead, they were fastened like a badge to their chests.

Between them, a body wrapped in emerald green silk rested in a finely carved mahogany casket, surrounded by lilies and goldenrod branches. Standing just to the side was a black-veiled figure, a child tucked to her hip, another clutching her hand.

Fletch's heart clenched at the sight.

In the two days since Dreythan had woken, it had come to dawn on her. The realization of Norland Wyntersoul's absence, and the reality of his death. It happened slowly, the numbness gradually receding to leave an empty place that ached in its wake. The whole of Iventorr felt empty without Captain Norland's enormous presence. Without his booming voice echoing off the stone walls, or the sound of his stomping feet making their way through the cobbled streets. The stillness that filled the place he'd occupied was cold and sharp, and jabbed when least expected.

It didn't feel at all like the grief and confusion that had followed Klep's death. Yet somehow, it was the same.

Skirting around the edge of the crowd, Fletch reached Petrecia as the woman turned toward her. Under the lace, her eyes swam with unshed tears, her cheeks pale. On her hip, young Solund stared, his bright blue eyes puzzled. Jormund, his elder brother, watched Fletch solemnly.

Wordlessly, she offered him her hand. He glanced up at his mother who nodded, then reached up and clasped her finger with his as Iventorr's bells rang the second afternoon hour.

As the final peal slowly faded, the doors to the dining hall parted and King Dreythan strode out. Black silk robes flowed around him as he climbed the raised platform's steps, silver trimmed hems shimmering. The ten emerald-set spires of the royal crown of Ivenhence were settled over his furrowed brow. He looked over the gathered citizens, his features somber.

"We have gathered here today," he said quietly, "to celebrate the life and to mourn the loss of a man whom many knew and loved. Norland, Captain of Iventorr's guard, the Forester's former head. Husband, father, son." Hesitating for the briefest moment, his eyes flitted over the crowd, then locked with Fletch's. Taking a deep breath, he finished firmly, "Friend."

She listened as his deep voice rolled over the crowd, every word distinct.

"Few of us knew his surname, but those of us who did were graced with a deeper understanding of who Norland was, of his honorable and courageous nature. He was born a Wyntersoul of the Wynterhead Clan — indeed, the son of its patriarch. Though the Great Slaving had ended more than a decade before his birth, many amongst his people bore resentment against Ivenhence and the Corwynter name for claiming the lands they'd once occupied. His father was not least among them.

"When a particularly harsh winter left the Wynterhead Clan weak and starving, tensions on the mountain came to a head. On the patriarch's command, the people began to arm themselves for an attack on Ivenhence.

"Though he had not yet come of age, Norland openly defied his father, telling any who would listen that attacking a people who had done them no harm would accomplish nothing. Desperate to prevent bloodshed and the loss of innocent lives, he challenged his father to one-on-one combat for the right to hold the title of patriarch."

Dreythan paused, crowned head dipping. "He only told me the story once," he said, his voice as heavy as his expression. "But it has always stayed with me. His father won the fight and, as is their custom, the Wynterhead Clan banished him from their mountain, never to return.

"But still Norland did not admit defeat. He traveled on foot for days, barely stopping to eat or rest, until he stumbled into Iventorr's throne hall. He warned my father, King Dreythas the Reclaimer, of the impending attack, begging him to send food and supplies to the foot of the mountain as a show of good faith. He was certain no lives needed to be lost, that no blood needed to be shed. That the people of his home were merely desperate enough and hungry enough to turn to violence for answers.

"The king had no choice but to listen to his heartfelt plea. When the Wynterhead Clan descended for their attack, they found a score of unarmed guards and ten wagons filled with goods at the foot of the mountain with my father at their head."

Raising his eyes to once again pierce the crowd, Dreythan's expression cleared. "Norland prevented a war between his people and Ivenhence. He was only sixteen years of age."

He went on to speak of Norland's seven-year term as a Forester, then of his five-year term as their Head, but Fletch found it difficult to focus on his words. She stood in the square beside Norland Wyntersoul's casket, his son gripping her hand as everything slowly shifted. The world came into sharp focus yet drifted hazily by. She tried to bring her mind back to Dreythan's voice, to the stories he was telling of the man who'd been his closest friend and most trusted advisor, but all she managed was a vague sense of half-understanding, of partial presentness.

Her father's funeral had taken place in this exact spot. The platform had looked so large in her childish eyes, the young king so alone and far away standing atop it as he tried his hardest to give an appropriate eulogy to the man who'd been his father's dearest friend. She remembered feeling confused, afraid, and overwhelmingly isolated.

The small hand in hers tightened. Glancing down, she found Jormund staring at his father's silk-wrapped body, wiping his face with his sleeve.

He was experiencing the same loss she had at the same age she had. Peering quickly up at his mother and brother as if to make sure they hadn't seen him crying, he squared his little shoulders.

Her chest tightened, fingers gently squeezing his. It wasn't fair that so young a child should have to bear such a weight. It wasn't fair that his father was gone.

Dreythan's tone had changed. She straightened, swallowing.

"Norland's life ended too soon," he was saying, his eyes fixed on the silk-wrapped figure below him. "Your life ended too soon, my friend. And as such, you left much behind which you still wished to accomplish. There is not a doubt in my mind that you wished to reconcile with your people, the Wynterhead Clan, and that you wished to repair the relationship between them and Ivenhence. I make this oath to you and to your memory, Norland Wyntersoul. I shall not rest until the Wynterhead Clan and Iventorr can call each other brothers. I shall make every effort to mend past hurts between us, to provide the means for your people to reach a new understanding of peace and prosperity." Raising one fist to clench over his heart, he bowed his head. "This I swear."

Head still bowed, the king descended the steps to stand opposite Fletch beside Norland's casket. Even though he didn't meet her eyes, a wordless feeling, a connection, spanned between them. A bridge of togetherness amid the pain and sorrow, of warmth and love in the chill emptiness of grief.

The four Sentinels turned as one. Gripping the carved handles on either side of the casket, they lifted it off its cradle and stepped forward, the crowd silently parting before them.

Fletch fell into step beside Dreythan and Petrecia, Jormund still solemnly holding her hand. Others fell in behind as they strode through the quiet, empty streets, tugging cloaks and scarves close against the cold breeze as they wound their way towards the royal garden. As the casket-bearing Sentinels passed beneath the garden gates, the crowd behind drew to a halt. The people gathered as closely to the gate as they could without crossing the threshold, watching as Dreythan, Fletch, and Norland's family traversed the leaf-strewn garden.

Beneath the ancient oak tree waited a freshly-turned heap of rich brown dirt and a long, narrow, deep hole. The lid of the mahogany casket was leaned carefully against the oak's trunk, as if acting as a wooden headstone.

The Sentinels paused just in front of the hole, and Fletch's heart twisted sharply. Matteo Alwick and Darvick Hammerfist left the casket in the hands of Aeda Yewmaster and Harrild Hammerfist and approached the lid, each taking one side. Slowly, respectfully, they guided it up and over Norland's body. When it was settled into place, they met each others' eyes with a nod.

It was time.

Distantly, Fletch felt the small hand slip from hers as Jormund stood beside his mother. She released a deep, shaky breath she hadn't realized she'd been holding, the hollow in her chest yawning wide.

Taking the coiled ropes that lay waiting beside the open hole, the Sentinels looped the hooked ends through the casket's handles, kneeling in unison to either side of the hole.

Dreythan stood beside Fletch, his warm hand finding hers as the Sentinels gently lowered Norland Wyntersoul to rest in his grave.

To King Dreythan Dreythas-son, rightful ruler of Ivenhence and its lands,

It is with deepest regret we find ourselves with no choice but to inform you that your cousin, King Morthan Morthas-son, is not what he seems. Though few here in Ilumence remember the tales of old or the truths behind those tales, those of us who do are alarmed and appalled by Morthan's recent actions and wish to warn you against him.

Since the death of his father, Morthan has shown little to no interest in shouldering the responsibility of ruler. He has left the governing of the kingdom to us, his three advisors. He does not sleep and does not eat. Perhaps most alarmingly, he spends much of his time consorting with an unsavory woman named Nilith, sending missives to unknown peoples and locations.

Two moons ago, an armed force attacked a Thissian border outpost. According to eyewitness accounts, the attackers were wearing Ilumencian royal armor. Gorvannon blamed us for the attack.

At that time, we attempted to contact your royal person by messenger, but he went missing upon reaching the Pass between Mount Valer and Mount Norst.

Other attacks at different points on the border have occurred since then, each carried out by men dressed in Ilumencian armor. As such, tensions between our nation and Thissa have reached a breaking point. Gorvannon will not believe the attacks are not sanctioned by the council unless we can provide proof otherwise.

While searching for the party responsible for these attacks, we happened across a pile of missives in the royal office. Many of them were addressed to King Morthan from you, but several were drafts of letters which Morthan had begun, then discarded. In these missives, he claimed that Gorvannon was attacking our borders, not the other way 'round.

I beg your forgiveness for my forwardness, my lord, but these are unprecedented times. It is my belief that Morthan himself has instigated these attacks on Thissa, and he is using them as a guise to draw himself closer to you.

He has only just left for Ivenhence on your invitation, and I pray to Ivere that I am wrong regarding his intentions. It is my belief that Morthan has given his soul to Kazael and has been Turned into an Unbreathing. I believe he means to release Kazael from his prison.

Please, Your Majesty. Use caution. Even if you do not believe the legends of old, I am convinced Morthan means you harm.

Corwel Kindlar, Third Advisor to the Crown of Ilumence, Duke of Mooreland.

King Dreythan Dreythas-son,

It is clear you are unaware of the game Ilumence is playing. My borders have been attacked seven times in the past two moons. Each time by a score of men wearing Ilumencian armor, each time at night and without warning. Fifty-three of my people are dead.

I have only just opened and read the most insulting missive I have ever laid eyes on, written in your hand and addressed from you. Judging by the tone of your past letters, it is clear that you have a spy in your midst, and one skilled in the art of forgery. Since my spy-master agrees,

Ivenhence is off the hook. But consider this a warning: war with Ilumence is coming. If you have people in your sister-nation you care about, get them out of there. Now.

Our borders are now closed, and our seas have been barricaded. No Ilumencian or Ivenhencian merchants will be allowed to pass.

I only warn you because you seem like a decent sort. Don't contact me again. There's no possibility for a trade route unless you want to supply your sister-nation's enemy.

Gorvannon, High Commander of Thissa

Dreythan stared from one missive to the other, slowly shaking his head.

"We found them in his quarters, sir," Harrild Hammerfist said darkly. "He was simply sitting there, all these letters and scrolls piled around him."

Raising his eyes to the foot of the throne's steps, Dreythan stared at the white-haired figure that knelt there, swollen-jointed hands clasped in manacles. Beside him rested a wooden chest, filled to heaping with rolls and bits of parchment.

"Brinwathe, Head Librarian of Iventorr," he said. The syllables left a bitter tang on his lips. He had leaned on this man, depended on his wisdom and knowledge.

Yet here he was, a traitor to the throne.

Beside the weathered old man, Fletch frowned, peering at a sheaf of papers as she rustled through them. "I suppose this answers many of our questions." She glanced at Brinwathe, her undamaged eye narrowed. "You... you were the one who removed the materials concerning Unbreathing from the library, weren't you? Fifteen years ago, before the assassinations."

"I was," he replied, his hoary voice creaking in the still air.

Dreythan frowned. For a man being accused of treason, he was strangely calm. "You were acting under Morthan's direction?" he pressed. "Did you not question the reasoning?"

"I did," Brinwathe admitted. "But I had only just arrived in Iventorr at the time, my lord. I was... deeply rooted in the

Ilumence Loyalist way of thinking." After a brief pause, he added, "I believed I was erasing the lies the former slaves had told themselves during their darkest hours to cling to some semblance of sanity. That I was wiping the slate clean, allowing them to forget the monsters they invented."

Dreythan cocked a brow. "You speak as if your 'way of thinking' has changed."

The figure before him didn't respond. He shuffled in place, head dipping.

"How many letters have you kept from me over the years? How many have you altered, forging the penmanship of the sender?"

"I did not count them, my lord," the old librarian said. "But they are all here. All the originals, that is." He chuckled weakly. "I was nearly found out by Anshwell when they visited my quarters unexpectedly a few moons ago. After that, I tried to destroy it all, but could not bring myself to. There is a profanity in destroying the written word."

"But not the word of former slaves who gave everything for their freedom."

His words echoed sharply off the stone walls.

Brinwathe shook his head. "I only took the materials. I did not destroy them. You can find them in the bottom of the chest."

Shooting a doubtful glance at Dreythan, Fletch stooped over the chest. Though her plaster-encased arm was bound to her ribs, she rummaged through the container with the other, setting stacks of papers and scrolls aside in her search for the bottom.

"And how many messages did you write using my hand? Or my father's hand?" Dreythan asked over the rustling of parchment. Rising, he settled into his usual pacing track on the top stair. "How many times did you debase the royal seal of Ivenhence?"

"Only once, my lord. Two weeks ago. I... sent one to Gorvannon in your hand."

"And what did that missive say?"

"I was as blatantly insulting as I could be, my lord. King

Morthan had made it clear he wished Sentinel Wyndshaper gone from Iventorr upon his arrival, and that he wished Gorvannon incensed against Ivenhence." The old man hesitated, then continued, "I made it seem that you were boasting of your successful trade negotiations with the Isles and with Ilumence, that you dared Gorvannon attend your trade summit. I... I also insinuated that you suspected him of the attempts on your life. When I was certain Gorvannon's blood would be boiling, I finished by flaunting the relationship with the Wyndarin and their recent visit."

"That must have been why he sent this reply." Dreythan glanced back down at the letter, at the neat rows of characters perfectly spaced and ordered. "Gorvannon could not have realized it, but by mobilizing his navy, he was acting as Morthan's puppet." To Fletch, he added, "What better way to lure Fletch out of Iventorr than to place her mother and her mother's people in seemingly grave danger?"

Though her eyes met his, Fletch didn't answer. Placing the papers back in the chest, her forehead creased in a frown, she absently brushed her bruised throat with her fingers.

Dreythan's chest tightened. Turning back to Brinwathe, he said, "But I still do not understand, Brinwathe. Why, after over fifteen years of peace in Iventorr, after becoming Head Librarian and making our kingdom your home, would you betray us?" He swallowed the words that nearly followed, hands clenching. *I trusted you, leaned on you. Gods, but I leaned on you.*

"It makes no difference now," the old man murmured, his chin dipping even further toward his collarbone. "The Ilumencian royal line is broken. If what I hear is true, 'twas broken even before I left Ilumence all those years ago."

"It makes a difference to me."

Fletch's voice cracked like a whip through the still throne room. Startled, Brinwathe raised his head, his cloudy eyes crashing into hers.

"It makes a difference to Captain Norland," she continued as her stare burned into him. "It makes a difference to twenty-three valiant guards. To Klep Ironshod, to Dreythan's father, Dreythas." She swallowed hard, livid fire pooling in her eyes. "And to my father, Kell Wyndshaper. All of whom died because of your treachery."

"Indeed," Dreythan agreed. The pure, livid fury in Fletch's eyes lit something in him. He stopped pacing, the fire in his gut growing to a roaring furnace. "Well said, Fletch. It does make a difference, traitor Brinwathe."

The librarian flinched at the word, but didn't drop his gaze, transfixed by the blaze that crackled in Fletch's face. "Very well," he whispered. "I did not know Morthan meant to take your life, my lord. That day in the Pass. I was told you were to be captured, threatened, but that you would be allowed to return to Iventorr to relinquish rule to the Ilumencian crown." Meeting Dreythan's eye, he crumpled, shoulders bowing. "When you returned with young Wyndshaper, when I heard of Unbreathing assassins, I... I convinced myself it was a misunderstanding. The guards must have been asked to surrender, and had refused. But when I heard of the black arrows used... I of course thought of the weapons Purveyn Holden had made under Morthan's commission, fifteen years ago."

"And Parfeln? What did he think of this development?"

"We agreed it had been wise of him to destroy the arrows that felled King Dreythas and Kell Wyndshaper. Parfeln scoffed at the idea of Unbreathing, but... he had not read the accounts I'd stolen from the library. He had not seen the stories of the survivors. If he had, his conviction that such monsters were a fairytale might have been swayed." The librarian paused, ghosts flitting behind the curtains of his milky eyes. "Time and again, no matter how old the former slave or what horror they had experienced, they described the Unbreathing the same way. Yellow eyes, teeth and nails that stretched into fangs and claws when roused. Faster and stronger than any man, especially in the light of the moon. Weakened by silver. I had begun to doubt my own belief that the slaves had made up these monsters to justify their suffering." He shook his head. "Thus, I wrote a missive to Morthan, alerting him to the presence of a newcomer in the castle, one who claimed to sense Unbreathing. I asked him if the ambush party in the Pass had been as she claimed, and mentioned she was returning to Herstshire as a messenger.

"Morthan's reply was dismissive. He admitted he was using Unbreathing, but said they were merely effective mercenaries. But when Forester Wyndshaper returned injured..." He hesitated. "I spoke of my concerns to Parfeln. He refused to listen. At that time, I... I swore it all off. I didn't want harm coming to the people I'd grown to know and care for." Liver-spotted face dissolving in a mass of melancholic wrinkles, he added, "Parfeln wouldn't hear of it. He... he must have told Morthan of my perceived treachery. Weeks later, a man in a black cloak and robes woke me in the dead of night. He threatened my life if I didn't comply with Morthan's needs, and promised to keep watch to ensure I spoke of our interaction to no one." Brinwathe shuddered, his jowls wobbling. "His eyes... they were yellow, as yellow as a cat's."

He fell silent for several minutes, the manacles around his wrists clinking as he shifted.

"What then?" Dreythan prompted.

"Klep Ironshod was attacked, and an Unbreathing spy found and slain, my lord. I hoped to Ivere it was the same that had threatened me, but... there was no way to be sure. So I simply waited, avoiding Parfeln, sending Morthan updates as demanded. Then the Wyndarin came, and they spoke of Purveyn the Fletcher." His throat bobbed. "Parfeln wrote Morthan himself to warn of Matteo Alwick's mission to Wuthera. When Matteo returned, we had no idea what had transpired whilst he was away. Parfeln nearly lost his wits. He was certain we had been found out, that Captain Norland was simply waiting for us to break." Straightening as much as his rheumatism would allow, Brinwathe gave a slow nod. "I was not as certain, having been privy to Morthan's cruelty. But I gathered all the evidence I still had in my possession, sorting it by addresser and date. I did not wish record of it to be lost, even if Morthan was to take the Ivenhencian throne." He cast a glance at the chest of papers, something akin to affection sparking on his aged face. "Such things are vital to the annals of history."

Dreythan's feet slowed to a stop as he stared down at the wrinkled little man before him. The man he'd depended so heavily on without even realizing it, the librarian who was always there to fetch the records he needed or to explain the syntax or context of a specific word. The man he'd learned his kingdom's own history from.

It was enough to make him ill.

"Take him away."

He could hardly bring himself to watch as two guards escorted Brinwathe, Head Librarian of Iventorr, out of the throne hall.

"To think," Harrild muttered. "Parfeln sent a sun jay warning Morthan of Matteo's mission to question Purveyn. He must have believed Purveyn's family would not come to harm. And yet... Parfeln practically sentenced his own brother and his family to death." He glanced sharply up, then wilted. "I suppose I simply find it hard to reconcile that the men I knew for years would be capable of such things."

Collapsing back into the throne, Dreythan grunted, "As do I, Harrild. As do I."

"Are you all right?"

At Fletch's soft inquiry, heat sprang to his ears. "I shall be," he replied. Peering around Harrild at her, he raised a brow. When she nodded, he said, "Before I dismiss you to your post, Sentinel Harrild, there is another matter I — we — wish to discuss."

"'We'?" Harrild repeated, a smile breaking across his pockmarked face. "Gods, but that does my heart good to hear. I'm at your service, my lord, my lady."

Fletch's cheeks pinked. She flashed a glance at Dreythan, and he gestured encouragingly.

"Yes," she faltered. "I've... been thinking, these last few days.

Since Captain Norland's funeral."

Something in her face shifted at those words. Squaring her shoulders, she continued, "If Vvalk returned forty years after his defeat at the Battle of Reclamation, there's no reason he shan't return again. And when he does, there is no knowing when it will be, or what he will do to try to release his Master, Kazael. We need to be prepared for his return."

Harrild was already nodding. "I've thought much the same, my lady. Missives are being written to ask those willing to join the castle guard." He inspected her face curiously. "But you have something else in mind?"

"I do," Fletch said.

The way her eyes sparkled when she spoke of her passion... Dreythan's insides kept turning to molten pudding every time he watched it. It made it wonderfully difficult to concentrate.

"'Tis possible there are Wynd-bloods scattered across Ivenhence," she continued. "Like my father, who was called a bastard in Ilumence and given a bastard's name. Perhaps they seek community, family. If we could send word across the kingdom to these individuals, let them know they are needed, that they're welcome, some of them might heed the call." Giving an audible gulp, she finished, "'Tis my hope we could form a new division of the castle guard, one specially trained to detect Unbreathing, tasked with preserving the history and knowledge of Iventorr. A division of Wynd-blood soldiers."

"An excellent plan," Harrild said, his hazel eyes shining. "If you were going to ask for my help training them, say no more, my lady. I shall aid in whatever way I can."

Fletch's face softened into a grateful smile. "That's exactly what I was going to ask. Thank you, Harrild."

"We have already spoken to Treasurer Anshwell regarding this," Dreythan added. "As they are acting Head Librarian. They are preparing messages to send across Ivenhence, and require the aid of a few of your guards to accompany their messengers."

Harrild saluted smartly, his fist snapping to his chest. "Of course, my lord. I'll see to it immediately." Pausing, he gave Fletch a wry smirk. "A new division of the guard, eh? I've the perfect name for them."

She grinned back. "Oh? Let's hear it, then!"

"I must refuse, my lady. You would forbid me from using it."

With that, he left, chuckling as if immensely pleased with himself the entire stretch of the throne hall aisle until the door closed behind him.

"I wish I had thought of that," Dreythan muttered ruefully. "An excellent idea." Hoisting himself from the throne, he descended the steps, stopping by Fletch's side. "Would you like to take my arm, my lady?"

In response, Fletch closed the remaining floor between them, slipping her hand into the crook of his elbow. It was strange how at home her hand felt there. As if it had been made to rest in that very spot.

Then again, everything about her felt like home.

"Shall we go review those missives, my lord?" she teased, drawing another smile to his lips.

His hand closed gently over her fingers on his arm as he bent to press a kiss onto her cheek. "Yes, indeed," he said softly, delighted by the color that swept over her cheeks. "Come, my love. Let us summon the Wyndshapers."

Kate Argus is a reader, a dreamer, and an advocate for equal human rights for all. The Wyndshaper is her first novel, but she has plans to write many more. Kate currently resides with her husband and their two fur children in Ossian, Indiana.